W9-BRI-911

Praise For

THE
FIVE STAGES
of
ANDREW
BRAWLEY

"*The Five Stages of Andrew Brawley* broke my heart, then put it back together again. I truly loved this book." —Bruce Coville

"A wonderfully written book that is more proof that the genre of 'LGBT YA lit' simply knows no bounds." —Brent Hartinger, author of *Geography Club*

"*The Five Stages of Andrew Brawley* is as inventive as it is moving. A beautiful book." —Trish Doller, author of *Where the Stars Still Shine*

Also by Shaun David Hutchinson
The Deathday Letter
fml

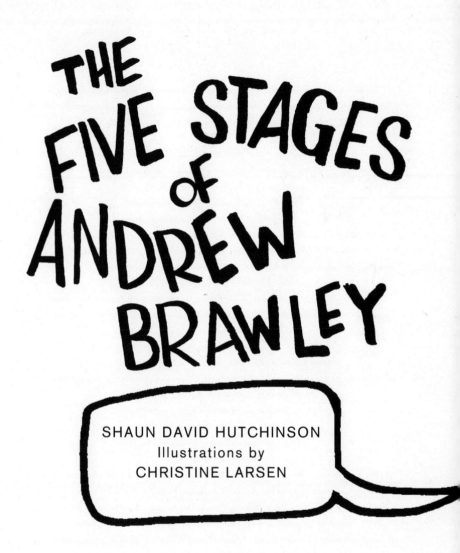

THE FIVE STAGES OF ANDREW BRAWLEY

SHAUN DAVID HUTCHINSON
Illustrations by
CHRISTINE LARSEN

SIMON PULSE
New York London Toronto Sydney New Delhi

SIMON PULSE

An imprint of Simon & Schuster Children's Publishing Division

1230 Avenue of the Americas, New York, NY 10020

First Simon Pulse hardcover edition January 2015

Copyright © 2015 by Shaun David Hutchinson

All rights reserved, including the right of reproduction in whole or in part in any form.

SIMON PULSE and colophon are registered trademarks of Simon & Schuster, Inc.

For information about special discounts for bulk purchases, please contact Simon & Schuster Special Sales at 1-866-506-1949 or business@simonandschuster.com.

The Simon & Schuster Speakers Bureau can bring authors to your live event. For more information or to book an event contact the Simon & Schuster Speakers Bureau at 1-866-248-3049 or visit our website at www.simonspeakers.com.

Designed by Regina Flath

Cover illustration and lettering copyright © 2015 by Christine Larsen

Cover image is used for illustrative purposed only; any person depicted in the image is a model.

The text of this book was set in Adobe Garamond Pro.

Manufactured in the United States of America

2 4 6 8 10 9 7 5 3 1

Library of Congress Cataloging-in-Publication Data

Hutchinson, Shaun David.

The five stages of Andrew Brawley / Shaun David Hutchinson ; illustrations by Christine Larsen. pages cm

Summary: Convinced he should have died in the accident that killed his parents and sister, sixteen-year-old Drew lives in a hospital, hiding from employees and his past, until Rusty, set on fire for being gay, turns his life around. Includes excerpts from the superhero comic Drew creates.

[1. Hospitals—Fiction. 2. Grief—Fiction. 3. Gays—Fiction. 4. Orphans—Fiction. 5. Comic books, strips, etc.—Fiction. 6. Runaways—Fiction.] I. Larsen, Christine (Illustrator), illustrator. II. Title.

PZ7.H96183Fiv 2015 [Fic]—dc23 2014022200

ISBN 978-1-4814-0310-8

ISBN 978-1-4814-0312-2 (eBook)

This one is for Nara Star, my own personal superhero

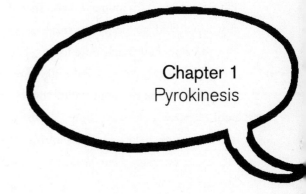

Chapter 1
Pyrokinesis

The boy is on fire.

EMTs wheel him into Roanoke General's sterile emergency room. He screams and writhes on the gurney as though the fire that burned his skin away burns still, flaring deep within his bones, where the paramedics and doctors and nurses crowding around him, working desperately, will never be able to extinguish it.

The boy looks my age, seventeen. His hair, where it isn't singed, is the color of autumn leaves. The kind of leaves I used to rake into piles with my dad and take running jumps into.

I can't see the boy's eyes from where I'm hiding, but his voice is a chain. It grates as agony drags it out of his throat. The skin on his legs and part of his chest is charred black.

The scent of burning lingers in my nose, and even as bile rises into the back of my throat, I can't help thinking of all the times I barbecued with my family during the summer. Mom would squirrel away extra food in the back of the fridge because Dad always burned the chicken.

It's late, and I should be gone, but I can't take my eyes off the boy. I'm a prisoner of his animal howls. There is nowhere in this hospital that I could hide to escape his screams.

So I stay. And watch. And listen.

A girl runs in, arms windmilling about. Screaming words that I barely hear over the sound of my own heart thudding. ". . . in the pool . . . party . . . he was yelling . . ." The paramedics restrain the girl, and she shrinks. She's a broken mirror. The pieces are just reflected bits of us: our anger, our horror, our fear, borrowed and returned. She can keep mine.

I focus on the boy.

The biggest concern is protecting his airway. I know that. It's basic stuff. If the boy breathed the fire, it might not matter what his skin looks like. That his screams reach every corner of Roanoke's claustrophobic emergency room is a good thing. When he stops screaming is when I'll worry.

The doctors and nurses huddle, discussing their plan of attack, maybe; praying, maybe. Mourning, maybe. The boy needs miracles. The storybook-magic kind.

One of the doctors—an octopus of a woman working with all eight arms simultaneously—cuts away the ruined bits of clothing and peels them back like ragged strips of wallpaper. The boy moans.

I turn away. I'm not prepared for this. I only came to the ER to say hi to the nurses and see if anyone had blown off a finger while lighting fireworks. Today being the Fourth of July made my chances of seeing a grisly Roman candle accident pretty good.

But this is bad. This is so much like that night.

The small emergency room can hardly contain all the people crowded in it. The walls are white. The floors are white. The drapes that cordon off the exam rooms are eggshell, except for one space reserved for small children. That curtain is decorated with tiny faded yellow ducks. The nurse's station is a stumbling block perched in the middle of the ER, and all the doctors and nurses are forced to dance around it. The nurses complain, but it's a fixed point in space. Immovable.

Like me.

My calves ache from crouching, and my shoulders are stiff. I fear that if I move, I'll be seen, and tonight I want to remain invisible. The boy on fire needs me to stay. He needs me to be witness to his pain. It's an odd thought to have, but I'm growing used to the odd thoughts that invade my brain these days. Every day.

Like how the ER smells remind me of an Italian grinder. The kind that's smothered in vinegar and mayo and too much oregano. Usually the emergency room is a stew of bleach and blood and whatever rotten odors the patients carry in with them. But not tonight. The boy isn't just burned. He's cooked.

I turn back to the scene, hoping that they've finished peeling him. He moves less than before. He cries less. Maybe the doctors gave him something for the pain. Except he and I know that some pain burrows so deep, no narcotic can ever soothe it. It's etched on your bones. It hides in your marrow, like cancer. If the boy survives, this pain is a memory he won't want.

I'll remember it for him.

Steven startles me from behind. "Drew? What're you doing

here?" Steven is twiggy, with a bulbous nose and a hairline that he left in high school, along with the rest of his good looks.

"Hey, Steven," I say, playing it nonchalant. I stand up slowly, not taking my eyes off the burning boy, and hide my anxiety behind a lopsided grin. "I was on my way home, and I thought I'd stop by and say hi."

"Bad time, kiddo." He's cradling an armful of sterile gauze and looking where I'm looking. The boy screams. Steven flinches. Sometimes I think he's too sensitive to be a nurse.

I nod my head absently, letting Steven's words settle into my ears but not really hearing them. I try to reply, but the fire in the boy's screams sucks all the oxygen from the room.

Steven glances at the bandages in his hands and says, "I should go."

"Me too," I say. "I'm working breakfast tomorrow. See you then?"

"Sure." Steven's blue eyes light up at the mention of food. "Tell Arnold not to undercook the eggs. Runny eggs are disgusting."

The boy screeches, and Steven goes. He walks apologetically and disappears into the tumor of people surrounding the boy.

I stay. The doctors and nurses press bandages to seared skin. After his airway, fighting infection is their next priority. I can't tell how much of the boy's body is burned, but it's enough. Soon they'll wheel him to another part of the hospital. I might never see him again. I don't even know his name.

But I have to go. Death will appear soon, as she always does. She might take the boy, she might not, but I can't be around when she comes. She arrived late before and didn't get me. But she won't make the same mistake twice, and I'm not yet ready to leave.

No one sees me take off. I navigate the hospital on autopilot.

There are doors through which only hospital workers are allowed to pass, but I make my way invisibly. I imagine I can't be seen, and I am not seen. The hospital walls have no memory. They would crumble under the weight of so much suffering. It's better that they forget.

On the first floor, far past the surgical ward, is a section of the hospital abandoned in the middle of renovations, left to decay when the economy collapsed and the money ran out. Naked beams and partially erected drywall rot like forgotten bones. Dust and neglect fill the air. No one comes here except me. No one even remembers it exists.

I grab the flashlight that I leave by the door. It casts a shallow sphere of illumination. Enough to drive the shadows back, but not enough to banish them completely. Sometimes I try to trick myself, imagining that I'm at my old house in my old bed and that the others are asleep in their bedrooms, dreaming sweetly. But it's an illusion that rarely lasts long.

This is home now.

I trudge to the farthest corner, to the only room that's even remotely finished. It has four walls and a knobless door that I tape shut. Most nights it feels like a prison.

My bed against the far wall is a pile of lumpy, stained sheets that embraces me with all the comfort of a sack full of rocks. My pillow is a laundry bag stuffed with discarded scrubs.

I pop in my earbuds and play some music. It's in Spanish, so I don't understand the words, but the lazy, metallic twangs of the guitar are soothing. The sounds of the hospital can reach me even here, and I can't sleep with the gasping and wheezing all around me, with

5

the wraiths that haunt the halls, chattering through the night like a million cicadas.

Today was long, and I'm tired. It's barely eight in the evening, but I can't keep my lids from sliding closed. More often it's the reverse, and I stay awake all night, begging for sleep to take me.

Exhaustion is a relief.

Before I lie back and let reality slip away, I retrieve a small tin from beneath my pillow. It's the color of sun-kissed skin and weighs less than it should. I dig my fingers around the edges and remove the lid.

The first thing that hits me is the rich scent of leather. Old leather. Leather that was loved. I open the faded brown wallet and linger over the picture in the plastic window. Then I fold it closed and put it beside me. Scattered at the bottom of the tin are two gold rings, one toy horse, and a gold cross. I don't touch those.

I replace the lid and settle against my makeshift pillow, clutching the wallet and gazing at the picture until I fall asleep.

But my last thoughts aren't of the smiling family in the photograph. They're of the boy on fire.

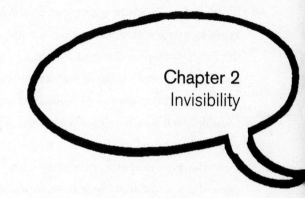

Chapter 2
Invisibility

I don't dream much anymore; I draw instead.

I spill my graphite nightmares onto rough pages that I scavenge from recycling bins in the billing department. And I listen. I listen to the scraps of words and whispers that float about on the cool, antiseptic air. I watch the flickering images that appear and disappear at the corners of my eyes. Sometimes I hear nothing for days, and then it'll all rush in like a tsunami that washes over me and never recedes. Reality becomes twisted until my world and the world of memories, where my family is still alive, blend together and I don't know what's real.

And then there's the world I create.

My superhero has a name: Patient F. Before I arrived at the hospital, I barely drew at all. Just doodles on the edges of textbook pages. But now I draw constantly, filling the gaps between minutes with stark lines and harrowed eyes. Even when I don't want to.

I've been working on Patient F's story for about a month. It begins before Patient F is captured by the RAND Corporation for experimentation. It begins when he's still a man in a suit, doing the kinds of boring things that men in suits do. The things that no one writes about because they know that boys don't really have nightmares about clowns or three-eyed·tentacled beasts that rise from deep within volcanoes. When boys wake up screaming in the night, it's because they know that, one day, they'll have to grow into men who wear suits and spend their days doing boring things that cause them to rot from within, so their skin withers and blackens and cracks, leaking out their juices until they finally lie decaying and putrid, forgotten by a world that deemed them unworthy of remembering.

It begins there because it's important to know that a superhero with no past began as a man with no future.

Patient F is unstuck from time. Temporally freed as a result of the pain inflicted upon him by the doctors in red lab coats with the six-inch needles and the shiny bone saws. He sees what he was and what he will become and all the moments that connect those two points. Patient F sees the whole of his existence spread before him like dots on a Pac-Man board that must be devoured before the ghosts catch him and end the game.

When Patient F opens his eyes for the first time, he's been Patient F for his entire life. He knows who these men are and what they've done to him. He remembers the man in the suit, even though the rest of the world has forgotten him. He knows every person he's lost and every person that they'll take from him. Patient F has a list of people to kill. He begins with the doctors in the red lab coats.

And he moves on from there.

The hospital is quiet this early in the morning. It's sleeping. Despite that, there are always a few people shuffling about—nurses and doctors and orderlies—but I've learned their routines. Heisenberg searched for the chaos present in ordered systems, whereas I've found the order in chaotic systems. Chaos is an excuse for people who don't have the patience to see the patterns.

There are showers not far from my room that are usually empty. They smell of feet and deodorant, and steam lingers in the air like a persistent fog. Despite the emptiness, I wash up quickly to avoid being caught, and then ransack the lockers. I tell myself I'm not a thief, even as I thieve a white T-shirt from locker 13 and a tiny iPod from locker 33. I only steal out of necessity. The iPod I have is almost dead, and no one ever thinks to bring a charger. I got that iPod from locker 21; tomorrow morning, I'll return it. Doctors have more important worries on their minds than misplaced gadgets.

I dress in the white shirt I liberated from the locker and jeans that I took from the lost and found. Sometimes I think of myself as a savior of the lost, a caretaker of the found.

When I've dressed and brushed my teeth and raked a hand through my increasingly unruly hair, I sneak through the hospital and head for the cafeteria. Roanoke General is a sprawling, lazy building that suffers from lack of planning. Unfinished wings sit forgotten, wheezy and sick. There are so many hallways, new nurses and doctors are jokingly given a spool of thread on their first day. They laugh it off but surely wish they'd paid more attention when they receive their first emergency page and spend ten minutes trying to escape the labyrinth.

I have a map in my head so that I never get lost. I know where all the abandoned rooms are, where the maternity ward is, where the ICU is, where they keep the sick kids, and where they hide old people who probably won't ever again see the outside world. The hospital is my ocean, and I am its Sir Francis Drake.

No one pays attention to me. I walk with my hands in my pockets and my head down, and people pass without a second glance. Some know me, some are too busy reading charts or tapping away at their phones, but most are indifferent. I have a theory about that. I think that people who help others for a living—doctors and nurses and firefighters and police—carry only so much goodwill inside them. Once it's depleted, they have to wait for the well to replenish itself, so they use it sparingly and only on those who need it most.

A young man walking down a hospital hallway at five in the morning isn't anyone's priority. Sometimes, though, I wonder if people can see me at all. Occasionally I consider standing in the middle of the emergency room, waving my arms and screaming as loudly as I can just to see what would happen. But I never do. It's far too risky.

Arnold is waiting for me when I slip under the metal gate and into the dim cafeteria. He insists that everyone call him Arnold instead of Mr. Jaworski, and he pronounces it *Ah-nold* when he's trying to be funny. He's rarely funny, though not for lack of trying.

"You're late," Arnold says. He fakes anger but can't pull it off. It's the beard and the belly. Even as he stands by the deep fryer with his hands on his hips, trying to frown, he looks more like a swollen pink Gumby than the man who pays me cash on the sly to serve reheated hash browns.

I don't answer him, just get right to work refilling the condiment containers and turning on the heat lamps. The caf smells like fried bacon and eggs, and possibly marinara. The blend of aromas makes my stomach rumble. If I could sleep here, I would. The rest of the hospital reeks of that antiseptic tang, but the cafeteria is an oasis in a desert of smells.

Aimee is in the back doing prep work. She hardly ever says two words to me and doesn't eat where anyone can see her. I had a dog like that once. We adopted him from a shelter the day before he was going to be put down. The workers said he'd been abused.

I've never seen a mark on Aimee's whip-thin body but, like her eating, I'm sure it's happened, whether I see it or not.

Arnold is whistling this morning. Sometimes he sings; sometimes he hums. This morning, he's whistling. He makes up tunes from scraps of songs he hears on the radio. The notes are never quite right but somehow sound okay together. Not that it would matter if they didn't: Arnold is as shameless as he is tone deaf.

I work quietly to avoid having to talk to Arnold. Even more than singing, he loves to talk. During my interview, he didn't ask me one single question that he let me answer. Instead, he filled the time telling me about his wife, who is a lawyer, his son, who is going to be a doctor, and his master's degree in literature. The only thing I found especially interesting was that Arnold spent six years in college yet works in a hospital cafeteria. I haven't asked him why, though. We have an unspoken agreement about secrets.

When it's time to open up, Aimee works the cash register while I serve the food. It's a thankless, boring job that allows me to spend time listening. Despite being in plain sight on the other side of the sneeze guard, ladling watery eggs onto plates, the moment I don the ridiculous hairnet Arnold insists I wear, I become nobody. It's better than being invisible.

Most of the talk revolves around which doctor is sleeping with which nurse, or who accidentally left a sponge in a patient, or how many times patient so-and-so rang the call button in the middle of the night when they should have been sleeping. It's mundane stuff that I don't care about, and today I use the repetitive movements of filling trays to work myself into a trance as I sift through the buzz of conversations, listening for any mention of last night's burned boy.

He's been on my mind since I left the ER. Carved into my brain and left to fester.

Being burned scares me. There was a guy named Smitty who worked at Station 9, where I volunteered as a junior firefighter. One of the coolest guys I've ever met. He spent his off hours riding motorcycles and jumping out of airplanes and climbing mountains without a safety harness. Smitty wasn't afraid of anything. Nothing.

Except being burned. As a rookie he got caught under a fallen beam in a burning house. It took three guys to pull him out, but the fire had already charred his back. Smitty showed me pictures of his burns and described in relentless detail the endless debriding and skin grafts. He told me that there were days when he never stopped screaming. Days when he would have welcomed death.

And I can't help wondering if that burned boy is welcoming

death now—even as Arnold snaps at me to refill the bacon.

But I know he isn't, and can't be. Because Death is in the corner, eating a fruit cup.

It's risky standing here staring at her. Death's got my name on her list, and though I'm in disguise, it's only a matter of time before she sees through my mask and discovers not a young man who serves slimy hash but a young man she was meant to collect.

"Boy, if you don't stop staring past me, I'm going to reach across that glass shield and grab a handful of your hide."

"Hey, Jo."

Jo is one of the ER nurses who sometimes lets me watch the good cases. She's built for sumo wrestling, with grabby brown eyes and a smile full of braces. I learned the first time I met her that she is not the kind of woman you trifle with. She never quits, won't take no for an answer, and would knife you for a Butterfinger.

"Are you planning on feeding me anytime soon, or am I going to have to speak to your manager?" Jo frowns with her whole face.

I toss the spoon into the eggs and cross my arms over my chest. "I reserve the right to refuse service to anyone," I say. "And that includes uppity nurses."

Jo and I stare at each other across the sneeze guard, neither blinking, neither bending. It's the Berlin Wall of sneeze guards. I study every line on her face. I would bet an entire day's pay that each one corresponds to some patient she lost. Someone she went home and shed tears over while burying her sorrow in a pint of Phish Food and a couple of hours of bad reality TV.

Each one of those lines has a name. One of them might be the name of my burned boy.

13

"I'm too hungry to play your games today, Drew." Jo rolls her big brown eyes and nudges her tray with her hip. "Load me up. And don't be stingy with the bacon."

Steven slides into place beside Jo and grabs a bagel with a pair of plastic tongs. He's different from how he was last night, springier in a way that makes me think he could have been a ballet dancer instead of a nurse.

"Don't listen to mean old Jo," Steven says. "She's just cranky because she got stuck cleaning up explosive diarrhea instead of watching the fireworks."

Jo slaps Steven's arm as I pile food on both of their trays. Jo and Steven eat equal amounts, but somehow every ounce sticks to Jo's ass like a blood-hungry tick, whereas Steven seems incapable of gaining weight—a fact that he likes to exploit, especially around Jo, and especially when there's cake.

The two of them bicker while I serve. I'm about to ask what they know about the boy from last night when Emma squeals "Drew!" and runs up to the counter. I think she'd hug me through the glass if she could.

"Heya, Emma," I say, and wink at her. Emma's a sweet girl raised on sitcoms and infomercials. She's the opposite of Jo, who wears her worries on her skin. Emma hides behind a wide smile and gracious eyes the color of a blue-raspberry slushy.

I come out from behind the counter to give Emma a hug. Beneath the sharp scents of antiseptic and latex, Emma always smells like sugar cookies.

"No hug for me?" Jo asks.

"The boy's afraid of getting lost in your mountainous

bosom." Steven ducks out of the way of Jo's backhanded slap.

Before releasing me, Emma crushes the wind from my lungs. I catch Arnold glancing down his nose at me from behind the line, so I run back to my station.

"How are you today, baby?" Emma asks.

I shrug. "You still not eating carbs?" Emma shakes her head, so I dump a double helping of eggs onto her plate.

Jo tries to sneak a piece of bacon off of Emma's tray, but she's not nearly as stealthy as she believes herself to be. "Jo, get your thieving fingers off my bacon before I break them."

"So," I say before Jo can start a fight with Emma, who despite her size is a fierce combatant. "Anything good come in last night?"

The three nurses look at each other before sliding their trays toward the cash register. Jo takes a fruit cup from the cold case like it can balance out the seven hundred grease-laden calories she's about to inhale. Steven tears off half the top of his bagel and stuffs it in his mouth. Emma's eyes brand them both traitors until her pink face lights up.

"There was the one guy. The guy with the cut on his arm." She blinks rapidly in Steven and Jo's direction. It takes them a second to catch on to her ham-fisted subject detour.

Steven snaps his fingers, nearly tipping over his orange tray. His grace, it seems, has deserted him. He swallows that doughy bite of bagel and says, "Right, the Mexican guy. With the arm lac."

Jo laughs like she has a mouthful of bees. "I think you about scared him back across the border when you showed him the catheter." She hands Aimee her credit card and says, "See you tomorrow morning, Drew?"

15

"Maybe." I rarely commit to anything these days.

Steven waits for Aimee to ring him up before handing her some bills that he pulls out of the waistband of his scrubs. The ER's standard-issue scrubs are a violent shade of fuchsia that the nurses universally despise.

When Steven steps out of the way to allow Emma to pay, she sighs. "You want to know about the boy from last night, don't you."

"Emma . . . ," Steven says.

Don't talk about patients: That's one of the first things they told us when I was a junior firefighter. They drilled it into our heads. Whether you're a doctor or a nurse or a paramedic, you're not supposed to discuss patients with anyone uninvolved in their care. Privacy laws and some such.

But I doubt that's why they're hesitant to talk about the burned boy.

"He'll hear the details eventually." Emma sighs again. "Some kids from his school lit him on fire." She dumps it right out there, no sugar coating, which is odd since she loves sugar so much. "They doused that boy with alcohol and lit a match."

Steven is eyeing me warily the same way my mom did the first time I watched a horror movie. I begged her for weeks to let me watch *Dream Terror IX*. When she finally relented, she sat beside me with one half-covered eye on the movie and the remaining uncovered eye on me, waiting for me to tell her that the movie was too scary. I never flinched, but I had nightmares for a month.

If Steven's afraid I'm going to have nightmares about the burned boy, it's already too late. Anyway, I've seen the effect; I may as well learn the cause.

16

"Why did they burn him?" I ask.

Steven gives in. "The police are saying it could be a hate crime."

"Aren't all crimes hate crimes?"

"Because he's gay," Steven says.

"Oh."

Now I understand why Steven and the others wanted to keep this from me. They didn't want me to make it personal.

But knowing now that someone *did* that to him—it makes my memories of last night even more tragic. It's as if the new knowledge travels back in time to rewrite the gravity of his situation.

"Did you know him?" Emma asks, and I wonder why. Maybe I've let too much emotion onto my face.

"We don't all know each other," I snap.

Steven tries to lighten the mood with a chuckle that comes out an octave higher than his normal laugh. We all know it's forced, but we play along—Emma because she doesn't know any better, and me because, now that I have the information, I'm not sure what to do with it.

The burned boy isn't just another hospital tragedy, a Fourth of July accident. He's a victim.

I point at Jo, who's glaring at us with naked ire. "You should eat before your food gets cold."

Emma picks up her tray like it's all no big deal. It's nothing. The burned boy is nothing. I wish I knew her secret. "Bye, cutie. See you later."

"You betcha," I say, trying to mimic her detachment.

Steven hangs back. When Emma's out of earshot, he says, "I didn't want you to find out like that."

"It's not like I know the kid." Which is true—I don't know him—but that doesn't make his pain any less real.

"I should go," he says. "Are you sure you're all right?"

I slap on a smile and wave Steven away. "I'm good."

Steven nods and turns to join Emma and Jo. When he's taken about two steps, I blurt out, "What's his name?"

"Drew . . ."

"I'll find out anyway."

Steven hangs his head, staring into his runny yellow eggs. "Rusty," he says. "Rusty McHale." He shuffles to his seat, but I notice that he no longer appears interested in eating.

A couple of doctors enter the line, chatting about a particularly interesting liposuction. I tune out.

The burned boy has a name now. I start to wonder how he's doing, and I notice Death getting up from her table in the corner. She's got long, dark legs and a floral-print scarf tied around her neck. She gathers her neat trash and deposits it in the wastebasket before striding away. I hope that she's not going to visit the burned boy.

Rusty.

"Do you know her?" Aimee asks. That's the most words I've ever heard her string together at once. She lives in Monosyllabia, in a house of yeses and nos.

I glance at Death's now-empty table. "No," I say. "And I'm doing my best to keep it that way."

18

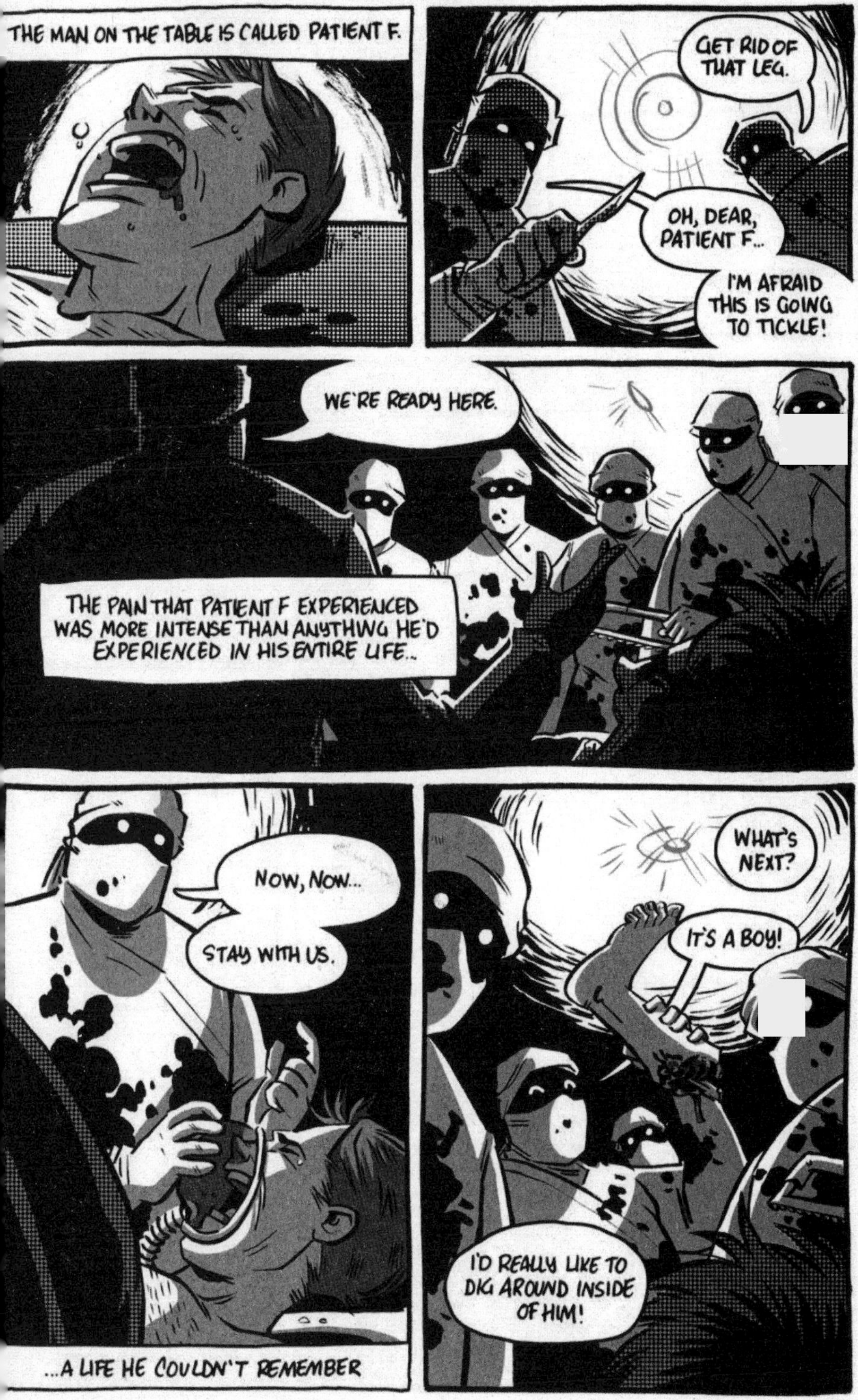
THE MAN ON THE TABLE IS CALLED PATIENT F.
GET RID OF THAT LEG.
OH, DEAR, PATIENT F...
I'M AFRAID THIS IS GOING TO TICKLE!
WE'RE READY HERE.
THE PAIN THAT PATIENT F EXPERIENCED WAS MORE INTENSE THAN ANYTHING HE'D EXPERIENCED IN HIS ENTIRE LIFE...
NOW, NOW...
STAY WITH US.
...A LIFE HE COULDN'T REMEMBER
WHAT'S NEXT?
IT'S A BOY!
I'D REALLY LIKE TO DIG AROUND INSIDE OF HIM!

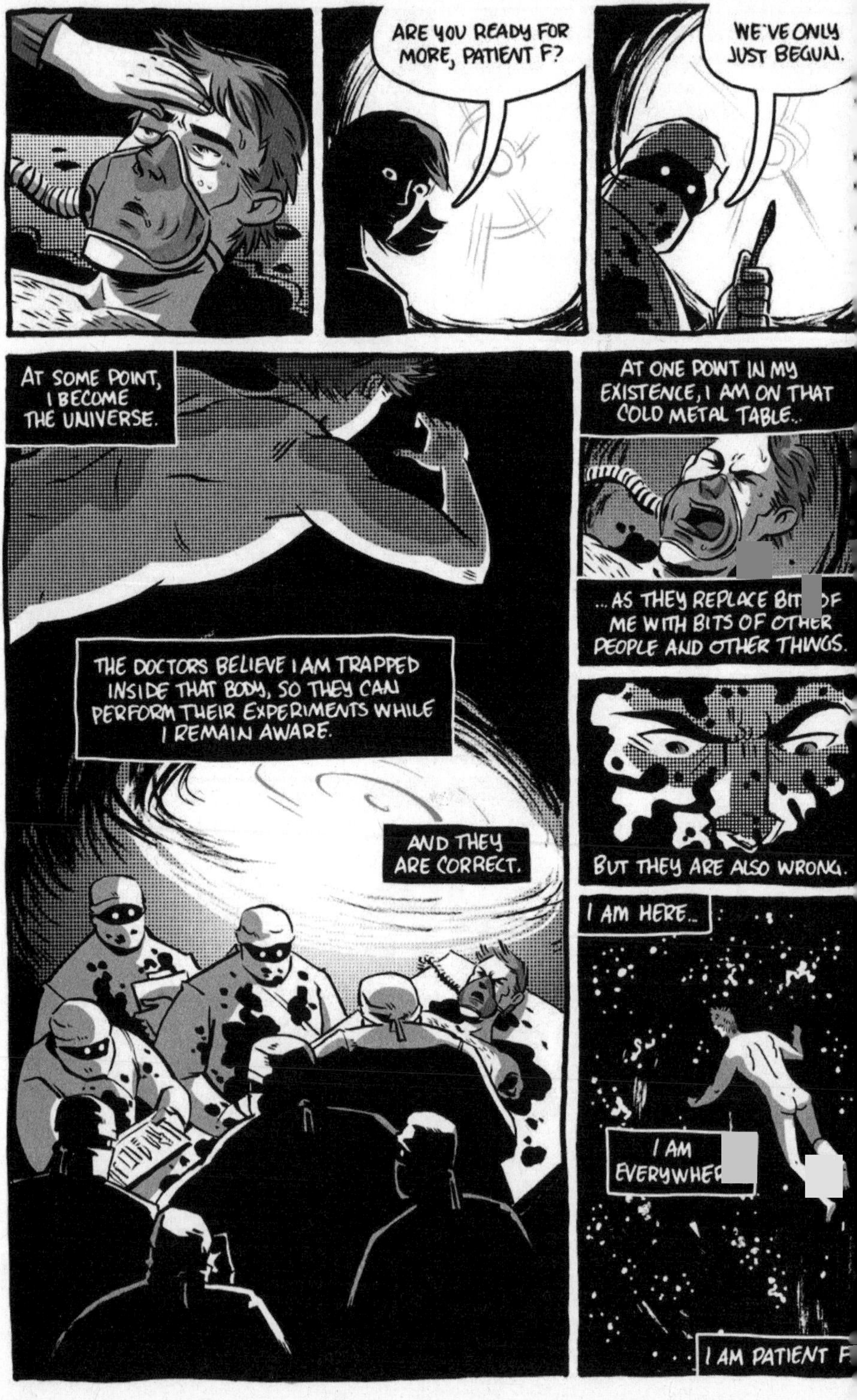
ARE YOU READY FOR MORE, PATIENT F?
WE'VE ONLY JUST BEGUN.
AT SOME POINT, I BECOME THE UNIVERSE.
THE DOCTORS BELIEVE I AM TRAPPED INSIDE THAT BODY, SO THEY CAN PERFORM THEIR EXPERIMENTS WHILE I REMAIN AWARE.
AND THEY ARE CORRECT.
AT ONE POINT IN MY EXISTENCE, I AM ON THAT COLD METAL TABLE..
...AS THEY REPLACE BIT OF ME WITH BITS OF OTHER PEOPLE AND OTHER THINGS.
BUT THEY ARE ALSO WRONG.
I AM HERE..
I AM EVERYWHER
I AM PATIENT F

Chapter 3
Superhuman Intelligence

People are fed, and my job is done.

Arnold pays me before I leave. "Explain to me again why I'm risking my livelihood by paying you under the table?" He hands me the envelope, and I don't bother counting the money inside before I stuff it into my back pocket. It's always all there, and the cash, while nice, isn't important.

"My parents won't let me have a job," I say. "But I need the money for college." All I had to do at the interview was mention college, and he practically fell over himself to give me the job.

"Where do your parents think you are when you're here?"

I tuck my sketchpad under my arm. It's bursting with Patient F drawings and notes. Not that I need the notes. "Visiting Grandma."

"Ah," Arnold says. "You really have a grandma here?"

"Duh," I say, with a smirk. "Room 1184. Eleanor Brawley."

"I might check."

"Be my guest," I say. "Your sauce is boiling." I point at the biggest pot of marinara sauce I've ever seen, happily bubbling away on the stove, spitting flecks of orange and red oil at the wall. Arnold mutters something under his breath that might be a swear but probably isn't. I'm fairly certain that I've never heard Arnold swear. Not even the day I dropped an entire tray of macaroni and cheese on the floor. I swore. Arnold made a lame joke.

While Arnold tends to his sauce, I sneak out. The hospital smell clobbers me as I pass from the cafeteria into the clean white hallways.

I wander, not entirely sure where I'm going. I'm a sailing ship letting the winds take me where they will. And in those winds, I hear the whisper of Rusty's name, which is how I end up standing outside the ICU, peeking through the gap between the double doors.

The ICU is where they deposit the desperately ill, the patients whose grasp on life is tenuous and liable to slip. The ones who are most likely to receive a final visit from long-legged Death herself. That's why I don't spend much time in this section of the hospital.

I turn to leave. Rusty is just a poor burned-up boy who probably won't survive the day. I've got no reason to stay.

Except I don't move.

The hallway in front of the ICU is the Doldrums, and I am adrift.

The double doors open inward. I slide against the wall to avoid being seen. A nurse in sky-blue scrubs wheels an elderly woman wearing an oxygen mask down the hall without so much as a glance for me. As the automatic doors begin to close, I slip through them and into the first empty room. The ICU is arranged similarly to the ER, an oval room situated around a desk area like an egg-shaped wheel.

But the ICU is nicer, newer. There are monitors everywhere, beeping and chirping to remind the nurses that their patients are still alive.

Two nurses staff the monitors with an economy of movement that I find both admirable and terrifying. They're more robot than person. They don't chatter or joke like my nurses in the ER do. The ICU nurses barely speak, and when they do, it's always in serious tones.

If one of those nurses finds me here, I'll likely wish Death had found me instead.

I peek through the beige curtains to see if I can figure out where they're keeping Rusty. There's an enormous monitor hanging on the wall bearing a list of names and vital stats. I look for McHale and find him. He's just a series of numbers. 97. 100/65. 97.7. 225. Heart rate, blood pressure, temperature, and maybe his room number. I'm not sure if those numbers are good for the burned boy, but I know they mean he's still alive.

The nurse who left with the elderly woman returns with a Styrofoam cup breathing steam. Probably coffee. None of these nurses look familiar, but that doesn't mean I've never seen them. I usually pay as little attention to them as they do to me.

The nurse says something to the others that I can't hear, but they respond with terse nods.

Coffee Nurse goes into a room while the others wait outside. She returns, ushering along two people, a man and a woman, both frayed. They barely exist, clinging to the here and now by their brittle fingernails. I look at the number on the wall: 225. Those must be Rusty's parents. They're old, but not as old as they appear to be: sixty-five at forty.

The other nurses slip quietly into Rusty's room while Coffee Nurse speaks to the McHales. Rusty's parents cling to her words as if they're the only port in a storm. I imagine her saying, "Your son is in good hands. You're tired. Go to the cafeteria and get some coffee. Maybe something to eat." I should warn them to avoid the spaghetti.

As Coffee Nurse leads the McHales away, the other nurses wheel Rusty out. I barely glimpse him, but I hear him moaning. The McHales hesitate and turn back toward their son. Coffee Nurse firmly guides them out the door, allowing them no opportunity to falter. Whatever is about to happen, she wants them elsewhere. Possibly for Rusty's sake, likely for their own. It's killing the McHales to leave, but they do. Maybe they go to the cafeteria. Maybe they flee the hospital, never to return. I couldn't blame them for it.

Coffee Nurse speaks to the others before they wheel Rusty away. When they've gone, she hangs her head. The things I imagine she told herself on her coffee break—that the boy is her job and not a child—aren't the armor she needs them to be. In her position, it's a weakness to care so blatantly.

The screams begin a moment later. Inhuman, monstrous howls. Surely it's an animal those nurses are torturing and not my burned boy.

But of course it is him, and there's no way to lie to myself about that.

As Rusty's shrieks devolve into frantic cries, calling out for the cruel parents who abandoned him, Coffee Nurse brushes the imaginary wrinkles from her scrubs and trudges toward the wicked place to which her cohorts have taken Rusty.

Only a minute more, and I can't take it. My fists are clenched, my knuckles white. My fingernails dig into the fleshy parts of my palms, leaving little half-moon indentations that will fade away painlessly. Unlike Rusty's screams, which follow me even as I run out of the ICU and far down the hall.

There's only one place I want to go. I lean against the wall for a moment and catch my breath, trying to unspool the line tightening around my lungs. Putting Rusty out of my mind isn't easy, or even possible. I try to imagine that he's Patient F fighting against his bonds as the doctors in red lab coats experiment on his broken body, but imagining Rusty as a superhero doesn't make his pain any less real.

My feet take me to Pediatrics. Everything here is brighter, livelier. The rest of the hospital is painted to remind people that they're in a Serious Place where Serious Things happen and Serious People work, but Peds is an entertaining jumble of primary colors and clowns and flowers and toys. It would be the coolest place in the hospital if it weren't for the sick kids.

Nurse Merchant sits at a small, unobtrusive workstation, filling out charts. Down here, they do their best to avoid reminding patients that they're in a hospital, but it's a badly staged illusion that people can't help seeing through.

"Hey, Nurse Merchant," I say. I try for a smile, but my lips barely twitch.

"Drew." Nurse Merchant has got enough smile for both of us. She moves with a mom's sincerity, though I'm not sure she's old enough to be anyone's mom. "How are you, sweetie?"

I tuck my hands into my pockets and shrug a little. "Good, I guess."

Nurse Merchant sets aside her pen and offers me her full

attention. She's pretty and reminds me of Marilyn Monroe, except that Nurse Merchant has brown hair that she wears pulled back. Sometimes I try to imagine her outside the hospital, but I can't do it. Like me, she lives here.

"That's good," Nurse Merchant says. "How's your grandma?"

"Still in a coma." The joke falls flat, so I quickly change the subject. "How are Trevor and Lexi?"

"Trevor had a rough night, but Lexi was up with the sun."

"As usual," I say about Lexi, though lately it applies to Trevor, too. "Can I see them?"

Nurse Merchant looks toward Trevor's room. "Better give Trevor more time to sleep. But Lexi could use the break. She's studying. Again." Nurse Merchant emphasizes "again," and I don't have to ask what she means.

"I'll take care of it," I say, my smile coming more easily.

"Good boy. See if you can get her to eat, too." Nurse Merchant returns to her charting, and I walk to Lexi's room. I'm not family, so technically I shouldn't be here, but the rules are more flexible in Pediatrics. Anything that makes the kids happy is welcome, and that includes me.

The blinds in Lexi's room are wide open. The blinds are always open, even at night. The view's not so great; there are some power lines, a nondescript grayish office building, and a run-down Chick'n Shak. Not more than two miles away is the ocean, but you can't see it from Lexi's room. The limited view isn't even worth the effort to keep the shades open, but Lexi refuses to close them and has vowed everlasting torment upon anyone who tries.

Lexi isn't the kind of girl you expect to have cancer. She isn't plucky or strange. She doesn't have indie cred or a brilliant ray of sunshine that beams out of her ass no matter how bad things get. She's bookish and eager and the kind of girl who likes getting extra English homework over long holiday weekends.

"What's up, A-Dog?" Lexi asks. She doesn't even look up from the textbook she's devouring with her bloodshot brown eyes. She's skinnier than a spaghetti noodle, and a bowl of oatmeal sits untouched on the tray by her bed. I want to grab the spoon and force-feed her, but that's not the way to work Lexi.

"A-Dog?" I ask from the doorway.

"No good?"

"I like Drewfus better."

Lexi glances at me out of the corner of her eye. "Why am I not surprised?"

"Because you're the genius who knows everything." I step into the room and rub Lexi's bald head before she has the chance to stop me.

"How come people are always trying to rub my head? I'm not Buddha, bitch."

I wriggle my eyebrows suggestively. "Bald girls are hot."

"Please." Lexi leans back against the pillow but doesn't close her book. I bet she's thinking that she can sneak-read a line while I'm talking.

"No joke." I pull up a chair and rest my feet on the edge of her bed. Lexi's room is small but warm. The walls are faded yellow, and there's a Sesame Street mural in the corner. It's odd having a giant Elmo looming over me. Sometimes I feel like he's going to pull away from that wall and tickle *me*.

27

"Trevor said he thought you looked great sans hair," I tell Lexi. "Of course, that was before I told him that when your hair grows back, you'll probably end up with some wicked sideburns."

Lexi sits up, knocking over her book. "You did *not!*"

"Huge muttonchops."

"You're evil."

I nod. "Superhero, supervillain—it's a pretty fine line." I try to twist my grin into an evil sneer, but I think I just look deformed.

"You write anything new?" Lexi asks, pointing at my sketchpad.

Lexi knows all about Patient F. That's how we met. I was in the cafeteria working on some sketches when Nurse Merchant noticed me. She has a brother who draws, so she sat down and asked me about my work. I didn't want to tell her about Patient F—I was embarrassed, you know?—but she has a way of getting people to do things they don't want to do. Maybe that's her superpower. After I showed her Patient F, Nurse Merchant told me about a girl up in Peds who might enjoy my stories. I think, in her own misguided way, Nurse Merchant was trying to play hospital matchmaker, unaware that Lexi and I were clearly not a match.

But I went to Peds anyway. Lexi still had some of her hair then. The chemo and radiation were eating away at her body, and she barely knew I existed, but I told her all about Patient F—all that I'd written to that point, anyway. We've been friends ever since.

"Not really," I say. "I'm working on the beginning again."

Lexi rolls her eyes. Without eyebrows, she reminds me of a Muppet. "You've got to learn to move forward, Drew. That's your problem, you know?"

I'm not sure what to say, so I keep my mouth shut.

"Did you hear about that boy who got lit on fire?" Lexi asks.

My stomach clenches, and I forget to breathe for a second. I hope that Lexi didn't notice, that my emotions didn't betray me, and I nod, wondering how Lexi heard about it. Peds is so insulated from the rest of the hospital. The nurses here are a different breed. Nurse Merchant would never fraternize with Steven and Emma and Jo, with their childish, gossipy ways.

"It's all over the news," Lexi says. "He was at a Fourth of July party, and some kids doused him with alcohol and set him on fire."

"Yeah, I heard about it." I came here to escape Rusty, but I soak up every detail, unable to stop myself. Even when the anger threatens to cripple me.

"They have some suspects but no witnesses." Lexi tilts her head to catch my eyes, but I look away, stare out her window, imagining I can actually see the ocean. Maybe that's what Lexi does, why she keeps the blinds open.

A voice in the hallway catches my attention. Death is hovering around Nurse Merchant's station, chatting all friendly. At least that means she's not with Rusty. I keep my back to the door so she doesn't see me.

"It's all anyone talked about at breakfast," I say, distracted by Death. "Kid got burned—buttered toast, please."

"Oh," Lexi says. I think she's finally caught on that I don't want to discuss Rusty. "Did you and Trevor really talk about me?"

I'm listening for Death's next move. Her heels click-clack across the floor, and it sounds like she's coming my way. If she catches me, *I'll* be buttered toast. Every muscle in my body clenches and my heartbeat trebles. I expect that, any second, I'll feel her cold, bony hand on my shoulder as she hauls me off to her lair.

But Death detours into Trevor's room. She spends too much time in there these days, but it doesn't surprise me. One day soon, I imagine she'll claim Trevor as her own. For now, though, he belongs to us.

"Drew?"

"Yeah?"

Lexi frowns at me for not listening. "Did you and Trevor really talk about me?"

"Trevor and I talk about a lot of things, Lexi," I tell her. "Maybe you were one of them. Maybe you weren't. Either way, we definitely didn't talk about how skinny you're getting." It's the kind of answer that I know will drive her nuts. "Anyway, I have to run." I don't want to be around when Death leaves Trevor's room.

Lexi slides her book back into her lap and eyes the oatmeal. "Fine. I have a lot of work to do anyway. I've got to finish the decorations for Trevor's party."

"You work too much," I tell her.

"It's all I have." She looks down at her book. "You and Trevor and work."

I want to tell her that she could have so much more if she focused on the now and less on the future, but I can't risk staying. My chair scrapes across the floor when I put it back. "See you tomorrow."

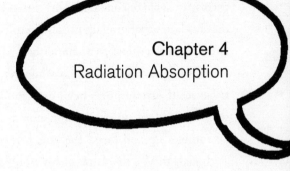

Chapter 4
Radiation Absorption

Today is a very special day.

I stand on the roof of the parking garage and stare at the world beyond the hospital. It's early, and mist clings to every car and building and random stranger wandering down the lonesome two-lane streets. Sometimes whole days pass where I don't see the outside world at all. I lose myself in the rhythm of the hospital and the people who walk its halls, lost in their own routines, oblivious to the futile nature of their jobs. Sometimes I forget that I wasn't born in the bowels of Roanoke General, that I came from *out there*. That there is a whole universe beyond these walls, churning along without me.

I think I could stay on this roof forever, surrounded by the smell of concrete and hot summer air. In Florida, summer arrives before the dawn. By the time the sun comes up, the world is sweat soaked, and people hide in air-conditioned bubbles. I don't mind it. It's better than the cold.

I can't stay up here forever, though. The world *out there* isn't real. Not anymore. Not for me. For me, there is only this hospital, these people, and one very special day.

I run down the stairs, taking them two at a time, relishing the permanence of concrete under my feet as I leap down and land hard, the shock reverberating up my legs, reminding me that I'm still here and that I have things to accomplish.

Visiting hours aren't for a while yet, so I stop by the cafeteria to see if Arnold needs help, but I'm glad it's my day off when I see Arnold's foul, summer-storm mood. I watch from the gates as he rumbles up and down the line, throwing trays of food around as though they're the cause of his troubles. I've seen him annoyed before, but I've never seen him truly angry. I hope I never see it again.

"You don't want to be here." Aimee's so thin, she barely displaces air, which is why I didn't hear her come up behind me.

"Who pissed in his cornflakes?" I'm afraid to take my eyes off of Arnold. He's a one-man hate machine.

"No one." Aimee has a hook nose that's accentuated by her sunken cheeks. When she frowns at me, I feel like she could be terrifying if she just put some effort into it. "Today is his son's birthday."

"Oh." I want to press her for more information, but Aimee slips under the gate and hurries into the caf, a brave, lone warrior. I could join her, help her negotiate Arnold's rage, but I know I wouldn't be doing it to help Aimee, that I'd only be doing it to find out why Arnold is so angry, and there are more important things to do today.

I spend the rest of the morning staying out of the way. Death isn't the only person searching for me, and a shiftless boy is bound to arouse suspicion, so I walk with purpose. I'm grateful when nine o'clock rolls around, so that I can gather my helium-filled tools of war and invade Peds.

With my hard-earned cafeteria wages, I bought a few gifts from the shop. Chocolate, mostly. There weren't a lot of options. I suppose there aren't many things that sick people need. Stuffed animals and chocolate. I'm not sure Trevor will appreciate a teddy bear, no matter how cute its button nose.

Nurse Merchant is doing her rounds when I stroll in with my balloons and bags. Tight lines crease her forehead. I'm not sure what to make of that. Is she angry? Annoyed? Have I done something wrong? Is something wrong with Trevor?

"Today's a very special day," I say to explain the balloons. "This is the day Trevor was supposed to die."

"Oh, Drew." Nurse Merchant puts her hand to her mouth and stands in the hall, so fragile that a soft breath could shatter her.

When Trevor was diagnosed with aggressive stage 4 leukemia, his doctor gave him six months to live. Today is that six-month mark. Lexi and I have been planning his very special day for a week. I've been sneaking her bits of colored paper, and she's been making decorations between bouts of marathon studying for classes that won't even start for another two months.

"Why didn't you tell me?" Nurse Merchant has regained control, but her expression remains grim.

"Is Trevor okay?" I ask. It's the only question that matters.

Nurse Merchant crosses the room to stand beside me. She's shorter than I am, but I still feel small. "Trevor's alive."

Not okay. Not fine. Alive.

"Can I see him? I've got these balloons and stuff." I hold up the gift bag. Its handle cuts into my fingers.

"Maybe you should visit with Lexi first," Nurse Merchant says. "Trevor had another rough night."

"But—"

She puts her hand on my shoulder, and it stops me midsentence. "I think he's awake, but he's not quite ready for visitors."

"Lexi first," I say, as if it were my decision. I glance at Trevor's room forlornly. Lexi came to the hospital before Trevor, but I have the sinking feeling that he'll be the first to leave.

Lexi is sitting in her bed with books spread across her lap. She looks healthier than she did yesterday—but barely. The sun streaming through the open blinds is an invasion of light that sears my eyes.

"Drew?" Lexi's smiling this morning. Her smile is her secret weapon. She pulls it out so rarely that just when I'm convinced it never existed, she flashes it and completely disarms me. Moments like this, it's easy to see why Trevor is so taken with her.

I toss the bag of goodies onto the chair and let the balloons bob around at the foot of Lexi's bed. "It's a very special day, right?"

Lexi's eyes fly open. "Oh!"

"You forgot?"

"I didn't forget," Lexi says defensively. "I'm just not quite finished." Lexi shoves her books to the floor and points at the wardrobe in the corner. "There's a plastic bag in there. Get it for me."

There are more clothes in Lexi's wardrobe than she could ever possibly wear. Sometimes the nurses encourage her to dress in regular clothes and walk around the hospital, ostensibly for exercise. But I believe it's so that she can pretend for a little while that she's a normal girl. Her mother feeds the effort by turning up with armloads of the kinds of clothes that "cheap hookers wear"—Lexi's words, not mine.

The bag she asked me to fetch is at the bottom of the wardrobe, on top of a knit sweater that's far too warm to wear now.

"How could you forget?" I ask, tossing her the bag. I don't mean to sound accusatory, but anger clings to my words like sticky tar.

Lexi doesn't look me in the eyes when she says, "I lost track of time." She pauses. "The days all just run together, Drew."

"Were you doing schoolwork?" I glance at the books on the floor, and I know that it's killing her to leave them lying there. Every textbook is a sacred tome to her. Might as well set fire to a Bible. "School doesn't start for weeks."

"But I want to be ready."

"You'd rather be ready for something you may not even get to attend than something that's here now?"

Lexi stops cutting the banner. "This isn't my life, Drew. My life is out there."

"Your life isn't out there until *you're* out there."

Nurse Merchant wanders in and instantly gauges the room. She looks at me and at Lexi and says, "I'm not letting either of you near Trevor with this kind of negative energy." She busies herself taking Lexi's blood pressure and temperature before she moves on.

"Need some help?"

Lexi nods at me, and I take up a pile of the colored paper. Most of the decorations are done. It's just a matter of cutting them out. We work side by side and seem to have struck an unspoken truce.

By the time we're finished, Lexi is lecturing me about feminism in *The Canterbury Tales*. I do my best to nod along and pretend I care, even though I'm not really paying attention because I'm too anxious to visit Trevor. When Nurse Merchant finally tells us that we're allowed to go to Trevor's room, my gratitude is boundless.

Trevor Guerrero looks defeated. There's a picture beside his bed of a boy with bushy blond hair and a confident smile. He's cradling a football and looks like he's ready to tackle the world. I can't comprehend that the boy in the picture and the broken boy in the bed are the same person—until he smiles. Then I know.

"Droopy Drew." Trevor sounds like he gargled broken glass. "Balloons?"

Lexi wheels her IV stand into the room and starts hanging our decorations—signs that say GLAD YOU'RE NOT DEAD! and CANCER, SCHMANCER. She keeps glancing over her shoulder at Trevor but doesn't say anything to him yet.

I tie the balloons to Trevor's bed rail and hand him the bag. "Balloons *and* chocolates," I say.

Trevor struggles to sit up, but he can't and surrenders. Bones outline his pale, damp face, and beads of sweat roll down his smooth head. "Just 'cause you brought me candy doesn't mean I'm putting out." Every word is agony for him. I can see it in the way he flinches and curls in on himself.

"Not even one little smoochy?" Lexi makes kissing noises as she draws the blinds open with a flourish.

"Trevor isn't my type," I say. I toss him the chocolates. "No nuts."

Lexi laughs—a pained sound, like a tortured cat. Everything about her is amped up right now, and I think it has to do with her proximity to Trevor. Her crush isn't of the subtle variety.

Trevor's quick on the uptake. He grabs his crotch and says, "I got your nuts right here, dude." Then he laughs too, but laughing is difficult for Trevor. It's a marathon. I watch the rise and fall of his chest to make sure that he doesn't lag too far behind his breathing.

He coughs and looks ashamed. "I had asthma when I was little," he says. "Grew out of it, you know?"

"Just breathe," Lexi says. She's parked near the window, but I can see that every fiber of every muscle is poised to spring to Trevor's side if necessary.

"Whenever I marched onto the football field, I wondered if that would be the day that God stole my breath again." Trevor digs into the gift bag and pulls out a CONGRATULATIONS ON YOUR NEW BABY mug to go along with the chocolates. "Thanks, Droopy."

"Today's a very special day!" Lexi exclaims out of the blue. I know she's trying to bring some levity to the situation, but she's doing a really terrible job. "Drewfus tells me you think I'm going to grow a pair of nice hairy sideburns."

Trevor's chalky skin turns strawberry red. I imagine that, before he got sick, he was the kind of guy who never blushed. The girls threw themselves at him, and he kissed them all and made them cry.

"Droopy said that," Trevor says. "Not me."

"I plead the sixth." I hold up my hands.

"The fifth," Lexi says in her most teacherlike voice.

I chuckle. "Six is higher, and I need all the protection I can get. You're scary."

"You want to talk scary? You should see the wig my mom bought me." Lexi tosses out that little grenade and then sits back to watch the shrapnel fly.

Trevor gapes at Lexi, disbelieving, and then he cracks up laughing. This time, the laughter rolls through his scrawny frame until it twists him into a knot and he starts coughing. The coughing seizes him, shaking his body like a matchstick house on a foundation of sand.

I turn to get Nurse Merchant, but Trevor points at the water glass, and I fetch it instead. After a couple of sips, he says, "You gotta get the wig."

Lexi's shoulders are high, tense; she isn't sure she should relax yet. She's ready to back me up with more water if Trevor needs it. "No way."

"Come on," I say. "How bad could it be?" Except that I've met Lexi's mother, and I'm pretty sure I have a good idea exactly how bad it could be.

"Anyway. It's my very special day." Trevor has pulled out the big guns, and he's a crack shot.

Lexi pretends to think about it, but I know there's no way she can refuse. It's all pretense at this point. "Fine. But only this one time, and don't you dare laugh at me." She points at us both to make sure we know we've been warned, and then she drags her IV stand out of the room.

The moment Lexi's gone, Trevor begins adjusting his nasal cannula and fussing over his hospital gown. "I can't believe you told her that I thought she was gonna grow monster mutts."

Trevor's heart rate spikes, and I can't help smiling. "Dude, she likes you."

"How can she? Look at me." Trevor's lost about fifteen pounds since he checked into the hospital. I used to call him Skeletor, until it stopped being funny. "She likes that guy," he says, motioning at his picture.

"You *are* that guy."

Trevor frowns because he knows I'm patronizing him. But what else can I do? He's dying.

"Senior year was supposed to be the best year of my life. That's what everyone said. But I'll be here." He thumps a fist against the side of his mattress.

"Alive," I remind him.

"This ain't living, Droopy."

I'm not sure what to say. He's right about everything.

Lexi saves me when she returns wearing something that looks like a scraggly, dead raccoon on her head. The wig is bushy and brownish and hangs limply around her face. I prefer her bald.

"I think you have it on backward," I say.

"Thanks." Lexi stands in the doorway, adjusting her wig. "How about now?" She strikes a pose that makes her look like a funhouse-mirror reflection of a supermodel.

Trevor, who's been staring with his mouth hanging open for the past ten seconds, finally finds his tongue and says, "Dead cat?"

"I was thinking wet dog," I say.

Lexi endures our wisecracks with her arms crossed over her chest and a deadly frown. "Anything else?" Now she's daring us to mock her, and Trevor rises to the challenge.

"I don't know, Drew. She's getting a bit snippy, so we might want to cut this short."

It's not particularly funny, but Lexi grins, and we all start laughing. We can't stop. The laughter lightens the mood of Trevor's very special day—until he starts coughing and we have to call the nurse.

• • •

39

Nurse Merchant kicks me out after a couple of hours because Lexi and Trevor need their rest. I haven't visited Grandma Brawley in a few days, so I wander toward her room. The nurse at the desk recognizes me, even though I don't remember his name. There are too many nurses at this hospital to remember them all.

I try to sneak by Mr. Kelly's room, but he's awake and yells at me from his bed. "Andrew! Andrew, they're trying to kill me!"

Mr. Kelly is hooked up to more wires than a marionette. He's a wrinkled bag of apples with white hair in his ears and nose, and none on his head.

I duck into Mr. Kelly's room but stay near the door. "I don't have time to chat today, Mr. Kelly."

He points at the tray on his table. "But they're trying to kill me. Look at this swill."

I lift the top off the tray. Green beans and apple juice and some beige-colored meat. There's even pudding for dessert. "I've built up a tolerance. I'll take it if you want."

"Take it." Mr. Kelly waves his bony hand at the tray. "My Gloria is bringing me a burger. A burger!" He yells loud enough for the nurse to hear. For the whole hall to hear, really. Too bad nobody's listening.

I pick up the tray and head for the door. "Thanks, Mr. Kelly. Enjoy your burger."

Grandma Brawley is in room 1184. She's a tiny woman with silver hair that spills out over her pillow like tinsel. Her chest rises and falls with the sound of the equipment that monitors her vital signs. The only time she moves is when the nurses come in to change her sheets or exercise her limbs to make sure she doesn't get bedsores.

Other than that, she's a sleeping princess. A fairy tale that someone forgot to finish.

"Trevor's probably going to die," I tell her matter-of-factly. I tell Grandma Brawley everything. She's a vault. Best secret keeper ever. She even knows how I ended up in this hospital. But she'll never tell.

"And Lexi's in love with him but won't do anything about it. She doesn't know how to live in the moment." I shovel Mr. Kelly's food into my mouth, trying not to taste it on the way down. It's worse than Arnold's cooking, which is saying quite a lot.

"Trevor doesn't have the confidence to tell Lexi that he's in love with her, too. They've spent so long being sick, they don't know how to be in love."

I call her Gran even though she's not my grandma. I have no idea who she is. The only indication of her life outside this hospital room is the picture frame by her bed with a lock of red hair pressed between the glass.

"I wish I could do something for Trevor." As I say the words, I realize that I *can* do something. Not much, but for someone like him, every bit of joy counts. As soon as I finish eating, I start sketching.

It takes most of the day to finish the drawing. When I finish, I run out of Grandma Brawley's room, through the halls, hoping I'll make it to Peds before visiting hours end.

Nurse Merchant is still hanging around, chatting with another nurse. "Oh dear, Drew," Nurse Merchant says when she sees me. "I'm afraid I can't let you in to see Trevor."

I hold out the folded piece of paper, the one I've been working on for hours. "Come on, I only need two minutes." I try to flash my winningest smile, but I can already sense that something is wrong.

41

"Trevor's on a ventilator."

I drop my sketchpad and paper. I don't know how I'm still standing. Nurse Merchant is by my side in an instant.

"But today's a very special day," I whisper.

"I know, sweetie."

The other nurse is mute, but Nurse Merchant knows what to do. She wraps her arms around my shoulders and hugs me.

"What happened?" I ask, though I'm not sure I want the answer.

Nurse Merchant sighs. "Being sick is exhausting, Drew. Sometimes the body needs help. That's what the ventilator's for. It'll help Trevor breathe so that he can save his strength."

I slip out of her hug and pick up my drawing, hold it out to Nurse Merchant. It's Trevor, dressed like a superhero, ready for battle. He looks fit and powerful and alive. Just like in the photograph. "I wanted Trevor to see himself the way we do."

Nurse Merchant nods. "Why don't we leave it in his room so that he can spot it right when he wakes up?"

I don't think I'm strong enough to see Trevor like this. I was in his room once when he coded. That was when I could barely tell he was sick. We were playing cards, and Trevor was alive. Then he wasn't. I huddled unseen in the corner while the doctor shocked Trevor's quivering heart back to life. When he opened his eyes, he laughed. The fucker actually laughed.

But he's not laughing now, and I can hardly stand to look at him with that accordion tube snaking out of his mouth, machines forcing his lungs to expand and contract.

Nurse Merchant rests her hand on my shoulder. "I know it's tough."

I put the drawing on the edge of Trevor's mattress and retreat to the door. "I've seen worse."

"That shouldn't be true for someone your age," Nurse Merchant says.

And she's right. But it doesn't change anything. Words never do.

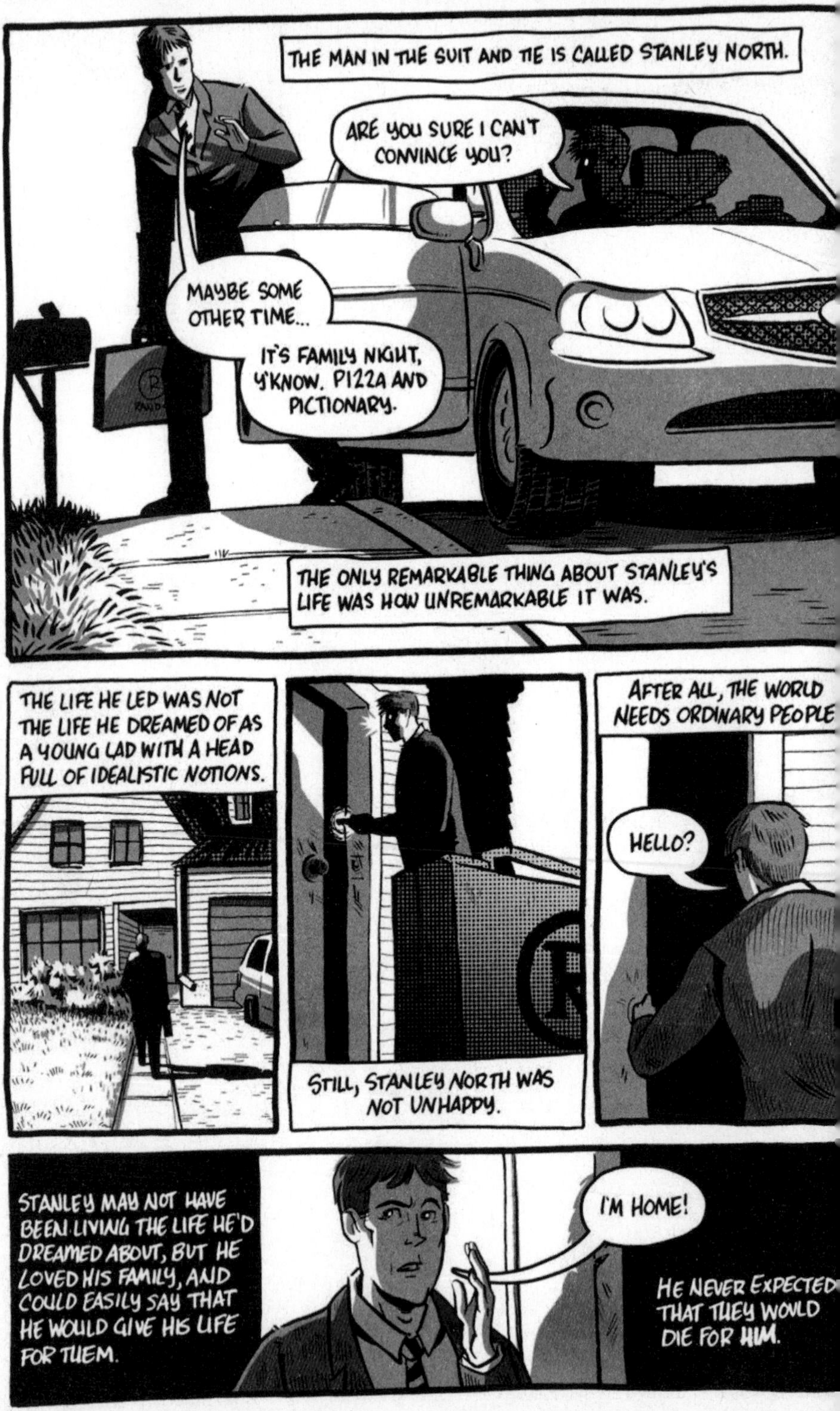
THE MAN IN THE SUIT AND TIE IS CALLED STANLEY NORTH.
ARE YOU SURE I CAN'T CONVINCE YOU?
MAYBE SOME OTHER TIME...
IT'S FAMILY NIGHT, Y'KNOW. PIZZA AND PICTIONARY.
THE ONLY REMARKABLE THING ABOUT STANLEY'S LIFE WAS HOW UNREMARKABLE IT WAS.
THE LIFE HE LED WAS NOT THE LIFE HE DREAMED OF AS A YOUNG LAD WITH A HEAD FULL OF IDEALISTIC NOTIONS.
STILL, STANLEY NORTH WAS NOT UNHAPPY.
AFTER ALL, THE WORLD NEEDS ORDINARY PEOPLE
HELLO?
STANLEY MAY NOT HAVE BEEN LIVING THE LIFE HE'D DREAMED ABOUT, BUT HE LOVED HIS FAMILY, AND COULD EASILY SAY THAT HE WOULD GIVE HIS LIFE FOR THEM.
I'M HOME!
HE NEVER EXPECTED THAT THEY WOULD DIE FOR **HIM**.

Rye Public Library

964-8401

1/3/2017 2:31:55 PM

****

Title: The five stages of Andrew Brawley

Item ID: 34602002413253

Due: 1/31/2017

Beyond the Binding 1/19 at 6 30 PM

Cookbook Club 1/23 at 1PM (Sign up Required)

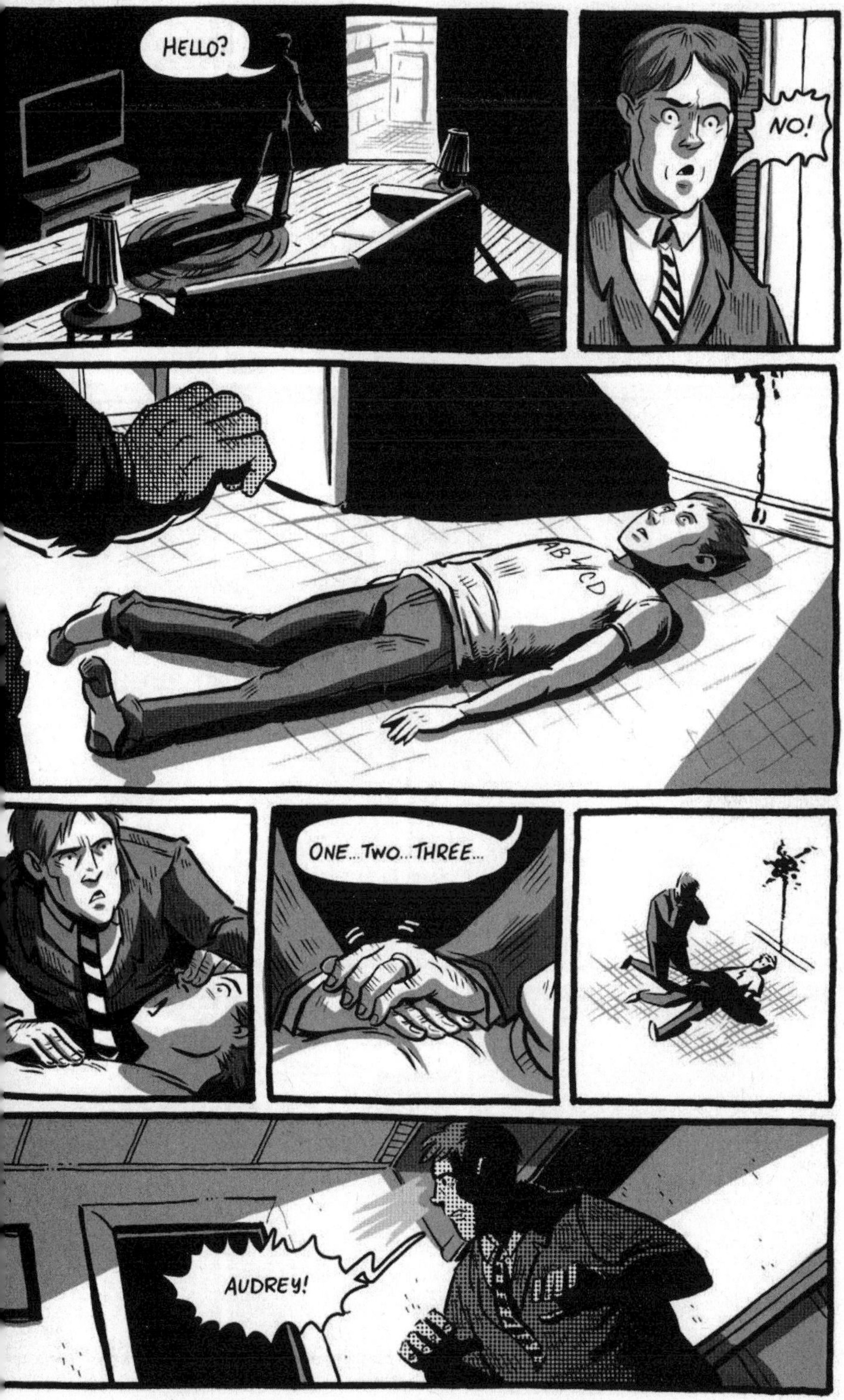
HELLO?
NO!
AB4CD
ONE... TWO... THREE...
AUDREY!

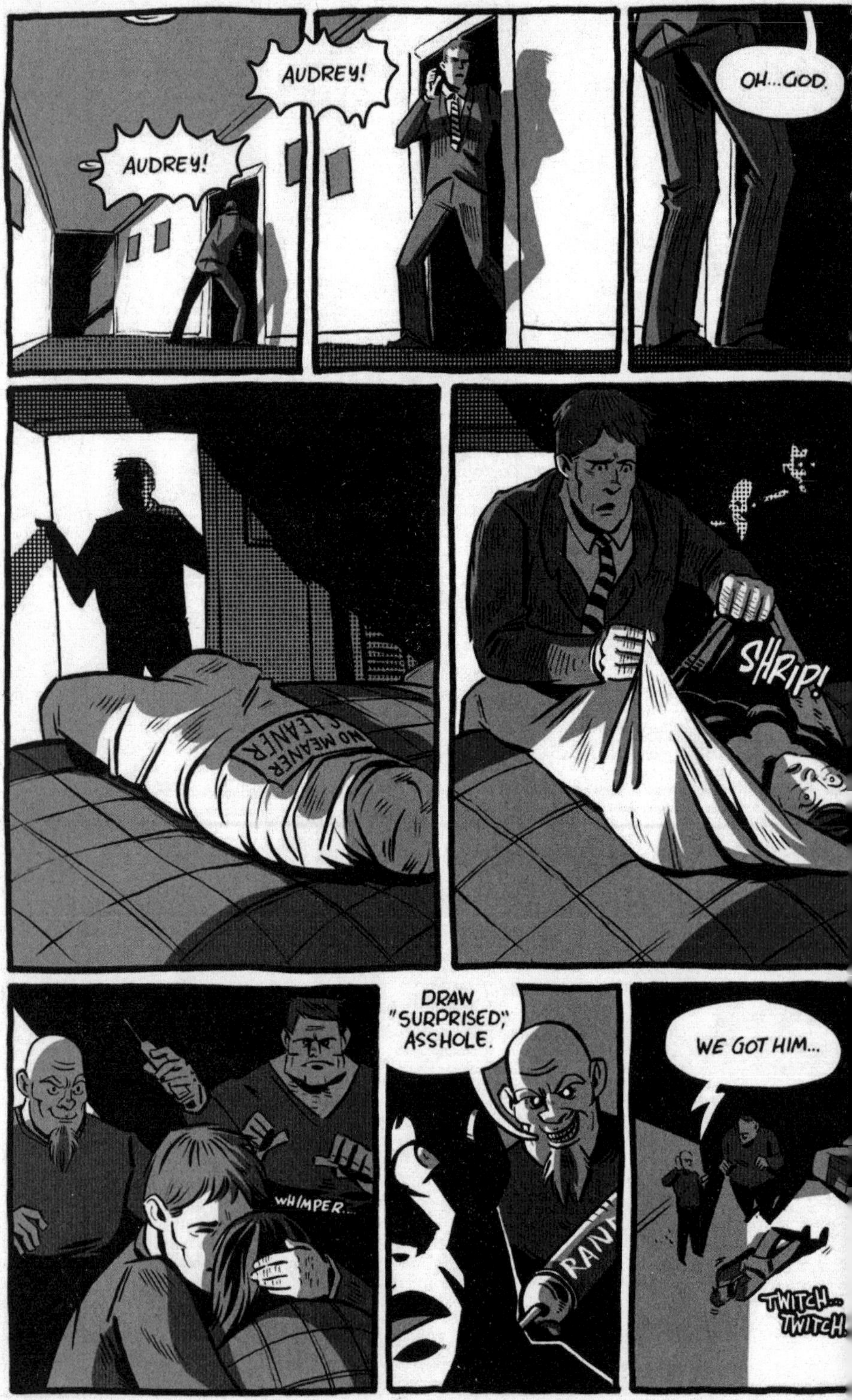
AUDREY!
AUDREY!
OH...GOD.
NO MEANER CLEANER
SHRIP!
WHIMPER...
DRAW "SURPRISED," ASSHOLE.
WE GOT HIM...
TWITCH... TWITCH.

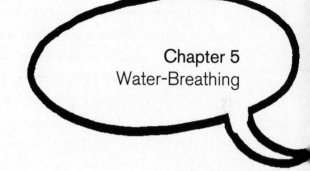

Chapter 5
Water-Breathing

Patient F is an enigma even to me, his creator.

I sketch in the cafeteria because I have nowhere else to go. With the events of the past week fresh in my mind, I'm in no mood to socialize, but I don't want to be alone, either. Every time I close my eyes, I see Rusty burning. Every time I open them, I see Trevor in a state of half death, gasping for breath that doesn't come. It's been a couple of days since I've visited either of them. For all I know, Death could have carried off one or both. She's ruthlessly efficient.

But I think I would know.

Patient F is my only distraction. When I'm drawing, it's as if I, too, become unstuck in time, sharing in his dark adventures, bathing in the same blood. Lexi was right about one thing: I spend too much time focusing on his origin. The problem is that I'm unsure where to take Patient F next, and he's not talking. Who can guess the desires of the dead?

"Why didn't you tell me you could draw so well?" Arnold sits down with a thump and scares me so badly that I break the tip of my pencil and smudge the panel I was working on. I try to mask the murder in my eyes, but it doesn't matter: Arnold is oblivious.

I pull out my earbuds and shove them in my pocket. "Because I didn't want people bothering me to draw stuff for them all the time."

Arnold fires off a laugh like he thinks I'm joking. "I don't suppose you'd give the menu board a spruce." He hikes his thumb over his shoulder at the black dry-erase board. It looks like it hasn't been used in decades and displays the same picture as the day I was hired: a constipated fish that Arnold must have drawn with his feet while blindfolded.

"No," I say. With most people, if you avoid eye contact, they'll take the hint and leave. But Arnold isn't like most people. We're alone in the caf, and he's determined to annoy me.

"You'd be doing me a huge favor. I don't know if you noticed, but I don't draw so well."

I glance at the board again. "What? No, that fish is a real winner. It belongs in the Louvre."

Arnold misses my sarcasm and beams from behind his bushy beard—which grows more unruly every day. "I did take an art class in college. Easy credit, lots of pretty girls."

"Oh, yeah? So are you a breast or a thigh man?" I ask, trying to embarrass him. It works. He blushes fiercely.

"No changing the subject." Arnold wags his finger. "Now, about that board . . ."

I drop my pencil. I'm not going to get anything done until I (A) agree to draw on his board or (B) dodge the question until he gets so angry that he storms off. I'm game for plan B except that it runs the risk of also costing me my job, and I need my job to avoid suspicion. Working for Arnold gives me a reason to be in the hospital. Without it, people might notice that I never seem to leave, and that I resemble a certain missing boy—and that's a gamble I'm unwilling to take. "If I do it, will you leave me alone?"

"Yes," Arnold says. "Let's get started. You can draw tomorrow's menu." He beelines for the board before I have a chance to change my mind.

I gather my pencils and sketchpad and follow. He shows me where the markers are and tells me to draw vegetable lasagna and meat loaf.

While I work, Arnold babbles about his family. His wife keeps telling him to stop wasting his life working in a cafeteria, cooking substandard food.

"If you're so smart, then why *are* you here?" I quickly draw the outline of a meaty loaf in an appetizing shade of neon orange.

"I could ask you the same thing," Arnold retorts. He busies himself disinfecting the counters. It's past closing, and I should be long gone.

"No fair evading the question, *Ah-nold*."

This makes him laugh. He's the inquisitive type, and I know that someday he'll figure out the truth about me. For now, he's happy to talk about himself. "I make good food for people who have terrible heartache. They grieve for their loved ones, and I do what I can for them: I feed them." It sounds like something Grandma Brawley would say—the Grandma Brawley I've cooked up in my mind, anyway.

49

I scribble some finishing touches on the vegetable lasagna. It looks more like two slices of bread hugging a jumble of emo veggies. Not a terrible drawing—definitely better than Arnold's fish—but not my magnum opus.

"Calling it good food is a bit of a stretch, don't you think?" I ask. Arnold belly-laughs, and I say, "Seriously, though, you could teach or write a book or something."

"I like it here."

"Sounds to me like you're hiding." I don't mean to say the words; they just jump out of my mouth. It's not so much that I regret saying them but that they come dangerously close to violating our unspoken agreement.

Arnold tosses his rag into a bucket of bleach water and pops open the cash register. "The menu board looks good. How much do I owe you?"

Despite that it's late and Arnold is annoying me, I still don't want to be alone. But I can tell when I'm being dismissed. "How about I just take the leftover doughnuts off your hands and we call it even?"

Arnold acts as though he's thinking it over, but he's already closing the cash drawer. "You drive a hard bargain, Andrew. The doughnuts are yours."

The emergency room is quiet this time of the night, and Steven, Jo, and Emma are gathered around the nurse's station, staring at something that I can't see but assume must be pretty amusing by the way Steven is cackling like a cartoon villain. I stand off to the side, just watching the three of them. They're a makeshift family. They take care of each other, laugh with each other, and if Steven weren't gay, they'd probably sleep with each other too.

They make me long for my family. My friends. The people in my life that I cared about without reservation. I have Lexi and Trevor now, but it's not the same because they have their own people outside these walls.

There's the hospital, and there's everything that happens outside it. My ER nurses and Lexi and Trevor and the burned boy Rusty—they all have lives *out there*.

Everything I have is in here.

"Surprise!" I say, and stride forward, offering up the doughnuts in outstretched hands. "I come bearing gifts."

Steven leaps to his feet, trying to look busy. When he realizes that I'm not one of the doctors, his momentary terror is replaced by a smile wide as the Grand Canyon. "Hey, Drew. What are you doing here so late?"

Emma turns the laptop toward me. "Have you seen this video? This chick's a one-woman library of Joss Whedon characters." She snorts and laughs. "Seriously, she went into a grocery store and slayed a box of Count Chocula."

Jo rolls her eyes. "I don't get it." She spies what I'm carrying and says, "You gonna show us the goods or just tease us?"

I lift the lid and expose the sugary treasures inside. "I got glazed for Steven, jelly for Jo, and sprinkles for Emma."

Emma squeals. "Yay! I'm so totally eating carbs again."

"Carbs everywhere—beware," Steven says. He strolls to the box, looking rather uninterested. "What makes you think I like glazed?"

"Because you like shiny things." I nudge the box. Steven daintily picks up the glazed with his first finger and thumb and tears off a bite.

Emma kisses my cheek in thanks, and that only leaves Jo. "Come on, Jo. You know you want it."

"Sugar, I'm on a diet." She reaches behind the counter and pulls out a rumpled plastic bag of carrot sticks.

"Come on," I say, pushing the box closer and closer. "Don't deny your high-fructose desires."

Jo wavers. Steven and Emma watch while they munch happily on their doughnuts. Jo reaches out but retreats. She reaches out and pulls back again. The third time she reaches out, Emma sticks her hand into the box and says, "Well, if you're not going to eat it, I am."

"I will cut you, Emma." Jo snatches the jelly doughnut and savors a slow, sugarlicious bite.

Steven's practically on the floor now, convulsing with laughter, and I can't help smiling. Soon, we're all sitting around the laptop, eating doughnuts and watching funny videos. It's barely ten, and there's only one patient in the emergency room, a regular who gets dumped off by the police whenever they find him passed out drunk in a parking lot. As we're finishing a clip of a blind dog that spends five minutes running into walls, the phone rings and Steven runs to answer it.

"Any news on the burned kid?"

Emma sighs while Jo sneaks another doughnut. "He's doing better than expected. Third-degree burns over most of his legs, some of his torso, and his right arm. He's pretty lucky." She glances over her shoulder. "Steven's been taking shifts in ICU. I think it hit him pretty hard."

Before I can ask any more questions, Steven strides into the room looking deadly serious. "Incoming! I already paged the doc."

Jo pushes me toward the wall. "Stay here and out of the way." She purses her lips and frowns. "Better yet, you should probably leave."

There's no way I'm leaving, but I make myself small and try not to be seen. It's sick, but I hope we're in for something gory. A splintered bone or a bloody gash that needs a slew of stitches. Anything to get the taste of the burned boy out of my mouth.

Emma, Steven, and Jo glove up and prepare for the incoming patient. Steven's rattling off the details, but I'm so busy fantasizing about someone else's pain that I don't hear them. The nurses look so grave, which only excites me. It's not like I'm some gore hound, but the rush of an emergency leaves me no time to dwell on my own tragedies.

My breathing is rapid, and my stomach is tangled and sick with anticipation. I love the moment right before all hell breaks loose. The calm before the proverbial shit storm.

The doctor waltzes into the ER, pulling on gloves and calling for the situation. He's a little man with razor burn and tufts of hair sprouting out of the neckline of his scrubs. Probably the kind of guy that no one paid attention to in high school, but here, now, he's God.

The automatic doors open, and time dilates.

"Three-year-old male . . . respiratory arrest . . . down eighteen minutes . . . no rhythm . . . CPR performed in the field." The paramedics roll the stretcher into the emergency room, and everyone springs to action. The latent energy in their bones is released in one

53

brilliant, near-acrobatic display. The medics are still performing CPR on the tiny bundle in the stretcher. One guy stands at the head with a tiny ambu bag while another stands at the chest, performing compressions.

"Pool?" Steven asks.

"Bathtub."

"How long was he in the water?" The doctor's voice is emotionless. He follows the stretcher into the room.

"The mom says only a minute," the medic says between compressions. "But he was cold when we got there."

They transfer the body onto the bed and push the stretcher out of the way. Jo and Steven and Emma work as one graceful unit, attaching wires to the boy's body, continuing CPR, fetching anything and everything that the doctor calls for. The paramedics are extraneous now, but they have paperwork to fill out.

I have to remind myself to breathe, because every time they inject something into the boy's line or push air into his lungs or check his always-absent vital signs, I feel like I'm the cold one. The dead one. It could be me on that table. It should be me.

And this goes on for hours. No, minutes. But when you live it, it'll feel like hours. You'll beg for it to be hours. You'll tell yourself that this all took place in a parallel universe where seconds are minutes and minutes are hours. That the doctor and nurses have been trying to revive that little boy for longer than is humanly possible. Because there's no way that anyone would give up on a child in less time than it takes to microwave popcorn.

"Time of death," the doctor says, "is ten twenty-nine." He yanks off his gloves, tosses them to the floor, and walks away.

54

I can't stand without the wall, so I lean and wait while the paramedics trade paperwork with Emma. And I watch that body sleeping on the bed, small and still as a doll that I saw once at a garage sale. It was an ugly, plastic, scuffed-up thing that I couldn't imagine anyone ever wanting. But beat up as it was, I knew that, at one time, someone had loved it.

After the paramedics leave, the emergency room returns to status quo. Just Steven and Emma and Jo and me, and the nearly empty box of doughnuts. Only now there's a dead toddler not twelve feet from where I'm leaning. My legs still feel wobbly beneath me.

"I want . . . ," I say. "May I try CPR?" The words fall out of my mouth and hit the floor. My brain is disconnected. I don't even remember thinking that I wanted to try to perform CPR on the little boy, but once the words are out there, I know that I *need* to try.

They look at me as if they'd forgotten I ever existed. Emma covers her tiny cry, and Jo buries her fists in her hips and I know she's thinking that if she were my mother, she'd tan my hide for staying when she told me to leave. But I don't care. They don't understand. I'm supposed to be here, supposed to do this.

"Please?"

Steven shakes his head. "Not a chance," he says, but there's a moment of hesitation when he looks from me to the boy with the tube poking out of his mouth and back to me, and I think that maybe I do have a chance.

I'm not sure if I can stand without the wall.

The twelve feet between me and the boy isn't really twelve feet. It's a hundred miles, and I'm pretty sure that I can't span them. Not even if I crawl. Except that I'm walking. One foot in front of the other.

"You've let me take vitals before, and I'm already CPR certified. I need to know what it feels like on a real person . . . so that I don't freeze when it counts." I'm talking underwater. Words are bubbles that grow from my lips and drift to the surface.

Steven's face is a mask of ache. He's a crumbling tower. "That's a person, Drew."

"Not anymore," I whisper, but even I don't believe it. Watching CPR is one thing. I've practiced on dummies and I've seen it done in the field on ride-alongs, but I've never done it on a real person. Not even when it could have made a difference. "I have to do this."

My feet shuffle my reluctant body across the floor. I'm floating. I'm in the room. By the bed. I'm not looking. I can't make me look.

I don't know what changes Steven's mind. Maybe it's the rawness of my voice, the determination I wear over every inch of my skin. Maybe Steven sees more than I give him credit for. I don't know. Maybe I never will.

"If you're alone," Steven says mechanically, "compressions are the most important part of CPR. You have to keep the blood circulating." I've heard all this before. Compressions at a rate of one hundred per minute. Sing "Stayin' Alive" to keep the rhythm. Then Steven says, "Go on and put the heel of your palm between its nipples."

Steven doesn't refer to the child as a he, but he *is* a he. A he with black hair and black eyebrows and brown eyes and blue skin. Little, little, little. Too little. Too late.

"Nipple line," Steven repeats. I glance back at Jo and Emma for help, but they busy themselves avoiding me and Steven.

I obey. Memories batter the wall I've built up against them. I don't want to touch the dead baby he, but I do. His skin—it's not like they say in movies. It's a raw porterhouse. Cold and damp and so, so dead.

"With a child this young, you can use one or two hands," Steven says. "Compressions should be about one-third to one-half the depth of the chest, or two inches in this case." Steven's voice is monotone and steady as if we're discussing the proper procedure for changing a car's oil.

"Yeah," I say. My voice breaks.

"Go ahead and press down."

Pushing is difficult. The boy resists. I lean into it, putting my weight behind my hands.

Push.

One and two and three and four.

I mumble the words to "Stayin' Alive" under my breath, almost laughing at the lunacy of using disco to stave off death.

And five and six and seven and eight.

Vomit oozes out of the boy's mouth, foamy and gray. There are some carrots and maybe some squash. It's all squashed.

"If you had a partner, they'd be at the head, bagging the patient." Steven's still lecturing, but I'm not listening. He's not human anymore. He's dead eyed and automatic, and guilt gnaws at me for getting us both into this.

The song sticks in my brain; I keep repeating the same words. They can't bring the boy back, but maybe they can shield me from the horror of this moment. Under my hand, his ribs crack and splinter. I stop, stumble backward into the wall. The boy sits up and sings along.

I throw up in the trash. Some lasagna, water, pretzels. I make an inventory of everything I've eaten over the last couple of days and look for it at the bottom of the bin.

"Drew?" Steven rubs my back and I force myself not to flinch.

"I'm fine."

"I should never have agreed to that."

Jo can't ignore me anymore. Her shallow well has refilled, or it's deeper than I thought. She hisses at Steven and then says, "Drew, are you—"

"I'm fine!" I scream, and wipe my mouth with the back of my hand.

"Where's my baby?" a woman wails through the window at the admitting desk. "Where's my Emilio?"

Emma rushes off to intercept the parents, and Jo says, "I'll get Dr. Gelbwasser." Steven ushers me out of the room and closes the white drape behind us. I'm sure he's regretting his decision to let me practice CPR on the boy, but he doesn't seem to suffer for dead Emilio as he does for Rusty. Maybe he sees something of himself in my burned boy the way I see pieces of Cady in Emilio. Maybe hell is seeing the lost loved painted over the faces of the strangers we meet.

"Emilio," I say. The mother is too young for this kind of pain. She's rabid, clawing and kicking and screeching at Emma. Her world is behind that sheet—shattered and broken—and she will spend the rest of her life trying to piece it back together.

"She's going to want to see him, isn't she?" I ask.

Steven nods. "The hardest thing is for a parent to lose a child."

I slowly back away. "Unless it's the other way around," I say. And then I run.

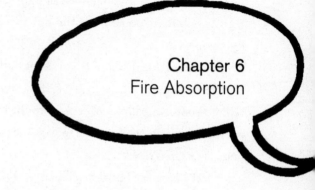

Chapter 6
Fire Absorption

When I was young, I ran because my bones hurt.

I was ten, and the doctors said that it was a growth spurt, that I'd get over it. Moving helped, so I ran anywhere and everywhere that I could. My dad called me the Man in Motion. Running became my obsession. I thought I could outrun the pains of growing.

Maybe if I run fast enough now, I can outrun the dead boy on the gurney. Outrun my thundering heart and his tiny baby hands and my own hurt. Everything hurts. But I realize that I'm not running from the boy. I'm running from the memories. From the guilt. No matter how far or how fast I run, I won't ever escape this pain.

When I reach the ICU, I stop. Beads of sweat collect in my eyebrows and run down the sides of my nose, tickling my face. I hadn't meant to come here. I've been avoiding this place, yet here I am.

There's a space between the doors, and I peer through. The ICU is quiet and dark. One nurse sits, watching the monitors.

Rusty's still in there, beating and breathing and fighting.

There's no way for me to sneak in without opening the doors, but my need to see Rusty eclipses my fear. I need to know that someone in this hospital is going to be all right. Sometimes I wish I were Patient F so that I could move through the walls and no one would know.

I am not Patient F, and I cannot move through walls, so I wait. Eventually, the nurse gets up and heads toward the bathroom, muttering about something under her breath. I don't have the time to wonder what's on her mind. As soon as she's gone, I open the double doors and slip inside.

I feel like a cat burglar, walking on tiptoes, creeping along as quietly as I can to avoid detection. There should be another nurse around here somewhere, but I don't see anybody else in the hall, and I sneak into Rusty McHale's room.

The moment I'm in Rusty's room, I know what the nurse was muttering about. It was about him. Rusty. His moans are a rip current that pulls me under, tumbles me, and tries to drown me. They ebb and fade and rise again, a cacophonous symphony of pain, pain, pain. Maybe the nurse didn't go to the bathroom after all. Maybe she just needed to escape this awful place and this awful noise, the way my own brain is telling me to flee.

Only I don't. I can't. Not twice in one night.

Rusty's room is nothing like Lexi's or Trevor's. There's nothing of the boy here. No photos or flowers or balloons. There are machines. There are two chairs. There is a sink. On the wall across from the door, there is a window with the blinds pulled low. And in the bed, there is a boy on fire. His right arm and chest are wrapped with ban-

60

dages, and I can't see his legs under the blankets, but they're elevated so that he forms a human V.

He finds no peace in sleep. His pain ages him. Steals into his dreams. He can't fight this pain, because it's intangible. All he can do is try to survive it.

The nurse's shuffling footsteps scratch across the floor, and I duck down beside the bed, putting Rusty between the nurse and me. It's lonely down here, and I wish that I'd brought some music, but I suppose that if Rusty can't escape his pain, neither should I.

Still, I need to fill the silence.

"My parents died," I hear myself saying all of a sudden. "My parents and my little sister, Cady." My voice is a whisper, and I'm not sure Rusty can hear me, but part of me hopes he can, that maybe my voice will help him forget his pain, if only for a moment. "Right here in this hospital, they all died."

Time tries to drag me back to that night, to that second, but Rusty anchors me here. His nightmares keep me safe.

"I huddled in a corner, forgotten, all cut up and dirty and half-dead. I watched Death take my whole family. One by one. First she took my dad. Then my baby sister. Then my mom." Walking through the memories is like walking over hot coals. The faster I do it, the less it hurts. But less is relative.

"Dad was the worst. Cut up and broken, his head split like an egg. He was dead as the medics brought him through the doors. Cady went next. Her little body lost too much blood. I maybe could have saved her if I—" My voice breaks, but I can't stop. "Mom held on the longest. She was always the fighter in the family. But in the end, Death took her, too."

Rusty's moans crescendo, and I hear the nurse get up from her chair and head our way. I burrow deeper into my hiding spot, make myself as small as I can, wishing for invisibility.

"I'm so sorry, baby," the nurse says. She's standing at Rusty's other side, her clean white sneakers peeking beneath the bed. "Your morphine is turned up as high as it can go. Just try to sleep." Her voice is worn out, thin. Rusty is dragging her to the edge. She stands there for just a moment longer and then leaves. I hear her feet slowly padding back the way she came.

"Death would have taken me, too," I whisper once Rusty's moaning has faded—more likely from exhaustion than relief. "But she was late. And now I live here, hiding from Death, trying my best to keep her from catching me." I reach for his unburned hand. It's soft, and his fingers are long like a piano player's. My own look clumsy and stubby in comparison.

"Just hold on," I tell him. "One day soon, you'll get out of here, you'll leave, and you won't remember this pain."

Rusty squeezes my hand and, shocked, I look up. He's staring down at me with a desperate look in his eyes.

"It's okay," I say. My voice trembles, now that I know he's listening. "I'm a friend."

Rusty's hazel eyes grow wider, then relax. He hasn't got the strength to fear me. But his grip is still tight. He's crushing my bones, and I let him. What do I need my fingers for, anyway? If Rusty wants to transfer some of his pain to me, so be it.

We remain there, Rusty on the bed and me on the floor, connected by eyes and skin, gripping each other in the quiet night as if we're afraid that we'll go spinning off into the void of the universe if we let go. I wish there were some way to take Rusty away, to build a new world for him, a world where he's safe.

Reality is so raw, so coarse. It's like acid, eating away every day at our nerves. I hurt how he hurts, and I would do nearly anything to end his pain.

"Don't let them take me," Rusty says. The words form lightly on his lips, and I catch them before they rise like dandelion seeds and float away.

I search Rusty's wounded eyes, looking for the truth, and I find it: Down under the morphine haze, buried beneath the layers of agony, is fear. Fear of the people who hurt him, fear of death, fear of *out there*. I couldn't save Emilio and I couldn't save my parents or little sister, but maybe I can save Rusty.

It won't make up for what I've failed to do, but it's a start.

"Okay," I promise. "Cross my heart and hope to die."

Chapter 7
Death Sense

Death likes scrambled eggs.

She sits in the corner of the caf talking to a ponytailed doctor who looks like she's on her way to a soccer game rather than an appendectomy. They've been chatting for an hour over cold eggs and plain oatmeal. I wish I knew what they were saying. Reading lips is more difficult than it looks in movies. The only words I make out from Death's glossy red mouth are "grapes," "digger," "pirate," and "shriven." Either she's far more dangerous than I thought, or I suck hard at lip reading.

Rusty's parents are here too, along with the girl that I saw in the emergency room the night he came in. I don't try to read their lips. There's nothing to read. They eat their breakfasts with their heads bowed. Silent. Slow. As if Rusty is already gone. An hour from now, if you ask them what they ate, I doubt they'll remember.

I'm not working this morning, I'm only pretending to work so that I can keep an eye on Death. Ever since the night that she failed to take me, I've done my best to avoid her by hiding in plain sight. Even when police came, flashing that crappy picture of me from when I was fourteen and had acne and shorter hair, no one knew I was the boy they were searching for because I was smart and gave them no reason to suspect. But now, things have changed. I have to protect Rusty, and that makes the game far more dangerous.

I stayed with him all night, then slipped out when the day nurses arrived. He didn't say anything more. It wasn't necessary. Rusty doesn't want to go, so I'll make sure that Death doesn't get her manicured fingernails anywhere near him—even if it means that I have to track her all day.

The thing about Death is that she's predictable. She eats every morning at seven thirty. Usually alone, but sometimes with her friend. Maybe they play tennis together or belong to the same gym or share an occasional kiss in an unlit hallway when the days at the hospital feel too long to bear. Death never leaves. Death lives here. She's married to her job.

Arnold sidles up next to me and admires my handiwork. He's smiling today and singing some rap song that he must have heard on the radio. The tune is catchy, but the words make no sense.

"It's funny," Arnold says. "Is that chicken *supposed* to be angry?" He tilts his head to the side and regards the dry-erase board like it's a Picasso.

I put away the markers, but I keep one eye on Death. She and her doctor friend are doing more talking than eating, so I should have plenty of time before she leaves.

"The chicken on the left is being nice," I say. "And the other one, with its wings crossed, is upset." I tap the board. "Sweet and sour chicken."

"You are brilliant!" Arnold exclaims, drawing unwanted attention. "I especially like the vegetables wearing bow ties."

"There's not much I can do with vegetarian bow-tie pasta."

"No," Arnold says, "it's perfect." He's trying too hard. Something about him isn't quite right. He's like one of the songs he hums—slightly off. "Are you sure you don't want to stay and work today?"

I shake my head and gather my sketchpad so that I'm mobile. "I made a promise to a friend."

"I understand. But come back later."

"Why?"

A line is forming, and Aimee looks overwhelmed. Arnold scowls at her and turns to me. "I have books for you to read."

"I'm not really a reader, Arnold."

He points at my sketchpad. "If you write stories, you read stories. Come back later."

Agreeing is the only way he'll leave me alone. When he's gone, I steal a glance at Death and her companion. Death is laughing. I try to imagine their conversation, but for the life of me, I can't think of what might make Death chuckle. The business of soul taking can't be that amusing. I wonder if Death was late retrieving me because Cady told her something funny. Maybe I'm alive because my sister took too long to die. Cady was hilarious. For a six-year-old, she had a way with words. Like the time she told me, "I think it would be fun if we played checkers, but instead of checkers we use waffles, and instead of playing with them, we eat them." Cady and I never got to play checkers with waffles. I would have liked to.

"Drew?" Emma snaps her fingers in front of my eyes, and I realize that not only am I staring at Death, but Death is staring back at me. I fake a yawn to cover.

"Hey, Emma," I say, looking around for Steven and Jo. "Where's the rest of the Scooby gang?"

"Gone home," Emma says. Her eyes hang, and her smile is blurry. The night has not been kind to her. "Do you know that woman?"

"Sure, we go way back."

Emma frowns. I sneak a glance at Death again, and she's still staring at me.

I think about running. Taking off and spending the rest of the day in my dark hole with my lumpy mattress. I haven't slept and I'm exhausted. Maybe I could rest up and shadow Death tomorrow. Except I promised Rusty, and if Death took him while I napped, I'd never forgive myself.

"About last night," Emma says. "The little boy."

I hold up my hand and cut her off. "Forget it."

"No," Emma says. "Steven should never have let you do that."

"I twisted his arm," I say, my tone more lighthearted than I feel. "I needed to know how to do it on a real person. I had a chance once and . . . I couldn't do it. So . . ." I shrug and clear my throat. "I needed to do that last night."

Emma takes studied measure of my words, as though she's trying to determine whether I'm being honest. "You hungry?" she asks finally.

"I could eat."

Emma and I pass through the line, filling our trays with dubious breakfast foods. I'm not particularly hungry, but eating with Emma gives me one more reason to stay in the caf watching Death. She's no longer staring at me, which is a relief, but I'll have to be more careful if I'm going to keep her away from Rusty and avoid being caught.

We sit a couple of tables away from Death and the doctor.

"Oh my God. Carbs!" Emma guides a hero's forkful of hash browns into her mouth and groans with pleasure. It's kind of obscene, but it makes me laugh. Until that moment, I didn't know how badly I needed to laugh. She gulps her coffee while I nibble at my eggs.

"How can you drink that coffee?" I ask. "It smells like motor oil."

Emma inhales the steam, closing her eyes as if this is some kind of ritual that must be observed in order to fully appreciate the exquisite aroma and taste. I know for a fact that Arnold pays pennies for the stuff, and it tastes like swill.

"One day, when you're older, probably around college, you'll discover the joys of coffee. It's an elixir, Drew. Better than sex."

I stare at Emma's cup dubiously. "Nothing is better than sex."

"You're cute, Drew," she says between mouthfuls of egg. "And you have so much to learn."

"But sex—"

"Rocks," Emma says. "It does. But there are so many things that are better."

I had the sex talk with my parents when I was thirteen, so I know the ins and outs of it. Plus, you know, there's porn on the Internet. And sex has been my holy grail practically since puberty, and here's Emma telling me that it isn't the apotheosis of the adolescent experience I'm expecting it to be.

"Like what?" I ask. "What's better?" It's a challenge.

Emma shrugs. "A fresh cup of gourmet coffee, for one. A bubble bath. Getting a foot massage while watching a new episode of *Big Brother.*"

My fork pauses halfway to my mouth when I realize that Death and her companion are no longer at their table. I glance around and spot Death getting a refill on her coffee.

I don't have much time, so I cut to the chase.

"A bubble bath is better than sex?"

"God, yes." Emma's eyes glaze over and her shoulders slump, as if she wishes she were soaking in her tub right now. "Especially after a long day in the ER." She smiles. "There are so many things that are better: chocolate cake, a shot of tequila, kissing—"

"No way is kissing better than sex. I know all about kissing. I've had a boyfriend."

The thing I love about nurses is that nothing fazes them. Emma—sweet, sweet Emma—could go from discussing Shakespeare's sonnets to describing a gnarly case of genital warts without so much as a hint of embarrassment. She could probably even draw you a picture of them. "Let me tell you about kissing, Drew. If you're in a relationship and the kissing isn't the best part, run."

"But it's just kissing," I say.

Emma pushes her empty tray toward the center of the table and leans back in her chair. Her muscles unravel under her scrubs. It's probably the first time she's relaxed in nearly twelve hours. "People don't talk about that one great orgasm they had on top of the Eiffel Tower. In movies, long-distance lovers don't see each other across a crowded airport, run to each other, and start bumping uglies on the baggage conveyor belt. It's all about the kiss, Drew. Sex is biological. Kissing is art."

Death pays Aimee for the refill and heads toward the door. I tense up.

"Maybe you just haven't been having good sex," I say. I'm not looking at Emma anymore.

"True. But that's not the point." I catch Emma staring at me the way I'm staring at Death. "Why do you keep watching Miss Michelle?"

"Miss Michelle?"

"The social worker?" Emma's looking at me like I'm crazy, and Death is getting away. "She does grief counseling and works with kids—oh, Drew, do you need to talk to her about last night?"

Miss Michelle may be her mask, but I know her true face. Her real name. Death wears stockings and a pencil skirt, but I see through to her cold, dead core.

"I have to go, Em. I'll see you soon." I don't wait for her to reply, just gather up my sketchpad and escape as quickly as I can without resorting to a flat-out run.

Trailing Death isn't easy. She weaves through the hospital like she's wearing roller skates instead of high heels, barely pausing to take a breather or speak to anyone. The doctors and nurses we pass all seem to treat her with deference bordering on fear. Sure, maybe they know her as Miss Michelle, a woman who visits children, reassures parents, helps in the transition of grief, but they've got to notice that everywhere she goes, death follows.

And today, everywhere Death goes, I follow.

It doesn't take long to figure out that we're going to Peds. Dread parches my throat, and I wonder if Death is going to visit Trevor. I haven't seen him since they put him on the respirator. The guilt is suffocating. I drag my feet as I walk, hoping Death will take a last-minute detour, but we arrive at Peds, with its blatant attempts to emulate real life, and Death immediately begins talking to Nurse Merchant. I duck into Lexi's room.

Lexi is sitting on her bed with her knees pulled up to her chest, flipping through a stack of flash cards thicker than my arm. It's cloudy outside, so only a few stray beams sneak through the dirty-cotton clouds and into the room.

Everything is neat and in its place, except for one noticeable thing: The wig has been flung across the back of the chair. It still looks like a taxidermist's castoff.

"Hey, Lexi." She's glaring at me like I should feel ashamed—and I do.

"He got off the respirator this morning," she says without a greeting. Every word is a bullet aimed somewhere especially painful: knees, stomach, groin.

I move into the room and lean against the wall so that I can keep one ear open for Death. She's still outside gabbing with Nurse Merchant about color palettes for her new bathroom. Regardless of whether she's here for a friendly visit or to take Trevor's soul, I need to stay frosty.

"I was busy," I tell Lexi. It sounds lame even to me.

Lexi grits her teeth and flips through her cards too fast to actually be studying them. "Do you think he's going to die?"

"Yes."

"Drew!"

"Eventually," I say, but Lexi glares at me with more hatred in her eyes than I've ever seen before. I almost wish that I could bottle that

hate and stuff it in Patient F. If he had hatred like that inside him, maybe he could move on from his pathetic beginnings.

"I'm sorry, Lexi. He's supposed to be dead already. That's why the other day was all balloons and decorations and scary wigs."

She turns from me.

I should've lied to her, told her that Trevor was going to be fine. People tell harmless lies all the time. If I'd lied to Lexi, I wouldn't have to see that look on her face now. The one that says I've destroyed her.

Lexi's mother saves me by storming into the room like a mad cow. "Drew Brawley? How the hell are you?"

Mrs. Kripke is a faded beauty queen. Literally. She was Spring Queen or Summer Cream Corn Queen or something like that when she was Lexi's age, and her entire life since has revolved around that one glorious moment. She wakes up every day and dresses like she's on her way to a pageant. She has the smoky eyes and bloodred lips, as well as a bosom squeezed so tightly that her breasts look like they're trying to escape, and she's clearly never met a bottle of hairspray she doesn't want to make sweet, sweet love to.

"I'm well, Mrs. Kripke," I tell her.

Lexi cringes like she wants to crawl under the covers and hide. I step away from the wall and wedge myself between Lexi and her mother, but Mrs. Kripke pats my cheek and shoves me out of the way. She starts toward Lexi but then detours, grabs the wig off the back of the chair, and begins brushing it out with her manicured fingernails.

"Alexis, sweetheart, you have to take proper care of this." Mrs. Kripke is all smiles as she sits down, pulls an industrial-size hairbrush out of her bottomless purse, and brushes out the wig in earnest. "Bald girls don't win beauty pageants."

"Did you bring the books I asked for, Mom?" Lexi redirects her annoyance with me to her mom, and I have to admit I'm grateful for that.

"Forget about your books, darling. We need to work on your look. Get you out of this dreadful hospital gown." Mrs. Kripke sighs, and it sounds like the air hissing from a bike tire. "The only good thing to come out of this cancer is that we finally got your weight under control."

Normally I'd agree with anyone who says that Lexi spends too much time studying, but Mrs. Kripke grates on my last nerve. Add that to the fact that I feel guilty as hell for what I said earlier about Trevor dying. "I think bald is kind of hot. And smart girls are totally in right now."

Lexi slides me a smile on the down-low, and I rest assured that all is forgiven. Mrs. Kripke, on the other hand, wrinkles her nose and says, "Honey, no offense intended, but that is why you are a queer and I'm a former Miss Winter Garden Orange Grove Queen."

"Mom!" Lexi launches into a lecture about the appropriateness of words like "queer," but I'm not listening, because Death is on the move. If she goes into Trevor's room, all may be lost. Just because I think that he's going to die soon doesn't mean I want him to, and it doesn't mean that I won't try to stop it from happening by any means necessary.

I'm holding my breath as Death walks toward Trevor's room. At the last minute, she ducks into the room next to his, and I heave a sigh of relief. That room belongs to a ten-year-old boy named

Jesse who has a shattered femur. I wasn't in the ER when Jesse came in, but Jo told me that boys don't get breaks like that falling out of trees.

"I have to go," I say to the Kripke ladies, and dash out the door before either can protest. Nurse Merchant waves as I beeline for Trevor's room. She's on the phone, so she doesn't say hello, but I know she'd make me stop if Trevor wasn't well enough for visitors.

The blinds in Trevor's room are closed, and it feels like Death *has* been here. Trevor is sunk deep into the bed, clutching the TV remote, flipping through channels. A picture of me framed by "Have you seen this person?" sails past, but Trevor doesn't even notice. He looks pale and broken. Nurse Merchant said that the respirator was supposed to help Trevor breathe so he could save his strength, but he looks weaker than ever.

"Miss me, Droopy?" Trevor asks when he notices me. His voice is harsh, like he swallowed a bucketful of drywall screws and chased it with a bottle of Tabasco.

"No way. This is totally a pity visit." Trevor and I bump knuckles. I hold back for fear of breaking him. "I had to escape from Lexi's room."

Trevor tries to laugh, but it's all breath and no sound. "She badgering you about proper grammar in your comic book again?"

"She covered half of the pages I gave her to read with red ink," I say. "But it's worse than that: Her mother's here."

"Yikes." Trevor grimaces. Last time Mrs. Kripke visited, she tried to dress him in these baby-blue capri pants.

I plop down in the chair, prop my feet up, and try to pick out Death's voice next door. Jesse's squeaky treble soars and dips, while Death's syrupy tones provide a deep undercurrent to the conversation—not unlike the sound of waves crashing on the beach.

It's a thought that I hate myself for having, but I'm glad that Death is in Jesse's room and not here. I don't know Jesse like I know Trevor. I'd rather Death took no one at all, but if I have to choose, Trevor is my boy.

"Drew?"

"Sorry," I say. "I was thinking about how Lexi's mom kept trying to force her into that wig."

Trevor laughs and coughs and laughs again. Every time he coughs, it sounds like he's tearing long strips of construction paper. "I bet her mom has a matching one." Trevor primps his invisible hair and says, in a scratchy falsetto, "Oh, look at me. I'm Mrs. Kripke, and I wear a rat on my head."

"Would you like some cheese?" I say, joining in. "Mmmmm. Cheese."

"I was Miss Creamed Corn USA when I was only one year old, and I can still fit into that swimsuit." Trevor throws back his shoulders and tosses his head, striking an awkward pose that's one part Mrs. Kripke, two parts praying mantis. And I can't help laughing. I cover my mouth with my arm to keep from losing it, but I nearly fall out of the chair, which makes Trevor laugh too. We laugh so hard that I'm the one who can't breathe, and Trevor offers me a cup of water.

"You know," Trevor says, once I manage to stop laughing for half a second, "they make wigs for girls to wear down there."

I sip at the lukewarm water. "You mean, like, *down there?*"

Death and Jesse aren't talking anymore, but she hasn't left his room yet.

Trevor nods. "They're called merkins."

"You made that up. Who would want extra crotch hair?"

"Maybe bald girls." Trevor is avoiding my eyes and fidgeting. "Do you think Lexi's bald down there, too?"

I smack Trevor's leg and regret it when the pain crosses his face—pain he won't complain about because he doesn't want me to think he's weak. I could straddle him and beat the crap out of him, and he wouldn't make a peep. "I don't know, dude. Go ask her."

"She wouldn't tell me."

"Well, she definitely won't tell me," I say.

"Come on. Having a gay dude for a friend has got to have some perks."

Death's high heels click-clack in the hallway, and I know that my time is limited. I hate leaving Trevor like this, but I'm still on a mission. "You really like Lexi, don't you?" I flick my eyes to the doorway. Death has stopped to chat with Nurse Merchant again.

"Don't."

"Trevor."

"I said *don't*." Trevor stares at the windows. The blinds block everything out, but it's like he's got x-ray vision and can see through them, the same way Lexi can see the ocean even though it's out of sight. "You know how Lexi is always looking out the windows or sitting near them?"

"Yeah," I say.

"It's because she doesn't belong here. She's got worlds inside her, and being sick is just holding her back. She's gonna beat it, dude. She's gonna beat it and grow back her hair and laugh at that fucking wig one day. She's gonna get out from behind these walls and crack the goddamn world wide open."

Trevor grapples with his breath for every word, and I'm smart enough not to interrupt him.

"But I'm dead. They're trying some experimental shit on me, but I'm not stupid. I'm good as gone."

"Dude—"

"Don't bullshit me," Trevor says. His eyes are flat, cold. "Before I came back in here, I found this bill in my mom's office for a burial plot. A grave, Droopy. My grave. Even my folks know the truth, and my only goal right now is to keep breathing long enough to see that girl escape this hospital."

I don't know what to say. Trevor is proof that you don't need superpowers to be a hero.

Death heads for the exit, and I hesitate. Trevor's spears me with those empty eyes of his, but I don't have a choice. I really have to go.

"You're not going to die," I tell him from the doorway. "I won't let you." I leave before he can argue.

Death is ahead of me, and I almost lose her. It's because I don't recognize where we are—and that's saying a lot. I know this hospital—I *own* this hospital—but Death veers into a hallway that I've never been down before, and I'm lost.

It's another unfinished section of hospital. Where drywall is actually hung, it's unpainted, gray, and sad. There are strips of plastic sheeting draped everywhere, making it look like a maze inside a maze. I have to follow the sounds of Death's heels on the concrete floor because I can't see her anymore. I'd have to creep much closer to keep her in sight, and I don't want to risk discovery.

I turn a corner and am suddenly staring into the hospital's chapel.

It's a somber, cramped room filled with pews, five on each side. From this side of the doorway, I can't see Death, but it makes sense that she'd come here. She and God probably have an arrangement.

The wisest course of action would be for me to backtrack and hang out in the hallway until Death is finished here, but my curiosity gets the better of me and I go inside.

The chapel carpet reminds me of the mud-colored rug at my old high school, and the walls are painted dark maroon. There's an altar at the front covered with signs of different faiths. Death is kneeling in front of the altar, and a middle-aged man with curly, receding salt-and-pepper hair kneels beside her, whispering in her ear. He's wearing a long cream robe and reminds me a little of Super Mario.

The moment I step inside, I realize my mistake and turn to leave, but the chaplain glances over his shoulder and catches my eye and, for some reason, I feel obligated to stay. Death is too busy talking to notice me, so I slip in and sit in the corner pew. I keep my head down, put my sketchpad beside me, and pick up a Bible. I'm on Death's turf now, and I want nothing more than to run, but that would draw unwanted attention.

While I wait, staring blankly at the Bible on my lap, I think about Trevor and Rusty and Patient F. Maybe I've been unable to figure out what Patient F is supposed to do next because I assumed that everything he had was gone. His family is gone—that's true—but Patient F is unstuck in time. What if he could bring all the people he loved forward in time—snatch them from the moment before the accident and put them into the bodies of people in Maligant City? Then he could save them over and over again. Patient F could spend the rest of his life saving his family, and they would never have to die. Not really.

"Hi there."

Death looms over me. I didn't hear her approach. My fear reflexes kick in, and they scream at me to run, run away as quickly as possible. Outwardly, I struggle to remain calm.

"Hi," I say, keeping my eyes on the Bible, giving off *leave me the hell alone* vibes as I fold in on myself.

"I know who you are."

I freeze. The game is over. I thought I was being cautious, but Death has been on to me all along. "You do?" I swallow.

Death nods. "You work in the cafeteria. Andrew, right?"

"Yeah," I say, hiding the insane relief that floods my body. Death sits down beside me. She moves like a dancer, and tear tracks mar her face—wet roads that begin at her eyes, curve around her cheeks, and fall off the cliff of her chin. It shocks me, but I figure that if Death can cry, maybe we all have a chance for redemption.

"My name is Michelle." Death offers me her hand, and I take it. It's warm; her grip is sure. "May I call you Andrew?"

"Andrew, Drew, Andy. Whatever."

Death smiles like I've made some kind of joke. "Are you okay, Andrew?"

I shrug. "Sure. Why wouldn't I be?"

Death glances around the chapel. She seems at home, like this is her sanctuary. If she lives anywhere in the hospital, I imagine it's here. "People often come to the chapel when they're worried about someone."

"Why are *you* here?"

79

"God helps me make sense of the world." She says it so simply that I know, for her, it must be true.

I return the Bible and prepare to bolt. I feel trapped in this room, even with Super Mario at the front, acting like he's busy, though he's clearly eavesdropping.

"Clarity can't undo the bad things that have already happened."

"No . . . it can't," Death says. "What bad thing happened to you?"

"I have to go." I stand, but Death blocks my way. If she knew who I was, who I really was, she'd bag, tag, and whisk me away for sure. It was a terrible idea to follow her here.

"Do you believe in Jesus, Andrew?"

"I believe in all paths to God," I say. "Except my own." I edge past, trying not to touch her. "Thanks for the talk."

Death grabs my arm before I can run away. She holds me, and for a long, dark moment, I'm sure I'm sunk. She's going to take me, then she's going to take Trevor, and then she'll take Rusty, too, for good measure.

I've failed. Broken all my promises.

But Death doesn't take me. She stands up slowly, reaches into her purse, and pulls out a card.

"God doesn't always answer his phone. But I do." She tucks the card into my moist palm.

I hustle out of the chapel, trying not to look suspicious, though I know I must.

It's not until I'm safely hidden in a supply closet near the ICU that I realize I left my sketchpad behind. It's a casualty of war. I can't go back for it right now.

For the rest of the day, I loiter around the ICU. It's too dangerous to continue following Death, so my fallback plan is to make sure that Death doesn't come anywhere near Rusty. She knows my name now, which means I have to be doubly careful.

I've evaded Death once. I can do it again. I won't let Rusty go without a fight.

TIME EXISTS, NOT AS A PATH ALONG WHICH YOU TRAVEL, BUT AS A SINGLE IMAGE TOO LARGE FOR MOST PEOPLE TO SEE ALL AT ONCE. FORTUNATELY, I AM NOT MOST PEOPLE.

I CAN'T SAVE MY FAMILY FROM THIS FATE, BUT I CAN STEAL THEM FROM THIS POINT IN TIME.

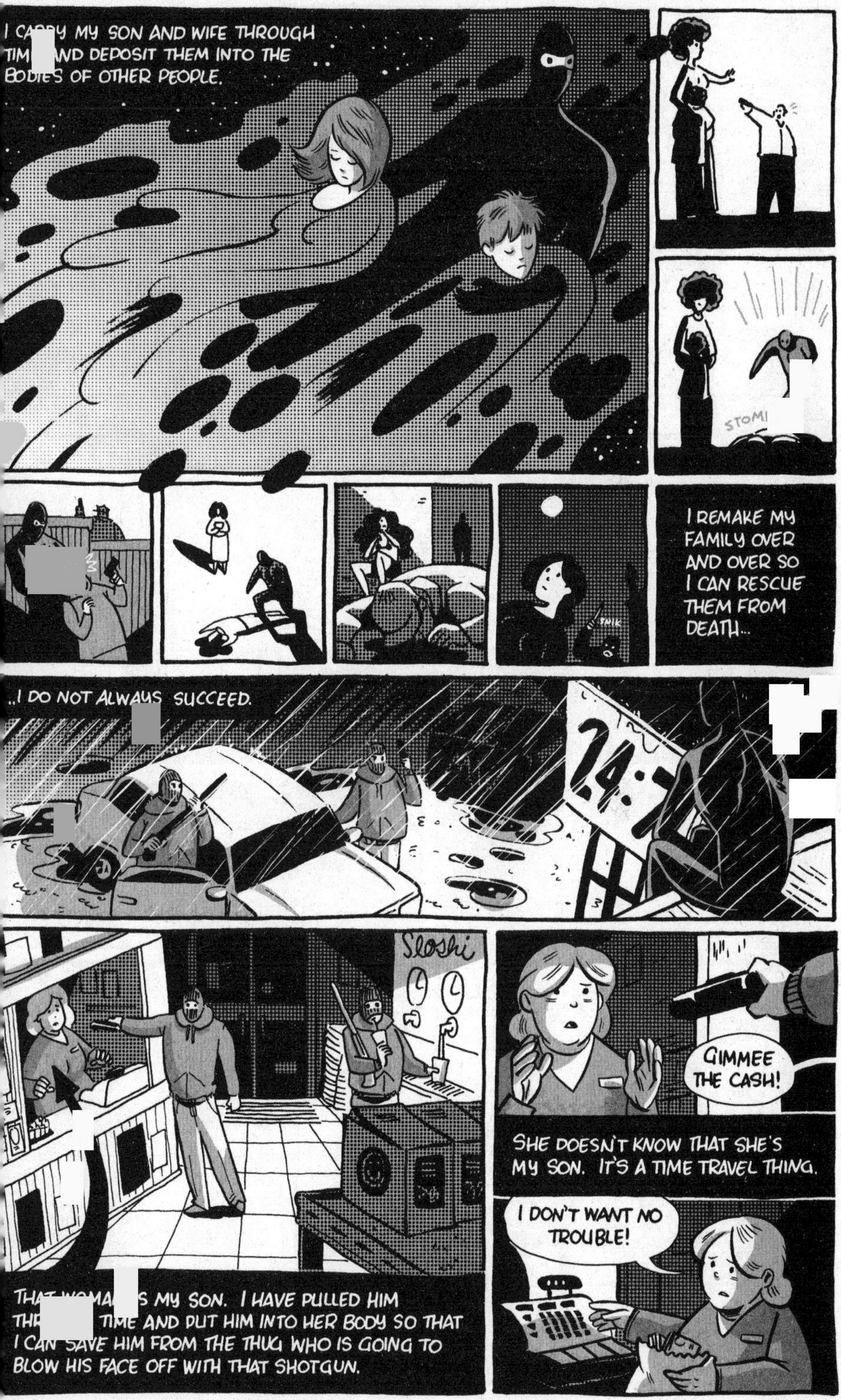

I CA Y MY SON AND WIFE THROUGH
TIM ND DEPOSIT THEM INTO THE
BODIES OF OTHER PEOPLE.
STOM
I REMAKE MY FAMILY OVER AND OVER SO I CAN RESCUE THEM FROM DEATH...
..I DO NOT ALWAYS SUCCEED.
24:7
Sloshi
GIMMEE THE CASH!
SHE DOESN'T KNOW THAT SHE'S MY SON. IT'S A TIME TRAVEL THING.
I DON'T WANT NO TROUBLE!
THAT WOMA S MY SON. I HAVE PULLED HIM
THR TIME AND PUT HIM INTO HER BODY SO THAT
I CAN SAVE HIM FROM THE THUG WHO IS GOING TO
BLOW HIS FACE OFF WITH THAT SHOTGUN.

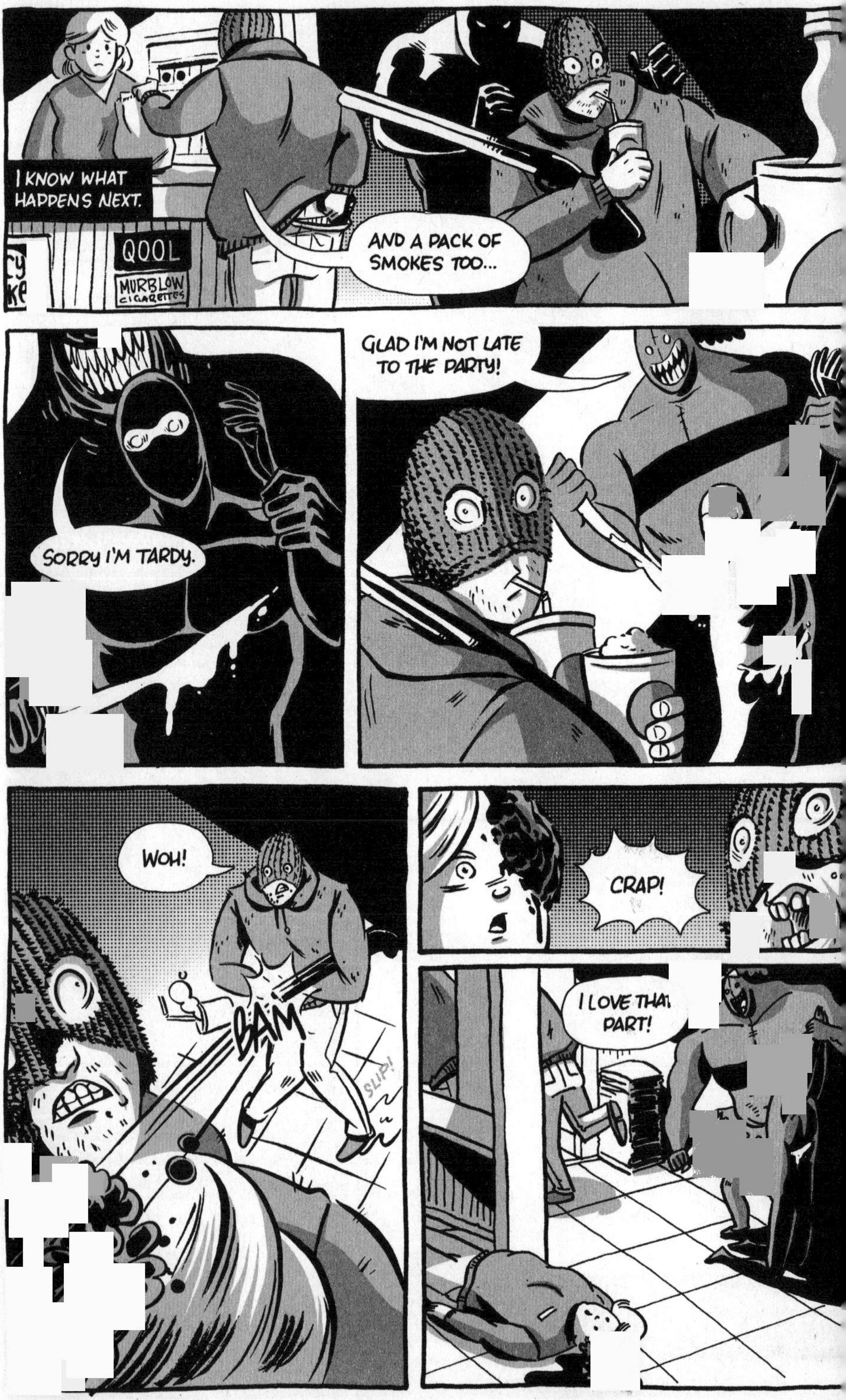
I KNOW WHAT HAPPENS NEXT.
QOOL
MURBLOW CIGARETTES
AND A PACK OF SMOKES TOO...
SORRY I'M TARDY.
GLAD I'M NOT LATE TO THE PARTY!
WOH!
BAM
SLIP!
CRAP!
I LOVE THAT PART!

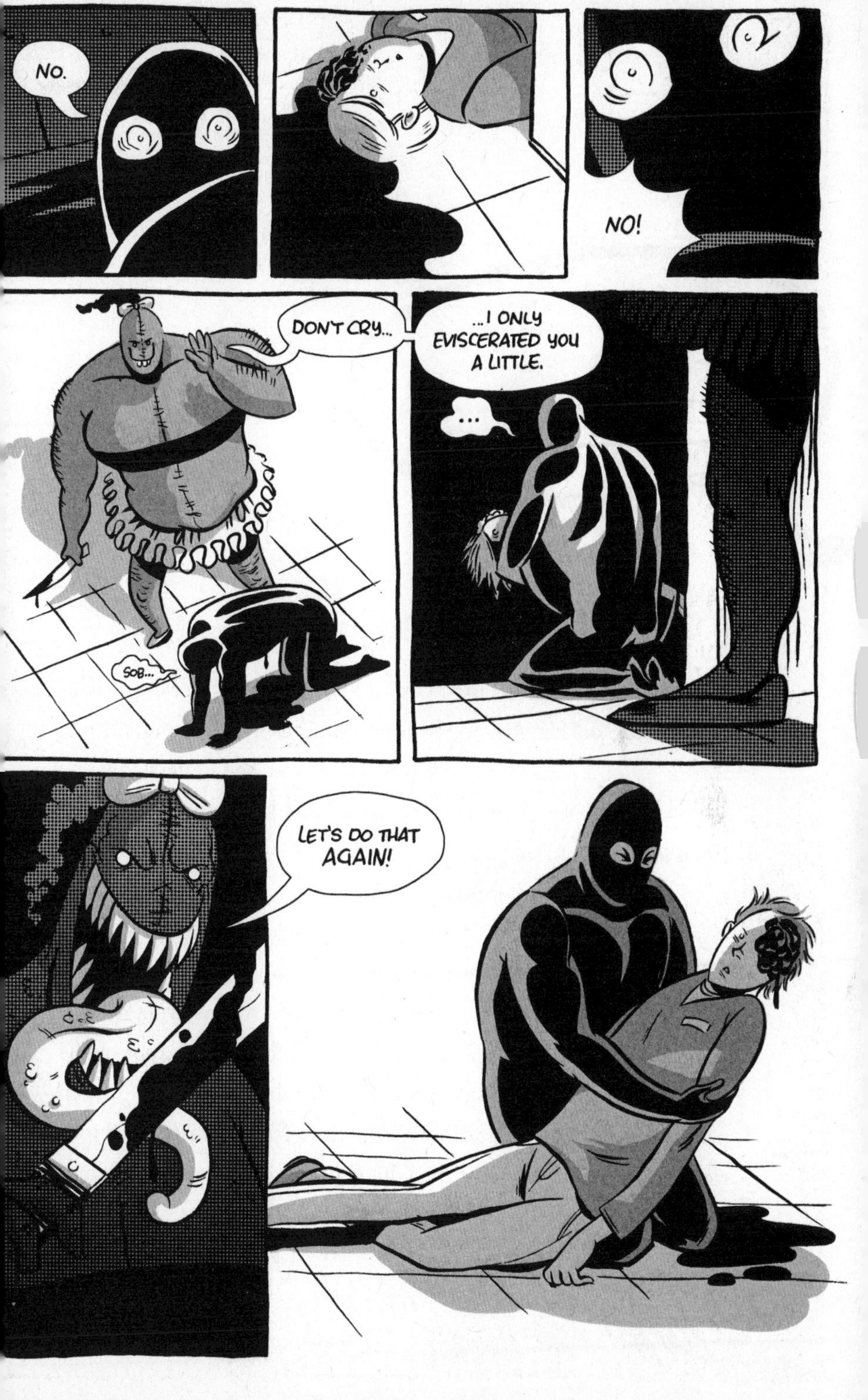
NO.
NO!
DON'T CRY...
...I ONLY EVISCERATED YOU A LITTLE.
SOB...
...
LET'S DO THAT AGAIN!

Chapter 8
Enhanced Agility
and Stamina

The elevator doors open into the warm, moist air.

"Have a little faith," I tell Lexi as I wheel out of the elevator, but I'm not sure she has any. She believes in things she can hold, dissect, absorb off of a page. She trusts bridges because she understands the math that underlies their basic structure and keeps them aloft even when they seem to defy gravity.

But people aren't bridges. There's no equation for deciphering human motivations. People are unpredictable. Even when you believe that you've managed to figure a person out, based on long and thorough observation, they still manage to surprise you.

We wheel into the waning sunlight that bathes the roof of the parking garage. A two-foot-high wall marks the boundaries, to keep people from driving their cars over the side. Trevor whistles and rolls right up to the edge. It isn't the Chick'n Shak or the office buildings or the pothole-filled parking lot below that makes him whistle, that steals his breath and forces him to cough.

"I haven't seen a sunset since I got here." Lexi sighs, rising out of her wheelchair to stand beside Trevor's. They're bound fast to each other's orbits, and neither seems to realize it.

"It looks like the burning heart of God," Trevor says.

I never thought of a sunset like that, but the way it smolders, pink and low, I'll probably never think of one any other way again.

"I didn't bring you sick bastards out here to watch the sunset," I say. We have just about an hour before the sun disappears below the horizon, which is covered by blue-gray clouds like bruises on the sky. But I know damned well that, if I let them, Trevor and Lexi will sit there and watch every infinitesimal movement of the sinking sun, their own bodies inching ever closer until, finally, their twin orbits disintegrate and they crash into each other. I'd be okay with that on any other day, but that day is not today. Today I have plans.

"Then why'd you bring us here?" Trevor asks. He's mesmerized by the sunset, but there's this undercurrent of anger to his voice, like he's mad that I've reminded him of the world *out there*.

I turn from my sun-struck friends and run to grab the supplies I stashed up here this morning. For two days, I watched Rusty and Trevor dutifully, making sure that Death kept her distance, taking breaks only to work my shifts for Arnold—if I stopped showing up, he'd worry, and he'd talk, and the last thing I need is for people to talk about me—but today is Sunday, and even Death has to take the day off occasionally.

"Hockey," I say, holding three broomsticks, and a tennis ball that I rescued from the lost and found.

"Dude!" Trevor spins in his chair, the sunset forgotten, and holds out his hand. I toss him the ball, and he deftly plucks it out of the air. The natural athlete still exists, buried under countless layers of chemotherapy and self-pity.

"Are you sure this is a good idea?" Lexi asks for about the tenth time since we escaped.

"No," I say. "This is probably *not* a good idea. Nurse Merchant is probably going to flay me alive, Trevor is probably going to wind up so exhausted that he'll sleep for a week, and you, my dear, are probably going to sunburn your beautiful scalp."

"Then let's go back," Lexi says. "Before anyone realizes we've gone."

There's no talking to this girl sometimes. I pass Trevor a broom. "Go on, then," I say.

"Yeah." Trevor tosses the ball in the air, catches it, and balances it on his fingertips before rolling it down the back of his hand.

Lexi huffs, sits down in her wheelchair, and pushes herself a couple of feet before I say, "But don't act like you're leaving because of rules and regulations. We know the truth." That stops Lexi cold.

"The truth?"

"The truth."

Lexi slowly turns, her face framed by the red-hot embers of the setting sun. I've awakened the sleeping dragon. She's the goddess Kali now. The destroyer of worlds and young men's hearts. "And that is?"

I allow a smile to settle slowly across my face, enjoying each second of Lexi's indignation. "That you know I'm going to kick your ass in hockey."

For a minute, I think that Lexi won't rise to the bait. Trevor has stopped playing with the ball. He's watching Lexi for signs that her nigh-invincible armor might actually crack. There's silence up here. No beating hearts, no breaths. Just a trio of kids who should all be dead.

"You're toast, Drewfus," she says, flashing me that rare smile. "Prepare to be annihilated."

Trevor whoops. Game on.

We play until the sun is but a memory to the sky. Lexi surprises me and Trevor, proving that she's more than a bald bookworm with an acid tongue. She handles the wheelchair expertly, pivoting with jaw-dropping skill. In the end, she manages to score more goals than me and Trevor combined.

Trevor tries his best. His eyes gleam with a predatory energy that says it doesn't matter that we're friends, or that he's harboring a titanic crush on Lexi: He will devour us both for dinner.

Unfortunately, Trevor's body doesn't have the strength to back up his convictions. He sweats through his white T-shirt, which sticks to his bony chest like damp tissue.

I should call the game, but Trevor is determined to score on Lexi. She lounges in her wheelchair like a lazy scarecrow, holding her broom across her lap, using her feet to roll the chair back and forth in front of the blue-lined parking spot we designated as the goal.

"I'm gonna get you this time, Kripke," Trevor says. His voice is scratchy. It jumps in his throat like a needle on a damaged record.

"Let's just can this," Lexi says. "You need to get back to bed."

I flinch. That's the worst thing Lexi could have said. But she's in an impossible position. If she continues playing, he'll never score, and this will go on all night. If she lets him score, he'll know it and never forgive her. And if she doesn't play at all, Trevor will feel cheated.

"I've got some sodas over here," I call, but they're not listening to me. I don't exist anymore. Not to them.

Trevor toys with the ball, sweeping it with his broom, containing it to an area just to the side of his wheelchair. His movements are sluggish, his arms limp. "This one is mine," he says. He said that about the last three.

I can't allow him to fail. If Patient F were here, he'd see the future. He'd know that Trevor is going to hit the ball and that it's going to fly wide. He'd know that missing again will shatter Trevor's pride, leaving him with one less reason to open his eyes in the morning, causing Trevor to spiral down, down, down, until he simply stops. Stops caring, stops fighting, stops waking up.

"Prepare for humiliation, Lexi." Trevor pulls back on the broom. His muscles have atrophied. So little of their former strength remains that they strain under the slight weight of the broom. In the night, under the light of the universe, Trevor's scars shine like constellations.

It's pretty clear that Lexi understands her predicament. She knows that letting Trevor win would be worse than defeating him, so she prepares to destroy him. Her face hardens into a rigid mask. It's the same face she wears when she's studying, the same face Trevor wears now. Death before defeat. Sports or academics, they're opposite sides of a fiercely competitive coin.

Trevor swings.

The broom hits the ball, but the head is turned slightly, and it begins to veer.

I'm already moving. I was moving before Trevor made contact.

Lexi wheels herself into position to protect her goal, knowing full well that she won't have to. She's done the math.

But she didn't figure me into the equation. I throw myself into the path of the ball. I snatch it from the air and twist my body, using the ball's momentum to throw it over the edge. I stumble against the wall and catch myself before I tumble over. The ball sails in a graceful arc, disappears into the dark abyss. The *out there*.

"What the hell, Droopy? I totally would have made that shot."

"You wish," Lexi says.

I lean against the wall and fold my arms over my chest. "I'm bored. And I brought snacks."

Trevor wheels to the edge and peers over. "Can't you go get it? I would have scored that time."

Lexi wheels herself beside him. "I would have blocked it."

"You would have *tried*." Trevor is breathing so hard that his whole body shakes and shudders.

"The ball is gone," I say. "Let's grab a drink before I take you two crazy kids back to your rooms."

I feel the pull of gravity, the pull of the world beyond these walls, the catchy three-chord siren song attempting to lure me to the other side. I step away from the edge, fall back into the safety net of my reality here.

Lexi is the first to follow me, and I hand her a Coke. It's lukewarm now, sweat beading the outside of the can, but she cracks it open and gulps it down. "Come on, Trevor."

Trevor is still gazing into the abyss, and I worry that it might be gazing back.

Everyone will leave this hospital at some point in time—one way or another—except me. But I'm greedy to keep my friends here. To stop Death from taking them. It isn't so much to ask. I only want three: Rusty, Lexi, and Trevor. Death can take the rest.

"I would have made the shot," Trevor says one last time. He wheels around and doesn't look me in the eye when I hand him a Coke.

"Yeah, but only because I was tired," Lexi says. She tosses me a *yeah, right* glance on the sly.

"It *was* a good shot," I say, and Trevor grumbles something unintelligible. But I can tell, by the slight smile crouching at the corner of his mouth, that he's already rewriting the memory, convincing himself that the ball really was on a trajectory for the goal.

"Hell yeah, it was," Lexi says. She holds out her Coke can and waits for Trevor to clink it. I clink it too. "To Trevor!"

"To Trevor!"

I toss Trevor a packet of sour-cream-and-onion chips, which he tears into like a crazed piranha. "Where'd you get this haul?" he asks, spraying chips down the front of his shirt.

I sip my Coke and eat some M&M's, the chocolate mixing with the aluminum zing of the soda into some kind of crazy acid swirl. "Vending machines."

"Mom doesn't let me have cookies," Lexi says. She's been eating the same tiny cookie for the last five minutes, nibbling at the edges, licking the chocolate with the tip of her tongue. "Food is the enemy, every meal a war, and the battlefield is my ass."

"Your mom's crazy. You're beautiful." Trevor flushes the moment he voices the words, and they hang out there between us all like a rudderless zeppelin. I'm waiting to find out if they'll burn up like the *Hindenburg* or somehow manage to stay aloft.

Lexi holds the cookie in front of her eyes, avoiding Trevor's gaze, and then she pops the whole thing into her mouth. She chews, her face a study in ecstasy. It's uncomfortable to watch someone enjoy something so much. I eat another handful of M&M's and look away.

After that, the silence is too awkward, so I tell them my idea about Patient F plucking his family from time and putting them into the bodies of people in Maligant city.

"It sounds like purgatory," Trevor says when I finish. "Patient F, trapped in Maligant City, being stalked by the Scythe, trying to atone for his sins by doing good so that he doesn't end up in hell. Totally purgatory." Trevor coughs and sips his Coke. I should have brought him water.

"You don't believe in all that, do you?" Lexi asks.

"All what?"

"God, heaven, hell."

Trevor shrugs. "Sure. Don't you?"

"No way. When I die, I die. There's nothing out there."

"That's sad," Trevor says. "I have to believe this isn't the end all of everything. Otherwise, this pain, this bullshit, life, isn't worth it."

"You think this purgatory place is real?" I ask Trevor.

He nods. "Sure. Good people go to heaven, bad people go to hell, and sometimes the people who aren't ready for either—they hang around in purgatory until they are."

"Nonsense," Lexi scoffs.

"It's not nonsense, Lexi," Trevor says. His voice is scratchy and low. "When I die, I sure hope that I'm going to heaven."

Lexi doesn't respond to that, and neither do I. How can we? Lexi wants to—I can see it in the twitch under her eye. The scientist, the

93

rational heart that pounds in her chest, wants to tell Trevor that there is no God; there is no heaven or hell or purgatory. There is only *this*. But she bites her tongue, unwilling to murder his hope.

"We should go back," I say. "Nurse Merchant is probably freaking out."

We leave the brooms behind, and I help Trevor roll his chair into the elevator. A thoughtful silence shrouds our journey back.

"You'll go to heaven, Trevor," Lexi says, when the elevator stops at our floor. She holds the doors open with her foot but doesn't wheel herself through. Her whole body hesitates, and I don't understand why. I can't wait to return to the hospital, to the familiar smells, the winding hallways, the chilly lights. "You're too good not to." She sighs and then finally exits.

People watch us as we move through the hospital. They look suspicious. It's long past visiting hours, and we look strange: me pushing Trevor, Lexi wheeling herself. Her upper lip is beaded with sweat, and her flowery yellow top is damp. If I could push them both, I would.

Peds is in chaos when we creep near the entrance. Nurse Merchant hasn't left, even though her shift ended an hour ago, and there are two other nurses I don't recognize rushing around, along with a security guard, a doctor, Lexi's mom, and a couple that I assume are Trevor's parents.

Nurse Merchant is on the phone talking quickly and with her hands, waving them around like an orchestra conductor. Mrs. Kripke is shouting at anyone who will give her half a moment's attention. Trevor's parents hold each other and stare into space.

"Shit," Trevor says.

"You hang back," Lexi says to me. "I'll tell them it was my idea."

"Thanks for today, Droopy." Trevor bumps my fist and wheels himself the last few feet into the ward, followed closely by Lexi.

I hide behind a tall cart filled with empty dinner trays and watch the scene unfold.

Trevor says, "What's up?" and the room erupts with questions and shouts. Nurse Merchant hangs up the phone and descends upon Lexi and Trevor with her stethoscope and thermometer. The security officer demands to know where they were. Lexi fends off the inquisition with noncommittal answers like "I don't know" and "just hanging out."

"Do you know how much worry you caused me?" Mrs. Kripke shrieks. She's clutching that god-awful wig like a security blanket. She doesn't wait for Lexi to answer before sweeping her girl into her arms, ignoring Lexi's protests, and hugging her tightly. I can't tell if Mrs. Kripke is happy to see Lexi or attempting to suffocate her.

"Sorry, guys," Trevor mutters to his parents. He's sagging in his wheelchair, as if his skeleton is too weak to support his weight. Trevor's parents loom over him. It's almost creepy, the way their arms are crossed over their chests. I've never seen Trevor's parents before. They don't look much like him. His mother is blocky, like an unfinished marble statue, with the same shiny blond hair Trevor has in his picture. Trevor's dad is tan and leathery with a bushy black moustache and shoulders that roll forward so far, they're becoming hunched.

"They called us at work," Mr. Guerrero says. "We had to close the store an hour early." His voice has a hint of an accent he's clearly worked hard to eliminate.

95

Mrs. Guerrero strokes Trevor's cheek with the back of her hand. I close my eyes and imagine that I can feel the soft skin of her fingers. My mom used to touch my cheek like that—when I was four and my closet was full of monsters.

"I'm sorry," Trevor says again. Mr. Guerrero fights to remain angry, but his brittle resolve collapses, and he falls to his knees in front of his son, weeping. A few moments later, Nurse Merchant wheels Trevor to his room.

"We were so worried about you," Mrs. Kripke is whining to Lexi. Lexi has been deposited back into her wheelchair, and her mother arranges the wig on Lexi's head so that the curls brush the tops of her shoulders. Wig or not, Lexi really is a beauty queen.

I wait for Lexi to rip the wig off her head, fling it at her mother, and wheel back into her room to seek refuge with her books—but she doesn't. She patiently allows her mother to adjust the wig and doesn't even complain when she uses spit and the hem of her blouse to clean some smear of imaginary dirt from Lexi's forehead.

"I love you, Mom," Lexi says, and it's so sincere, so real, that my world tilts and I feel hot and sick.

I bolt down the hallway, not caring if anyone sees me. It's a race to the bottom, and I'm going to win. I blow past two doctors, and it's like a wind has torn through the hospital halls. I'm too fast for them to see, faster than the speed of sound. Fast enough to outrun this pain.

When I reach my room in the unfinished wing, I fall down onto my mattress and pull out the tin box. My body is wracked with sobs, my eyes blind with tears. The walls of this room bend and breathe; they collapse in around me, so close they press my skin. There's no door, no windows. There's only me and this mattress and this goddamn picture. The picture of my family that's always here waiting for me, even though they never will be. Not ever again.

Because they're dead, and it's my fault.

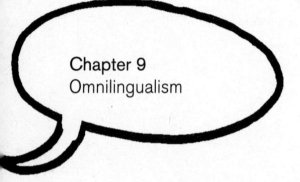

Chapter 9
Omnilingualism

Being without my sketchbook makes me twitchy.

The nightmares gather behind my eyes, crowding out reality, until all I see are the monsters lurking in dark corners, the Scythe hiding behind every curtain, Death standing in front of me with an empty tray and a hungry look in her eyes.

"Andrew?" she asks. "Is everything all right?"

No. Nothing is all right. I want to scream at her. I want to bludgeon Death with my cold steel ladle and force her to return my family. My thoughts are tearing at the seams of my body, trying to squeeze out and expose me, but I wrestle them back and calmly say, "Do you want Swedish meatballs or vegetable fried rice?"

Death takes her tray of greasy Swedish widowmakers to her usual table in the corner and eats with one eye on me and one eye on a stack of files. A list of names. She gives me the creeps staring at me like that, and I wonder if she knows my true face the way I know hers and is merely toying with me because she enjoys the hunt far more than the kill. Either way, I am no one's prey. She'll take me one day for sure, but she won't be laughing when it happens.

The day passes quickly, and I finish my shift. Arnold tries to hand me a book when he pays me, but I wave him off and leave. I can't function like this. I need my sketchpad.

I screw up my courage and trek through the unfamiliar passages that lead to the chapel. I haven't come here since the day I followed Death because . . . well, I don't know why. This is a place of God, and He and I aren't exactly on speaking terms these days.

Trevor believes in all that heaven and hell and purgatory stuff. Lexi believes in quiet oblivion. I'm not sure what I believe. Heaven is a nice thought. If I knew, really knew, that my parents were hanging out in paradise, sipping rum runners while they waited for me, maybe I'd let Death catch me so that I could be with them. But I don't know that. I can't. This could be purgatory. Or hell. Maybe there is no single answer. Maybe our beliefs decide our fate after death.

The chapel hasn't changed, except this time it's empty. It's a cold room in spite of the warm colors. The walls are faded, the wooden pews are dull. The chapel feels wheezy and insubstantial, like Grandma Brawley—a room hovering on the edge of life, unaware of the day-to-day grief and happiness occurring around it.

My parents were seriously lapsed Catholics. They kept a Bible on the bookshelf, and both had grown up attending mass and confessing their sins to deaf priests. They even kept a crucifix on their bedroom wall. But they never passed on their beliefs to me or Cady. I always thought, if Jesus really was the son of God, even he would find all the rituals oddly macabre.

"I knew you'd return."

The chaplain startles me, and I turn around so quickly that I stumble into him. We both fall into the pews, and I grunt and scramble to my feet, helping the chaplain rise in the process. Even I know it's rude to knock over a priest and not offer him a hand back up.

"Sorry," I mumble.

"No, no. It's my fault. Shouldn't have scared you." The chaplain's got a sleepy voice, like he just woke up from a solid nap. "I'm Father Mike."

Father Mike looks much as he did when I first saw him, though up close he seems less comical. His cheeks are dotted with razor burn and acne-scar craters. He's also shorter than I thought, but the way he carries himself—his squared shoulders and straight back—makes him appear taller. He gives off a smooth, quiet confidence that I don't believe is posturing.

"Andrew," I introduce myself. "Or Drew or Andy. Whatever."

"Andy," Father Mike says. "I found your sketchbook. You're quite talented."

"Did you read it?" I glance around for my sketchpad but don't see it.

Father Mike climbs the two steps to the draped altar and reaches behind it. He draws out my sketchpad and offers it to me, only there's no way I'm going up there. Aztecs cut people's hearts out on altars like that.

"Did you dream up that Patient F story?" Father Mike asks.

"I guess. I mean, yeah, I wrote it." My hands twitch at my sides. This strange little man is holding my sketchbook hostage, and there's nothing I can do about it. I wonder how many heaven points I'd lose for decking a priest. "May I have it back, please?"

Father Mike opens my pad and flips through the pages. I feel the clean white paper pulling at me; I want to siphon off the night-mares that have bred uncontrolled inside me and imprison them between its covers. I need a quiet place to draw more than I need air to breathe.

"Answer me one question, and I'll return it to you."

"I really have to get going," I say. "Lots to do." The more Father Mike touches my pages with his stubby, oily fingers, the more I want to beat him into a coma, but this man is friends with Death, so I have to keep my cool.

"It's one question, Andy." Father Mike closes my sketchpad and dangles it in front of his chest like bait.

I scowl at him and pace down the aisle. "Fine," I say, resigned to the fact that answering him may be the only way to escape. "One question."

"Wonderful." There's laughter in Father Mike's eyes, caught up in the fine wrinkles that grow from the corners of his eyelids and spread like rays of light. Father Mike doesn't move any faster than he needs to. At first I think it's because he's messing with me, but I real-ize it's because he lacks urgency, which I suppose makes sense. Why hurry when you have all of eternity at your disposal?

He flips through the pages until he finds the one he's looking for. "Patient F is on the run from the RAND Corporation, and they've sent their deadliest agent, the Scythe, to capture him."

"Yes," I say.

"And Patient F can move through time, but he only chooses to remember certain aspects of his life." Father Mike rifles through the pages again. "For instance, he knows the names of all the men who were involved in murdering his family, but he doesn't remember how they killed them, or why."

"Correct."

Father Mike looks up at me. "Why doesn't he want to know?"

"Guilt," I say, and hold out my hand.

But Father Mike makes no move to return my sketchpad. He isn't even looking at me anymore. He's staring at a page: Patient F is tearing out the skeleton of one of the men on his list. Outside the building, the Scythe is preparing an ambush. My pencil strokes are heavy, dense.

"But why?" Father Mike asks. "Why does he feel guilty?"

I drop my hand to my side but remain standing. "He blames himself for the deaths of his wife and child."

"How can he know that for certain if he doesn't know how or why they were killed?"

"What more does he need to know?" I ask. "They're dead, and he's alive."

Father Mike nods slightly, his eyes still glued to the book. He flips through the pages again. "So he feels guilty for surviving?" He looks up, stares right into my eyes. Father Mike's got these blue eyes like I've never seen before. They're flashlights, shining their holy light into corners of my soul that I don't necessarily want illuminated.

"It's more complicated than that." My legs are tired, and I slip into the cramped front pew, squirming to find a comfortable position. "Patient F *is* responsible for their deaths."

"Why?"

"He just is!"

"That's silly." Father Mike tilts his head and raises his eyebrows. Maybe he's waiting for another explanation, but I haven't got one. "Survivor's guilt is understandable. I deal with families who blame themselves for losses they couldn't possibly have prevented." Father Mike touches the pages. He runs his finger lightly over a heavy pencil stroke. "But the revenge—Patient F's obsession with dragging his family through time over and over so that he can save them—it's bloody masochistic."

I struggle to find the words to explain it properly. If I had my sketchpad, I could draw what I mean for him, but he doesn't seem to want to release it. "Patient F is protecting his family the only way he can."

"But they're stand-ins. Ersatz duplicates. His wife and son are still dead. These people, they're not really his family."

"Maybe not technically," I say. "But they're his to protect. His responsibility."

"He's the one who's putting them in danger in the first place." Father Mike holds up the pad and points to a frame where Patient F is tearing his wife through space and time and dropping her into the body of an elderly woman on the street, who's about to be robbed.

"They were already in danger," I say. "Look at the old woman. Whether his wife is in that body or not, the old woman is getting jacked."

Father Mike studies the frames. "It's still masochistic," the chaplain says. "And I don't buy it."

I get up and snatch the sketchpad from Father Mike. "It's not for you to get. You're just some priest who read something that didn't belong to him. What do you know about comic books anyway?"

I turn to storm off down the aisle, but Father Mike clears his throat with authority—the way my father used to clear his throat when he knew I was trying to pull one over on him—and it stops me short.

"I'm not saying the story is bad. Far from it."

"Then what are you saying?" I won't give Father Mike the satisfaction of me turning around to face him.

"Only that . . . someone who goes to such great lengths to avoid death and save people who aren't even really his family—he isn't acting out of guilt alone. He's punishing himself."

I hesitate, then glance back over my shoulder, almost afraid to look at him. "Punishing himself for what?"

Father Mike shrugs. "It's your comic. You tell me."

Chapter 10
Time Travel

My feet don't listen to me.

Instead of running somewhere quiet to immediately start sketching, I end up hanging around the ICU, watching people go in and out of Rusty's room. Mostly his parents. They're haggard and thin. They almost look worse than Rusty, and they barely leave his bedside. It's like they're funneling years of their life into Rusty so he'll get well sooner. But I think if that were possible, more children who got hurt would end up as orphans.

The girl's here too. The one who was with Rusty in the emergency room that night. She doesn't look broken anymore; she's purpose made flesh.

Rusty's parents call her Nina, and she's rebuilt herself. Now she's full of rage, aimed at the monsters who put Rusty here. Nina doesn't look like the crusading, angry type, though. She's unassuming—dowdy, even. Her brown hair hangs in a limp ponytail, and her clothes look like she pulled them from her closet at random. She's pretty, but she walks and dresses as if she's unaware of it.

Nina spends hours on her cell phone giving interviews to reporters, talking about how little the police have done to track down the boys who set Rusty on fire. From her chatter, I learn that there were no witnesses. That three boys doused Rusty with alcohol and set him ablaze. Rusty claims not to remember the identities of his attackers, but it's an established fact that he's been bullied since his freshman year. The police have suspects but haven't arrested a soul.

Everyone scatters during Rusty's burn care. His wretched screams rip through the ICU and linger like radiation, and I wonder how the nurses bear it. Then I see one of them, good old Coffee Nurse, tucked away in a corner, sobbing. She probably thinks no one can see her, but I do. From the empty room that I'm hiding in, I see her.

The last time I was in the ICU, this room was occupied. Today it smells like bleach. The bed is stripped, and the machines are all silent. The room feels the void left behind by its last occupant; I feel the walls searching, groping for a warm body to protect. They have me instead.

I nod off, curled up in a corner on the floor, and wake up in the dark. It was stupid to fall asleep, but at least I wasn't caught. If I had been, Death would have descended upon me and spirited me away—that's for sure. I still have her business card in my pocket, and sometimes I think it would be easier to call her and end this game.

When I've stood, stretched, and cleared my head, I peek out the door and, spotting no nurses, dash across the ICU into Rusty's room. There's still heat coming off his body, but he looks better. The ban-

106

dages are clean, and his face is less tortured. He still moans, but his voice is softer, like he's moaning more from habit than anything else.

"Hey, buddy," I say. "Sorry I haven't visited lately." If Rusty hears me, he doesn't acknowledge it. "I've been watching, though. Making sure Death doesn't come around and get you. So . . . I've kept my promise."

I lean against the wall, folded into a blind spot. For a moment, I just stare at Rusty, memorizing the slant of his eyes, how his wave of red hair crashes over his forehead, the way his unburned left hand twitches in his sleep as if he's playing the guitar.

"I wish I could go back through time," I tell Rusty. "I'd kill the guys who did this to you." My voice breaks, and I feel a sharp pain in my chest. It's like a shard of glass is burrowing through my rib cage. I can't bear it: the thought of someone actually lighting another person on fire, of watching the orange and blue flames lick away the layers of another human being's skin—the fat bubbles underneath, and the poor soul can't do anything but scream in absolute fucking agony. After a while, maybe he can't even scream anymore.

It's a horror beyond imagining.

Not even in my nightmares.

When Rusty doesn't respond to my words, I wedge myself between the wall and his bed, settle my sketchpad over my knees, and work on Patient F. The nightmares I've been hoarding flow out through my fingers and flood the blank pages. I lose myself in the story of Patient F and his revenge, and of the Scythe's wicked games. It's all out of order but, if you think about it, life's like that some-times. Even though the man Stanley North and his perfect family are in the past, he has to earn them in the future. Killing the men on his list isn't really revenge, it's just the price Patient F pays for bygone happiness.

The nurse checks on Rusty, and I curl into a ball and hide. Under the bed, I see that she's got thin ankles, and she taps her toes to music only she hears while she fusses with Rusty's IV.

After a minute or two, she leaves, and Rusty says, "I know you're there." He whispers so softly that I'm not sure if it's my imagination playing tricks on me. "Hey," he says, a little louder this time.

"I'm here," I say, so that he doesn't raise his voice again. The nurse's station isn't that far away. "I'm Andrew. Or Andy or Drew. Whatever."

"Rusty." It costs him to speak, to say his name, but he sounds better than Trevor. When Trevor talks, it requires all his strength, and even then I'm not always sure it'll be enough. Rusty just sounds weary, burdened by memories.

"Why are you here?" he asks.

"I don't know." Maybe it's not the right thing to say, but it's honest, and I think that he deserves as much honesty as I can give him. "You look like you could use a friend."

"Friends let this happen to me," Rusty says.

I look up, and he's looking down. But not at me, at his right arm and his chest and his legs. He doesn't see the bandages, only the burns. If Patient F is unstuck in time, Rusty McHale is stuck in one moment.

I try to give him my friendliest smile. "I wanted to be a firefighter . . . once."

"Lucky me."

I sit silently beside Rusty's bed, thinking of something to say that won't sound cliché. By now, I'm sure he's heard everything: how he'll be all right, and that everything happens for a reason. Those sorts of sentiments are bullshit. Even the people who say them don't believe them. Not really. They want to believe, but there are too many villains in the world and not enough heroes for anyone to truly buy into the scam that is hope.

"You know why this happened to me?" Rusty asks. His question is a challenge. I look at him, and this time he *is* looking at me, craning his neck so that he can see my face. I scoot back so that he doesn't have to work so hard.

"Yeah."

"And?"

"And what?"

"You think I'm some kind of pervert?"

"No," I say.

Rusty looks away, rests his head upon his pillow.

"Not everyone is that closed-minded," I tell him.

Rusty chuffs. "Yeah, right."

"No one's ever set *me* on fire," I say. It's direct and maybe a little cruel, but Rusty needs an anchor.

"Get out," Rusty says.

I reach up and take Rusty's hand. He pulls away, and my sweaty fingers slip through his. "Just because some ignorant assholes hated you enough to do this doesn't mean that everyone will." I stretch my arm up farther and grab Rusty's hand again. This time, he doesn't let go. He squeezes my hand tightly—so tightly, it hurts.

"You got anything to read?"

The sudden change of subject surprises me, but I'm grateful.

"No," I say, shaking my head to refocus. "But I've got this comic I'm working on. I could tell you about Patient F."

"Yeah," Rusty says. "Okay."

Throughout the night, I tell Rusty every story I've ever written about Patient F: how he was born; his life before, when he was a man in a suit; and the experiments performed on him by the men in red lab coats, the ones who turned the man in the boring suit into Patient F. I tell Rusty about the names on his list, and the people he saves, and about the Scythe, who hunts Patient F through the streets of Maligant City.

At some point, Rusty falls asleep—I don't know when—and I realize that I'm talking to myself.

"I killed my parents, you know."

I've never spoken the words out loud. They sound bare, hollowed out. They deserve better than to be whispered in a dark room to a sleeping boy. "I told you they died here in the hospital, but I left out that it was me who killed them. This was the last place they were alive, and now they'll never leave. And neither will I. I don't deserve to. There are people looking for me—at least, they *were* looking for me—but they'll never find me. Anyway, I'm pretty sure they've given up."

I don't know what I want. Absolution? From Rusty? I barely know the guy. And I don't think he's in a forgiving mood right now anyway.

"I'll see you tomorrow night," I say.

There are no nurses at the station when I peek around the corner. They're either on rounds or fetching supplies or doing another of the hundred things they accomplish at night while their patients sleep, lost in the snores of the machines. I scurry for the exit, anxious to escape before any of the nurses return.

"I heard you in there," says a familiar voice.

I freeze at the double doors. My instincts urge me on, but I ignore them and turn around. Steven is standing a couple of feet away with his arms crossed over his chest. "Oh, yeah?"

"You're not supposed to be here. The ER is one thing, but this place . . . if you get caught . . ." There's something different about Steven, and I don't mean the blue scrubs he's wearing instead of his usual fuchsia ones. He's quieter, smaller. He moves delicately, as if the floor is fragile ice that we're all in danger of plunging through.

"He needs friends."

Steven doesn't argue—how can he? Knowing he's not alone is as important to Rusty's survival as the antibiotics they pump into him. Steven drops his arms, his shoulders. He's defeated. "You've got to be more careful."

"I'll try," I say.

"You'll have to do better than try."

I look toward Rusty's room, remembering the way he squeezed my hand. "I won't let anyone hurt him."

Steven nods silently and creeps back to the nurse's station as if I'm not here. I can only guess at Steven's motives for not ratting me out, but I think it has everything to do with Rusty. Maybe he needs Rusty to live as badly as I do. Maybe for very different reasons. Or maybe he knows that just living isn't enough and he thinks I'm the person who can give Rusty something worth living for.

Finding something to live for is hard enough for *me*. I'm not sure how I'll do it for another person. But I damn well have to try.

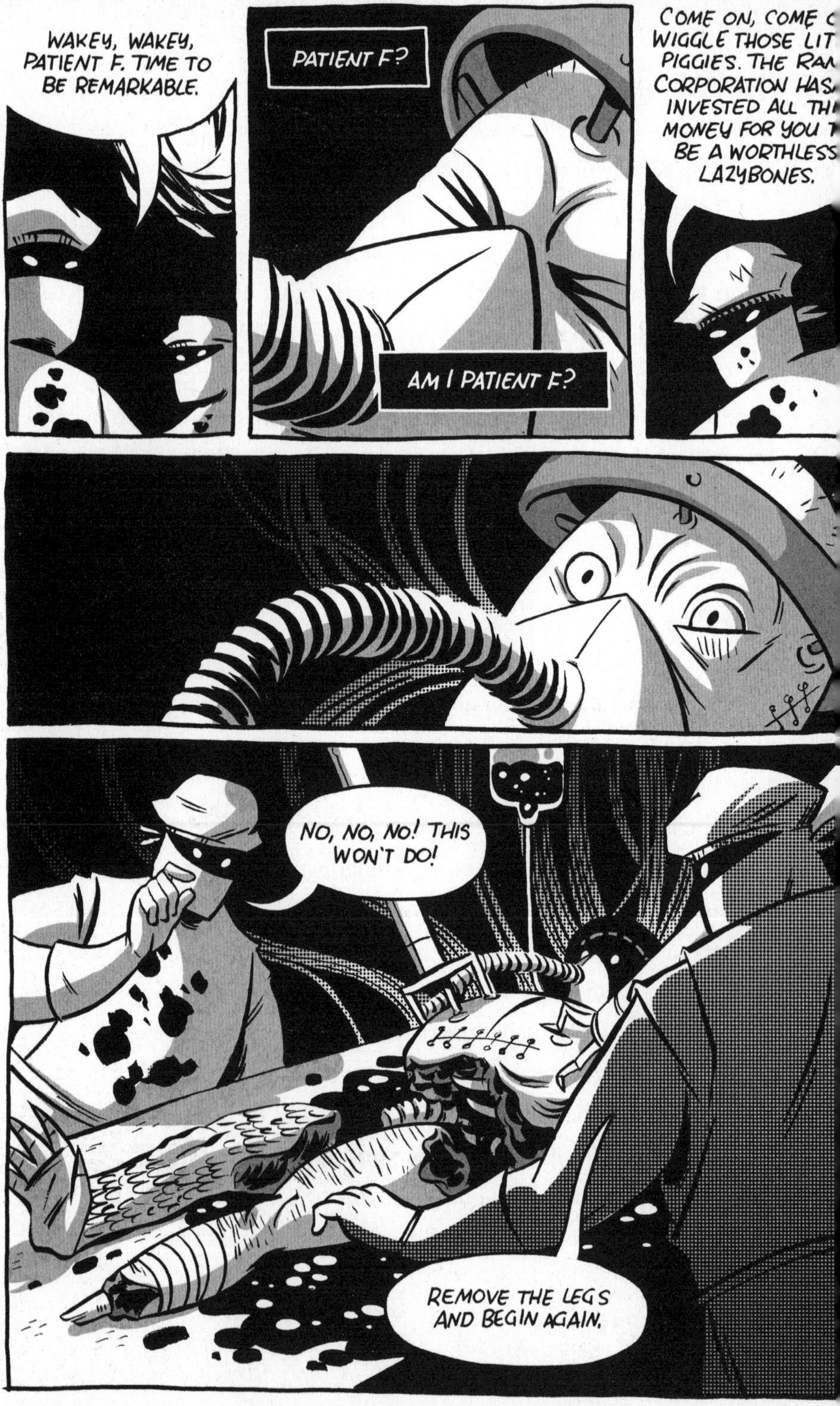
WAKEY, WAKEY, PATIENT F. TIME TO BE REMARKABLE.
PATIENT F?
AM I PATIENT F?
COME ON, COME C WIGGLE THOSE LIT PIGGIES. THE RA CORPORATION HAS INVESTED ALL TH MONEY FOR YOU T BE A WORTHLESS LAZYBONES.
NO, NO, NO! THIS WON'T DO!
REMOVE THE LEGS AND BEGIN AGAIN.

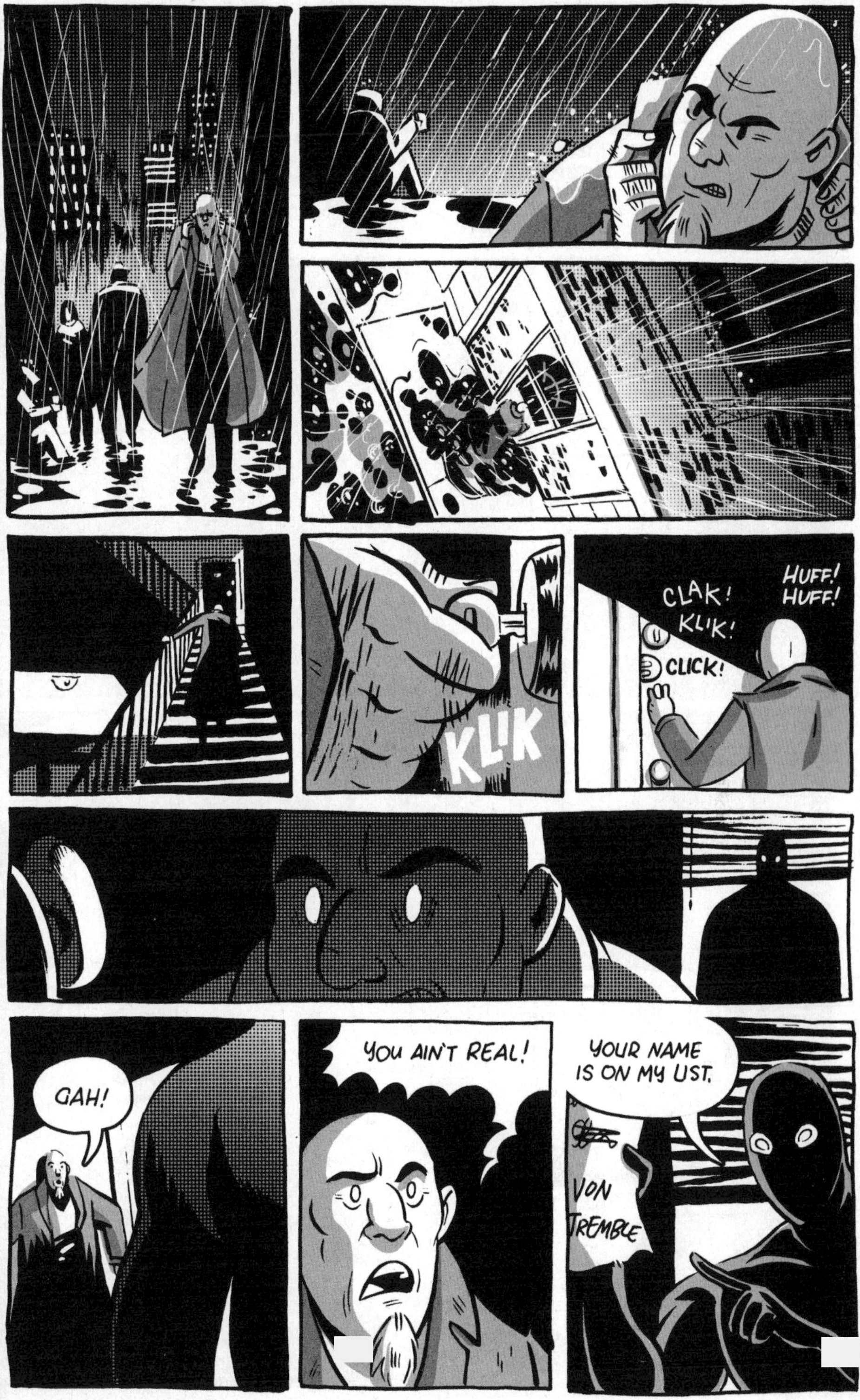
KLIK
CLAK!
KLIK!
CLICK!
HUFF!
HUFF!
GAH!
YOU AIN'T REAL!
YOUR NAME
IS ON MY LIST.
VON
TREMBLE

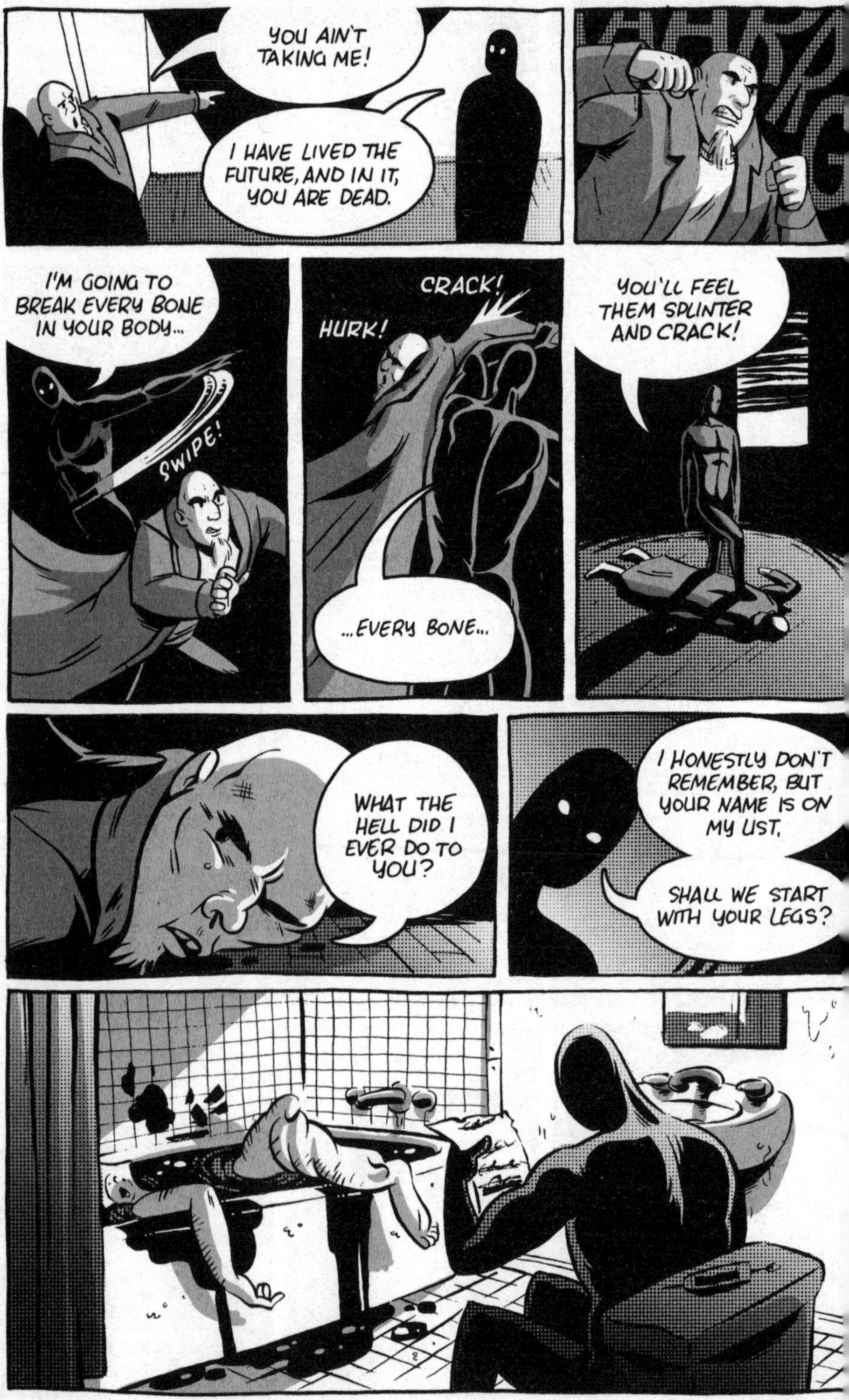
YOU AIN'T TAKING ME!
I HAVE LIVED THE FUTURE, AND IN IT, YOU ARE DEAD.
I'M GOING TO BREAK EVERY BONE IN YOUR BODY...
SWIPE!
CRACK!
HURK!
...EVERY BONE...
YOU'LL FEEL THEM SPLINTER AND CRACK!
WHAT THE HELL DID I EVER DO TO YOU?
I HONESTLY DON'T REMEMBER, BUT YOUR NAME IS ON MY LIST.
SHALL WE START WITH YOUR LEGS?

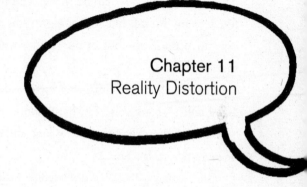

Chapter 11
Reality Distortion

I hate chocolate.

Beginning just before Thanksgiving and continuing through the holidays, my mom made sweets nonstop. Fudge, coconut balls, buckeyes, truffles, cookies. She'd sit on this little pink-painted stool in front of the stove and stir chocolate, humming songs that I can't remember. Back then, I thought they were annoying. Now I'd give anything to hear them.

For weeks, the sickening smell of chocolate permeated the house. It was like this suffocating blanket that you couldn't find your way out from under. By the time Christmas rolled around, you could've withheld all my presents and I still wouldn't have eaten any of it.

Whenever I smell chocolate now, I'm sucked back to those days. The days when my mom sat on that stool, stirring a batch of chocolate with her wooden spoon—the one with the charred end—and humming. It's the only way I get to see her now.

Sometimes, memories are all that keep me going, and I can't help wondering what keeps Rusty going. What he holds on to. I'm afraid if I don't find out, I'll lose him forever.

"Try some fudge." Arnold shoves a piece of dark brown, crumby fudge at my mouth like he's going to force-feed it to me if I don't say yes. Walnuts rise out of the sickly sweet bar like surfacing submarines.

"Pass." I hand a woman her credit card along with the receipt and a polite "thank you." She hardly notices me.

Arnold offers the fudge to my one and only customer. "Fudge?" he says. "It's on the house."

The woman doesn't acknowledge Arnold either. She's Rusty's mother, and she comes into the cafeteria every day at 4:35 for dinner, fills a tray, sits at a table for an hour, and then throws the food away without taking a bite. I'm not entirely sure she's even aware of her surroundings. Each day, she's older and farther gone. Occasionally, Rusty's friend Nina or Rusty's father joins her; usually she's alone. Her boy, that's what she clings to, and I get the feeling that if Rusty died, his mother wouldn't outlive him long.

"I need a new book, Arnold." We're in that peculiar time between lunch and dinner. The cafeteria is mostly empty, but the competing smells of fresh dinner foods wage war in the air.

"I gave you one on Tuesday." Arnold pops the fudge into his mouth and grimaces. "Yum." He spits it out into a napkin, wadding the whole mess up and tossing it in the trash. "Too much . . . something."

"That was Tuesday. This is Saturday. I need a new book."

"You finished *1984*?" I nod. "And?"

"It was a book," I say. "A long and boring book." In fact, the only thing I actually enjoyed about it was the person I read it with. But I keep that to myself.

"Boring? You thought *1984* was boring?"

"Didn't you?" I busy myself checking the hot trays even though they're full of food and ready for the dinner crowd. The truth is that I can't stop thinking about Rusty. Reading to him the last few days has been the highlight of everything.

Arnold looks like I just turned on the gas oven and tossed in a match. He's so shocked, he can barely speak in full sentences.

"But *1984* . . . it's a classic."

"Which is just a fancy way of saying 'boring.'" I lean against the counter. "What's the big deal, anyway?" I'm not sure why Arnold's getting his tighty whities in a twist. It's a book. I read it because Rusty asked me to, and I did so happily. The longer I read, the more content he looked. Each sentence more powerful than morphine. I dreaded the last page more than Death.

"When my son, John, read it," Arnold says, "we talked about it for days. We even started speaking in Newspeak until Mrs. Jaworski threatened to make us cook our own meals if we didn't find a new book."

"Good thing I'm not your son."

Arnold's eyes go flat. I screwed up. It was a joke, and not even a good one, but the emotion drains from his face—his passion for books, for being here and talking, all gone. The man standing before me is polished steel, and that's my fault. Only, I don't know why.

But Arnold will be back to his old self soon enough. It's not the first time I've pissed him off, and I'm guessing it won't be the last.

117

The dinner crowd hits full force, and neither of us has a second to spare for anger. I dish out food and ring up customers, while Arnold charms his hungry patrons, sharing his smiles with them but not with me.

After the rush dies, Arnold hands me my cash for the day and tells me to get lost. A few slow-eating stragglers remain, but Mrs. McHale is gone. I haven't seen Death either, and that worries me. She could be with Rusty right now, but he was doing so well last time I saw him that I doubt it. Besides, I'm hungry and won't be any good to Rusty if I pass out.

I grab some food and sit at a table in the corner, studying my most recent Patient F panels. In some ways, Patient F and Rusty are so alike, but at least Patient F has his revenge to keep him focused on living. I'm not sure what Rusty has, if he has anything at all. I know that his parents love him, and that his best friend, Nina, would do anything for him, but hopelessness infects him like an insatiable virus that devours all the good in his life, excreting fear. Fear of living, fear of dying, fear that he's going to disappoint the people who love him, and even fear that their love is not enough. I see it, I recognize it. I draw that same hopelessness in Patient F's eyes.

Father Mike strolls into the cafeteria, and I slouch, hoping he won't see me. But he waves right away. I sigh as he grabs dinner and heads toward my table. "Hi, Andy."

"Father Mike." I keep my words clipped and try to send out major *go away* vibes, which obviously don't work since Father Mike flounces down into the seat beside me and digs into his steamy potpie. All I want to do is finish eating so that I can visit Rusty, not spend my evening listening to Father Mike babble.

"How have you been?" I don't know why Father Mike is asking, so I'm unsure how to reply. The way he shovels food into his mouth makes me think he's genuinely curious. Or hungry. But I can't forget that he's friends with my nemesis: Death.

"Okay, I guess." I try to cover my drawings with my arms, but Father Mike has already seen the sketchpad. He watches me while chewing a mouthful of potpie, wearing a goofy expression like he's been huffing incense. He makes a grab for my sketchpad, his fingers harboring little bits of mushy peas and carrots on them—and I slide it off the table into my lap.

"Just curious to see if you've come up with anything new. I'm a bit of a comic-book junkie."

"Seriously? You?" I stifle a laugh, but the truth is that the thought of him holed up in his chapel reading comics doesn't surprise me.

Father Mike smiles and breathes out a long sigh, clearing decades of dust from his lungs. He leans back in his chair and closes his eyes for a moment, summoning the memory. "I used to have a huge collection. Golden-Age stuff. Superman, Batman, Sub-Mariner, Human Torch. Nowadays, I read more modern books. *Kick-Ass* and *Fables* and *The Walking Dead*, but I miss the old stuff."

While I can't deny that I'm intrigued by the idea of this short, round, balding priest who's into comic books, Rusty is waiting for me to bring him a new story to read. Steven told me that every time the ICU doors open, Rusty looks to see if it's me. That's a weight I'm not sure I'm able to carry. I'd love nothing more than to spend the rest of my life reading to Rusty, but it's not enough. Eventually, he'll get bored and slip away from me.

Then again, Father Mike might have an idea how to keep Rusty anchored. A priest must know everything about life and death. Or more than me, anyway.

"What happens to people who kill themselves?" I ask. He was right in the middle of a story I wasn't paying attention to, and the question pulls him up short.

"Come again?"

"Suicides. What happens to them?"

Father Mike scrubs his face with his hand and pushes his tray to the center of the table. Clearly, this was not the direction he expected our conversation to take. "Suicide is serious. Taking your own life is considered a mortal sin."

I shake my head, worried that he thinks we're talking about me. "What if you don't kill yourself?" I say. "What if you just stop wanting to live?"

"I'm not sure that's the same thing."

"Isn't it? I mean, if something really bad happened to you and you stop trying to live, isn't that the same?"

Worry lines crease the corners of Father Mike's eyes. "Maybe, but I have to admit that I'm a little confused here, Andy."

There's no easy way to explain this without talking about Rusty, but Rusty's secrets aren't mine to tell. Anyway, I enjoy having him to myself. So I say, "Just . . . how can I find a way to make someone want to live who maybe feels there's nothing worth living for? Like Patient F." I put my sketchpad back on the table and slide it to him.

Relief floods his face now that he thinks we're talking about Patient F. The hypothetical discussion about suicide wasn't about me, but about a character in my book.

He wanders through the pages for a moment. If the drawings

are too graphic for him, it doesn't show on his face. Not that it's any worse than flesh-devouring zombies, but still, he's a priest and I'm not sure how much exposure he's had to the real world.

"Your Patient F reminds me of the way they draw Batman now," Father Mike says. He closes the sketchpad and puts it on the table between us. "All anger and rage and revenge. He saves Gotham from the monsters but destroys it in the process. That bothered me in the movie, you know? Sure, he stops the Joker, but at what cost? Life is about more than hate. It takes more than anger to make a hero."

"What does make a hero, then?"

"Love."

"Oh, come on." At first I think he's messing with me, but when he just gives me this *you heard what I said* look, I know he's totally serious. "Superheroes are supposed to be badass, Father Mike, not all lovey-dovey."

Father Mike rolls his eyes. "You don't listen well, do you?"

I can't help laughing a little. "You sound like my dad."

"I'd like to meet him sometime."

I ignore the comment and say, "We were talking about superheroes."

Father Mike pauses, serious, like maybe he's going to press me about my father, but he doesn't. "In order for a hero to be a true hero, he's got to have something worth living for. He's got to love something."

This isn't helping. Part of me wishes I'd never brought it up. I know he thinks we're talking about Patient F, but telling me that he's got to have something to live for in order to have something to live for is like telling me water is wet because it's water.

"In the movies, Batman cuts himself off from the people who care about him and from his own feelings, and, in my opinion, he becomes worse than the bad guys. Patient F is in danger of heading down the same path."

"He saves his family," I say. "Drags them out of the past and puts them into people from the present. He loves them enough to do that."

Father Mike shrugs. "And he spends the rest of his time gutting his enemies without even knowing why. And the people he saves, they're not his family, are they?" He glances at my sketchpad again, and it's like he's trying to see through the cover to each page beneath. Then he looks at me the same way and it makes my skin itch.

"Sure they are."

"No, Andy, they're not."

"You just don't understand."

"Maybe not," he says. "But his family is gone, and nothing is going to change that. He's got to stop living in the past and focus on the present. He's got to find a way to live for now. That's how Patient F becomes a hero."

Suddenly, I feel like we're not talking about Patient F anymore, and I just want to bail, but I'm afraid that will make him suspicious, so I choke out a laugh. "You really suck at this," I say. "That's probably why you got sent here instead of to a real church."

Father Mike pushes my sketchpad all the way across to me. "I requested to come here."

"Yeah, well, that's weird. Anyone who chooses to spend all day hanging around a place full of the sick and dying is weird."

"I agree."

That's it. I grab my pad and get up, but I trip over the chair behind me. Father Mike watches me as I fight gravity and sort myself out. I feel his eyes all over me and I wonder if he really can see all my secrets.

Arnold is waiting for me near the menu board, which features yellow noodles and a chicken bathing in a giant pie. He shoves a worn book into my hands. "*Frankenstein*. You'll like this one."

"I think I read this."

"Read it again." He looks like he wants to say more, but his tongue is choked with lingering anger and the words go unsaid. He leaves me standing by the board more confused than ever.

When I was fourteen, I went through this awful phase where everything my parents did annoyed me. I thought they were these terrible tyrants out to make my life perfect hell. Thankfully, I got over that. And even though I never considered my parents even remotely close to cool, I came to believe that they had a better handle on life than me, that they'd figured it out. When the world felt like a wasteland of suck, I held on to the hope that one day I would grow up and have all the answers, just like my parents.

As I look over at Arnold and then at Father Mike, I realize that adults are just as fucked as the rest of us. No one really grows up. No one unravels all of life's many mysteries. They just grow older and become better liars.

Chapter 12
Time Freeze

Trevor looks like shit.

There's no kinder way to say it. Trevor is my friend, and I hate seeing him like this. He's hooked up to more wires than Pinocchio, and he eats through his IV now. I didn't think it was possible for him to lose any more weight, but this hospital seems keen on proving to me that things can always get worse.

Trevor tries to sit up when I first walk into the room, but I wave him back and lean against the door frame, trying to conceal my shock at his appearance. His skin is as pale as the underside of a frog, and his cheeks have sunken in. He's emaciated.

The blinds are open, probably Lexi's doing, and the early night sky is almost as bright as day.

I had a couple of hours to kill before I could see Rusty, and I decided to come here. There was a time when here was the only place I wanted to be.

"Hey, Droopy," he says, and mutes the TV. "Long time."

I pull the chair out of the corner and sit, propping my legs on his bed. "Sorry, dude. Been busy. Work and Grandma. You know."

"Oh, I know," Trevor says, forcing his thin voice to sound suggestive. "Lexi reckons you've met a guy."

She's too smart for her own good. "Obviously she's got too much time on her hands if she's dreaming up that crap."

Trevor limps through a chuckle. "No way, Droopy. It's all over your face. What's his name?"

These are the kinds of questions I expect from Lexi, not Trevor, but it's clear that he's hungry for more than just food.

"You remember that kid who came in a couple of weeks ago, the one who was set on fire by some of his classmates?"

"That guy?" Trevor gapes at me.

I shrug. "I read to him sometimes. Steven—the ER nurse I told you about? He's been picking up some shifts in the ICU, and he lets me visit Rusty. That's his name, by the way. Rusty McHale."

"You like him," Trevor says. It's not a question. More like a friendly accusation.

I'm not sure how to respond. Maybe I do like Rusty. He's more than an ordinary patient to me, more than someone I just read books to. But it's all so confusing. This isn't high school. Things are more real here. Falling in love would complicate my life. Not that I love Rusty or think he loves me. See? Complicated.

So I say, "I don't want him to die."

Trevor gazes at me with his huge, watery blue eyes. They've always been big, his eyes, but now that his face is little more than a skin-draped skull, they look bigger than the moon.

"I was dating this girl when I got sick," he says. "Sick the second time. I beat the leukemia when I was six. Trounced it. Me and my parents figured we'd beat it this time too." Trevor tries to sit up again, and I help him with the controls on the bed. "My parents are good people—just so you know—they'd be here if they could. But somebody's got to pay for this palace."

"I know about your parents," I say, but I realize too late that Trevor's not saying this stuff for my benefit so much as for his own. Maybe it's something he needs to remind himself of on rough days like these.

"The girl's name was Siobhan." He grins. "Isn't that a great name for a girl? Siobhan Fitzpatrick. She had long black hair down her back, shiny and soft and always smelling like mangoes. Sometimes I was afraid to touch it. Like I might ruin it. And her eyes were this brown, like suede. Plus, she was smoking hot."

"Of course she was," I say, grinning back.

Nurse Merchant pops her head in, gives us a wave when she sees that we're talking, and disappears.

Trevor closes his eyes, and after a couple of seconds pass, I think he's fallen asleep. It wouldn't be the first time. It's different now, though. Now I worry about what happens if he never opens his eyes again.

"Trevor?"

"I'm here," he says. "I was just remembering her." He looks at me. Maybe through me. "We had all these plans. We were going to be the prom king and queen. We were gonna drink ourselves silly and road-trip to crazy places like Arkansas or Canada." He turns his head toward the window, and yellow light bathes the stark planes of his face. "I thought I loved that girl."

126

"So, what happened?" I ask. Trevor has joked about girls before, but he's never mentioned Siobhan.

"I got sick again. She was okay with it for a while, but watching a person rot is tough. My hair fell out, and I dropped a ton of weight. She would call me to go to the mall, and I'd have to tell her that I couldn't get out of bed." Trevor sighs. "I broke up with her before I came here. We'd been talking, and she told me that she couldn't bear the thought of me dying. Like it was a foregone conclusion."

And then Trevor pins me down with his big blue moon eyes, and he says, "Love's more than holding hands and going to dances. It's two people who struggle to live, even when they should maybe both be dead. When maybe one of them would be better off dead."

I hold Trevor's stare, and neither of us speaks for a little while. I wonder what kind of man he would have grown up to be had he not gotten sick. Death makes philosophers of us all, but I think that Trevor would have always been the kind of man who looked beyond the curtain of blind mediocrity that most people are content to leave closed. I think Trevor would have been exceptional. Trevor *is* exceptional.

"You're wrong, Trevor." My voice is jarring in the silence.

"Come again?"

"You're wrong about love."

"What do you know?" He's bitter now. He should be bitter. His past and his future are both rooted in loss.

"Love isn't static. It's not about simply holding on. It's about action and consequence."

Trevor sighs. "I'm tired. I think I need to sleep."

I sigh too and nod my head. "Okay."

I get up and drag the chair back to its place. Trevor rolls onto his side and faces the window. The decorations from his special day still adorn the walls, but they're looking limp.

"You were right to let go of Siobhan," I say, "but that doesn't mean you don't deserve to fall in love."

"It wouldn't be fair to let any girl love me." Trevor mumbles to the wall. "I'm a heartbreaker, Droopy. Guaranteed."

"Her heart's going to break either way." I leave the room and stop at Nurse Merchant's station.

"How you doing?" I ask.

Nurse Merchant eyes me suspiciously. Trevor and Lexi took all the heat for sneaking out of their rooms—they denied I was even with them—but I think Nurse Merchant suspects the truth. "Fine, Andrew. You should visit Trevor more often." She massages her temples. "His doctors are hopeful about his new treatment, but you should still try to get by when you can."

"I'm keeping an eye on Death," I say. "I won't let her take him."

"Sweetie, when it's your time, it's your time. Death is the one thing none of us can escape."

That's not the sort of sentiment you'll find inside greeting cards, and her honesty is one of the reasons I love Nurse Merchant.

"Can I visit Lexi?"

"She'll probably strangle you if you don't." Nurse Merchant waves me toward Lexi's room and picks up her pen. "I've got all this paperwork to do."

"Thanks," I say.

Lexi's sitting on her bed, surrounded by books. There's an empty tray of food beside her, and she's wearing a bandanna. She's never worn a bandanna in all the time I've known her. It looks odd.

"Heya, Lexi."

"Drew!" Lexi tries to crawl out of the bed, but she's caught in a tangle of IV tubes and monitor wires and, of course, mountains of books, so I go to her and wrap her in a tight hug. When I step back, Lexi slaps my shoulder and says, "Where have you been?"

I walk around to the window and sit on the sill. The lingering heat of the day feels good on my back. I didn't notice how cold I was until now.

"Why don't *you* tell me where I've been?" I tease her. "According to Trevor, you have a theory about that."

Lexi doesn't even have the grace to look embarrassed, which is why I love her. "It's that Rusty boy, isn't it? The one who was . . . the one in the ICU?"

"Oh my God," I say, trying my best to imitate Lexi's excited tone. "He's so swell, and I think he's gonna ask me to prom!" Then I roll my eyes.

"Drew!"

"Lexi." I fold my arms over my chest and attempt to mimic my father's masterful face of disapproval. "Bullies set him on fire. I highly doubt he's in the mood to date. Anyway, I only read to him. I'm taking him *Frankenstein* after I leave here."

Lexi glows as bright as a star. She looks like I just told her that we danced the night away. Seriously, she's wearing a smile big enough to stretch across the sky.

"Will you stop staring at me like that?" I say. "We're just friends."

"Sure you are."

I point at her bandanna, hoping to change the subject. "What's up with that?"

Lexi touches it thoughtfully, as if she'd forgotten she was wearing it. "My hair is growing back. But it's all wispy and gross. This was my mom's idea. Her only good one."

"Can I see?" I don't know what makes me ask. Curiosity, yes, but there's something else. Lexi didn't go around bald because she was strong and proud. For Lexi, it was a protective measure, a wall that stopped people from asking her about her cancer. It didn't make her vulnerable; it made her untouchable. The bandanna is unexpected, and I'm dying to know what's changed.

"I'd rather not."

"Oh, come on."

"No." And that's that. Lexi owns the last word. She created it, patented it, and she'll murder anyone who tries to take it from her. "How's Grandma Brawley?" she asks, clearly better than me at changing the subject.

"Wanna go see her?"

Lexi grins. "Nurse Merchant is still mad at me for the last time."

"It's worth a shot."

It takes a lot of begging, but I use my considerable charm to convince Nurse Merchant to let Lexi accompany me to Grandma Brawley's room. I have a strict forty-five-minute deadline, though, and if we're not back on time, Nurse Merchant swears that she'll call the police. I believe her.

I wheel Lexi through the halls. This is like a vacation for her. She smiles at everyone, waves at the nurses and orderlies she recognizes.

Lexi's been in and out of this hospital often enough to know many of them.

The nurses on duty nod at me when I wheel Lexi toward Grandma's room, despite that it's close to the end of visiting hours. I try to keep quiet so Mr. Kelly doesn't notice us, but he's got a sixth sense, and he calls out from his room: "Andrew! Come here, Andrew!"

Sighing, I pull Lexi's wheelchair to a stop beside his doorway. "Can't talk today, sir. Busy, busy."

"The nurses are still trying to do me in, Andrew!"

Lexi turns around in her chair so that she can look at Mr. Kelly. She smiles. "Me too." She pulls off her bandanna to reveal thin fuzz on her scalp weakly working its way topside. "Just look what they did to my hair."

Mr. Kelly chuckles. "It looks beautiful. But better stay away from the orange Jell-O—just to be safe."

"Thanks." Lexi takes command and wheels herself straight into Grandma Brawley's room. By the time I follow, she's already got her bandanna tied in place.

"Not a word," she warns me.

"He's right, though. It's beautiful."

"Shut up." She rolls around to Grandma Brawley's window and throws open the curtains and the blinds. I stroll over to join her. The view is worse than Lexi's. The window looks directly onto an abandoned construction site. Rusted beams sit idle while the concrete silently crumbles.

"What's this?" Lexi asks. She's holding the picture frame with the lock of red hair.

"Did I ever tell you about my grandfather?" I ask.

Lexi shakes her head. "You never talk about your family."

I move the visitor chair so that I can sit across from Lexi. "Sandy Brawley," I say. "He and my grandma met when they were just fifteen, living in Hell's Kitchen. There was a war going on. World War II.

"Sandy and Grandma got married the day before he shipped off to the front lines. The war was near its end, but she knew there was still a chance that he wouldn't come home.

"Sandy only had two things to give Grandma: this lock of hair, and a tiny apartment that had belonged to his parents. It was a small place, barely big enough for the two of them, but it was his, and he gave it to her. There was this little window that looked out onto the street, and every day when Grandma got home from work, she sat in a chair and waited for Sandy to return." I pause to stare out the window for a long, dramatic moment.

"Nine months later," I continue, "she had my dad. And every night, she rocked him to sleep in the chair, waiting for Sandy to come home.

"There were letters at first, but then they stopped. No one could tell her anything. Everyone thought he was dead. But Grandma stayed in that chair, waiting for Sandy to come home.

"The war ended. My father grew up. He married my mom and had me." I tilt my head and smile. "And still Grandma sat in that chair by the window, with nothing but the lock of hair and a handful of hope. She refused to leave her post until finally she just couldn't take care of herself any longer. Dad had to put her into a nursing home. Even then, she sat by the window in her room, waiting for Sandy to come home."

I finish my soliloquy and look up to see tears running down Lexi's face. She's staring at that lock of hair like it's made of stardust. "Drew, that's so sad."

I nod my head slowly, sigh heavily, and then I bust out laughing. "I'm only kidding." I say. I laugh so hard that I start to snort. "I have no idea whose hair that is. And, anyway, that'd make me, like, over forty years old."

Lexi clenches her jaw hard. She returns the frame to the night-stand. "I hate you."

"Seriously," I say, "this isn't even my grandmother. She's just some lady I visit when I need peace and quiet from the likes of you."

"You are such a liar," Lexi says. But she doesn't wheel away. "It's still sweet. Even if it's not true."

"There's nothing sweet about it," I say, but I'm not laughing any-more. "If that story were true, it would mean she wasted her whole life waiting. Sometimes you have to seize life by the balls, Lexi."

She frowns, gazing at Grandma Brawley. "I know all that. But I still wish someone loved me enough to wait forever." She wheels back around the bed and right out the door. I jump up to chase after her.

"Hey, Lexi!"

She stops, spins her chair around to face me. "What?"

"There is."

"Is what?"

"Someone who loves you enough to wait for you. He's waiting harder than I've ever seen anyone wait."

Lexi's jaw trembles—I've blindsided her, but she refuses to show it. "Let's get back before Nurse Merchant goes ballistic."

"Yeah," I say. "All right." But I can't help thinking that if Rusty had someone like Lexi to hold on for, then maybe I could keep him from dying. Maybe he would see that the world isn't such a cold, dark place.

Only, I don't know anyone worthy of him.

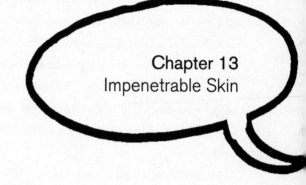

Chapter 13
Impenetrable Skin

Frankenstein is sweaty in my hand.

I wave at Steven as I pass through the ICU's double doors and head straight for Rusty's room. When Steven's not around, I have to be sneaky, but that doesn't happen often anymore. I guess we share the same mission. I'm not sure I trust Steven to stop Death from taking Rusty, but he's better than nothing.

Something is out of place. I notice it right away, before I take ten steps into the ICU. It's laughter.

Usually the ICU is a mechanized symphony, an orchestra composed of IV drips and heart monitors and respiratory machines. It is the music that keeps the patients alive. There's rarely laughter. There's rarely anything to laugh about. But there it is: an airy chuckle darting through the sterilized air on hummingbird wings. Zoom, zoom, zoom.

The closer I get to Rusty's room, the more distinct the laughter becomes. And then I see the girl. Nina. My instinct is to run, but my feet ignore my brain's flight response, and I barrel right into Rusty's room with my sketchpad in one hand and *Frankenstein* in the other.

Nina is in bloom. Her brown hair hangs loose upon her shoulders, and she's wearing a tight-fitting tank top and some hip-hugging jeans. This is not the same girl I saw a little while ago barking at reporters on the telephone, nor is it the same shattered soul who accompanied Rusty into the ER that night. This girl is fun and flirty. She's the kind of girl who shops first and worries about the credit-card bills later. Is it an act? A mask she wears for Rusty? Or were her other two faces the masks?

Rusty breaks into a smile when I blunder into the room. I'm not used to seeing him in so much light. He's wearing these pressure bandages over his regular bandages that look like black sleeves. Steven tried to explain it all to me once, the details of Rusty's burn care, but I didn't want to know. Details are how doctors make patients less than human, and I don't want to dehumanize Rusty.

"Well, hello there," Nina says. She stands tall, almost as tall as me, and folds her arms over her chest. "I think you might have the wrong room."

"This is my friend Drew," Rusty says.

Nina looks me up and down, her lips pursed. She disapproves; that's her job. "You're the one who's been reading to him." She relaxes a hair, but I sense that her ease has little to do with me and everything to do with maintaining her current mask. "Isn't it a bit odd, you being here so late all the time?"

I feel like a burglar who has bungled the job and is standing at the business end of some seriously pissed-off homeowner's shotgun.

One wrong move and Nina might decapitate me and slam-dunk my head into the hazardous-materials bin.

"I work in the cafeteria," I say. "And I want to be a doctor, so sometimes I volunteer in the emergency room. It's only for the summer. It's not like I live here or anything."

Rusty snorts and starts coughing. Nina's right there with water, and Rusty sips some out of the straw. He reminds me so much of Trevor; they're on the same road traveling in opposite directions.

"What's your name?" I ask.

"This is my bestie, Nina." Rusty seems to have recovered, but he keeps glancing in my direction.

I told him that I lived here in the hospital. I also told him that I killed my parents. But he hasn't asked me questions about any of that stuff in the week that I've been coming up here to read to him. I assumed it was because he wanted the favor returned.

Nina sticks out her hand, and I shake it. She's got a firm grip hiding inside her tiny fingers. I don't flinch. "You really shouldn't come here so late, Drew. Rusty needs his rest. He's got interviews tomorrow."

"I told you that I'm not doing any interviews."

"People need to know what happened to you," Nina insists. She's wearing her other mask now, the soldier. "How are the police ever supposed to arrest those boys if you don't talk about it?"

Rusty turns his face from Nina. His heart-rate monitor spikes, and tears form on the edges of his lids, collect there like raindrops on a windowsill. "Don't you have to get home?" he asks, his voice gruff.

The muscles in Nina's jaw pulsate. She's going to crack a tooth if she's not careful. She glances at me, and I can't tell if she's looking for backup or someone to blame. Finally, she sags. Defeat lops two whole inches from her height. I feel bad for her, but my relationship with Rusty is tenuous. I read to him. I protect him from Death. It's not like, over the last week, we've become soul mates.

"Tomorrow, Rusty." Nina gathers her purse and mopes toward the door. Before leaving, she turns to me and says, "If you keep him up too late tonight, I'll pull out your fingernails one at a time. *Capisce?*" She sounds like she's trying to mimic a mob-movie villain, and she's doing a damned good job.

I wait for her to walk through the automatic double doors of the ICU ward before I finally exhale the breath I've been holding. "Well, she's interesting," I say.

Rusty chuckles. This is the most I've seen him smile since we met. "She means well. Ever since . . . this . . . she's started acting like everyone who comes within ten feet of me is an enemy. And she's always trying to pressure me into talking to reporters."

I watch Rusty when he speaks. It's an effort for him to move air through his lungs. Steven told me that Rusty was lucky he didn't burn his airway badly, but it still pains him. "Why don't you do the interviews?" I take my usual seat on the floor by the bed.

Rusty shrugs.

"But maybe if people see how hurt you are, a witness might come forward."

"Drop it," Rusty says. His voice is clipped and cold, but he shakes his head. "Nina can be exhausting." The laughter that filled the room when I arrived has fled with Nina. Maybe she's better for Rusty than I am. Or maybe the smile he wears when she's around is a

138

mask too. Maybe they're both pretending to be happy for the other's sake. Either way, I can take a hint.

I look up at Rusty and smile. A real smile. "I told you I'd come."

"You bring the book?" He reaches over the side of the bed, and I give him *Frankenstein*. "First *1984*, and now this. I didn't peg you for a classics guy."

"I borrowed it from a friend."

This is how our conversations go. Small talk followed by reading. I'm afraid to know too much about him—or to let him know too much about me. Knowing leads to caring. And I lose everyone I care about.

"Do you really live here at the hospital?" Rusty leans over the side of the bed, looking down at me with those hazel eyes of his. They fluctuate. Sometimes they're more green than brown, sometimes more brown than green. But they always look like the ocean this one time I saw it in the summer, blanketed by massive clouds of nomadic seaweed.

"Yeah," I say. "I suppose."

"Why?"

I bite my fingernails, a habit my dad helped me break when I was little by dipping the tips in Tabasco sauce. "Why do you want to know now?"

Rusty shrugs, but he doesn't stop staring at me. He's trying to read me like the books I read to him. "It's just odd. You spending so much time in the hospital, and that nurse guy out there seems okay with it."

"He's got his reasons."

"What are yours?"

There's no way Rusty's going to let this go. He's used to getting what he wants. You can always tell that about a person. Most people aren't direct when they want something. They try to bribe you or guilt you or scare you into bending to their will. But people used to getting what they want are direct. They know you'll give in eventually; no subversive tactics are necessary.

"This is the last place my parents and sister were alive." Saying it out loud doesn't hurt like I thought it would. It hurts more. "There was a car accident and they died and it's my fault. This place, it's all I've got." I don't realize I'm crying until I taste tears on my lips. "I was supposed to die too, but Death was late to get me. I hid then, and I've been hiding ever since. If she discovers me now, she'll take me away, and I'll never see my family again."

"Why wouldn't you see them again?" Rusty asks. He's still trying to read me, and I wish he'd stop.

I answer anyway. "Guys who kill their families go straight to hell. No passing Go, no chance for redemption."

"Oh." Rusty lies back, and any moment now he's going to call for Steven. He's going to tell him that I'm a psycho who needs to be pumped full of mind-numbing drugs and locked away for the rest of my life.

I tense my muscles to run.

"Do you know why I don't want to leave?" Rusty asks.

I blink at him, confused by the turn in the conversation. After a long moment, I say, "Because you'll die *out there*."

Rusty looks at me again. It was the right answer, but maybe it wasn't the one he was expecting. Maybe he expected me to say something about fear or pain, but we both know the truth: Death is

140

the only thing waiting for Rusty McHale beyond these walls.

"You know what happened to me?" he asks.

"Yeah. But I'd like to hear it from you."

"I'm so tired of telling people about it." Rusty's voice is languid, tangled in the pain medication. It's often a battle for him to keep from succumbing to sleep, but I want to keep him here for a while longer.

"I told you about my parents."

Rusty frowns. "Was any of it true?"

"All of it." Something about Rusty makes me want to tell him more—everything, maybe—but right now I think what he needs is someone to listen.

It's difficult for Rusty. He clears his singed throat and tries to prop himself up higher, but the effort makes him wince. As drugged up as he is, pain still bleeds through the haze. He's like Patient F on the operating table, surrounded by the men in red lab coats. He can't escape the pain; it's woven through the fabric of him.

"People always guessed that I was gay." Rusty starts off slowly, choosing his words with care. "Not like I'm flaming or anything— or that it'd be bad if I were. It was just the worst-kept secret at my school. I never dated girls, Nina was always my bestie, and I sucked at sports."

I laugh. I can't help myself. "Sucking at sports doesn't make you gay."

"No, but it makes you a target," Rusty says, and the smile dies on my lips. "The bullying started freshman year. I took this AV class. I'm totally into movies and filmmaking, and I thought it would be fun. I read the morning announcements over the TV system, and I guess I talk kind of funny—"

"No you don't," I say. "You talk nice. I like the way you talk."

Rusty looks at me looking at him, and he doesn't smile the way I expect him to. Maybe he's not sure whether I'm telling the truth or just humoring him. The thrum of his voice and the way it curls around the edges makes me think of the whitewater rafting trip my dad took us on last summer. Of this one waterfall that tumbled us all over the edge, leaving us soaking and laughing so hard. When Rusty speaks, it reminds me of a time I was happy. How could I not like that?

"Anyway," he says, "I wound up on this hit list that a bunch of kids were passing around. It had the names of different students on it and a corresponding number of points you could earn for punching them in a public place. Bonus points for pulling it off in front of a teacher. Double bonus points for doing it in class."

"That's nuts," I say. "There's no way anyone got away with that."

"Rich kids can get away with anything." There's acid in his words. "The rest of us are on our own."

I bow my head. "So you ended up on this list. . . ."

"Fifty points," Rusty says. "That's how much the beatings I took were worth. Each. Their favorite place to punch me was in this long hallway that connects the two campuses of my school. It's so narrow that you can stand in the center and touch both sides. And it's dark, too. I'd be trying to get to class, and the punch would come from out of nowhere." His voice breaks, but he continues. "Usually they'd punch me in the nose or eye. Occasionally a cheap shot missed and clipped my ear. I started taking the long way around, but they always found me."

I try to brush Rusty's hand, but he flinches and pulls away. "We can just read."

"You wanted to know." Rusty's fighting the lure of his pain meds, and I'm torn between wanting to know what happened and wanting Rusty to rest, to stop hurting for a little while.

"The bullying continued sophomore year. Teachers and the administration caught on to the list, but the guys, they just moved to something else. For the first part of eleventh grade, it was a game called Sack Tap. I got hit in the balls so many times that one of my testicles nearly ruptured. I wore a cup to school for the rest of the year."

Rusty sips his water. "It was always something. I lived in constant fear of what was going to happen next. Do you know what that's like?"

I nod. I do.

"I doubt it." Rusty frowns. "Anyway, it was Fourth of July, and I'd been invited to a party at this guy's house. They never invited me to anything, so I figured it had to be a prank. But Nina told me that her friend Lena said that everyone felt bad. That we were about to be seniors and it was time to put the past behind us.

"By then, my being gay wasn't even a secret anymore. I hadn't dated any guys, but if someone asked me, I told them the truth. You know—" Rusty's words catch in his throat, and I'm poised to call Steven.

But Rusty barrels on and I'm in awe of his tenacity. "I think maybe I hoped that I could have just one good year. Everyone says that high school—senior year especially—is the best time of your life, and I wanted that. I wanted it so badly."

"And they lit you on fire," I say, trying to cut to the chase to spare Rusty from having to go on.

He leans over the side of the bed and looks at me, like he's begging me to let him finish.

Slowly, he shakes his head. "No. Not right away. At first, it was cool. I had some drinks, chatted with people. I had friends, you know? It's not like I was a complete social pariah. But I'd never been part of the crowd. It felt damned good to belong for once." Now Rusty's whole body trembles. "I don't know whose idea it was, but some of the guys grabbed me. They stole my clothes, tore them off of me, and just fucking left me there. Naked. In front of everybody. Nina was making out with her newest boyfriend and didn't even know what was going on. Everyone laughed. People who didn't even know me thought it was the funniest thing they'd ever seen. I was humiliated. I screamed at them and tried to get my clothes back, but they tossed them around until some genius finally threw them on the roof."

"Why didn't you just leave?" I ask.

Rusty chuckles, but there's no mirth in his voice. "It's so dumb. I'd had a couple of drinks and didn't want to drive."

"Then what happened?"

"What do you think happened?" Rusty glares at me. "I got my clothes back. I had to use the pool skimmer to drag my clothes off the roof. With everyone watching. You can't really hide your junk when you're trying to maneuver a fifteen-foot-long pole." Rusty gulps more water. Some of it trickles over his chin.

I don't want him to finish the story. I know how it ends. I remember his screams. Hearing the whole truth makes it so much worse. Those boys didn't just jump him and set him on fire. They tortured him first. For years. Rusty had been burning for a long time before they actually set him aflame.

"Nina tried to find me afterward, but I wanted to be alone. The party was at this girl Cassie's house. There was a big yard, so I sat out in the dark, trying to sober up enough to leave.

"That's when they got me. They snuck up from behind and splashed me with something. I couldn't see their faces. God, they were laughing so hard. I don't remember hearing the lighter, but one minute I was wet and the next I was burning. Oh, fuck, I burned."

Rusty's not even trying not to cry. "I never felt pain like that before. The world compressed into this small, dense pocket of agony. Nothing—nothing—existed outside of my pain."

"Rusty."

"But you know what the really messed-up thing is?" He doesn't wait for an answer. "I remember this one thought. I remember thinking that as bad as being on fire hurt, at least I didn't hurt inside anymore."

"Rusty—"

"I don't remember the rest. Nina says I ran into the pool. The doctors say that saved my life and that it's a miracle I only got burned on my legs and chest and arm." He holds up his bandaged arm. "But, you know, this doesn't feel like a miracle."

"Rusty," I say for the third time. "I don't want to hear this anymore."

"Yeah." He looks down at me, and if he's got any pity in him, he's not showing it. "I just figured you should know."

"That I should know what happened?"

"That you should know why I don't want to leave," he mumbles. "It's like you said. I'm afraid I'll die out there."

I don't know what to do. There's nothing left for me to say. But now I know that we both lost something *out there*. Something that we'll never get back.

"Don't you want to know who did it?" Rusty asks. "I'll answer if you ask me."

I think for a second. If he told me, I could tell Nina and she could tell the cops. Maybe that's what Rusty is hoping for. But those people can't hurt Rusty in here. I won't let them. "The who isn't important. Only what happens next." This time, when I put my hand through the bed railing, Rusty twines his fingers through mine.

"Will you read to me now?"

"Of course. Although, now, *Frankenstein* seems like a terrible choice."

Rusty laughs, and I laugh, but we can't clear the fog of guilt and sadness that blankets the room, thick in the air we breathe. I pick up Arnold's book and read until Rusty falls asleep. Then I read some more.

Death isn't taking him.

Not tonight. Not ever.

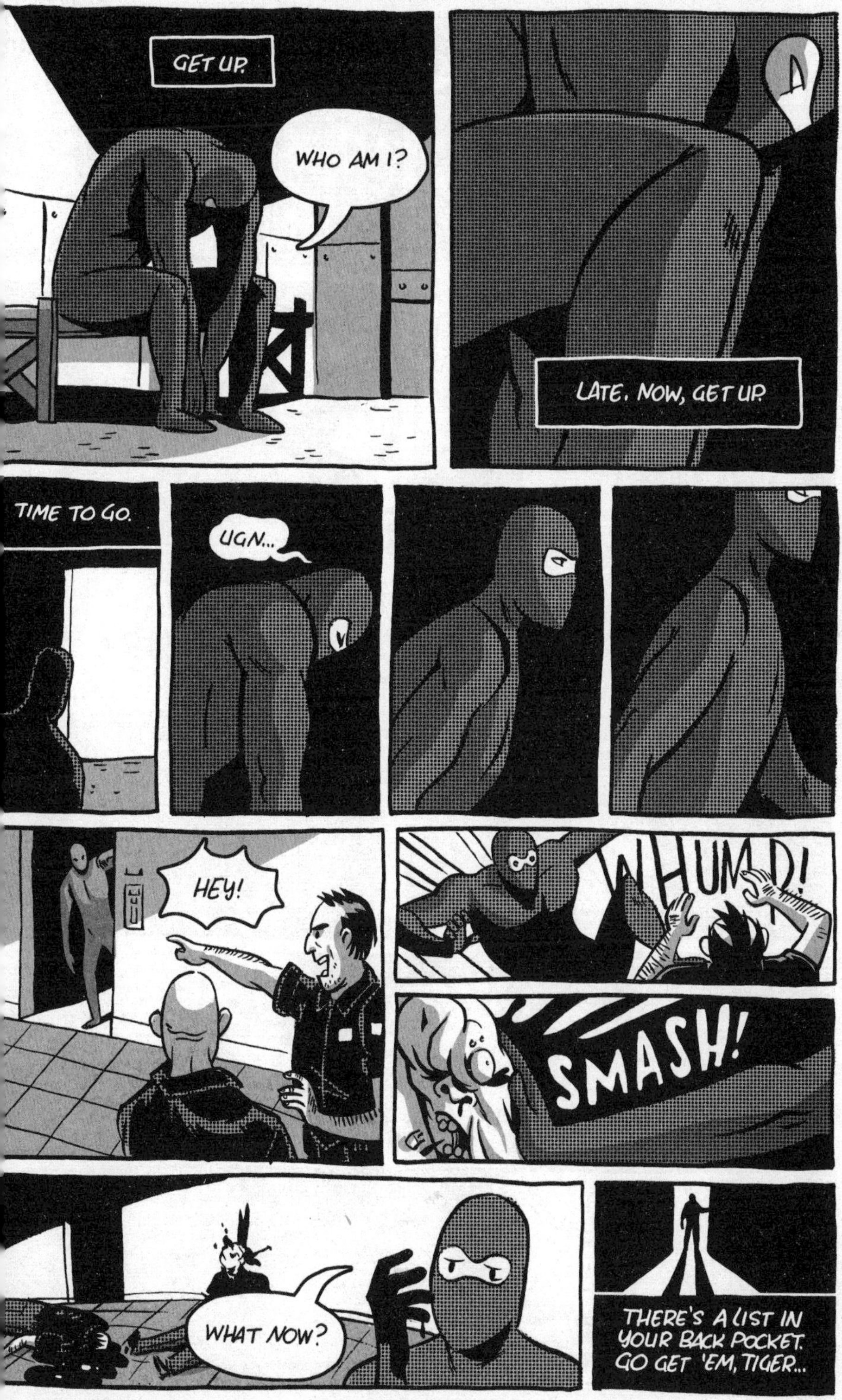
GET UP.
WHO AM I?
LATE. NOW, GET UP.
TIME TO GO.
UGN...
HEY!
WHUMP!
SMASH!
WHAT NOW?
THERE'S A LIST IN YOUR BACK POCKET. GO GET 'EM, TIGER...

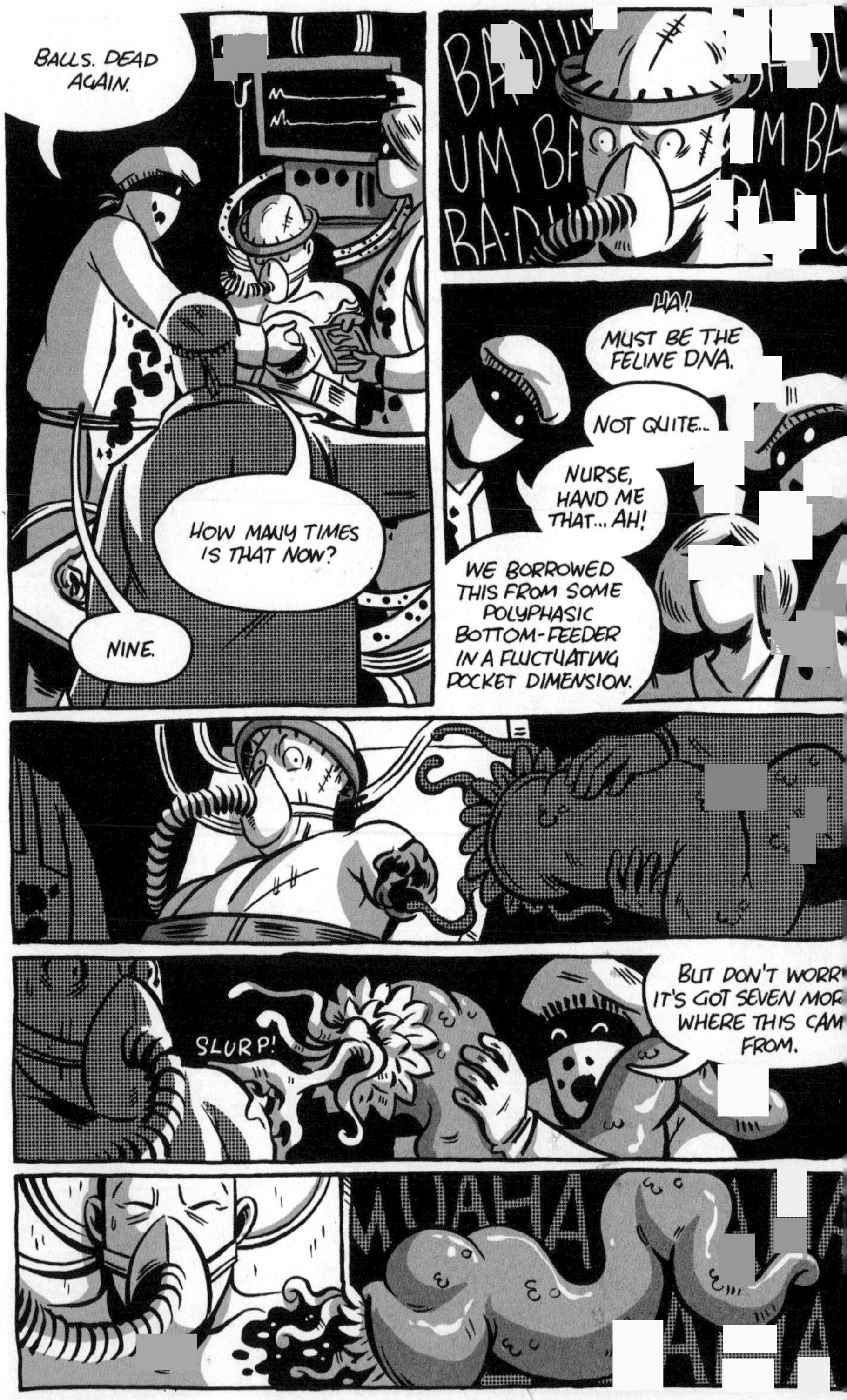

BALLS. DEAD AGAIN.
HOW MANY TIMES IS THAT NOW?
NINE.
HA! MUST BE THE FELINE DNA.
NOT QUITE...
NURSE, HAND ME THAT... AH!
WE BORROWED THIS FROM SOME POLYPHASIC BOTTOM-FEEDER IN A FLUCTUATING POCKET DIMENSION.
SLURP!
BUT DON'T WORR IT'S GOT SEVEN MOR WHERE THIS CAM FROM.

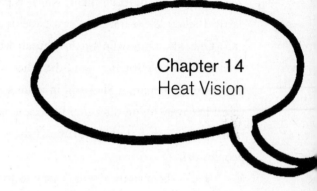

Chapter 14
Heat Vision

The ER has moods, and tonight it's bored.

Jo leans against the nurse's station with half a jelly doughnut hanging out of her mouth, staring at me like I just told her that the world is going to end in thirty seconds.

"What?"

Maybe it was a bad idea to mention that I'm never going to let Rusty die. But I said it, and now I have to deal.

Emma goes about her business, restocking the exam rooms and making sure that everything is in its place. Sometimes I wonder what her house looks like. Does she outline the position of every item in her home so that, if anything moves while she's gone, she'll instantly know? Or is she a closet slob? Some people are like that. They show one face to the world and keep the other hidden. Like Death and Miss Michelle.

"Steven says that boy's doing good," Jo says. "But burns are tricky, Drew. Gotta be careful of infections. If death takes that poor, sweet boy, there ain't nothing you can do to stop it."

I sit on one of the wheeled stools and spin in slow, small circles. The ER has been quiet all night, which is partly disappointing and partly a relief. We've only had two patients in the last ninety minutes. One was a guy who cut his thumb while slicing onions—he needed two whole stitches—and the other was a woman complaining of stomach cramps. She's still in exam 4 waiting for someone to wheel her away for an ultrasound. Occasionally I hear her groaning from across the hall, but I've mastered the art of blocking out other people's pain.

"That's where you're wrong," I say to Jo. I know who Death is, and I'll keep her away from Rusty with a baseball bat if necessary. But Jo keeps giving me funny looks, and if she asks too many questions, I could be in serious trouble. It was hectic that first night I came to the ER, and no one paid me any mind, seeing as my mom and dad and baby sister were dying all over the place. It was easy for me to vanish, but it's still possible that Jo, or any of the nurses, caught a glimpse of me. And I could accidentally trigger that hidden fragment of a memory if I'm not careful.

"It's commendable, what you're doing for that boy," Emma says as she comes out from behind one of the eggshell-colored curtains. She's looking flirty tonight, like she came straight to work from a bar. "But I think what Jo is trying to tell you is not to get too close."

Jo finishes devouring the other half of her jelly doughnut. "Don't tell me what I'm trying to say. I know what I mean to say, and I think I said it well enough for the boy to get my meaning."

Emma shrugs and moves on to arranging the charts so that they're flush with the edge of the desk. She doesn't look Jo in the eyes—the way an animal trainer might not make eye contact with a lion—but the muscles in her cheek twitch as if they're short-circuiting. "I'm only trying to help. It's not healthy to get so close to a patient who might die."

"Why not?" I ask, hoping to break the tension.

Jo's face softens, something that I usually only see when she's dealing with a kid. When it comes to regular patients, Jo is a bull. She gets the job done quickly, efficiently, and without taking any crap. But when a kid comes into the ER, Jo's demeanor flips like a coin. Heads to tails, like that. She's patient and compassionate, and she even moves a little slower. That's how she's treating me now.

"Drew, if you want to be a doctor or a paramedic or even a nurse someday—and I hope to Jesus that you change your mind and become a teacher instead—then you have to learn how to distance yourself from patients. Never let it be personal."

"Like Steven has?" I ask.

Emma nods. She and Jo have gone from being combatants to sisters in arms. "Exactly like Steven."

I give myself another whirl on the stool and extend my legs so that they swing a circle like a compass needle. The world looks different when you're spinning. Colors run together in the most amazing ways. Everything bleeds into everything else, and you get this idea that maybe there are no differences between any of us. That if everyone everywhere spun, we'd all see that we're connected.

"But if you love someone, isn't the risk worth taking?" I ask when I come to a stop, but before everything separates again.

"Who said anything about love?" Jo furrows her brow. "I didn't say anything about love."

Emma kneels in front of me. Her eyelids glitter with this blue eye shadow like morning dew. "Are you in love with that boy who got burned?"

"With Rusty?" I ask, surprised. "I hadn't . . . I don't . . . I wasn't talking about me."

Jo shrugs at Emma. "Then who're we talking about, Drew?"

"Trevor and Lexi, of course."

Emma juts out her lip and cocks her head to the side. She's gone from a state of concern to a state of confusion. "Your friends in Peds?" I nod. "Well, why didn't you say so?"

"I just did."

"Boy." Jo stabs me with her eyes, and the way she says "boy" makes me feel like I narrowly avoided a backhanded slap. "You had me worried."

I want to go back to the part where they thought I might be in love with Rusty and ask them how I'd even know something like that. I've never been in love—I don't mind admitting it—and I'm not sure I'd recognize it even if I were up to my waist in the stuff.

But if I backtrack now, I'll never get them to help me figure out what to do about Lexi and Trevor.

"It's only that I know they care about each other. More than care. If they were out in the real world, they'd be boyfriend and girlfriend for sure."

Emma goes back to straightening things. "What's the problem?"

"I'm not exactly certain," I tell them.

Jo reaches into the doughnut box she hid under the counter and grabs the chocolate one that I chose specifically for her. The jelly was for Emma, but she's back off carbs. "How are we supposed to help you if we don't know what the problem is?"

I shrug. "It's complicated."

"Uncomplicate it," Jo says.

I think for a moment, try to come up with the right words. "Lexi's too focused on the future to realize that there's a guy right here in the present who wants to be with her, and Trevor's convinced that he's going to die, and doesn't want to put anyone through the pain of losing him."

"That's not his choice to make," Emma says.

"I know," I say. "I also know that if I could get Lexi to see what's right in front of her eyes, she'd choose ten minutes with Trevor over a whole lifetime without him. But I don't know how to get through to either of them."

Jo licks the chocolate off the ends of her nubby fingers and stares down her nose at me. She's got this superior gleam in her eyes that suggests she doesn't have time for my foolishness.

"You need to get them on a date," Jo says, like she's stating the obvious.

Emma squeals and claps her hands together. "A date! That's perfect. I can decorate the cafeteria. I have a disco ball!"

"Of course you do." I sigh. Before she launches this crazy plan into orbit, I say "There's no way I'm going to be able to get them out of Peds for a date." I tell them about kidnapping Lexi and Trevor and playing hockey on the top floor of the parking garage.

"Well, that was a stupid thing to do," Emma says as she smacks me on the shoulder. "Sweet but stupid."

"More stupid than sweet," Jo says. "And, yes, I'm talking about you."

"Anyway," I say. "They took the blame to keep me out of trouble, but I think Nurse Merchant suspects I was the ringleader, and it's impossible that I'll be able to sneak them out a second time."

"Nothing's impossible," Emma says. "Difficult, yes, but never impossible."

The idea of tricking Lexi and Trevor into going on a date is deceptively simple and simply brilliant. If I can get the two of them together for some romantic one-on-one time, they'll be forced to admit how they feel about each other, and the rest will fall into place.

It's the details that scare me.

"Who does the overnights in Peds?" Jo asks Emma. "Is it Perez? Tell me it ain't Perez."

Emma shakes her head. "Cho."

Jo breaks out into a self-congratulatory smile. It's so wide that I can see her gums. "We can take care of her." Jo rubs her hands together. "She's got a crush on our boy Steven."

"You think you can convince him to help?" Emma asks.

"Oh, I can. I *will*."

"Guys," I say. I'm feeling a bit anxious and lost. In under a minute, we went from a question to a hypothetical plan to suddenly calling in favors so that we can kidnap my best friends from their rooms and play matchmaker. I'm not sure what I expected when I brought up the topic, but this was not it. "I don't know. Is this the right thing to do?"

Emma and Jo stop their scheming and face me full on. I feel so small on my stool with the two of them looming over me.

"This is a great idea," Emma says. "We can throw them the perfect date."

"But what if Trevor's right?" I ask. "I mean, he *is* dying. Is it wrong to encourage Lexi to fall in love with him if he's going to die?"

"Baby," Jo says, "if Lexi is in love with this boy, there isn't a thing in the universe that's going to keep them apart."

"But it's not fair. He shouldn't have to die at all."

"You'll get no argument from me, but you asked us if love was a risk worth taking, and the answer is yes." Jo shrugs. "If everyone waited for a no-risk situation, no one would ever fall in love."

I look to Emma, and she nods her agreement. "We'll help you, Drew. Don't worry." She pats my shoulder.

A sudden sense of purpose blossoms in my chest, and I remember now what Father Mike said about Patient F: He's got to have something worth fighting for. Something worth living for. The same is true of Trevor. If he and Lexi were together, he'd have a new reason to keep fighting to stay alive.

"Andrew Brawley?"

A shiver squirms up my spine, and the hair on the tips of my ears stands on end. I know that voice. I recognize the ginger-scented perfume.

Death is here.

Slowly, I turn around, unwilling to abandon the safety of my stool. Death stands on the other side of the nurses' station with her arms folded over her chest. She's frowning at Jo, Emma, and me. She looks confused, and I only have a small window of opportunity to stop this situation from spiraling out of control.

"Michelle? What're you doing here this late?" Jo glances over at the exam room housing the woman with stomach pains.

Death—still staring at me, not at Jo or Emma—says, "There's some information missing about the Ramirez boy." She purses her lips and shakes her head. "I'm sorry, but what is *he* doing here in the middle of the night?"

Jo looks like her head might explode. It's never been particularly official, my volunteering in the emergency room, but I can tell by the way her neck muscles go taut that Jo isn't going to stand for anyone telling her what she can and cannot do. Which is why Emma steps in.

"Mr. Brawley is interested in becoming a doctor, so he joined the volunteer program. He's really very smart and quite helpful."

"It's"—Death looks at her watch—"It's after ten."

Emma looks embarrassed. "That's my fault. He stopped by after working in the cafeteria to bring us a snack, and we started discussing the appropriate circumstances under which to use a defibrillator on a patient."

"Right." Jo grunts, nodding along. "This knucklehead thought you could shock a heart with no rhythm back to life. Isn't that a hoot?"

"Jo and I were explaining that you can't shock a heart in asystole, only ventricular fibrillation or pulseless ventricular tachycardia. We must have lost track of the time." Emma makes her way toward me as she talks, and wraps an arm around my shoulders like a blanket. Or armor.

Death stands there, hands on hips, regarding the three of us with unconcealed suspicion. "Come with me, Andrew."

156

"Uh . . ." I stand and take a backward step. "I should really be getting home. My parents are probably wondering where I am."

"Are his release forms on file?" Death asks Emma. "Surely you haven't been letting him volunteer without filling out the appropriate release forms?"

Her questions are met with stony silence. I first ran into Emma while working in the cafeteria. We chatted about how I wanted to be a doctor, and she invited me to visit the ER. They've never questioned why I keep returning. All they've demanded for my continued presence is a steady supply of doughnuts.

"I'm sure I filled out something, right, guys?" I edge slowly away, preparing to make a break for it when Death attacks.

Death walks around the station, reclaiming the space I put between us with only a few high-heeled footsteps. She's right in front of me. Her brown hair is pulled back into a severe ponytail, drawing up the corners of her bloodshot eyes, and her knee-length skirt makes her legs appear far longer than could ever be possible. She towers over me.

"Come with me, Andrew. We'll contact your parents and sort this out."

"There's nothing to sort. And my parents are busy." One step back.

"I can reach them." Death extends her hand.

Jo glances from me to Death and back to me again. "Andrew, maybe you'd better go with her. You can fill out all the release forms and come back tomorrow."

Traitor. Jo's trying to save her own skin. Maybe I don't blame her. Maybe I do.

"Michelle," Emma pipes up—sweet, dependable Emma. "Honestly, Drew's been no trouble at all."

Death points her fiendish gaze at me. Her eyes are like cold, dead suns drifting in an empty void of nothingness. And that's what I'll be if she takes me. A void. Nothing. "I've noticed that Mr. Brawley seems to spend an unhealthy amount of time in this hospital, and I simply want reassurance from his parents that they know and approve of his whereabouts."

Emma sighs, looks at me apologetically, and gives Death a nod. It was such a little nod that it was almost imperceptible. But I saw it. Emma sold me out to my nemesis.

"Jo's right, Drew. The faster you clear this up, the faster you can return."

I take another step backward and hit the wall. There's nowhere else for me to go. "I don't want to go with her," I say, but my champions have forsaken me. Patient F would battle his way out, slicing off arms and legs, taking no prisoners. But I am not Patient F.

"We're only going to my office, Andrew," Death says. "Please don't force me to call security."

I know it's a bluff. She won't call security. Death is greedy and wants me all for herself. But I can't run, because I'll never be able to return, and I can't leave with Death, because she might discover who I really am. Either way, I risk losing everything.

Emma and Jo regard me curiously, as if they're beginning to have their own doubts. I want to hate them for their betrayal and cowardice, but I can't. I don't.

All my hatred is directed at Death.

"Fine." That's all I say before I fly out of the emergency room, leaving Death to catch up.

I don't know exactly where her office is, but I know where the administrative offices are, so I make my way there on autopilot while my brain works in a hyperpanic to invent a story that will cover my tracks. My fear, now that Death has my scent, is that it won't take her long to realize I'm the guy who got away from her—the wayward soul she's been hunting all this time.

Death doesn't run to catch up with me. She glides across the floor as if it's a frozen pond, skating smoothly over the surface until she draws up beside me and matches her stride to mine. We don't speak as we walk. The only sounds are the clicking of her heels and the uninterested grunts of hello from passing doctors and nurses. She subtly takes the lead. I'm not stupid. Death is handling me.

"Here we are." Death leads me into a room, a hole in the wall, really. There are no windows. Death lives and works in a coffin.

The office is small, maybe the size of Lexi's room, but dominated by a cheap particleboard desk piled high with folders and loose papers. There's paperwork everywhere, even on her keyboard and spilling over the top of her monitor.

This is not what I expected. This is not the well-groomed woman who sits quietly at lunch reading through folders, meticulously eating.

Death is overworked. Death is a slob.

"Have a seat, Andrew." Death points to one of the two chairs positioned at the front of her desk.

"I'd rather stand."

"Suit yourself." She settles into the nearest chair and crosses her left leg over her right. She lets out a sigh that causes her whole body to shiver. "My apologies. It's been a very long day."

"Maybe I should leave, then." I glance at the door.

"Not so fast." Death stares at me, unsmiling. "First, tell me why you spend so much time in this hospital." I swear she hasn't blinked once since she snuck up behind me in the ER.

I rest my hands on the back of the chair. It feels safer keeping something solid between us. "I work for Mr. Jaworski in the cafeteria."

Death nods. "I know, and I'll be speaking to him tomorrow."

My palms are an ocean of sweat, and I wonder if Death can smell my terror. Does she know that Arnold is paying me under the table? If not, what will she do when she finds out? Maybe she already knows everything and is merely toying with me. "I work in the caf, and my grandma is in long-term care."

"You mean Eleanor Brawley?"

That stops me cold. She knows about Grandma Brawley. I am Death's plaything.

"Andrew," Death says, "it's admirable that you visit your grandmother and that you spend time with your friends in Pediatrics—heaven knows those kids need all the friends they can get—and that you work and volunteer. But I worry about you spending too much time here."

I clear my throat, swallowing the lump in it. "It's . . . it's summer," I say. "Lots of free time. And these people are my friends."

"Don't you have friends outside the hospital?"

I can't read her, can't figure out what her endgame is. She hasn't mentioned Rusty yet, which means she might not know that I visit him. Protecting Rusty is as important as protecting myself. "I have friends out there." My trembling legs threaten to give out, so I slide around the chair and sit. "Do you?"

"We're not talking about me."

I lean back, resting my elbows on the arms, trying to appear casual, even though my heart is racing and my pits are drenched in sweat. "It's only fair."

Death looks thoughtful, as if she's trying to determine what to do with me. "Andrew, this is my job. I'm a counselor. I help people."

"There are people outside the hospital who need help too."

"There are people everywhere who need help. But this is where I work." She closes her eyes and takes a deep breath. When she opens them again, she says, "All right. Let's just call your parents. If they don't mind you being here, and you fill out the proper volunteer forms, I'll consider the matter settled." She reaches for the phone on her desk.

"Wait. They're sleeping."

"What's the number, Andrew?" Death stares me down, and her commanding tone offers no quarter.

"I won't spend so much time here anymore."

"The number."

"Please."

Death lifts the receiver just as the cell phone in her hip holster vibrates. She ignores it the first time, glaring at me instead. Her eyes are pinpoints. She knows. The expression on her face insists she *knows*. Maybe not everything, but she knows there's something *to* know, which means she won't ever give up trying to find out what that something is.

"You going to get that?" I ask, barely able to keep my voice from cracking.

Death answers the call. I can't hear what the other person is saying, but she nods a couple of times and then says, "I'll be right there." She returns the phone to the holster. Looks at me.

"Stay," she orders. But she doesn't move. She's poised to move, but she remains half in her chair, half out of it. "I'll be five minutes."

"Okay." I keep my voice small, submissive, so that maybe she won't hear my lie.

Death leaves without another word. I monitor the sound of her footsteps as they fade and disappear. My first instinct is to bolt, but the lure of those folders on her desk is too strong. I need to know if she has any paperwork about me, so I rifle around.

I don't recognize any of the names. I assume they're people who are or were in this hospital at one time or another. Maybe they're people that Death is scheduled to take.

I'm about to make my exit when I find names I do recognize. It's my family's folder, stuffed into the middle of a stack. Unimportant to anyone but me. I open it up and let its contents spill out onto the paper-littered desk. I start reading.

It's just stuff I already know. How they died, who they were. Of course, there's no way these pieces of paper could ever truly tell the story of my family. They don't say that my father was a kind, compassionate man—except when sports were on TV and he became a lunatic. And they don't say that my mom was the worst cook in the United States of America—except when it came to chocolate. They don't mention how I was the only person in my whole family who could watch a horror movie without once covering up my eyes. They leave out that my sister, Cady, wanted to be a tightrope walker when she grew up and how she always worked without a net.

This file isn't the story of my family. It's just a file. I gather up the pages, start to put it back in the stack, when I glance up at her corkboard. There are layers of papers tacked to it. Memos and photocopies and pictures of a slobbery bulldog, but the corner of one catches my eye. I lift the papers covering it and tear it down. It's me. My face. My hair is longer now and unkempt, and they drew the eyes too far apart, but it is me. Only it says I'm missing. Not dead: missing.

My grandparents, my real grandparents, are all dead and I don't know who claimed the bodies of my mom and dad and Cady, but they never came to claim me. I doubt there's anyone looking for me. I doubt there's anyone out there who cares.

But if Death ever realizes that under my shaggy hair and dead eyes is the boy from the sketch, it will ruin everything. I'll have nothing left.

I take the folder and the missing poster and run out of Death's office. I find a cubicle with a shredder and I feed its hungry metal jaws. I watch as my family, my face, are sliced up into rubbish.

My family is dead, and I no longer exist.

I leave before Death returns.

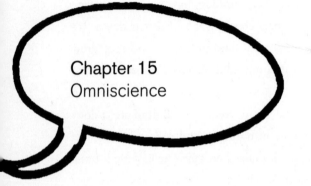

Chapter 15
Omniscience

Today, I'm the one whistling.

With my family's file and my sketch destroyed, I begin to feel that Death may never figure out who I really am. I'll never be truly safe, but I'm safer than I was last night. I wait until the breakfast shift is over before visiting Arnold. The moment he sees me, he shakes his head and points at the doors. "You can't work here anymore, Drew. I'm sorry."

Aimee is hunched over the cash register, peering at me through strands of hair that hang across her face. But it's not just her; I feel like everyone in the cafeteria is staring at me.

"Why not?" I ask, though I already know.

Arnold's face is red. "I can't pay you under the table. The law is the law."

"Come on, *Ah-nold*," I say. "You're not going to let some suit tell you what to do, are you? You need me."

"I could lose my job," Arnold says.

"Who's going to draw your menu board? I mean, come on, what are those?" Arnold must have drawn the picture himself, because it looks like a pair of testicles wearing chef hats are on the menu for today.

"Swedish meatballs. Bork, bork, bork." He wipes sweat from his brow with the back of his hand. His eyes are downcast, and he's fidgety. "Listen, I don't like this any more than you do. You're a good worker, but I have to think of my family. If you want to let me pay you like a normal employee, I'll rehire you on the spot." He spreads his hands, helpless. "Otherwise, I'm sorry."

This is exactly what Death wants. I'll fill out paperwork and she'll have my phone number and address so that she can call my parents. I wonder who else she's talked to. Will I be barred from the ER? Peds? Will Steven still let me visit Rusty?

Death is tricky, but I'm trickier.

"This is some 1984 shit going on here," I say to Arnold. "What would your son think of you bending over for Big Brother like this?"

Darkness descends over Arnold's face. Totally the opposite reaction I was hoping for. His lips purse, and his eyes tighten at the corners. Whatever love he had for me fled the moment I invoked his son's name.

"Good-bye, Andrew." Arnold's voice is clipped. He turns to leave, but I call out, "Wait!" and that holds him still for a second longer.

"I need the money, Mr. Jaworski. And I need more books. I'm almost finished with *Frankenstein*."

He keeps his back to me when he says, "I can't give you a job . . . but you can borrow books anytime."

He trudges away, shoulders slumped, like he's slogging through wet clay.

Unsure of my next move, I grab some lunch, make very small talk with Aimee, and snag a quiet table to work on Patient F. It's the only thing that will clear my head. I should stay out of sight, but the truth is that I kind of want to see Death. To let her know that she won't win. Which is stupid, really stupid, but this small defiance is all I have right now.

"Drew?" I look up, startled. Nina stands over me. She's got a tuna sandwich in one hand, her purse in the other. Her hair is tied back, and she's wearing a T-shirt and jeans.

"That's my name," I say, stilling my pencil over the paper. I'm trying to keep my face blank because I'm not sure what to make of Nina yet. She's the best friend, and she seems to be doing everything she can to make certain that the bullies who lit Rusty on fire are brought to justice, but something tells me her drive isn't entirely altruistic. There are two things that fuel the human soul to relentless action: revenge . . . and guilt.

Nina motions at the chair beside me with her chin. "Do you mind if I sit? I could really use a break."

"Go ahead." I start to put my sketchpad away, but Nina holds up her hands.

"Don't stop on my account." She steals a quick glance at the panel I'm working on, acting like she hadn't been looking over my shoulder for a good half minute before interrupting me. "You're quite talented. Rusty said so."

I'm not sure that I like that she and Rusty talk about me. Rusty is mine. I don't want to share him with anyone else. "I'm okay," I say.

"A little heavy handed on the shading. And the story is a mess."

Nina shakes her head. "Not according to Rusty. He said your—Patient F, is it?—stuff is twisted but really compelling."

"Compelling?" I ask. It doesn't sound like a word Rusty would use.

"Oh, yeah," Nina says, barreling right along. She peels the plastic wrap off of her sandwich. If she'd asked, I might have told her that no matter how bad Arnold's Swedish meatballs are, they wouldn't have, couldn't have, been worse than the tuna sandwiches.

"Rusty's really into books. He reads more than anyone I've ever met in my entire life. Did you know he got a perfect score on the verbal portion of the SATs?"

"I didn't."

Nina takes a bite of her sandwich, chews, and swallows. "He's a regular Einstein," she says, then makes a face. "Ugh. That's a terrible sandwich!" She takes another bite and grimaces. "Really bad. But I'm so hungry. Anyway, he's whatever the literary equivalent of an Einstein is. So if he likes your comic, it's got to be good."

I tap the end of my pencil against my cheek, waiting for Nina to get to the point. She doesn't seem like the kind of person to engage in witless banter without a reason.

"So." Nina grins. "Are you and Rusty, like, a thing?"

"A thing?"

"Like, a couple. You know?"

The question socks me in the gut. It's not what I was expecting. Does Rusty think we're a couple? I mean, I never dared think that he might, that he would feel the same way I do. Especially since I'm not even sure how I feel. It's my duty to protect him from Death. My feelings are irrelevant.

"Forget it. It's none of my business. I was only asking because he's really fragile right now, and I'd hate to see him get hurt." She takes another bite of her tuna sandwich before realizing that it's the same disgusting sandwich as before. I can see the battle waging on her face. She wants to spit the bite out, but she's afraid that might be rude. She swallows. I admire her courage.

"We're not a thing," I say. But I can't help wondering if we could be.

"Oh." If I didn't know better, I'd almost think she looks disappointed. This is the same girl who seemed like she wanted to punch me out last time I saw her. "Well, either way, just be careful with him, okay?"

"Rusty's stronger than you think." It's a stupid thing to say. I mean, of course he's strong. You don't survive the trauma of being turned into a human Molotov cocktail unless you're a fight-to-the-death kind of person.

"I know," Nina says as she eyeballs the rest of her sandwich. Her hunger is battling her revulsion, and I'm not sure yet which will win. "I just wish I'd been there when it happened."

I stop tapping my pencil. "You mean with Rusty?"

"I was late getting to the party. I only arrived a minute before the ambulance did." Nina wraps up the remains of her sandwich and pushes the gross mess to the side. "If I'd been there, I would have stopped it. I *would* have. And Rusty won't even tell me who did it."

"Maybe he doesn't know. They snuck up behind him."

Nina shakes her head, gives me a funny look. "He was burned from the front." She sighs and looks at her hands in her lap. "I think Rusty's scared. I think he knows who did this to him, but he's afraid they'll retaliate if he tells."

Nina keeps talking, but I'm stunned by this new knowledge. Rusty offered to tell me who had burned him the last time I was there. Part of me wishes I'd asked. Not that knowing would change anything.

But why would Rusty tell me that Nina was at the party if she wasn't? And how could he have been burned on the front of his body if the boys snuck up behind him? The questions zoom in my skull, pinballing about, demanding answers.

"It was good talking to you, Nina, but I have to run." I think I interrupted her, and she's kind of glaring at me, but I give her a little wave, grab my notebook, and take off to find Lexi. She's been watching the news coverage of Rusty's incident since it happened. If anyone can help me sort out what's true and what's not, it'll be her. But when I get to Peds, Lexi isn't in her room.

"Treatment," Nurse Merchant says. She's sitting at her station, bent over paperwork.

I turn toward Trevor's room. "How about Trevor?"

She smiles. "He's awake. But don't stay too long, Drew. He's had a rough couple of nights." She goes back to scribbling on her forms, as if I'm not even here.

If Death has spoken with her, Nurse Merchant isn't giving it away.

Trevor's eyes flutter open when I walk in, and he tries to grin. "Droopy Drew. What's up, buddy?"

"You look like crap." I toss my sketchbook on the bed. It bounces off of Trevor's legs; he winces. "Sorry."

"No big. It's the experimental protocol they've got me on. I feel like my bones are shredding. Like I'm made of bruises."

I go to the windows and throw open the blinds. It's what Lexi would do if she were here. The sky outside is streaked with gray clouds, and the sun is so bright that I have to shade my eyes with the back of my hand. "It sounds like the cure is worse than the disease."

Trevor struggles to sit up. I grab him another pillow and put it behind his back. "Thanks." He wriggles a bit to settle into a comfortable spot. "You got no idea, dude. If the cancer doesn't do me in, this shit they're pumping me full of sure will."

"You're not going to die, Trevor."

"Yeah. Right." Trevor fingers the edges of my sketchpad. "You see Lexi yet?"

I shake my head. "She's getting treatment." I look at Trevor, really look at him. At his thin frame and his bulging eyes and his pale, moist skin. "Why haven't you asked out Lexi yet?"

"Drew—"

"How come?"

"Where am I going to take her? We're in a hospital." He looks out the window, not at me.

"Lexi won't care about that." I fall into the chair, prop my feet up on Trevor's mattress.

He shrugs. "I care. I don't want this for her. I'm chained to this piece-of-shit body. She shouldn't be too."

I nudge Trevor's foot with my own until he looks at me. "That's not your choice."

"Whatever. She probably doesn't even like me."

Which I know isn't true. I also know that Trevor knows it isn't true. Whether he's waiting for me to argue the point or agree with him I don't know. Either way, it won't help him. There's only one way to help Trevor, and I'm not going to be able to do it alone.

"So," Trevor says, "did you come down here for a reason, or did you just want to torment me?"

"Definitely torment." I throw Trevor my biggest snaggletooth smile. "Actually, you've got your computer, right?"

"Yeah."

"Can I borrow it?"

Trevor points at the cabinet in the corner. "No porn. My parents use it sometimes when they're here."

I roll my eyes and retrieve the laptop. All of Trevor's clothes are folded on the shelves, untouched and unused. "As if."

"Sometimes Nurse Merchant makes this big production of closing my door and telling me that she'll be back in an hour. Like she thinks there's a chance I'm going to whack it in here."

"You haven't?"

Trevor shakes his head. "When your whole body feels like rotting meat, jerking off is the last thing on your mind." I start to laugh, but Trevor's staring at me, unblinking. His eyes are wide, even wider than normal, and his mouth is slack, like he's stuck in a moment between words, replaying the same second over and over. I'm about to snap my fingers and say his name when he goes into convulsions. He pitches forward and arches his back. His body becomes rigid as a corpse. The bed rattles and shakes. I scream for Nurse Merchant. She appears instantly, turning Trevor on his side, saying something to me—I'm not sure what.

I retreat into the corner, clutching the laptop to my chest.

Trevor moves further and further away. He and Nurse Merchant tumble down a long tunnel, and I can't reach them. There are more nurses now, and a couple of doctors. They're all shouting and poking Trevor while his body tears itself apart. The gravity between heaven and hell, between life and death, is fighting for bits and pieces of my friend.

Nurse Merchant takes my hand. I don't remember when she exchanged Trevor's laptop for my sketchpad, but I'm standing in the hallway hugging Patient F, wishing that I could pour my memories of Trevor thrashing about on the bed into the same stream of time Patient F uses to avoid thinking about his dead family.

"Drew?" A young orderly wheels Lexi into Peds. Lexi looks at me and swallows, then she glances at Trevor's room. "Drew?"

"He's alive," I say, but I can't say more. "I have to go."

I sprint through the halls, away from Lexi and Nurse Merchant and Trevor. I bust into the first bathroom I find and kneel at the toilet, puking up my lunch. Every time I close my eyes, I see Trevor slipping away, and a fresh wave of nausea wracks my body.

When there's nothing left in my stomach, I lean against the wall until the heaving aftershocks subside and I can breathe again.

I leave the bathroom and wander through the hospital, headed nowhere. Seeing Trevor like that has wrecked me. It's one thing to know, intellectually, that your friend is dying, and another to witness the process of death. I'm not sure I'm strong enough to watch it to the bitter end. I understand now why Trevor broke up with Siobhan and why he doesn't want to burden Lexi with his feelings.

But I also understand why it's more important than ever for him to tell Lexi how he feels about her. All of Trevor's very special days may be behind him.

I don't remember how I got here, but I'm standing in the chapel. There are a couple of people sitting in the pews—an older woman with her head bowed low and a man my dad's age just staring at the wall. I'm not sure how long I've been loitering in the doorway, but Father Mike sees me and waves me in.

I drag my feet. Father Mike is busy lighting candles on the altar. He's wearing a welcoming smile, but he's moving quietly, so as not to disturb the people seeking comfort in the silence. Still, his smile says enough.

"How are you, Drew?" He points to the front pew, and we sit together. He isn't in his robes today, just black pants and a black shirt and one of those little white collars.

"My friend is dying." The words spill out of my mouth. "I don't want Trevor to die."

Father Mike's smile fades when he realizes that I'm not here to seek advice about Patient F's next great adventure. I don't even know why I'm here. But it feels like one of the few safe places left in the hospital.

"Do you believe that God has a plan for Trevor?" he asks.

"I . . . I've always believed in free will."

"Having a plan doesn't mean that you can't make choices." He folds his hands, exuding a radiant calm. Gone is the funny man, the man who knows a shocking amount about comic books. In his place is the man of God.

I look down at my own hands. Still shaking. I can't erase the afterimages of Trevor from behind my eyes. But I focus on Father Mike's words and let him guide me back from the precipice. "I don't understand. Either God plans out our lives or he doesn't. We're trains on a track or we're pinballs."

Father Mike rests his hand on my arm and tilts his head so that he's looking me straight in the eyes. There's so much serenity there. His inner calm is contagious. I wonder how the mountains of tragedy don't wear him down. How supporting others doesn't leave him with a crumbling foundation of his own. I'm grateful for it, either way.

"It's more complicated than that," he says. "Think of God's plan like a road trip. You can follow I-95 all the way from Florida to Boston, or you can explore the back roads. You can get lost in a big city for a while, or you can spend your days stopping at antique stores in every small town you pass through. The choices you make on the way to your destination are yours. But where your path ends is in God's hands."

Tears gather on the edges of my vision. I can't stop them from falling. Don't want to. "So you're telling me that Trevor's going to die whether I pray for him or not?"

Father Mike takes my hands and folds them between his own. "Just pray, and I'll pray with you, and we'll leave the rest to God."

I close my eyes and slide to my knees. Father Mike kneels beside me.

"Father Mike?" I ask softly. "What does God want to hear?"

"The truth, Drew. Tell the truth."

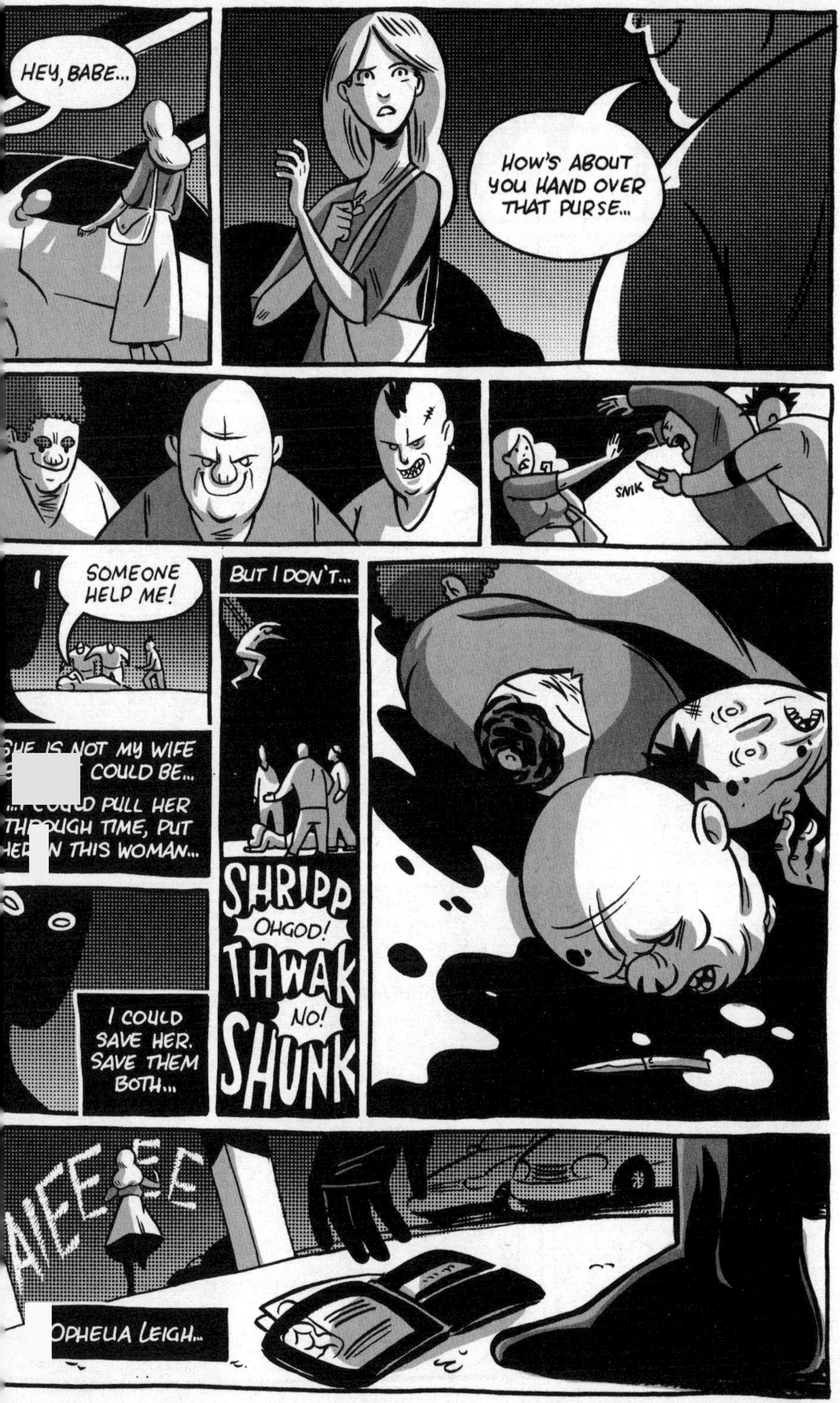
HEY, BABE...
HOW'S ABOUT YOU HAND OVER THAT PURSE...
SNIK
SOMEONE HELP ME!
SHE IS NOT MY WIFE
COULD BE...
...I COULD PULL HER THROUGH TIME, PUT HER IN THIS WOMAN...
I COULD SAVE HER. SAVE THEM BOTH...
BUT I DON'T...
SHRIPP
OHGOD!
THWAK
NO!
SHUNK
AIEEEEE
OPHELIA LEIGH...

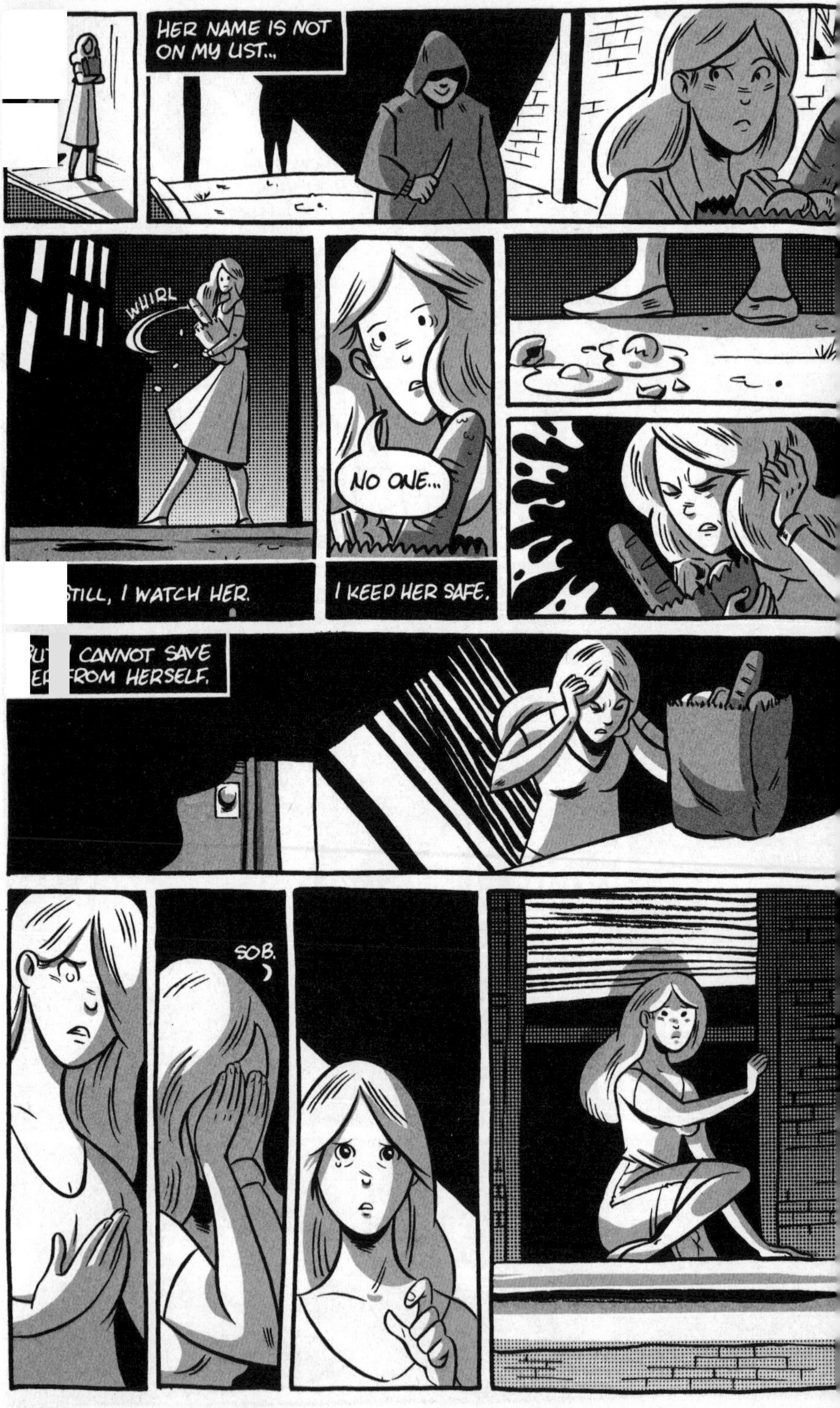

HER NAME IS NOT ON MY LIST...
WHIRL
NO ONE...
STILL, I WATCH HER.
I KEEP HER SAFE.
CANNOT SAVE
FROM HERSELF.
SOB.

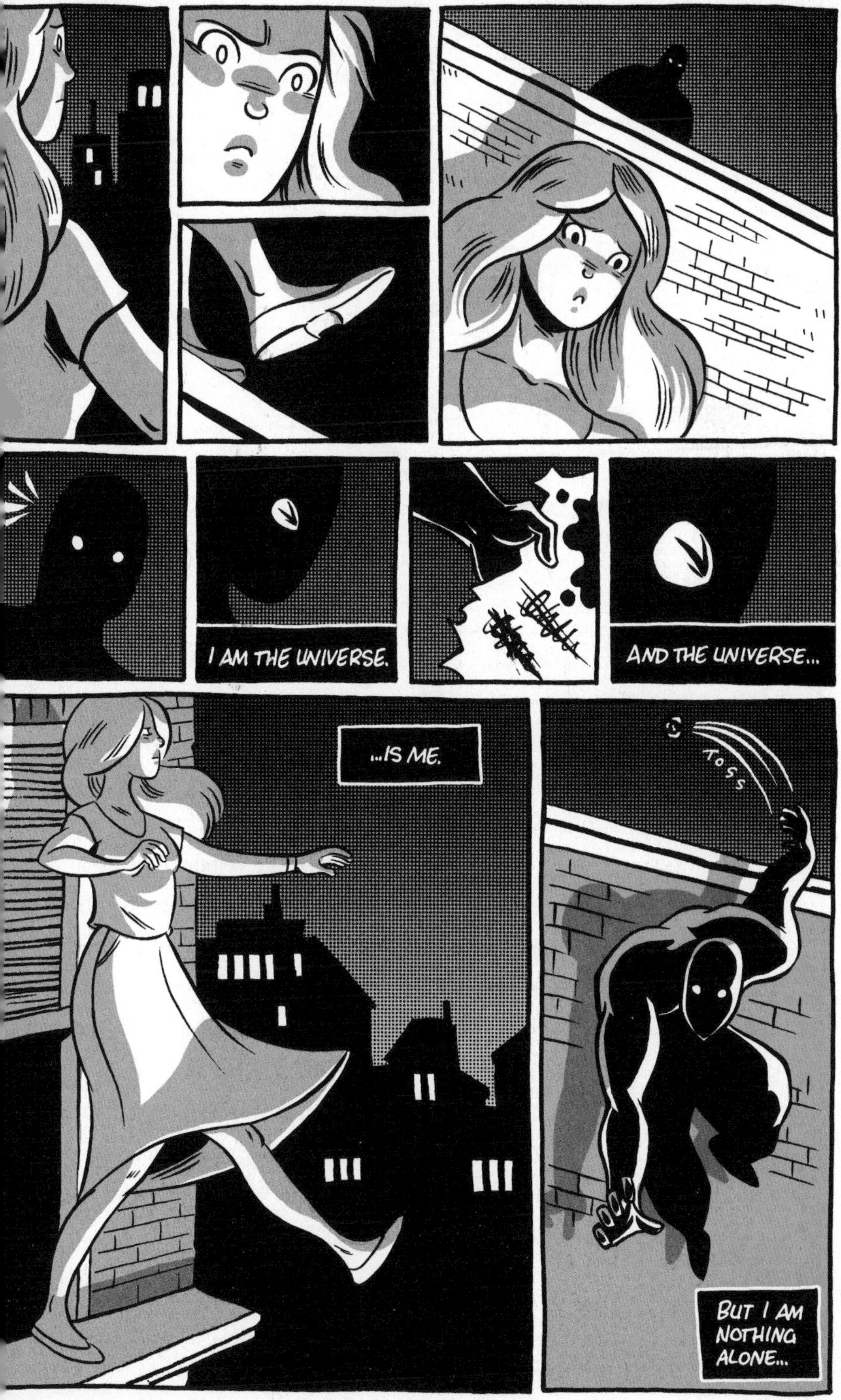
I AM THE UNIVERSE.
AND THE UNIVERSE...
...IS ME.
TOSS
BUT I AM NOTHING ALONE...

Chapter 16
Teleportation

Moving around the hospital becomes difficult.

No matter where I go, people stare at me; they take snapshots of me with their eyes so that they can file reports with Death. Somewhere, she sits on her throne of bones, waiting for me to make one more mistake. Then she'll snatch me up and take me away. Take me *out there.*

I'm not even sure what's out there anymore. I remember that first night. After I watched Death take Cady and my parents. The paramedics lost me in the confusion. Listening to Emma and Jo and Steven discuss the accident from my hiding spot in an empty exam room. I hated them then. The callous way they treated my baby sister as meat and not a little girl who loved to sing. The way they continued on about their nights like my family was little more than an interlude, a blip in their routine. The first chance I had, I ran. I found the unfinished ward of the hospital and tried to cry alone in the dark. But I couldn't. I couldn't cry.

The next night, I snuck out and found my parents in the morgue. I couldn't look at them. But I did cry. I cried so hard that I forgot my own name. When I was done, I realized that my parents were still here. And that as long as I was here and I remembered them, then they wouldn't be dead. Out there, time would pass and I'd forget, but here in the hospital, they'd always be alive.

Eventually I realized that Death had meant to take me, too, but that she'd been late. I know she'll find me in the end, but I'll evade her as long as possible. Her resources are not infinite. Death is a busy woman. But still, I spend a lot of time hiding out in my room, working on Patient F. He's continuing to move through the names on his list. The names of the dead. If a name is on his list, they die. He kills them. It's the way it works.

But since he met Ophelia, he's begun to think about things. Not about whether the people whose names are on his list deserve to die—they do—but about whether he deserves to live. When he's with Ophelia, Patient F feels the way he felt before, when he was a man in a suit with a boring job and a house and a family. He begins to wonder if he could maybe be that man again, for her, with her.

Except he's got too much blood on his hands to ever be happy again. It never washes off, that blood. It becomes part of his skin. It *is* his skin. It's all he knows.

I blink under the incandescent work light hanging from the wall and rub my eyes with my fists. An afterimage of the room floats on the backs of my eyelids. I don't even know what time it is. The battery has died on my iPod, and I haven't bothered to steal a new one. Doctors have bad taste in music anyway. So much country and gangster rap.

Since I can't remember when I last left my sanctuary, I decide it's time to visit Rusty. I know that I should check on Trevor, but I can't bear the thought of seeing him convulse again. Or of finding his room empty.

Instead, I head toward the ICU. When I exit my unfinished prison, the flood of sunlight momentarily blinds me. It's high noon, and the hallways are alive with people in motion. I alone stand still. It takes effort to find my way into the stream of people flowing by, but I do it, and I keep my eyes down and my steps quick. Death's minions are everywhere.

My stomach rumbles, and I figure I can make do with a snack. I grab some chips and mints out of the vending machine and then do a hair check in an empty room's bathroom. I'm starting to look terrible. I've never sported much of a tan, but these days I'm pallid; my cheeks are sprouting the beginnings of a scraggly beard, which both impresses and repulses me; and without a brush, the best I can do is wet my hair, now hanging in my eyes, and slick it back. The only good thing about my appearance is that I look less like the boy in that sketch with each passing day.

When I approach the ICU, I follow an orderly through the doors, but I'm stopped before I make it two more steps.

"I'm sorry," a nurse says as she scrambles out of her seat and rushes toward me. "You can't be here." She's young and energetic, like Emma, but she doesn't smell like sugar cookies.

"I'm here to see Rusty." I haven't done this before, seen him during the day. Officially.

The ICU looks different filled with people. ICU patients are on the precipice of life, staring down into the abyss, waiting for that one miracle to fend off death a while longer. And at night, you can feel the desolation drowning them, when they only have their own thoughts to grapple with. But during the day, there's a slick of hope that floats on top of all that fear. I don't think it's enough to save them, but it helps them want to save themselves.

The nurse is about to tell me to get lost when Nina trots over. "It's okay, Shari. He's okay." Nina puts her arm around my shoulders and smiles at Shari.

"Family only," Shari says, but she's already retreating.

"He's a cousin," Nina assures her. "Cousin Drew."

Shari cocks her eyebrow at me. "Rusty's got a lot of cousins."

Nina says, "Thanks, Shari," and drags me toward Rusty's room. "Rusty's going to be so thrilled to see you." She wasn't exactly the last person I wanted to see, but she wasn't the first, either. It should have occurred to me that she might be here, given that it's daytime, but I wanted to see Rusty so badly that I didn't think.

"Sorry for running out on you the other day," I say. "I really had to pee." *Pee?* I don't know where that excuse came from, but I already feel the tips of my ears burning, my cheeks turning red. "TMI."

"It's all copacetic." Nina herds me toward Rusty's room, and I stumble through the door. "Look who I found."

Rusty looks up and smiles. It's the greatest smile in the entire world. The dregs of horror from my episode with Trevor just dissipate in the air the moment I'm in the orbit of Rusty's bright, lopsided grin. I take in his face, every inch of it. The way his red hair falls naturally to the left side, the way his right eye doesn't open fully, the way the freckles down his unburned arm look like braille that I wish I could read.

"Heya, Rusty." My voice comes out shy.

"You left me hanging," he says. "Frankenstein's brother is dead, his father's maid is accused of the murder, and you left me hanging!"

I'm about to explain, but he's still smiling. He's joking. It's all I can do not to run over to his bed and hug him. I'm drawn like a magnet to his smile, his laugh, his everything.

"Rusty, are you going to introduce us?"

I turn around so quickly that I lose my balance and stumble into the door frame. Rusty's parents are sitting in the corner, eyeballing me curiously.

And just like that, Rusty's smile evaporates. "Mom, Dad, this is Drew. Drew, my parents."

I'm frozen. My limbs refuse to respond to the signals from my brain. Mr. and Mrs. McHale stare at me like I'm an invader, the enemy. I'm a fiend come to kidnap their son, to steal him away to my underground lair.

"Drew's great," Nina says. Her voice is an octave higher than normal, and it startles me back to reality. "He's an artist."

"Nice to meet you both," I mumble, waving at them weakly and trying to smile.

Mrs. McHale smiles like her son. "Nice to meet you, Andrew. We've heard so little about you." She gives me a wry grin.

"Rusty doesn't tell us anything." Mr. McHale coughs in Rusty's direction.

Rusty's parents look more alive than I've ever seen them before. They don't look like the haggard people I've spied on so often. I think it must be an act they're putting on for Rusty.

"Oh," I say. I figure they're waiting for me to explain my existence in Rusty's life. "Well, I'm working in the cafeteria for the summer, and my grandma is here too, so, yeah, I just spend a lot of time around the hospital. I was here the night Rusty came in, and I thought he could use a friend."

Mr. and Mrs. McHale examine me with curious eyes. But they're not the only ones. Rusty is staring at me too. I forgot he didn't know that I'd been there that night. I never told him.

"It's nice to meet a young man who visits his grandmother," Mrs. McHale says. "Rusty could learn a thing or two from you."

Rusty groans. "Jesus, Mom. His grandmother's in a coma. Noni Jean smells like cabbage, and all she talks about are her stupid dogs and their poop. Stitches pooped three times last I was there, and the way she talked about it, you'd think the stupid dog shat a log in the shape of the Virgin Mary."

"Rusty," snaps his father. "Language."

But I can't help laughing. Nina joins in, and soon we're all chuckling, except for Rusty's father, who doesn't seem to like me much. He keeps glaring at me with this permanent scowl.

"Why don't you join us, Andrew?" Mrs. McHale says. "We're about to play Trivial Pursuit."

"Yeah!" Nina says. "You totally have to play."

I look at Rusty, and he's wearing this look that says *I'm sorry.* Nina grabs the box and starts arranging the Trivial Pursuit board at the foot of Rusty's bed while babbling about how she's horrible at Trivial Pursuit but how Rusty is a phenom.

Rusty's parents drag their chairs closer and chime in with stories about how Rusty once came from behind to beat them all because he knew some obscure answer to a question about Antarctic animals.

Their voices become a buzzing in my ears, and the corners of my vision blur.

I'm back in the car with my parents and my little sister, and we're driving down a dark two-lane road. Mom wanted to stop for dinner an hour ago, but we were only a couple of hours from the hotel and I begged them to keep going because I needed to get out of this stinking car. Dad had a headache and I offered to drive.

Cady was trying to get us all to sing this song that she'd learned from the FitzBuzzies, a group of dancing and singing bumblebees who go on grand adventures to find the prettiest flowers in the world, but I didn't want to sing. Singing was for babies. My friends kept texting me from home; I was missing one of the best parties of my life to go on a lame trip to Florida with my family. We'd talked about going to Disney for years, but that was before I had friends, before my friends started throwing parties. I just wanted to get to the hotel room so I could find out if Nate Miller had shown up and who he'd brought.

My phone buzzed again, and my mom yelled at me not to look at it, but I already had it out—and Nina snaps her fingers in my face.

"Drew? Are you all right?"

Mr. and Mrs. McHale are staring at me, probably wondering if I'm on drugs. Rusty's got an inquisitive look on his face. He knows I went somewhere, but he's not sure where.

"I'm fine," I say. "I don't think I'm up for a game." I back toward the door.

"Why don't we go get some lunch?" Mrs. McHale says to her husband. He grunts something but stands without hesitation. "Sweetie, can we bring you back anything?"

Rusty shakes his head. I catch him exchanging a look with Nina right before she says, "Mind if I play third wheel? I'm starved."

"Let's shove off," Mr. McHale says. He nods at Rusty and stares at me—hard—as he passes by. I flatten myself against the door frame. I think maybe I should try to shake his hand, but Mr. McHale doesn't appear amiable to touching.

"It was very nice to meet you, Andrew," Mrs. McHale says. I get a sly smile from Nina as she skips out of the room.

Rusty waits until Nina and his parents are out of earshot before sighing. "I thought they'd never leave. I love 'em, right, but they're tiring." Rusty smiles at me again, that same brilliant smile.

I collect the Trivial Pursuit pieces and return the game to the box. "Sorry about earlier. I kind of zoned out."

"I get it," Rusty says. "You miss your family."

Rusty catches me off guard, like he'd seen inside my brain. But I don't miss them the way you miss a friend during the long summer months, while you're away visiting different parts of the country and they're stuck at home working at their parents' flower shop. I miss my family on an atomic level. The bonds that held us together were shattered, and now I'm incomplete. Radical.

I avoid Rusty's father's chair and sit down in the seat vacated by his mother.

"How you been?" I ask. It's not the kind of thing we normally talk about, but I've met his parents, and it's daytime. I've become part of his waking life. It feels like nothing is off limits now.

"Got some skin grafts scheduled," Rusty says nonchalantly. "They're going to peel some skin from my back and slap it on my legs."

185

I shift uncomfortably in my chair. The seat is fine, but Rusty's challenging me. It's in the way he looks at me, his eyes narrower, his hands curled into little fists. I should let this go, but I can't. "Good thing your back wasn't burned, then."

"Yeah," Rusty says. "I suppose."

"Nina having any luck finding the guys who attacked you?"

Rusty shakes his head. "Soon, a few days, maybe, they're moving me out of ICU into a regular room. A couple of weeks after that, maybe home." Rusty stares down at the gulf of blanket between his knees. "I don't want to go, Drew. I don't want to leave." He peers at me through dewy eyelashes. "I'm afraid I'll die out there. I really am."

I scoot my chair to the side of his bed, take Rusty's hand. It's clammy. "No one's going to hurt you," I tell him. "A promise is a promise."

We pull away from each other when Shari comes to hang a new IV and record Rusty's vitals.

"You'll never guess what I'm doing tomorrow night," I say once Shari leaves, to change the subject. Fear is still weighting Rusty down, but the truth is, I'm not sure that I *can* protect him from Death. I mean, I couldn't stop her from taking my parents or my little sister. I'm beginning to doubt that I'll be able to stop her from taking Trevor. Or—eventually—myself. I've lost my confidence. All my promises may come to nothing in the end.

Rusty's smile returns. It's not nearly full form, but it's waxing. "What are you going to do?"

"Remember how I told you about Trevor and Lexi? And how Trevor won't ask Lexi out because he's afraid of dying on her, and how Lexi's too blind to see that there's a really awesome guy right in front of her?"

"Yeah," Rusty says, though I'm not entirely certain he's following along.

"Tomorrow night, I'm setting them up on a date." I say the words out loud and feel immensely proud of myself. "I haven't worked out the details yet, but I'm going to make this happen."

Rusty touches the tips of my fingers. He's staring at me in this dreamy way, as though he's sleeping or his pain meds have increased. "Why is this so important to you?"

I shrug. "People deserve to be happy," I say. The real reason is less romantic. The real reason is that the sight of Trevor seizing reminded me how fragile his life is. The real reason is that, if I wait too long, Trevor will die.

But I don't tell Rusty those reasons, because then he'll know that I may not be able to keep all my promises.

"What about you?" Rusty asks. I almost don't hear his question because I'm too busy thinking about tomorrow night.

"What about me?"

Rusty fidgets with the ends of the blanket. "You got a boyfriend?"

I shake my head slowly. "Not currently," I say. "I had one once, but it didn't last. He had issues."

"Oh," Rusty says.

The mood in the room has shifted. Things are different now, and I'm not sure what's changed. My feelings for Rusty are intertwined with my fear and it's so confusing. I have to be his friend first, regardless of my own feelings.

"My friend Emma told me once that kissing is the best part of a relationship. She said that if the kissing wasn't the best part, I should run. Isn't that the weirdest thing?"

Rusty blushes. He gazes intently at every object in the room, while avoiding me. "I wouldn't know," he says finally. "I've never kissed anyone."

"Not *anyone*?" I don't mean to sound so condescending, but I'm shocked and can't help it.

"No, no one." Rusty stares at his hands. "Nina always tells me that I might not even be gay. She thinks it's not possible for me to really know until I've kissed a guy."

"So why don't you kiss one?"

Rusty finally looks at me, and he's got this fire in his eyes, this determination that scares me. I was right about him: There's fire hiding in his bones. "I want it to mean something. Like with Trevor and Lexi."

Silence fills the spaces between our words, and the spaces grow unbearably long.

"What's it like?" Rusty asks. "Kissing, I mean."

Now I'm avoiding Rusty's eyes. It feels odd talking to him about a guy that I only dated for a few weeks. But I can feel his stare, so I say, "It was okay, I guess. Let's just say that, with Nate, kissing wasn't the best part."

I'm so uncomfortable now that I want to crawl out of my skin and run away. But there's something about Rusty that makes me stay. That always makes me stay.

"How about I read some *Frankenstein*?" I say. The suggestion clears the awkwardness between us, and Rusty nods—a little too enthusiastically. I retrieve the book from his bedside table and find my place. "Are you sure you don't want me to get a less gruesome book?"

"Nah. This one is great." I'm about to start reading when Rusty says, "Oh, by the way, some woman came up here asking about you."

I gape at him, openmouthed, and fumble the book. It hits the floor with a smack that makes both Rusty and me jump.

"Woman?" I ask, coughing.

Rusty nods. "She was asking all sorts of questions about when you visited and what I knew about you. She seemed really curious. I didn't tell her anything." He glances at me sideways. "Everything okay?"

"Of course," I say, regaining my composure, picking up the book from the floor. "Everything's fine. The best."

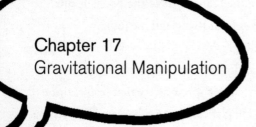

Chapter 17
Gravitational Manipulation

Love is for saps.

At least, that's what I used to think.

My parents were in love. I knew it subconsciously, but I didn't recognize the million little ways they expressed their love for each other. Like how my mom always bought my dad's favorite kind of cheese, Swiss, even though hers was Havarti. Like the way my dad forgot their wedding anniversary but remembered the songs that played on the radio the first time they kissed and the first time they made love and the first time my father drove my mother to the hospital to give birth. To me.

My parents didn't buy each other fancy gifts or take expensive vacations or plan elaborate surprises. They were simple people who showed their love in minute ways every second of every day.

That's how I know that Trevor and Lexi are in love. The way Trevor lowers the volume of his voice ever so slightly when he's talking about Lexi, as if he doesn't want anyone else to hear—not because he's ashamed but because he doesn't want just anyone to have those precious words. The way that Lexi opens Trevor's blinds when she goes into his room—not because she wants to see the world but because she wants to remind Trevor that it still exists, so that maybe—maybe—they can escape one day and see it together.

I see their love in the things they do that they aren't even aware of. Tiny touches and half winks and how one is always on the other's mind. Always.

Love isn't for saps. It's for people like my mom and dad. People like Lexi and Trevor.

Out there they'd be together—of that I'm certain. But it's different in the hospital. Their fear isolates them. Even when they share the same space, breathe the same air, they're alone. Lexi has her sights set so firmly on the future that she's afraid to embrace anything in her present, and Trevor is so certain he hasn't got a future that he's scared he'll drag down anyone he cares about.

They're both idiots. But I'm going to change that.

Arnold still won't let me return to work, but he and Aimee agree to help me with the date. I only ask to borrow the cafeteria for a couple of hours, but when I tell him my plan, he insists on putting together a special meal. I've tasted heroic portions of Arnold's "special meals," and I'm not ashamed to admit that I'm worried. Though I suppose if food poisoning is how the date ends, we'll count ourselves lucky that we're already in a hospital.

Jo and Emma volunteer to decorate the cafeteria before their shifts begin. They ask me for ideas, but I haven't got any and tell them to go wild. They're gleeful—manic pixies with more ideas than time or money will allow. Maybe I should rein them in, but I haven't the heart. Not even when Emma mentions her disco ball again.

Lovers infect those who surround them. Young lovers especially. And tonight, Arnold, Jo, and Emma are all terminal.

Convincing Steven to help is difficult. It's his night off, and he doesn't want to set foot in the hospital. I'm not too proud to beg or to admit that my entire plan falls apart without him. I strike straight at his ego. And it works, because it's true.

Navigating the hospital is more complicated now that Death is on to me. Even with my parents' file gone and that Missing poster destroyed, the hospital feels smaller. I peek around every corner, tip-toe, sneak. Death could be anywhere, everywhere, and I must be careful.

There's still so much to do.

Father Mike is kneeling in the front pew when I walk into the chapel at seven in the evening. I'm not meeting Steven until eight, but my construction-room prison was too confining. The shadows were too long, the ceiling too low. If I'd stayed down there one second longer, peering into the contents of the metal box, searching the faces in the photograph for some hint of absolution, I'd have gone stark-raving. I'm beyond forgiveness—not even God could pardon me, not that I believe He should.

Father Mike doesn't hear me, or he's too deep in prayer to bother with me, so I sit beside him and stare at the crucifix on the altar. It writhes. Squirms. Should I feel revolted? I'm uncertain. I prayed to God for Trevor, and it worked. This morning, he was alive and alert and bugging Nurse Merchant for second helpings of lunch, which was a lovely beef broth served with a side of apple juice and Jell-O and morphine. We didn't talk about the seizure, and I tried to erase it from my memory the way Patient F would have. Maybe I should pray for other things. Everything. But something tells me that I should hoard my prayers for dire times.

"How's your friend?" Father Mike asks. He looks like he's still praying.

"Taking the long way around."

"Good." Father Mike's words are clipped, and I feel like I've intruded on something important. He slides into the pew and looks at me. His eyes are spider webbed with red veins, and the lids droop, as if it's too much effort to keep them open. "Do you need something?"

I shake my head, wishing I'd gone to check on Emma and Jo rather than come here. "I wanted to thank you, I guess."

"I didn't do anything." Father Mike sighs heavily.

"God, then," I say.

He chuffs. "Yeah. God." There's something hollow in his voice. A hopelessness that I find unsettling.

"I didn't mean to bother you," I say.

After a moment, Father Mike shakes his head. "You're no bother." The tension in his body releases, and a smile even creeps to the corners of his mouth. But it's not wholly real. It's an act for my benefit. "I'm glad your friend is okay."

We stare at the crucifix for an uncomfortable span of time. I want to leave, but I think maybe this could be one of those dire times and that Father Mike might need my prayers or, at the very least, my company.

"I'm kidnapping Trevor—that's my friend—and setting him up on a date with my other friend, a girl named Lexi." I don't know why I tell him this, but his fake smile becomes real.

"That's nice of you. Really nice."

"Yeah. You can come if you want. Some of the nurses are already helping me, but more hands would be great."

Father Mike looks into my eyes, and it feels like he's looking deeper than that. He's a vulture picking over the corpses of my secrets. "I have to go home. But thank you."

"For what?"

Father Mike doesn't answer me. He gets up and walks toward the altar and disappears behind a curtain. I don't know if I'm supposed to wait for him to return, so I give him a minute. As I get up to leave, he reappears holding a bouquet of daisies and sunflowers. They're so alive, it's painful.

"Your friend should have flowers for his girl." Father Mike hands me the flowers and vanishes again. This time I know he's not coming back, so I go meet Steven. Guilt tugs at me for abandoning Father Mike, but his crisis will have to wait for another day. He's not dying and in love.

Steven is waiting for me in a hallway, leaning against the wall, a bag slung over his shoulder, checking his phone, trying to pretend that he has a place in the world *out there*, though I suspect that he, like me and Nurse Merchant, really only exists in this hospital.

"I can't believe I agreed to this." Steven punches buttons on his phone and slides it into the pocket of his scrubs, where it hangs low and heavy. "Nice flowers."

My guts are a quivering mass of excitement. This is about more than just bringing two friends together. It's my last-ditch effort to keep Trevor alive for a little bit longer. If anything can keep his heart beating, it's Lexi.

"Everyone knows Nurse Cho has a massive lady boner for you," I tell Steven. "She'll do anything you ask." I beg him with my puppy dog eyes, hoping he'll do anything *I* ask, and only feel slightly guilty about it. "Do you have the stuff?"

Steven rolls his eyes like I should know better. He tosses me his bag. "Hurry. I haven't had a night off in three weeks, and I actually have plans."

I don't call him on the fact that his plans probably involve a large pizza for one and a *Star Trek* marathon, because I really do need his help. Instead, I catch the bag and dart into the bathroom to change. Cho needs to believe that I'm a nurse or an actual volunteer or something. Of course, if Steven plays his part well, she'll be so distracted that she won't even notice I exist.

I don the blue scrubs and check myself out in the mirror. It's been so long since I've given my reflection more than a glance; I'm surprised by the sight of my own face. Hell, I could have left that sketch in Death's office and it wouldn't have mattered. I had this image in my mind of what I looked like, how I smiled, the stupid dimple in my chin. But that face is gone, replaced by something gaunt and hollow. I've aged decades in weeks. I search for me in the mirror. The real me. The me that had a sister and a mother and a father. The me who killed them and ran away. Only, he's not there. He doesn't exist. Maybe he was a mask and I'm what was left underneath.

I slide on the final piece of my disguise: a pair of black-rimmed glasses. I don't know where Steven stole them from, and I don't care. I push them up the bridge of my nose and imagine that I am Patient F: a man who is not a man. A gallimaufry of spare bits of other people and other creatures sewn together with twine into the semblance of a man. A man with no future, no past, and nothing left to lose.

Steven whistles when I exit the bathroom. My clothes, bag, and the flowers are stashed in a stall, behind a toilet. The janitors won't clean this particular hallway until about three in the morning: plenty of time.

"Schnazzy," Steven says. "Scrubs suit you."

The scrubs hang off my body like loose skin. The shirt's V-neck plunges too low, revealing the sunken-in hollow at the base of my neck, while the ass and crotch of the pants sag like a dirty diaper. "Did you steal these from a fat man?"

"They used to belong to Jo." Steven's laugh cannonballs into the hallway. It's a great laugh, but I feel a little weird wearing Jo's old clothes.

"We should take off," I say as I lead the way. Steven falls in line behind me.

When we arrive at Peds, Nurse Cho is filling out paperwork. She's a hyperalert young woman who manages to look simultaneously bitter and eager. Her movements are brisk, precise, while her red cheeks and lips carry a lingering smile. I don't come here at night, so I don't have a relationship with her like I do with Nurse Merchant. I don't even know what Cho's first name is.

The one thing I do know is that she's got a crush on Steven and a raging case of gay blindness. He could kiss an entire chorus line of men right in front of her and she still wouldn't have a clue.

This plan is bound to reinforce Cho's delusion, but other than pulling the fire alarm, it's all I had.

"You're up, champ," I say to Steven, and clap him on the back. He glares at me before approaching Cho, who's already beaming. I don't know what Cho sees in Steven. He's balding and bitchy, but she lights up at the sight of him. She drops what she's doing and touches her hair and her cheeks and her scrubs, checking to make sure that all is perfectly in place.

While they chat, I zone out. Around the corner, Trevor is resting. I hope that he's not having a bad night, because that would ruin the plan. It's the one variable over which I have no control.

I made a promise to Trevor that I won't be able to keep. Death is going to take him; I grow more certain of that daily. Even this plan is only a stopgap. If it works and Trevor and Lexi admit their love for each other, it might—*might*—buy Trevor some days, his foundering soul buoyed by passion.

But, eventually, Death will come. I've been deluding myself to think that she won't. That love, that anything, can stop Trevor's inevitable reaping.

I asked my father once why falling in love is such a big deal, and he told me that one day in love is worth a hundred days not in love. Maybe it's true. I don't know. I hope it's true.

Steven waves me over. "Sonia, this is Gus. Gus, Sonia."

Cho saves her smiles for Steven and glares down her nose at me. Maybe my disguise is transparent.

No, that's not it at all. I'm an intruder, interrupting her time with Steven. She's greedy. She wants him all to herself. I can relate.

"Hi," I say.

"If you get caught," Cho declares, "I'm saying you kidnapped them." That's all she tells me, and it's fair enough. Steven motions at me to go, so I do, commandeering a wheelchair on the way.

Trevor is flipping through TV stations when I enter. He looks different in the dark, blanketed in shadows and moonlight from the open blinds. His bones seem to gleam under his skin like long glow sticks.

"Droopy!"

I put my finger to my lips and slink around to his side of the bed. It only takes me a minute to transfer Trevor's IV to the pole on the wheelchair, but significantly longer to transfer him. Trevor doesn't weigh much, but every movement causes him pain. He winces and groans and sucks in his breath, and I think this was a bad idea and that I should call the whole thing off, but then Trevor looks up at me, not guessing what we're up to but anticipating that it's something exciting and devious, and he grins.

How can I possibly disappoint him?

There's no time to put together a perfect, date-appropriate outfit, so I just grab some clothes and toss them at him. He pulls off his gown, and I flinch when I see his body, pitted and bruised like rotten fruit, but I get to work helping him dress. We roll out of his room in under ten minutes, and Steven nods at me as I pass under the annoyed—but lust-filled—eyes of Cho. She's so smitten that Steven could have probably convinced her to fill the ward with bubbles.

Love is weird.

Trevor doesn't say anything until we're well out of earshot, and then he starts chattering on about how great it is to be out of that bed, asking where we're going, making guesses—though they're all wrong. His voice is strong, and he hardly seems like the same boy from a couple of days ago, with drool hanging out of his mouth and eyes rolled back into his head. He's rallying.

My mom used to say that about my baby sister at bedtime. Cady's head would loll about on her pudgy neck, and her eyes would be glazed over, asleep where she sat, until Mom tried to put her to bed. "Cady's rallying," she'd say when Cady demanded story after story, her appetite for anthropomorphic animals and their wacky adventures insatiable.

We stop by the bathroom, and I grab the flowers that Father Mike gave me. Trevor looks at me quizzically when I toss them in his lap, but he doesn't ask any questions. He's the perfect friend: up for anything and trusting through and through.

There's nowhere else to go but the cafeteria. Steven hasn't arrived yet, so I wait with Trevor in the hall.

"You look good," I say. The clothes I picked out in the dark aren't bad: a pair of jeans and a black polo shirt. They're too big, but his slouched posture hides it.

Trevor smiles. "Are you taking me to the prom? I definitely don't think I'm wearing the right dress for the prom."

"Smartass."

A pair of doctors walk by, barely sparing us a glance. To them, I'm just a nurse wheeling a patient.

"I'm sorry about the other day," Trevor says so quickly that it sounds more like "Isorryboutotheray." He wrinkles his nose and glances up at me through his eyelashes.

It would be easy to dismiss his apology. He didn't purposefully seize. It's not as if he saved the fit for the exact moment I was in there. I know that, and I know that Trevor knows it too, but it embarrassed him, just like it'll embarrass him if I don't accept his apology. So I say, "No problem, dude," so that we can both go back to pretending it didn't happen.

Trevor looks grateful and barrels along with the conversation. "What'd you need my computer for, anyway?"

"What?"

"You asked to use it before . . . you know."

Rusty. I'd forgotten. He said the boys who burned him had snuck up from behind, yet Nina had pointed out the obvious: Rusty was burned on the front of his body. I'd intended to look up information about the attack. Clearly, Rusty isn't being entirely honest with me.

"It's not important anymore," I say. I have secrets; Arnold has secrets; Father Mike and Steven and even Death have secrets. I can't begrudge Rusty his.

I hear Steven coming down the hallway because Lexi won't shut up. She's rattling off anatomy terms. Probably brought flash cards with her. Steven had strict instructions not to reveal where he was taking her or why, which is likely driving her crazy.

Trevor smiles. He hears her too. His ears are perfectly attuned to her frequency.

Lexi squeals when she sees us. She's wearing a light blue baby-doll dress and the mother of all grins. She may not be a beauty queen, but she is beautiful. More than.

"Wow . . . ," Trevor says, in a naked moment of awe. I push him forward and whisper *"flowers"* in his ear. He shoots me a suspicious look, but then his face relaxes. Trevor offers the bouquet to Lexi and says, "They're not nearly as pretty as you are, but . . . nothing is."

The kid is smooth.

Lexi doesn't say thank you. The way she glows as she presses her nose to the flowers and breathes them in is all the words she needs. I don't know where Father Mike found them—they could have come from the bedside of a dead person—but they're Lexi's now, more precious than school books.

I nod to Steven, and we wheel Trevor and Lexi into the cafeteria. At first sight, my mind is blown. Emma and Jo have transformed the utilitarian room into a fairy-tale wonderland. There's only one table, right in the center of the room. It's covered by a glitter-coated burgundy tablecloth, set with candlesticks and napkins folded into swans. The atmospheric lights are dim, with starlight from Emma's disco ball dancing on the floor. The rest of the cafeteria has dissolved into shadow.

"Dude," Trevor says. "What is this?"

Steven shakes his head and looks around, probably for Emma and Jo, but they're gone, their work complete. I'm going to have to buy them something better than doughnuts tomorrow. I'll never finish repaying them for this magic.

"Drew?" Lexi asks when I don't answer Trevor.

I keep my mouth shut until Steven and I park Trevor and Lexi at the table. The moment their wheelchairs slide in, Arnold appears wearing a white shirt and a bow tie, his beard neatly trimmed—and I'm speechless.

"Alexis, Trevor. Welcome to *Ah-nold's*, where your every wish is my command." He snaps his fingers, and Aimee trots out carrying two long-stemmed glasses filled with bubbly liquid. "Our finest sparkling grape juice."

"Droopy?" Trevor asks.

I shake my head, and Arnold continues: "For dinner this evening, you'll begin with a selection of cheese on toast points. Next, you'll have your choice of a creamy tomato bisque or a hearty Italian wedding soup. And for the main course, we have a tasty linguine with clam sauce or a nicely roasted chicken with wild rice." Arnold bows at the waist and winks at me before scurrying to the back.

There's so much love here that I can't bear it. "This should have happened a long time ago," I manage to whisper.

Lexi still looks confused. "What . . . what is this?"

Understanding has finally dawned on Trevor's face, and he's so near tears that it hurts. He smiles at Lexi and says, "Alexis Kripke, will you have dinner with me?"

For the first time, I think Trevor realizes that he's out of time. Everything since his very special day has been a loan. Maybe this will end in heartache, but it's better than heartbreak, because at least he'll have loved and been loved and risked something. It's why Trevor takes Lexi's hand now and kisses it.

Lexi melts. I don't exist anymore. Steven doesn't exist. There is only Lexi and Trevor and their very special night.

"I never knew how badly I wanted you to ask," Lexi says.

That's my cue. Steven and I retreat into the kitchen, where Arnold is cooking like a mad scientist. It may look like a laboratory, but it smells like heaven. "Nice spread."

"What do I know?" Arnold laughs. "They're grilled cheeses cut into tiny squares."

Steven chuckles and snatches one off of the tray. "You could feed them sawdust and they wouldn't notice."

I peer around the corner to see how the date is going. Trevor's talking, and Lexi's laughing, and they're touching and smiling and beaming. They're like stars, glowing and orbiting and burning oh so brightly.

"You did good," Steven says.

"Yeah."

"What's wrong?"

I shrug.

"It'll happen for you one day." Steven pats my shoulder. "You have to have faith."

"It's doubtful." I try not to sound like I'm digging for pity, because I'm not. I'm being honest. As honest as I can be.

"Come on," Steven says. "Things can't be all doom and gloom."

Arnold carries the first course out to Lexi and Trevor while Steven and I spy on them. They chuckle at whatever terrible joke Arnold tells them and then dig in to the food. Arnold returns to work on the soup, which smells garlicky and delicious.

"My mom loved me no matter what I did," I say to Steven. I lean against one of the prep tables and fold my arms over my chest. "When I really screwed up, she'd tell me that she loved me but that she didn't like me very much at that moment." I'm quiet, but Steven must sense that I'm not done, because he holds his tongue. "I know that God or Fate or whatever is out there loves me, but I don't think he likes me very much."

I'm not looking for answers from Steven, and he doesn't try to offer any. Instead he says, "Your mom was a smart lady. Being punished doesn't mean you should miss out on being loved."

I pretend to peek in on Trevor and Lexi, so that I can think about what Steven said. I'm not so sure he's right, but maybe he's not wrong, either.

The rest of the evening passes quickly for me. Arnold delivers each course, returning with empty plates. Lexi and Trevor's laughter fills the cafeteria until the walls are bursting with it. I've never seen either of them so happy. So full. Sometimes it's too difficult to watch. Sometimes it's too difficult not to.

When they finish dinner, Arnold surprises them with a blueberry pie that—thankfully—his wife made. It looks and smells so amazing that I steal a sliver for myself.

I'm not sure if Trevor kissed Lexi before the end. I wish I could make the night last forever, but eventually, Steven tells me that we have to take them back.

Trevor is silent as I wheel him to his room, but he's wearing the purest smile on his face that I've ever seen. On him or anyone. I don't think there's a force in the universe that could bring him down right now.

Cho glares at me as I push Trevor into his room. It's after ten, but I don't care. She can call Death and tell her what I've done. It was worth it. It doesn't matter if Trevor has one day left or twenty, each one will feel like a lifetime.

I help Trevor change back into his hospital gown, then slide him into bed, rearranging the tangle of tubes and wires. It doesn't take a nurse to know that he's exhausted. Happiness is all that's keeping him going right now.

Trevor grabs my hand as I head for the door. "Thank you, Droopy," he says. "Best night of my life."

I leave without saying good-bye.

My feet take me to Rusty. No, not my feet. My heart. My faith. Maybe God doesn't like me much right now, but fuck God. Rusty matters. I matter.

The nurse on duty looks up as I barge through the ICU doors

and stride into Rusty's room. He's sleeping sitting up, but he cracks one eye open when I walk in. The nurse barks questions at me, but I ignore her.

"Drew?" Rusty says.

He . . . Shit, he's so handsome. He's so broken. And I've never wanted to be with anyone more.

"I fucked up so badly," I say. "I don't deserve you," I say.

Rusty looks confused, clouded by sleep, but he's groping for awareness. "I like you, Drew. Maybe. I . . ." He shakes his head. "There's never enough time when you're around."

The nurse is yelling at me now, threatening to call security. Screw her.

Only we exist. Me. Rusty. Me and Rusty. I'm beside his bed. I'm kissing him. He's kissing me. His lips are chapped. He tastes like antiseptic. His tongue parts my lips, and his arms grope my shoulders and my back and and and.

We fall out of time. Past and present bleed into each other, muddying the waters of time until it's all the same; it's all now and perfect, and Rusty is so goddamn kissable. I have him, and I want more. He'll always leave me wanting more.

Rusty is pushing me away, telling me to run.

Security is coming, he says.

I need one more kiss.

I steal one more kiss.

And it's the best part of everything.

Chapter 18
Disintegration

Last night, my nightmares retreated.

Instead, the kiss infected my dreams. I lay in my bed with my arm pillowed behind my head, reliving the kiss. How it felt and how it tasted and how he made me feel normal for just a few minutes. How I'd do anything to kiss Rusty again.

The first time I kissed a boy, I was thirteen. He was fifteen. A friend of the family we fondly referred to as a cousin. I hadn't meant to kiss him, but we were wrestling over who got to be first player on *Super Roadcrash Extreme*, and he had me pinned down, his knees on my wrists, and a kiss just felt like the right thing to do. I never told anyone. He made me promise.

I thought I knew all about kissing—until last night. If a kiss like that is possible, if I was allowed to experience a kiss like that, I suppose God must not be too cross with me after all. Not that I'm admitting there's a God. Not that I'm saying there's not. But Emma was right: kissing is better than . . . anything. Everything.

My stomach is rumbling, and I can't remember the last time I ate. Breakfast should be just about over, so I get dressed and climb out of the darkness, walking through the halls with my head down until I get to the cafeteria. I can't be sure that the nurse in the ICU last night didn't report me to security. It's the kind of douche move that a nurse who doesn't know me would definitely make. But it was worth it to kiss Rusty.

It makes me smile to think of him. I'm wearing a smile to match the one Trevor wore.

Arnold is behind the line, scooping out helpings of eggs and chatting with customers. The cafeteria still feels special. The tables and chairs are all back in their places, but the air continues to vibrate with the laughter and love of Lexi and Trevor. I guess I'll need to thank them for demonstrating how happy a person can be. I'm not yet sure that I deserve happiness, but until God gives me a sign to the contrary, I'm going to seize it while I can.

"There are pancakes," Arnold says. He prepares a plate without any guidance from me and passes it under the glass. It's heaped with pancakes and bacon and eggs and some shredded potatoes. I can't eat all of this, but Arnold looks so cheerful. I know there's got to be more to him—a man who seems to own more books than a library and works in a hospital cafeteria—but maybe this is enough. He serves food to people with heartache, and that's all he needs.

"I can't thank you enough for last night," I say. "Trevor—"

Arnold beams. "And what about you? Mr. Steven told me that there is a special young man in your life as well."

Oh, God. My smile is bursting out of my face. My lips are stretched so high and so tight that the corners are going to touch my eyes. It's unbearable. It's awesome. I don't want Arnold to see it, because then Rusty will belong to someone other than me. Right now, he's mine. Steven knows, but Steven doesn't count, not really. But Arnold—Arnold is different. If he knows, he'll claim Rusty, claim us both. But, dammit, I can't help my smile.

"He's the boy with the books," Arnold says. He's not asking; he's piecing together all my steps from the last couple of weeks. I can see him trying to remember every look on my face and every word that I've said so that he can create a picture of Rusty in his mind. And of me.

"Yes," I say, and turn with my tray. "It's not a big deal."

"You're lying," Arnold calls in a singsong voice. He says it so loudly that the few people still in the cafeteria—nurses enjoying their coffee, doctors pretending to look busy, and families of patients trying to keep breathing—look up at me. It's more attention than I want.

"Don't you have some dishes to do?" I ask him as I walk to a table in the corner and set down my overflowing tray of food. When I sit, I glance up at Arnold, but he's gone, replaced by a middle-aged man with a turkey neck and a tattoo of a dragon on his biceps.

While I eat my pancakes, which are surprisingly good, I make up stories about the people in the cafeteria. It's a game that my dad and I used to play when we had a long wait somewhere. It was how I realized I loved telling stories.

"I'm not interrupting, am I?" Aimee, sans hairnet, stands at the table with a tray of food and a question.

"No, sit. I'm a little distracted today."

Aimee smiles. It's a tortured smile, a dress she doesn't get to wear often and isn't sure looks good on her. I could tell her it does, but she wouldn't believe me.

"What you did for your friends last night was nice." She puts her tray down and lowers herself to the chair. Her breakfast consists of an apple, a banana, some cantaloupe, and one lonely strip of bacon.

I lean back, and Aimee freezes, her watery brown eyes watching me, waiting to see what I'm going to do.

"Thanks for helping Arnold."

"I was grateful to have somewhere to be," Aimee says. I don't ask her what she means, because I don't think she'll tell me. She seems happy to eat in silence. I feel like a glutton with my still-full plate of food. I've been eating and eating, and it doesn't even look like I've made a dent.

Aimee is a dainty eater. She keeps her napkin in her lap but refers to it continually. The only thing on her plate she doesn't touch is the bacon, though I catch her staring at it a few times out of the corner of her eye.

"Do you want some of my bacon?" I ask, motioning down at my plate.

"No, thank you," Aimee says under her breath. "You should be nicer to Mr. Jaworski. He thinks of you like a son."

"He's got a son."

"His son is dead." Aimee gnaws the apple, crunching and crunching and crunching until there's nothing left but a browning core and some tiny seeds, which she lays out on the plate like corpses.

I shake my head. "No. You're mistaken. His son is a doctor, or he's going to be a doctor. That's what Arnold said."

"His name was John," Aimee says. "He was going to be a doctor but joined the army instead. He was blown up by a roadside bomb. There weren't enough pieces to identify. When they told Arnold, he had a heart attack and ended up here in the hospital."

I can't wrap my feeble brain around what Aimee's telling me. I think back to Arnold's anger on his son's birthday, how he keeps shoving books his son loved down my throat. I've been such an ass-hole.

"I didn't know."

"Few people do." Aimee pushes her plate away, taking a deep breath.

"You're not going to eat that?" I ask, nodding at her bacon.

"Not today," Aimee says. She lifts her napkin from her lap and carefully arranges it over the strip of bacon. She gets up and leaves the table without uttering another word.

My appetite, like Aimee, has fled.

I gather my tray and put the food into the trash, including Aimee's sad strip of bacon. It seems a shame to waste so much food, but I want Arnold to believe that I ate it. As I'm about to leave the cafeteria, I stop and run behind the line. The new guy doesn't even notice me. Arnold is in the back, up to his elbows in sudsy water.

"You can't be here," Arnold says over his shoulder. "You'll get me in trouble."

"I need to ask you a favor."

"No more favors."

"My friend, with the books," I say. "They're for him. I read to him. Only I'm not sure I'm going to be able to visit as often. So I was hoping, maybe, if you weren't too busy, that you could read to him."

I stop speaking, trying to gauge Arnold's response. He's scrubbing a pot over and over. I bet it's gleaming by now.

"His name is Rusty McHale. He's in the ICU. We're almost done with *Frankenstein*." I turn to leave.

"Drew—" Arnold's still scouring the pot. "Does he like pirates?"

I laugh. "Who doesn't?"

Arnold nods, and I leave. Maybe I don't want to share Rusty with anyone, with Arnold, but maybe that's too selfish of me. He's not mine. He's just a boy. And that was just a kiss. And it might have meant nothing. Or maybe everything. But I get the feeling as I leave the cafeteria and head to Peds that loaning him to Arnold was the right thing to do.

Nurse Merchant shakes her head when I set foot in her ward. "No, sir. No. You can't be here anymore." She's not joking or even smiling. She's right up in my face, yelling at me about kidnapping her patients.

Cho ratted me out.

"I can explain," I say, but Nurse Merchant doesn't want an explanation.

"These kids are sick!" she shouts. "You think you can do whatever you want with them, but they could die. And that would be on you, Andrew. Is that what you want? The only reason I didn't call security is because I know how much you mean to Lexi and Trevor."

I shake my head. "Lexi's fine. And Trevor needed time to fall in love. He's seventeen, and he'll probably be dead soon. Doesn't he deserve it?" When I say the words, I hate myself a little bit. I'll still try to keep my promise, still try to keep Death away from him, but where I should feel hope and determination I only feel dread.

Nurse Merchant purses her lips. The anger she wants to direct at me dies inside her, and she deflates visibly. "You're a good boy, Drew, but you can't do this again." She walks back to her desk and picks up a chart.

"I'm not good," I say, but she's stopped listening to me. And she hasn't forgiven me for taking Lexi and Trevor on a date last night. The goodwill I used to enjoy from Nurse Merchant is used up and gone.

There's a part of me that wants her to punish me. The part of me that doesn't deserve Rusty and needs an avenging angel like Nurse Merchant to come along and set the world right. Boys like me don't get to be happy. That's how it's supposed to be. I'm supposed to suffer in this hospital until the game ends, until long-legged Death finally realizes who I am and takes me away.

So, while I'm waiting for that inevitability, I go to Trevor's room.

Lexi has draped the wig over her IV pole and is dancing with it while Trevor laughs in his bed and her mother rolls her eyes from her chair in the corner. The room is so bright with the sunshine and Lexi that I have to squint. Lexi twirls around the room, dangerously close to becoming entangled in all the tubes and wires. Somehow she manages to stay free. Trevor grabs the edge of her gown and pulls her down to him, peppering her face with kisses, and their love makes the whole damn room glow even more.

They're so . . . happy. No. Yes. Yes, they're happy, but that's not it. They're so . . . *alive*.

Lexi throws down some tickles on Trevor, and he squeals before launching a counterattack. Mrs. Kripke halfheartedly tells them both to settle down and save their strength, but she knows that it's from this, from each other, that they draw their strength. Full stop. Period.

I did that.

And I don't think I can be part of it now.

On quiet feet, I back away from the room and leave the way I came, nodding good-bye to Nurse Merchant. It bothers me to think that I might never return to my friends, but they don't need me anymore. Despite my inadequacies, I seem to have kept my promise to Trevor after all. It doesn't matter whether Death takes him or not. In Lexi, he'll live forever.

Trevor is happy, and Lexi is happy. He's got a future, and she's anchored to the present, and I have no place in either. Not with them.

Mr. Kelly is yelling at the nurses as I make my way to room 1184. "Stop them, Drew! They want to do me in!" He's struggling against three nurses, two of whom are restraining him, while a third attempts to stick him with a needle. They ignore me. I don't look at Mr. Kelly. I walk by, straight into Grandma Brawley's room.

The old broad looks better. Her skin is pinker; her breathing is steadier. She needs only wake to leave. Part of me wants her to get well, to rise up and tell everyone that she has no idea who I am. It would solve all my problems. No more living in the hospital, no more "borrowing" iPods from doctors, no more keeping secrets, no more hiding from Death.

No more Rusty.

Rusty McHale is the one good thing I have. The only thing that belongs to me. And I'm pretty certain that I'm not worthy of him.

"What do you think, Gran?" I ask. "Is it possible for someone to be bad but still have something good in their life? I killed my family—why should I deserve Rusty? Why should I get anything at all?" I wait for an answer that doesn't come. It never, ever comes. Like the owner of that lock of red hair, my answer is somewhere *out there*. I think of her waiting, waiting her whole life, wasting her life waiting for Sandy to come home. And even though it's a fiction that I made up, I still hate her for it. I hate her for waiting for him and leaving me alone.

I don't want to be alone.

"Please, wake up," I beg softly. *"Wake up."* My voice is so small that I doubt she can hear it wherever she is. I sink to my knees and bury my face in the crook of her still, winkled arm. I need her to wake up and tell me that everything is going to be okay. That I won't always have to stand on the outside watching the people I care about die or be happy without me. Like my parents. Like Trevor and Lexi. Like Rusty.

I need it more than air. More than anything. I'm not sure I can go on not knowing.

Because I think Rusty will die if I stay with him. God knows I don't deserve him. Maybe I had it wrong. Maybe the only way to protect Rusty is for me to stay away. Maybe that's why Sandy stayed away from Grandma Brawley. He was like me. He didn't deserve her. So he left and never returned. Sure, she's alive, but is she happy? I don't know, and I need to know, and I cry for forgiveness, and I just want someone to tell me it's all going to be okay.

Father Mike is standing at the door when I lift my head. Snot dribbles down my lip, and my eyes are blurry with tears. He looks as lonely as I feel. Slowly, I rise.

"Sometimes I pray with them," Father Mike says. "Sometimes I pray for them."

I wonder how much Father Mike saw. As the desperate sadness passes, replaced by shame, I wipe my nose with the back of my hand. "She's my grandma," I say.

"No, she's not," Father Mike says. I freeze. "But I'm sure God won't mind you borrowing her."

"Do you really believe in God?" I ask, trying to change the subject.

Father Mike nods. "Today I do." He crosses his arms over his chest, not moving from the doorway. There's enough space for me to squeeze through if I wanted to escape, but doing so would put me uncomfortably within Father Mike's personal space.

"I should . . ."

"Don't leave on account of me."

"I'm not," I say, though clearly I am. Father Mike sucks in his stomach as I pass—a joke, maybe—and I say "bye" as I take off down the hall.

"Drew?" Father Mike calls.

I stop. Turn around.

"It's going to be okay."

He sounds so certain, I almost believe him.

Chapter 19
Berserker Rage

I wait for nightfall on the roof of the parking garage.

It's almost August, and the last swarm of lovebugs swirls around me, their tiny connected bodies a tragedy. They're born, they fuck, they die a horrific death splattered against an uncaring windshield. That's the cycle: The ones we love always die.

One day, I'll die too.

Rusty deserves better than that. He deserves someone who will always be there to catch him when he falls.

I wish I were that person, but I am not.

Arnold is leaving Rusty's room as I stroll through the double doors into the ICU. He's wearing a lazy smile, like the one my father wore after devouring a huge turkey dinner. Nodding as he passes, Arnold doesn't stop to talk to me, and I let him go. I no longer work for him; he no longer needs me.

Steven glances up from the monitors at the nurse's station. His face is unreadable. He doesn't wave or smile or anything before returning to work.

When I walk into Rusty's room, he's sleeping. His chest rises and falls steadily, and his mouth hangs open; a thin ribbon of drool leaks out. I think back to the nights I used to sit with Rusty and read to him. Before Steven. Before I could sit in a chair and be seen. I would wedge myself into the dark space beside his bed and lean my head against the cold metal frame.

"Is he gone?" Rusty asks.

"Arnold?" I say.

"Yeah."

"Yeah."

Rusty moves around above me. The sheets rustle, and the whole contraption shakes. "He showed up out of nowhere insisting that I needed him to read to me. He brought *Beowulf*."

"He works in the cafeteria," I say. "He's the one who gave me the books."

"He's a better reader than you are." Rusty is silent, and then he says, "But I hope that doesn't mean you won't still come."

The naked need in his voice is a baited hook he dangles before me, taunting me, daring me to bite. And I want to so badly.

"They're talking about moving me. Maybe out of the hospital, Drew." Rusty's voice is trembling. The words crumble as he says them, and he struggles to hold them together. "You told me that you wouldn't let them take me. You promised."

I can't see Rusty's eyes, and for that I'm thankful. Yesterday's kiss replays on my lips like a looped video, the memory stronger than reality. My lips want his lips. My hands, his hands. I want him on a quantum level, where we're already entangled. Where what happens to one happens to both.

"I killed my family," I say.

"You already told me that." Rusty shrugs like it's an unimportant fact, like the color of my eyes or something.

My memories are fuzzy because I've done everything I can think of to forget. I don't want them. I've tried to dissolve the details, rearrange the faces, even change the names. But the memories persist. I reach out for them now, because I want Rusty to know the truth. I need him to know the truth.

"I hated my parents, you know?" I say, speaking quickly. "My summer was all planned out. There were parties to go to and beaches to sleep on, and I was all set to volunteer at the busiest fire station in Providence, doing really hardcore shit." Once words begin to spill from my mouth, I can't stop them, or I don't want to. I'm honestly not sure. I only know that I won't stop until Rusty has heard everything.

"Dad surprised us with a vacation to Disney World. We'd make a road trip out of it, he said. A real family adventure. Maybe the last one before I trekked off to college. I tried every excuse to bail, but Dad held his ground and Mom pulled the guilt card. One last vacation with both of her babies, was that too much to ask? I felt like an asshole for hating them, but they were ruining my life.

"That drive felt like the longest hours of my life. We stopped at every cheesy tourist trap along the way. It was twenty hours of fast food and soft rock on the radio and road games, and Cady wouldn't stop singing. The car was this moving metal prison and I just wanted to be there already. Dad got a migraine and asked me to drive. It was that or stay at some bedbug-infested hick motel, and I was more than happy to do anything that got us to the hotel before I strangled someone with a seat belt. After a while, everyone dozed off and it was just me and the moon and a two-lane highway. I swear I only looked at my phone for a second. My friend Jack sent me some pictures from a party. Someone had brought a goat and . . . it doesn't matter. I'd drifted into the other lane and there was a semi. Fucking thing came out of nowhere. I swerved and ran off the road. The car flipped. I mean, I assume it flipped because, when I came to, I was upside down, my face all bloody, my cheek pressed to the roof."

Rusty sits silently, and I pause; my voice is breaking; it's broken. I clear my throat, blink rapidly to keep the tears at bay. *They're someone else's memories*, I tell myself. But that trick doesn't work anymore.

"They were sprawled out on the pavement," I say, swallowing a sob. "I could have saved them. I don't even know how I got them out of the car, but they would have been better off if I'd left them in there. Except for Cady. She was thrown through the windshield and into the ditch. She knew better than to take off her seat belt—I didn't know that she had. I never let her drive with me unless she put it on."

My body heaves with sobs now. They wreck me as I stumble through my memories of that night. I hoped maybe they'd have healed, but they've only festered, become gangrenous. But I can't bear to cut them off. They're mine to live with, my punishment from now until Death takes me, and likely beyond.

Rusty tries to touch me, but I flinch. "You couldn't have saved them," he says.

219

"I could," I whisper.

"It was an accident."

"You don't know," I say. "I trained for this. How to save lives. I . . . I tried to do CPR on Cady, but there was so much blood—she was drowning in it—and I froze. Fell back on my hands and watched her blood leak onto the blacktop. All my training, everything that I knew—and I let her die. I let them all die." I sit up, and I look Rusty right in the eyes, and I say, "Don't you see that I killed them? It was my fault. Everything is my fault."

Rusty shakes his head. "You were scared."

"Was I?"

"Yes!" Rusty says. "Anyone would have been. But you didn't kill them."

"I did," I say. "And if you don't leave, I'll end up killing you, too."

With his burned hand, Rusty strokes the bridge of my nose. He traces the lines of my lips and caresses my cheek. He searches my eyes with his—the hazel is more green than brown tonight. He's trying to find a way to forgive me for something he hasn't any right to forgive.

"You're right," Rusty says finally. "You did kill your parents. And if you let them take me from here, you'll be killing me, too."

"I miss them," I say, ignoring his accusation. "Being grounded for staying out late and the smell of Mom brewing coffee at five in the morning, and the way Cady's hair stuck up like fireworks when she got out of bed, but how she never stopped smiling, not even when she slept. There's a hole in me. A gaping wound. Every part of me misses every part of them. And it never stops hurting." A dry

220

sob shakes my bones, spreading from my chest like an earthquake. "I can't bear the thought of missing you, too."

Rusty is quiet. There are no more accusations. Letting out the truth hasn't healed the wound. That's a myth. Telling Rusty has made it worse. I'm bleeding out all over again.

"In tenth grade, I was so terrified of going to school that I threw up on myself," Rusty says. I'm not sure what he's trying to do, but I haven't the words to stop him. "It happened on the bus. Mrs. St. Charles rolled to a stop at the railroad track and opened the doors. But it was like my body kept going all the way to school, where I knew, I fucking knew, that Jaime Newton and Clive Downs were waiting for me in the locker room.

"I had P.E. first period with Mr. Callow, who believes that competition breeds superiority. It was beat or get beaten in his class."

The way Rusty talks about it is clinical, like how Steven describes a patient: This happened, and then this happened. I'm not sure what I'm supposed to feel, or why he's telling me these things. "Yeah, that's how high school is," I say.

"You sound like my dad." Rusty sneers. His lips shake, and he looks away from me. "But you don't know. Nobody knows. Not until they're covered in their own sick, running down the halls. Until they're the one on the floor, being kicked in the stomach so that the bruises won't show on their face. Until people whisper about them as they walk down the halls and someone paints 'cock gobbler' on their locker on Parents' Night."

Rusty's heart-rate monitor spikes, too fast. "That was my future, Drew. People beating me every second of every day, for the rest of my life. It didn't even have anything to do with being gay. . . . I was just different from them. And that realization, living with the knowledge that I'm always going to be on the receiving end of some asshole's sick, twisted mission to destroy everything and everyone that's not like him . . . it was too much. I couldn't bear it anymore."

"So you threw up?"

Rusty looks at me like he forgot I was here. "Yeah. But it's different in the hospital, with you. I feel . . . almost normal."

I don't know what to say. I swore to Rusty that I wouldn't let them take him, but I think getting away from me is the only way to keep him safe. He's got his parents. He's got Nina. My feelings for Rusty and my duty to keep him alive are at odds.

"About the other night," Rusty says. He's not trembling anymore. He's in control again. "The kiss, I mean."

"What about it?" I ask, wondering if it's the only thing he's been able to think about. The way it has been for me.

Rusty worries the corner of his sheet, the threads beginning to show wear. "Do you like me?"

"Of course I like you," I say immediately, knowing that he's asking more than I'm answering.

"Right," Rusty says. "But do you *like* me?"

I feel like I'm back in fourth grade. Nikki Baker slipped me a note asking if I liked her. She even drew little checkboxes under the question. But Rusty is serious, so I'm serious back.

"Yes," I say. I whisper. And my acknowledgment is a win for the part of me that lives for his smile, but it's a crushing defeat for the part of me that can't bear to see his pain.

"You came to tell me you weren't coming to visit me again, didn't you?"

I nod, unable to speak the words. "I'm bad," I say. "If I stay, bad things will happen."

"What if I don't care? What if I tell you that bad things are going to happen anyway?"

"I don't know." Confusion is a parasite that gorges on my brain. Words fail me.

But Rusty has words for us both. "I didn't mean what I said about you killing your parents," he says. He gulps and his Adam's apple bobs. "I was serious about me, though. If you let them take me away, I'm going to die." He lifts my chin and looks into my eyes. I see me as Rusty sees me. It's not real. I can't be that person. "For a while, I thought I'd be okay with that. Dying, I mean. An end to all pain. But then I met you." He leans forward and paints my lips with his lips. It's never enough.

I think of Trevor and Lexi and how happy they seemed this morning, how they were so alive, and I think—I want to believe—that I can have that with Rusty. But I don't deserve it.

"Rusty, I can't—"

"Let's run away," he says. "We'll leave the hospital together."

I think of Death closing in. Of her long fingers encircling my throat. "Better late than never," she'll say. And then she'll whisk me away like she did my parents, my baby sister Cady.

"I can't leave."

"Your parents aren't here anymore," Rusty says. His kiss is preferable to the harsh punch of his words.

"They're here for me."

"No they're not." Rusty clasps my hand inside his own. Both our palms are sweaty, our fingers grasping tighter than necessary.

"You really want to leave?" I ask. "Together?" I think of the love-bugs. Joined together, drifting on the wind. Their lives short and brutal but meaningful. I think maybe Rusty and I will be like that. Maybe our ends will be swift, but at least we'll be together. We'll go *out there* and face the unknown side by side.

"Yes," Rusty says. I know it's the truest thing he's ever said to me. "We'll run away. Disappear into the world. You and me. Rusty and Drew."

"Drew isn't my real name," I say, and Rusty replies by kissing me so hard that the blowback makes me dizzy. But I grab him behind his neck and kiss him back, our lips, our plans and desires, blurring into one nameless moment. The fire hidden in Rusty's bones flares to life and threatens to consume us, to turn us to ash with our fiery need.

I pull away. "When do we leave?"

"Now," Rusty says. "Let's leave now."

"Yes." I kiss him again. My hands find his hands and his chest and his back. I'm gentle as I touch the bandages, afraid of hurting him. "No," I say.

Rusty pulls back as if I've slapped him.

"We have to make sure that, when we leave, no one can find us." A plan is already forming in my mind. "We'll need money and supplies."

"How long will that take?" Rusty asks. His voice is shallow, panicky. I touch his hand to reassure him.

I try to think it through, but I'm dizzy with the taste of Rusty McHale. "A couple of days," I say. "Give me a week, and then I'll come back for you, and we'll leave together."

Rusty squeezes my hand. "I may not be here in a week. They're moving me."

"Three days," I say. "Hold out for three days and I'll come for you. I promise."

I no longer care whether I'm seen. Doctors and nurses hustle past me as I march toward my destination. The hospital walls breathe shallowly as I pass through them, aware of my plan, aware of my resolve. Once I made the decision to run away with Rusty, everything else ceased to matter. Not Trevor and Lexi, not Arnold or Aimee, not Steven or Jo or sweet, sweet Emma. Not Death. Not even my family. Only Rusty matters now. He and I will leave the hospital and disappear. The two of us together. We'll make our own family.

But before that can happen, I have to erase us. I have to make sure that Death can't follow our trail.

The administrative offices are dark. It's after midnight, and everyone's gone home. I briefly wonder whom Death goes home to. Does she have a husband or a wife or children or cats? Is there anyone who eagerly awaits her return? But those thoughts fade as I step into Death's office. There are more files than last time. Chaotic towers that threaten to tumble. Sheets of paper. People's lives.

The two files I'm looking for are on top of the desk. Prominently displayed. Rusty McHale and Andrew Brawley. She barely knows me and now she has a file on me. It's only a matter of time before she realizes the truth. I swipe the files and tuck them into the waistband of my pants.

I try to leave, but I can't.

This office belongs to the woman who took my family. She

robbed me of Mom's smile and Dad's long-winded speeches and Cady's nonsensical songs. They were my whole world and she stole them.

Miss Michelle.

Death.

I fucking hate her.

I shove the stacks of files, flinging them with all my strength. Papers sail into the air and arc back down, littering the chairs and the floor. My blood rushes in my ears, and adrenaline pumps in my veins, and I feel good. Powerful. I push the computer monitor to the floor, watching the glass pieces shatter and spill over the carpet. Rage takes hold, and I tear her drawers from the desk, raining pencils and pens and coins all around. I uproot the chairs, leave them lying on their sides.

When I'm done, I lean against the door, wheezing, admiring the destruction. And I laugh. Because fuck Death. She wasn't late at all. I was just too smart for her. And I'm too smart for her now.

I kick around the bits and pieces of Death's office until I find a pack of matches. I pull the files out of my pants. I know what my paperwork will say, and I don't want to read the words. But I open Rusty's file, curious.

My eyes are drawn to a highlighted phrase that reads "Injuries inconsistent with victim's account."

I blink, confused. What does that mean?

A flashlight shines down the hallway, and I hear the jingle of keys. I panic and run in the opposite direction. I run all the way up up up to the roof, and I don't stop until I'm there.

The night sky is dark, heavy with clouds. I put the files on the ground and stand over them with the matches. *Injuries inconsistent with victim's account.* I hesitate. But it doesn't matter, does it? Rusty was burned. It doesn't matter how it happened. All that matters is escaping, and leaving no traces behind.

With the acrid smell of sulfur in my nose, I watch our histories disappear. When Rusty and I run away from the hospital, no one will be able to find us.

Not even Death.

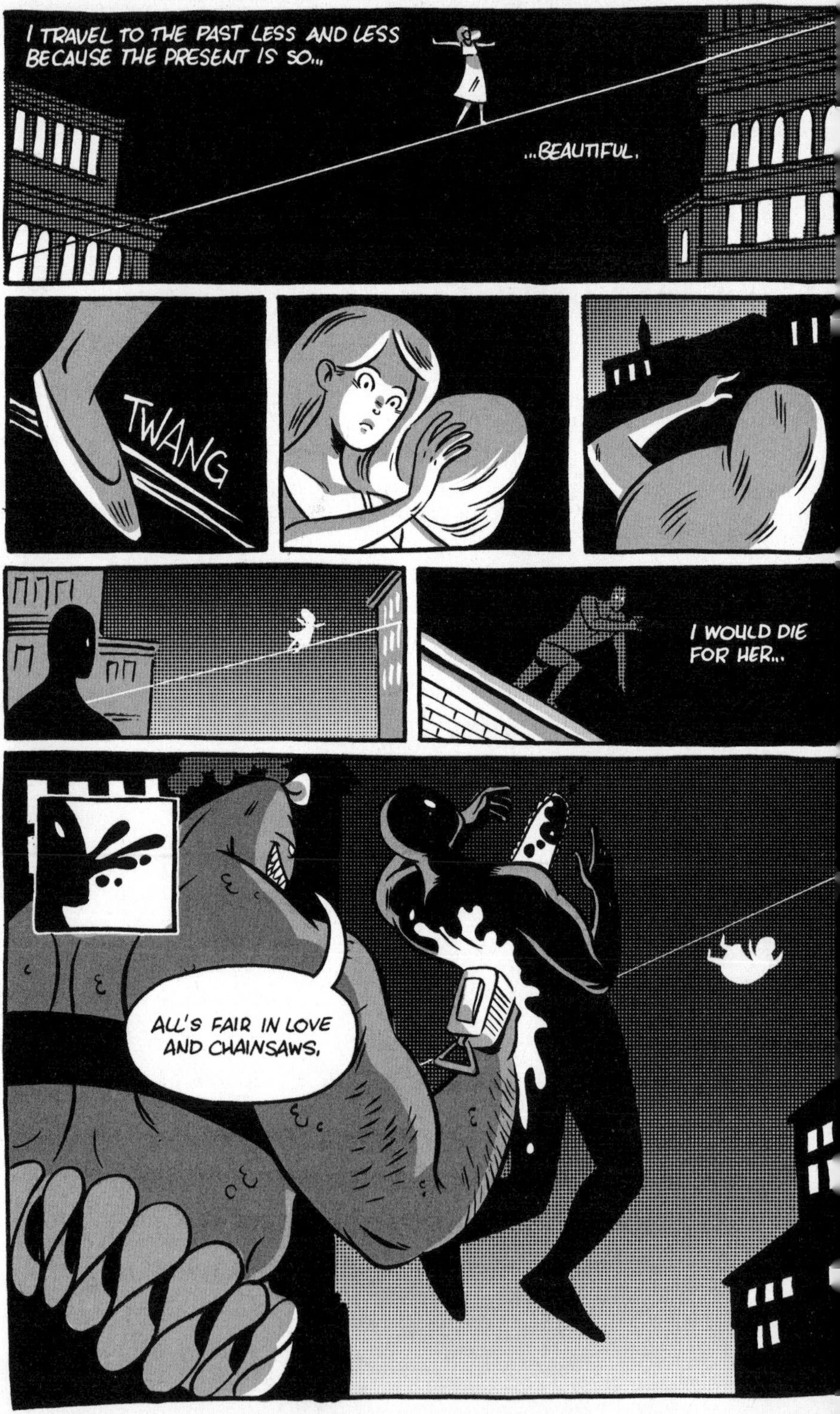
I TRAVEL TO THE PAST LESS AND LESS BECAUSE THE PRESENT IS SO...
...BEAUTIFUL.
TWANG
I WOULD DIE FOR HER...
ALL'S FAIR IN LOVE AND CHAINSAWS.

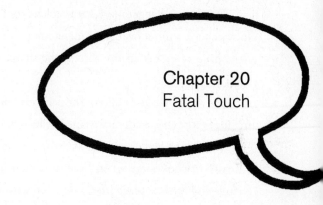

Chapter 20
Fatal Touch

By the end of the second day, I have everything I need.

I don't even call it borrowing anymore. I'm stealing. Outright. The thing is, I don't care. This hospital owes me, and I'm only collecting on that debt.

In the corner of my room are two backpacks filled with clothes, snacks, and music for the quiet nights. My big find was a wallet with four hundred dollars tucked inside. Under normal circumstances, I wouldn't have considered taking it—with all the iPods and clothes I've been hoarding, a wad of cash going missing will definitely raise suspicions—but tomorrow Rusty and I will be long gone.

Not seeing him has taken its toll. My heart beats in time to a rhythm I can't hear, and I think that it must be Rusty beating in the ICU, panicky, waiting to see if I'm going to keep my promise. But visiting him would be too risky. Visiting anyone would be. Instead, I stay in my hideout, drawing Patient F. I imagine a life for him and Ophelia outside of Maligant City. He does catch her, despite the Scythe. Patient F is invincible. He destroys the Scythe and saves Ophelia, and they begin life anew.

Though it's dangerous, I sneak to the roof of the parking garage to watch the sun set over the concrete horizon. The fear of going *out there* makes bile rise in my throat, the sharp acid of it burning my nose.

The world looks so alien. The seconds and hours that made up my life before the accident are faded celluloid, images that melt when I shine light through them. I shake when I think about taking care of Rusty. Fear chokes me when I consider running off and leaving my friends and the one place I feel safe, even with Death stalking me. At least with her I know my enemy.

Out there, my enemy could be anyone. Everyone. Except Rusty.

And that's the thought that anchors me. I'll have Rusty. My constant. Someone to watch my back. There's still a niggling suspicion about the truth behind Rusty's attack, but we can sort that out later. Or never. Who cares? No one will ever hurt him again.

As the sun disappears and night bleeds across the sky, my fear subsides until it's just another memory that I toss into the air, into the breeze that carries the smell of the ocean.

Tomorrow we leave.

I sneak back down, in the direction of my room, but my feet carry me to Peds. One last time. I know I shouldn't risk it, but I want to say good-bye to Lexi and Trevor. Now that they have each other, I'm not worried about them. They are each other's present and future. But I still want to see them, thank them for showing me what happiness could look like, and what it was worth risking.

Nurse Merchant isn't at her station. Instead, there's a small Hispanic woman who doesn't appear to be paying close attention to anything happening around her. I'm able to tiptoe to Lexi's room unseen. I'm working so hard to be careful that I don't notice the lights are out until I turn around.

Lexi's room is pitch black.

"Lexi?" I whisper.

The blinds aren't open. Something is wrong. In all the time that I've known Lexi, she's never closed the blinds. Not once, day or night. Not even when she changed clothes. She didn't want to shut out the world for one single second.

"Lexi!" I yell, not caring that the nurse will hear me. Not caring that Death may come for me. Not caring, not caring, not caring. Where's Lexi?

I stumble toward the light switch and jab it with my hand. The lights flicker and illuminate the empty bed, the sheets turned over and rumpled. Lexi's wig is still hanging over the back of a chair, and her SAT prep books are stacked on the table by her bed, and there's even a little bear nestled against the pillow that I'd bet my four hundred dollars Trevor bought her.

But Lexi's not here.

"Where the hell is Lexi?" I scream at the nurse, but she's on the phone now, staring at me with wide, scared eyes. She should be scared. I'll tear this ward apart if someone doesn't take me to Lexi now.

Each terrifying beat could be the one that causes my heart to explode as I imagine all the horrible places Lexi could be. I lean against the wall. It holds me up, saves me from crashing to the floor. My feet are useless now. Stupid, stupid feet.

"Droopy?"

Trevor ambles down the hall, blood from where his IV should be dripping off his fingers. Disconnected tubes dangle from his body. The nurse drops the phone and rushes to him, but he pushes her away with strength he shouldn't have. He stumbles to me and punches me in the stomach so hard that I double over, gasping for breath.

"She's gone!" he screams at me.

"Trevor?" I wheeze. His words confuse me. "Gone? Gone where? Home? Thank God. I thought—" I rub my stomach, trying to breathe. I'm not certain what I did to deserve that punch, but Trevor must have had a reason—

"Drew . . ."

The nurse runs back to the phone, and I know I need to leave before security—or worse—arrives to apprehend me. "I just came to say good-bye to both of you. You'll tell her for me, right?"

Tears bleed from Trevor's eyes. His lip trembles, and I can't believe he's getting this emotional just because I'm leaving. "She's gone, Drew. Lexi is gone."

"I know. You already told me."

"Dead," Trevor says. "Lexi's dead."

And I die too. Right here, right this second. Dead. I'm still breathing, still beating, still standing and talking, but dead. Except I'm not standing anymore. I'm on my knees. Pain rips through my legs, but it belongs to someone else.

Trevor's saying, "She's dead. Fuck, Drew, she's fucking dead," but the voice is someone else's and not Trevor's, and I scream back: "Stop saying that! If you say that again, I'll rip out your goddamn throat!"

Nurse Merchant materializes with her hand on my back, whispering "I tried to find you" in her soothing, maternal voice, but the words are so far away. So far. She tries to pull my arm around her shoulders and lift me, but the density of my grief glues me to the floor.

"Lexi's dead," Trevor says again. I lunge at him, fists swinging. He stumbles back, sobbing and trying to catch my wrists. I collapse to the floor again, crying. Sobbing.

And I see Death. "You did this," I yell. "You took her!" I scream. Death hovers in the air a few feet away from me, her black cape billowing in the foul, chill wind that sweeps through Peds. She's come for me like she came for Lexi. She's going to reap me, take my soul and lock it away.

"You can't have me," I say. "You had your chance."

Before anyone can stop me, I leap to my feet and run. I hear them chasing me, but I know this hospital inside and out. They'll never find me. Never.

Chapter 21
Resurrection

Death doesn't play by the rules.

It's almost three in the morning. For the last few hours, I've been hiding in the wardrobe of some woman who's on a respirator, trying to keep quiet, trying to keep still. Wondering how everything went so wrong.

Lexi wasn't supposed to die. It was supposed to be Trevor. Always Trevor. Not Lexi. She was the one who was going to leave and take on the whole bloody world. Tear it apart block by block and rebuild it better. It's who she was and who she wanted to be. This shouldn't have happened.

I have to know why.

Carefully, I crawl from the wardrobe and gesture a silent thank-you to the unconscious patient in the bed for granting me sanctuary. Moving around the hospital is going to be tricky now that everyone is looking for me. I could see it in Death's eyes earlier. She knew who

I was. I was the soul she'd lost, the one she was hunting. There would be no more guessing and no more games. She would find me and take me and put an end to it all. To me.

The hospital is quietest now. Doctors are catching what little sleep they can. Nurses are joking and finishing up paperwork and mainlining IV bags of coffee to keep dreams at bay for a few more hours.

I steal a pair of scrubs from a bin and put them on over my jeans and T-shirt. I keep my head down and walk. Not fast, not slow. Purposefully. As if I know where I'm going.

And I do. I know where I'm going. I was here once before. Once. That night. I didn't mean to see them. I only wanted to take those things that belonged to me. But they were there, and they were saying the most horrible things to me, and I swore that I'd never return.

Yet here I am. Standing before the cold metal doors. There are two tiny windows at eye level. I peer through to see if I'm alone.

I am. Alone.

I stand at those doors until the rest of the world turns to dust around me, until nothing is left except me and the doors and my fear of what awaits me behind them.

When I push them open, dead air rushes out like I've broken a hermetic seal. The morgue smells like iodine. A chemical bath of disinfectant. Not like the ER, where you can smell the mingling odors of the patients. The bodies here carry nothing of their former lives with them. They're scrubbed clean of *out there*.

The morgue is quiet but for a murmuring sound that reminds me of a typewriter. It's so low that I barely notice it, but it's there. A staccato whisper in my ear.

A table crouches in the middle of the room, and my friend lies upon it. She's the only body in the room tonight. Last time, there were three bodies. Two and a half, really. Now it's only Lexi. She's draped with a white sheet that tents at her toes and her breasts and her forehead, draping down to hug the rest of her body like first snow.

My feet are cemented a yard from the body. My eyes glued to the two fingertips of her left hand that are dangling from under the sheet. They're pale, more pale than Lexi had ever been in real life.

There are no windows down here. No way for her to see the sun or the skyline or the future. Her future. This is her future. A body and a box and a plot in the ground where Mrs. Kripke can visit and leave flowers, whisper story after story about her bygone days as a beauty queen. My only solace is that Lexi no longer has to worry about disappointing her mother. Lexi will always be a beauty queen now.

"Hey, Lexi," I say. My voice sounds cavernous in this room. It bounces off the body-size refrigerators lining the wall. "I'm so sorry." It's a stupid thing to say, and I don't know why I say it. She can't hear me or accept my apology. She doesn't even know she's dead.

"That's what you think, A-Dog." Lexi sits straight up, and the sheet falls into her lap. She's naked, with a gruesome Y-shaped incision that begins at her shoulders, meets at her sternum, and continues down her belly, where it disappears under the sheet. It's a bloodless wound but puckered where the skin was stapled back together.

For some reason, this doesn't shock me. I'm relieved, really. "Lexi?"

"In the flesh," she says. "Sort of." When she speaks, her mouth doesn't move. Her eyes are pasty and white, and she stares through me rather than at me. "It was a blood clot, before you ask."

"It was my fault," I say.

Lexi laughs, but it's a hollow, sick laugh that makes me want to puke. "Yeah, Drewfus, you caused the clot that killed me." She's quiet.

I shake my head. I want to run. Coming here was a terrible, terrible idea. "I should have prayed for you. Protected you from Death the way that I protected Trevor."

"Trevor's going to die too," Lexi says.

"I saw him earlier," I say. "He's okay. I think he's okay."

Lexi rolls her white eyes. "Not tonight, not tomorrow night. But eventually, Trevor is going to die. Like you. Like Rusty. Like everyone. Suck it up and deal."

"This isn't happening," I say.

"I think I was wrong about all that God stuff, you know," Lexi says. "I think I was wrong about a lot of things. But not about you, Drewfus. Never about you."

"I have to leave." I try to back away, but I can't move. "Let me go."

"You're so dumb," Lexi says. "Stupid, stupid, Andrew. Except, that's not your real name. I know everything now, including that."

"What do you want?"

"I want you to leave."

"I'm trying!"

"This hospital," Lexi says. "Leave tonight. Walk out the doors, into the world, and be afraid but be alive. Of us all, you're the only one who ever could."

I cover my face with my hands, trying to cry, trying to scream, trying to do anything that will break me free of whatever spell she's cast. Nothing works. I end up stepping even closer to her, my legs and feet beyond my control. "Fuck you for saying that. You don't know what's out there."

"But I know what's in here," Lexi says. "You've been here for so long, Drew, but your family's death was not your fault. My death is not your fault. Stop punishing yourself for living and start living."

I sink to my knees and feel Lexi's cold hand on top of my head. "Everyone I love is here." I look up. Lexi is staring down at me, staring down through me.

"No. They're not. Your parents aren't here. Your sister's not here. I'm not here. Soon, Trevor and Rusty will be gone too." Lexi's body shudders and her lip quivers. "If you don't leave, you'll be the only one left. Trapped here forever. All alone."

"I hate you," I say to her. But she's just a body under a sheet, and I'm just a boy on his knees who can't stop crying.

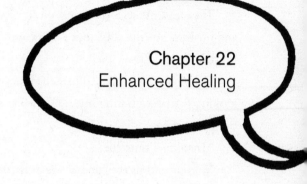

Chapter 22
Enhanced Healing

On the third day, I rise.

My mind is blank, consumed by the horror of Lexi. Destroyed by my own hubris. That I could ever leave this hospital, that I could ever live outside the walls, was folly. I'm no hero, no savior. I'm nothing but a boy, not even a man. A nameless coward who killed his family and hides from Death. Who brought Death to others instead of facing her myself.

This hospital isn't my purgatory. It's my hell. The punishment I deserve. I will stay here until the end of my days. Until the sun finally sets. Until the worms rise up and devour me. Until Death extends her long-fingered hand and drags me away.

At dawn, I go to the ER to see Emma and Jo. Steven is absent, replaced by a faceless man who looks at me with exhausted eyes before returning to his book.

"Boy, you are in it deep, aren't you?" Jo crushes my face to her chest, and I try to suffocate myself. My arms hang limply at my sides, unable to hug her back.

"Sweetie," Emma says. "We heard about *everything*." I don't know what version of the truth Death has told them, nor do I care.

They lead me to a stool and push me onto it. My knees bend, and my butt hits the vinyl, but I don't rest. "She's dead," I say. "Lexi. I didn't say good-bye."

Emma hugs me. She still smells like sugar cookies. "Police are looking for you," Emma says. "We won't mention you were here, but . . . maybe . . ."

"Thanks," I mumble.

"Steven told us the funeral was yesterday," Jo says. "He tried to find you."

I chuckle at the thought of Steven roaming the hospital, looking for me. Sometimes he gets lost in his own pants. Then I think about Mrs. Kripke alone at Lexi's grave, crying into her handkerchief, her giant hair unflappable in the wind, her makeup running down her cheeks like pats of half-melted butter.

I want to throw up.

"Drew?" Emma asks. She rubs my back and tries to get me to look her in the eyes, which I refuse to do. My body feels electrified, like I swallowed a ball of lightning and trapped it under my rib cage.

"I killed my parents," I say.

Jo turns from me. "I'm sure that's not true," she says.

"Jo's right," Emma says. "You're just not capable of anything like that."

I look up at Emma and Jo, and I want to believe them. I want to believe anything, but I think they're only patronizing a poor pathetic boy because they can't think of anything honest to say. I doubt they know who my parents were. "I wasn't here," I say, and leave.

The hospital halls are blossoming with the sun—growing weedy with doctors and interns and nurses—and my time is running out. Death will be patrolling the halls soon, and I need to return to my self-imposed prison. I stop at Peds and walk past Nurse Merchant, who's fresh on the job. She looks subtracted without Lexi. It's not one thing in particular, instead it's a sense of loss that ghosts her movements as if she's misplaced something valuable but can't recall what it was. I wait until her back is turned to sneak into Trevor's room.

Trevor is standing when I enter. On his own. No wires or tubes connect him to the hospital. His blinds are open, and he's staring out the window, resting his forehead on the glass, which I imagine is warm. He's wearing street clothes that hang so loosely on his body, they look like a scarecrow's hand-me-downs.

"Droopy," Trevor says. His eyes glimpse the reflection of me and then turn back to *out there*.

"Trevor."

Our hearts aren't in this. Our hearts belonged to Lexi, and she took them both when she died.

"You go to the funeral?" Trevor's voice is dead, but his body alive. The change is shocking. It was always the other way around.

I shake my head. "No. You?"

"My doctor wouldn't sign me out," Trevor says. "What's your excuse?" There's acid on his tongue. He's spitting venom, and I deserve it.

"No excuse."

"Figures."

Trevor and I stand in his room, he by the window and me by the door, trying to talk—and failing. I don't think either of us ever realized how real Lexi was, how she was the subject we talked about most. She was the glue, the dark matter. The miracle you can't see but which binds all things. Lexi was that. And more.

"I'm sprung," Trevor says. He turns around and eyeballs the blue duffel bag on his bed. The sketch I drew for him sticks out of it. There's not much else: some clothes and the decorations from his very special day. That seems so long ago now.

I whistle halfheartedly. "They're letting you out?" Trevor nods but doesn't look me in the eyes. "And the cancer?"

"Remission, supposedly." He shrugs and looks down at his arms, which are scarred and bruised, but whole. He's whole and new, and his entire life is spread out in front of him. But he's hesitant. He's alone, and I don't think he knows how to go on without Lexi.

Neither do I.

"That's awesome," I say.

"Yeah." Trevor walks around the bed to the wardrobe and pulls out the last of his clothes. I spy the outfit he wore when we played hockey on the roof. He ignores it and closes the door. "I'm supposed to start school in a couple of weeks. I should have done my homework like Lexi. . . ."

The picture of Trevor from before the cancer still stands by his bedside. "You going to play ball?"

Trevor shakes his head. "I'll never be that guy again." He notices me staring at the picture, and he picks it up and shoves it in the bag, crumpling the drawing. "You should have gone to the funeral. She loved you so much."

"I'm sorry."

"The fuck you're sorry," Trevor says. His voice is a sucker punch. "You're a fucking liar is what you are." He grabs the duffel bag and throws it at my head, but it flies wide and hits the wall. "Shit."

I chuckle. "So, not the quarterback?" Trevor shakes his head. "She liked it," I say. "That you were a football player. Thought it was hot."

"I was the kicker," Trevor says. "The guy who comes in to kick field goals and extra points. I barely saw an entire hour of actual play." His face is caught between embarrassment and anger.

"She wouldn't have cared." I pick up the bag, but it's open and the contents spill out. I recognize the wig immediately and pull it out. "Did you steal this from her room?"

Trevor practically leaps over the bed to snatch it back, but I hold it over my head, just out of his reach. He's breathless and falls into a chair. He mutters, "Asshole," and then, "Her mom freaked looking for it. Claimed that one of the nurses stole it."

"Dude! Seriously?"

"Mrs. Kripke was going to return it to the shop. Like it was just some dress that didn't fit, know what I mean?"

I toss the wig on the bed and retrieve the rest of his things from the floor. "There's something deeply twisted about you keeping that."

Trevor drags the hair into his lap and twines a lock around his finger. "I wanted something to remember her by."

"What're you going to do with it? Trot it out whenever you need a good whiff? Take it to college and Europe and your first apartment? Maybe you can get your future wife to wear it on your honeymoon."

"Maybe," Trevor says, defensively. "Anyway, fuck you, Droopy. You didn't even go to her funeral. I wanted to say good-bye, but I couldn't. You could and didn't. So unless you're buying me dinner, get off my ass."

"I'm sorry."

"No you're not."

"I want to make this right," I say.

"Yeah? Then how about you go back in time and make me never love her, you fucking prick. I was content. You made me love her. You made it real. And now she's fucking gone." Trevor turns to the window to hide his tears, but his shaking shoulders give him away.

"Trevor . . ."

"Go," he says, his voice rough. "My parents will be here soon, and the doctor will sign me out. You'll never see me again."

It's clear that I've done enough harm, and I turn to leave, but an idea takes root in my brain. Turning back time isn't in my skill set—I'm not Patient F—but I'm not totally useless.

"Meet me on the roof in ten minutes, Trevor."

"I can't."

"You're going to live," I tell him. "You can do anything you want."

Trevor's heavy-lidded eyes narrow and his lip curls in disgust. He'd like nothing more than to throw me through the window and dance on my broken bones. But he says, "Ten minutes, Droopy. Then I'm out of here for good."

"Okay," I say. "And, Trevor—bring the hair."

Trevor is standing at the edge of the roof, at the site of our one brilliant hockey game, peering into the nothing below when I arrive with Father Mike. The weather is clear, and a breeze blows in the ocean air from the east. It's exactly the kind of day that Lexi would have loved if she'd ever been able to detach herself from her books.

"You said ten minutes." Trevor balls his fist and takes a step toward us.

"I had to get someone." I point at Father Mike.

Father Mike mops his sweaty brow with a tissue that he slides into his sleeve when he's finished with it. "My fault," he says. "Though I'm not sure why." Convincing Father Mike to come without offering him a reason was difficult, as he was reluctant to leave his chapel unattended, but I told him that God would mind the shop in his absence and that I needed him.

"You brought a priest?" Trevor asks.

I shrug.

Father Mike shakes his head. "I'm Father Mike. You must be Trevor."

"How do you know my name?" he asks.

"Because I told him how crap you are at wheelchair hockey," I say. "He's a friend, Trevor."

Trevor eyes Father Mike up and down, trying to decide what to make of him. The pair of them are watching me, waiting for me to tell them why the heck I brought them here. My idea, which had seemed so clever in Trevor's room, feels a little morbid now, but I plow onward because I think Lexi would have approved.

"We're here to honor Lexi," I say. "To give her a proper funeral."

"You're crazy," Trevor says. "Nuts, bonkers, out of your fucking skull." He glances at Father Mike. "Sorry."

Father Mike chuckles and slaps Trevor on the back, as if they're old pals. "No worries, young man. I agree. This is bizarre. We haven't got a body."

I point at the wig in Trevor's hand. "We have her hair."

Trevor holds up the wig. "What? No."

"Lexi wouldn't want you carrying around fake hair for the rest of your life, Trevor." I hold out my hand, hoping that he'll turn over the wig willingly.

He holds up the hair and turns it around and around. Then he gazes back over the edge of the roof. "We were going to take a trip to Canada together."

"Canada?" I ask.

"Yeah, Droopy. Canada." Trevor's voice is rough and raw, and he hasn't let go of the hair. "Lexi told me that ever since she was a little girl, she wanted to visit. Now she'll never go."

Father Mike stands at the edge with Trevor. I join them and look down. One jump from here would probably kill us, and it would definitely hurt. "In heaven, you can visit any country you want."

Trevor clears his throat, and I wait for him to speak. I feel like I shouldn't say anything. "I was supposed to be the one to die. It was always supposed to be me. Isn't that fucked up, Father? Why'd God let that happen?"

Father Mike pulls a small Bible out of his pocket and holds it in front of him like a shield. "It's not your fault. It's nobody's fault."

Trevor glances at me. It's a knowing look. A bond over shared guilt. Shared love of an amazing girl.

"But why?" Trevor asks. "Why'd I get better when I should have died, and she died when she was supposed to be fine?"

"No one can know the mind of God," Father Mike says. "We have to trust that he knows what he's doing."

"Bullshit," I say.

Father Mike glares at me, but he doesn't reprimand. He knows that Trevor and I are beyond his ability to punish. "I like to think of God as an exceptionally smart scientist."

"Like Stephen Hawking?" Trevor asks.

"Yes," Father Mike says. "Now, I comprehend very little of what those scientists say, and I like to consider myself a smart man. But I trust that they know what they're talking about. And when they do things that scare me, like turn on a device that could potentially create tiny black holes capable of destroying the world, I have to have faith that those scientists have everything under control."

Trevor laughs. "Your priest is awesome."

"But they don't always," I say, when Trevor is done laughing. "Sometimes scientists get it wrong."

"Maybe," Father Mike says. "Or maybe they're simply so much smarter than we are that we can't fully understand their actions." Father Mike closes his eyes and turns his face toward the sun. "I see puppies and rainbows and bacon cheeseburgers, and I think, 'Gee, that God sure knows what he's doing.' Then things happen, like your friend Lexi dying, and it's tougher to trust his plan. But that's what faith is."

Trevor looks guilty. He shoves the hand not holding the wig into his pocket and stares over the edge. "Does that mean I'm supposed to be all happy that I lived and Lexi died? Because I can't. Because it sucks."

Father Mike sighs and takes the wig from Trevor. At first, Trevor doesn't want to surrender it, but he eventually does. "It means that those of us who are left behind have to live the best lives we can. Mourn her, but move on. Celebrate her by being great."

The words sting because I know that they're not aimed solely at Trevor. I can't think about anything but him right now. I'm here for him. For Lexi. "We should do this," I say, motioning to the wig in Father Mike's hand.

"You're not like any priest I've ever met," Trevor says.

"You're not like any cancer patient I've ever met."

"Cancer-free," Trevor says.

Father Mike grins from ear to ear. "Good for you. Now you have no excuse not to clean up that potty mouth of yours."

"What do we do?" I ask. I feel like maybe I shouldn't even be here. That Lexi was Trevor's and he loved her and I could have gone to her real funeral if I hadn't been a selfish jerk. But then Trevor smiles at me, like old times. "I don't know what religion Lexi was."

"She didn't believe in any of that supernatural crap," Trevor says.

I glance up at Trevor. "She changed her mind at the end." He gives me a curious look but doesn't ask how I know that, how I *could* know that. He just smiles.

"Her mom was Baptist."

Father Mike nods and says, "I think I can handle this." He

places the wig on the ledge and steps back. The gentle breeze stirs the strands, but it's not strong enough to dislodge it from its perch.

"We come here today to honor Lexi. . . ."

"Kripke," Trevor says. "Alexis Kripke." He frowns and wrinkles his brow, and he grips his temples, rubbing his scarred fingers over his stubbled scalp. "I don't know her middle name. I never asked. I don't know." He sheds tears and shakes with every breath he draws.

I pull Trevor to me and let him bury his face in my chest. "It's not important," I tell him. "You knew the stuff that mattered. Like that she loved you."

"And that she actually kind of enjoyed all that beauty-queen stuff," Trevor says. He sniffles. "She'd never tell her mom, though."

"She loved to eat honey out of the jar with her fingers."

"The first time she got her period, she was so afraid to tell her mom that she rode her bicycle to the store and asked some old lady in the deli to help her buy tampons."

These things make me laugh. With Trevor. For Lexi. For what a crazy, amazing, smart, and beautiful girl she was. I nod at Father Mike to continue.

Father Mike coughs and says, "We come here today to mourn the passing and honor the life of Alexis Kripke."

Trevor pulls himself together and faces the wig. He holds my hand, and we face it together.

Father Mike reads some verses from the Bible, some that I remember hearing when I was a kid and some that I've never heard before but that are soothing. I'm not sure if the Bible is a real book written by God or just a collection of stories for people who need help putting their hearts back together, but it's comforting, and I try not to think about it. Father Mike doesn't speak for too long. When he finishes, he smiles at Trevor.

"Lexi rocked," Trevor says. "She was smart and special, and she kissed liked whoa." He grins when Father Mike groans. "Lexi saw me for me. She didn't see my disease or the fact that I weighed less than she did. She saw *me*. She saw everyone, really. She saw right to the heart of who a person was and never judged them. Even Drew. She used to tell me that he was special. Broken but special, and that one day we'd never see him again because he'd finally gone out into the world to do something great. I always laughed, but I think she was right. She was always right.

"I think I loved that girl." Trevor looks at the wig and then out to the sky. "That's it."

I lean over and whisper, "I think she loved you, too." When I take Trevor's place, I don't know what to say. The wind is picking up a little, and I wonder if Lexi is up there or *out there* listening to us, watching us, waiting for us to move on. "I'm so sorry," I say.

"It wasn't your fault," Father Mike says.

"Not for that."

"Then for what?"

"For not doing something great."

Father Mike, Trevor, and I stand in a semicircle around the hair. It's the ugliest wig I've ever seen, but it was so Lexi. The way her mother chased her around her hospital room, trying to force it on Lexi's bald scalp. I think she would appreciate this. "You ready?" I ask, pulling the matches out of my pocket.

"May I?" Trevor asks. I hand him the matches. He takes a deep breath and marches up to the wig. He drags the match along the strike strip and watches it flare to life. He cups the tiny, fragile flame in his hand and says, "Bye, Lexi. See you in Canada." He tosses the match into the hair. The wig catches instantly, like a miniature flaming heart of God. The strands blacken and curl while sooty black cinders float away in the wind, toward the ocean.

Soon there's nothing left of the wig but the cap and some ash. I push the remains over the side, into *out there*, where they belong.

"I have to go," Trevor says. "My parents are probably freaking."

I offer Trevor my hand, and he shakes it. "Be great," I say to him. "For her."

Trevor nods and walks away. I know that I'm never going to see him again, and I think that's okay.

Father Mike rests his hand on my back. "I meant what I said about letting go and living."

When Trevor's gone, I look up at him and say, "People like me don't get second chances."

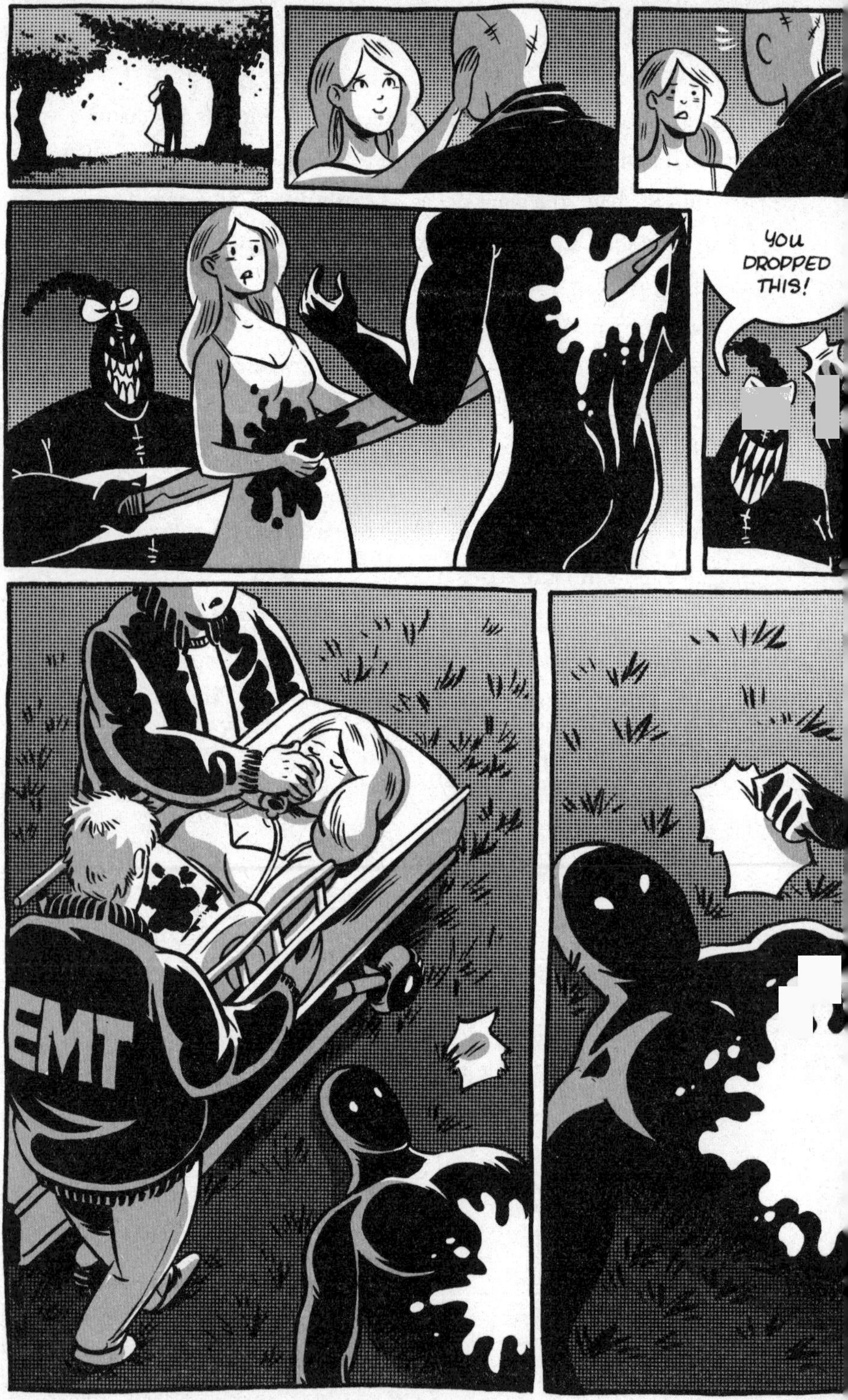

YOU DROPPED THIS!
EMT

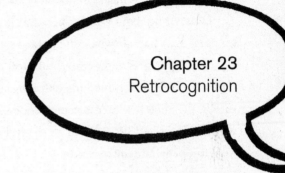

Chapter 23
Retrocognition

Without Trevor and Lexi, the hospital feels infinitely smaller.

I take satisfaction in knowing that Trevor is *out there*, going on. Living and doing all the things that people are supposed to do. I wish that Lexi were out there so they could face life together, but if my time in this hospital has taught me anything, it's that we so rarely get what we want. If Trevor survives long enough, he'll find a new girl, fall in love, and live happily with her. She won't be Lexi, but no girl could be. Not even the wig could have changed that.

I lose track of time in my unfinished prison. I only leave my filthy makeshift mattress to relieve myself. The pain is too much. My nightmares weave through reality until I am Patient F, on the table, surrounded by the doctors in red lab coats, screaming as they take me apart one limb at a time. When I wake in the dark, the nightmares don't recede. I seek comfort in my memories, but they are tarnished now. I've let everyone down. Trevor, Lexi. Rusty. He's gone by now, I'm sure of it. I was supposed to run away with him days ago. But I couldn't go. I don't deserve to escape. I thought that hell awaited me *out there*, but hell is here, around every corner.

I was wrong about Death. She wasn't late to get me; she was right on time. She's had me where she wanted me all along.

The nightmares never cease, and I feel myself being reassembled into something new, something unfeeling and impenetrable that can survive the nuclear winter to come. Not even my memories of Rusty, with his heart and his lips and all the feelings he has locked inside him, can penetrate my new skin.

Except, I think about him in that bed, waiting for me. Waiting for me to rescue him, thinking I'd abandoned him, that I'd let his parents take him away. And I realize that I owe Rusty an explanation so that he can move on. It's the least I can do.

The hospital is bustling, so I don't try to not be seen. I become part of the massive flow of characters running, walking, pacing, through the maze of hallways. People see me, but their eyes slide past because I'm not unique; I'm no one special. They see the old sketch of me that's been circulating the hospital while I was hidden away but don't connect it to the wretched creature in their midst. In that way, I am invisible. Not that I even care anymore. I focus on finding a phone so that I can get Rusty's number and call him. Try to explain why I didn't come.

"Drew?"

A hand grabs at my sleeve as I pass by. I keep going until the voice registers in my brain as familiar. I turn. Nina is sidestepping a wheelchair to get to me, her face a mess. Blotchy, red, her eyes are bruised and set deep. She's wearing clothes that don't match: capri-length jeans and a pink T-shirt with a black belt.

"Nina? What are you doing here?"

She yanks me around, drags me along behind her. Her steps are stony, wrathful. The click-clack damning me. We stop in a cold waiting room I've never waited in. There is only a small elderly woman here, clutching a tote bag full of green yarn.

"Where the hell have you been?" Nina asks. Her voice is an acerbic hiss.

"Lots of places," I say. She didn't know Lexi. Didn't know of her. The details won't make sense to her the way they will to Rusty. "I was going to see Rusty. Is he still here? You have to take me to him."

Nina crosses her arms over her chest, then drops them by her side, then crosses them again. Her eyes dart everywhere but won't meet my eyes. "He waited for you," she says. "When the doctors tried to move him out of the ICU so he could begin his physical therapy, he screamed. Rusty told them how much pain he was in. That bought him two more days."

"Two more days for what?" I ask, though I know the answer. My voice and tone are snappish because it's easier to be annoyed with Nina than admit how guilty I feel that Rusty waited and waited for me and faked being ill so that he could wait longer.

Nina sneers. "At first, I thought you were good for Rusty. He deserved to be happy and you made him happier than I'd ever seen him."

"I tried, I really did, but—"

"Well, he's dead, thanks to you." Nina says it quickly. The words have no spaces. They have no meaning. I look at her lips to match the shape of the words to the sounds that come out of her mouth because I simply cannot believe what I heard.

Blood stops circulating through my body. I feel it leave my face as I fall. Nina doesn't catch me, and I smack into the wall so hard that it feels like my cheek has shattered like an eggshell. I'm no longer attached to my body. The energy of me hovers over the meat sack I once inhabited, and I see the whole world, all time. Everything is spread before me like an ocean of laughter and madness and events that mean so little without context.

Rusty is the context that gives my life meaning. And Nina says he's dead.

"Are you okay?" Nina pulls me to my feet. I allow her to lead me to a seat across from the old woman, who is interested in neither her knitting nor us. My cheek throbs, and I wince when Nina touches it. "That's going to bruise badly."

"Rusty?"

Nina shakes her head. "He told me to tell you that he was dead. He said you deserved it." Her shoulders shake, and her lip twitches before the tears roll down the sides of her nose. "He was destroyed when you didn't show up."

My stomach drops. "But he's alive?"

"Yes," Nina says, sniffling and wiping her nose with the back of her hand. She snorts with a little laugh. "He is sick, though. Isn't that stupid? He faked it for two days and then developed a real infection, like his body was creating the reality to back up his lie."

"Nina, what the fuck happened?"

She loses her sad smile and glares at me. I know what she's

thinking: I have no right to demand anything from her. Or from Rusty. I don't need her to tell me that this is all my fault.

She sighs. "Rusty didn't tell me about your plan right away, only that you were supposed to come and that he couldn't leave without you. But I'm no idiot. He had a packed bag in his wardrobe, and he asked that man, the one from the cafeteria, to bring him a couple of books."

"Arnold."

"Yes," Nina says. "That's him. He reads to Rusty every day."

"Tell me Rusty is okay," I say to Nina. "Tell me." My cheek throbs in time with my rabbit heart, but I'm beyond pain.

Nina looks up at the old woman to see if she's listening to us, but that old woman hasn't so much as twitched since we arrived. "It was the day before yesterday. Rusty's parents were worried about him. He kept going on and on about how much pain he was in. They were hoping to get him out of the ICU so that he could begin putting all this behind him." Nina shivers. "Andrew, you should have seen how terrified he was. They haven't caught the boys who did it or made any arrests. The principal made a statement to the newspaper about bullying and doing everything they could to keep Rusty safe, but that's bullshit, and everyone knows it. School safety is a joke."

My heart is breaking inside my chest. I spin back through time until I'm standing by Rusty's bedside, watching him squirm and beg to be allowed to stay in the hospital so that he won't have to go back to school, while his parents and the doctors and the principal all tell him that he's going back, that he's going to be safe, even though they all laugh behind their hands with the knowledge that the bullies will get him, beat him, before the end of day one. I watch Rusty lie in the dark, long into the night, as he dreams up ever more disturbing ways for the bullies to torment him. In his nightmares, they resurrect medieval devices that stretch him and tear him into pieces and uncoil his meaty insides. He waits for me to come, waits for me to rescue him from the cruel hands of his foes, but I don't come, and he falls into despair.

"I'm not sure when the fake pain became real," Nina says, "but he developed an infection in his leg." She closes her eyes and tries to take a deep breath. "His doctors say he's not responding to the antibiotics, and they might have to amputate before it spreads."

"Where is he?" I ask, knowing that I have to see him.

It's like she doesn't hear me anymore. "He's not even fighting. He's given up. That's your fault, Drew . . . or whatever your name is. Rusty cared about you, and when you didn't show up he stopped caring about anything."

I grab Nina by the wrist. Her bones are iron. She's made of sterner stuff than even Patient F. "Where is he, Nina?"

"Still in the ICU. But you'll never get to him now. They've stationed a security officer outside his door."

I get up to leave, but Nina pulls me back down. "This is my fault, you know," she says.

"It's not." I narrow my eyes at her. "I told him I'd come, and I didn't." I don't bother explaining the reasons for my absence to Nina because she doesn't care about me or my feelings, only about Rusty.

"No. Before that," says Nina. "I made him go to that damn party. He'd never have gone if I hadn't bullied him into it." She realizes what she just said and looks embarrassed. "I knew about the boys and all the stuff they did to him, but I thought that if everyone could get to know Rusty like I know him, they'd see how great he is." Nina starts to shake with sobs.

I hug her and let her cry, her tears soaking my shirt. "You shouldn't have made him go," I say. She wails and clings, her nails scraping my skin. "But what happened would have happened eventually. Evil is everywhere, and no one can escape it."

Nina tries to claw at me as I push her away. None of this is about her. It's about Rusty, and right now he's languishing in a hospital room believing that I abandoned him. And he's right. There's a part of me that thinks I should leave him be, let him battle his demons and live or die on his own. But that is the part of me that is scared. A coward. The part of me that knows what I'm going to have to do to save him.

"When this is all over," I say to Nina, "he's going to need you. Try not to let him down again." My words are harsh and uncharitable, and they cut Nina to the bone, but her feelings mean little to me, so long as she protects Rusty.

Without giving her a chance to argue, I leave the waiting room. The old woman doesn't say good-bye.

I wait in Grandma Brawley's room because I don't want to cause a scene in the ICU. Mr. Kelly was sleeping and didn't yell at me about the nurses trying to kill him. Weirdly, I missed it.

"Who are you?" Grandma Brawley asks.

Her voice nearly knocks me out of my chair. I was trying to think of a better plan than the one I'd come up with, which is very likely to fail, and I didn't notice Grandma Brawley sitting up, staring at me with inquisitive brown eyes.

"Andrew," I say. "Andrew Brawley." The moment after I speak, I know I'm an idiot.

"Brawley, huh?" she asks. "So you're the boy everyone tells me is my grandson." I nod. "That's funny, because I haven't got any grand-children. Though, with that nose you do resemble my uncle Toby. Nobody liked him much."

"It's a long story," I say. Part of me wants to feed her some tale about us just having the same last name or being long-lost cousins, but she's keen. I can tell. She'd detect my bullshit before it left my mouth.

Gran laughs. "It's always a long story, kid."

Awake, Grandma Brawley looks different from how she did asleep. This is a woman you don't trifle with. She was no fairy-tale princess waiting for her prince to wake her with a magic kiss. She'd probably have broken the arm of any man who tried it.

"What're you doing in my room?" she asks bluntly.

"Waiting."

"We're all waiting," Gran says. "Who or what are you waiting for?"

I look at the picture frame with the lock of hair in it. "Can I ask you a question?"

Grandma Brawley thinks about it and then nods. "Go on, kid."

"Whose hair is that?" I point at the frame, in case she doesn't know what I'm talking about, but her mind is probably sharper than mine. This woman will be alive and kicking long after I'm dead.

"Why?" she asks.

Grandma Brawley is staring me down, and it makes me squirm. Maybe coming here was a bad plan. "I had this idea that it belonged to your long-lost love. A man who disappeared from your life, and you waited all your years for him to return. I imagined that the hair in the frame was all you had left to remember him by."

This makes Gran snicker. Then laugh. She's got a great laugh that fills the room and makes me want to laugh along with her, even though there's nothing funny in what I said. "You're a strange bird, kid. The nurses told me you spent a lot of time in here writing some kind of story. It's a good fiction but not the truth."

"Then what is the truth?" I ask.

Grandma Brawley reaches behind her for the frame. She traces the hair through the glass. "You'll never be more perfect than you are right now, kid. You're too smart to believe in all the bullshit but too naive to know that it's *all* bullshit. That's a great way to live. Everything is possible."

"But whose hair is that?"

"My daughter's," Grandma Brawley says. "I lost her too young."

"Oh," I say. "Can I ask another question?"

Grandma Brawley shrugs like she doesn't care either way, but I know she does. Only someone who cares could fake not caring so well. I feel like maybe it's a bond we share.

"How do you move on from something like that? How do you deal with losing all the people you love?"

"You don't," she says. "Not like everyone expects you to." Grandma Brawley sighs and rests the frame on the bed. "Life goes on with or without you, and that's just the reality of it. You never move on, you just keep moving forward."

"What if you don't deserve to move forward?"

Grandma Brawley touches the frame again. "The past is a cold place. No one deserves to be trapped there, no matter how terrible you believe your sins to be."

There's something in the way she looks at me that makes me think she knows about my parents and sister and the truth of why I'm here, living in Roanoke General, but she can't unless she heard everything I told her while she was asleep. I suppose anything is possible.

"Michelle," Grandma Brawley says, looking toward the door.

A chill enters the room, seeps into my bones, and my skin prickles. Death stands in the doorway in black trousers and a pale cream blouse that dips dangerously low. "You know each other?" I ask.

Gran nods. "I know her well." She winks. "But I don't suppose you're here for me, are you?"

Death shakes her head and says, "Andrew. I believe we have some things to discuss."

I take a deep breath and stand. It's a desperate plan. I may not be able to move forward, but Rusty shouldn't suffer for my sins. "I want to make a deal."

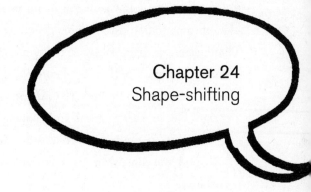

Chapter 24
Shape-shifting

Death and I barely speak.

The walls of Roanoke General groan as we pass: Death and Andrew Brawley. She's calm and quiet while I rehearse what I'm going to say, trying desperately not to gnaw my fingernails to the quick and give away my fear.

"I don't suppose I'll need to call the police right away," she says. Death's voice is raspy. She straightens her back obsessively, as though she's reminding herself not to slouch. These are the cracks in her foundation. The signs that Death, though patient, has grown tired of the chase.

"No," I say. I'm not sure if she'd be calling the cops because I trashed her office or because she thinks she'll need help removing me from the hospital. "Like I said, I want to make a deal."

Death nods. "Are you hungry?"

"I'm seventeen," I say. "I'm always hungry." Death chuckles at my joke, but the truth is that eating is the last thing on my mind. My serenity is a charade, the last act of a desperate man.

We enter the cafeteria, where Arnold and Aimee are working behind the line. Drawn on the menu board is a hideous illustration of some smiley, psycho tubes dancing on a grave of Technicolor blood. PENNE WITH VODKA SAUCE! the sign exclaims.

Arnold glances twice when I enter with Death, but whatever his thoughts, he puts on his best *Ah-nold* grin and says, "Drew! You like my sign? Get it? They're drunk and dancing."

"Yeah. You're the Jackson Pollock of cafeteria artists."

"Good morning, Mr. Jaworski," Death says, offering him a warm smile.

"Michelle. A pleasure, as always." Arnold glances at us together. "I didn't know you and Drew were friends."

"We're not," I say. "She's helping me with a problem."

"Rusty." When Arnold says the name, every instinct in my body screams that I should be with him right now. "He asked about you."

I take a tray and slide it down the counter. Alongside the pasta is a ghastly off-white concoction that looks like the end result of a bad case of E. coli. Steam rises from it, carrying the scent of garlic and onion. My traitorous stomach rumbles in response, and I can't resist. "Some of whatever that is," I say.

"Turkey tetrazzini. I didn't know how to draw that."

"Who would?"

Death coughs and slides her tray alongside mine. She takes a helping of the pasta, and we both grab some bread before Aimee rings us up. A knowing look passes between Aimee and Death, something that suggests that they're intimately acquainted, but they don't exchange a word that doesn't pertain to the food or the cost of the food or the paying for the food, until we're about to leave, and Death says, "Did you eat it today?" and Aimee nods yes. Death says, "Good for you." That's it. But Aimee beams like a supernova, blasting a rare smile out into the world for everyone to see, and for one shining moment, it's the most beautiful thing in the world.

The cafeteria is tidy and clean, evidence of a slow lunch, and Death and I take a table in the corner. I pick at the turkey tetrazzini with my fork, taking a tentative first bite before digging into it with a ferocity that would make Arnold beam with pride.

Death is a fastidious eater. She spears one piece of penne with the curved tines of her fork, runs it through the pinkish sauce, and then sniffs at it before putting it in her mouth. She chews that one tiny bite carefully before finally swallowing. It's a laborious process that she repeats ad nauseam until I finish my meal. The moment I rest my fork, so does she, making me wonder if she was only eating for my benefit. Does Death eat anything but human misery? Will she eat mine or must I carry it forever?

"Let's start at the beginning," Death says.

"The beginning of what?"

"Please don't toy with me." She pushes her tray toward the center of the table and folds her hands in front of her. "I've pieced together what I believe happened, and I simply need confirmation so that we may proceed."

Blood rushes from my head to my stomach to aid in the digestion of the heavy food I just wolfed down, and I feel exhausted. The resolve I had only thirty minutes ago crumbles in the face of my weariness. I can't remember the last time I slept without waking in the night screaming, or when my dreams weren't filled with shattered glass and loss and tears. I've shouldered the burdens for so long now that I never dared to imagine what it might feel like to share them.

But here's Death sitting before me, asking me to tell her everything. All I have to do is recite my story, let her take me away, and it will be over.

Only, I can't.

There's Lexi. There's Rusty.

There's the fact that I killed my parents. Directly, indirectly, they're still dead. That burden is mine until the end of days. Until darkness consumes us all.

"I'll tell you what you want to know," I say. "But, first, you have to do something for me."

Death narrows her depthless, feline eyes. "This isn't a negotiation."

"Everything is a negotiation."

"I could call the police," Death says. "I know you defaced my office. You could sit in a jail cell until you're ready to talk. Is that what you want?"

"Maybe you should," I tell her. "But you won't."

"Won't I?"

I shake my head. "No. You want me to come with you willingly."

Death's face is stony. I can't tell if she's angry or upset or shocked that I called her bluff. She could fade into the wall for all the emotion she shows. "What do you want?"

"To see a patient. Rusty McHale."

"He's not allowed to have any visitors except immediate family."

"It hasn't stopped me before."

Death purses her lips. "I know. And your friend Steven has been suspended for allowing it."

"That's not fair!"

"This is a hospital, Andrew, and there are rules."

I do my best to stuff my anger down, down into my toes. Negotiating with Death requires calm.

"Please. I need to see him."

Death's icy visage cracks. She stares at me over the table, which seems to be growing longer and longer, putting distance between us, an impassable gulf. Before she even speaks, I know what her answer will be.

"I'm not doing this for you," Death says. I hold my breath, unable to believe that my plan has succeeded.

"But you'll do it? You'll take me to Rusty?"

"Against my better judgment." Death stands up, and I swear I hear her tired bones creak. "However, after, you and I *are* going to talk."

As I follow Death from the cafeteria, I'm not sure what terrifies me more: explaining to Rusty why I never came, or explaining to Death why I never left.

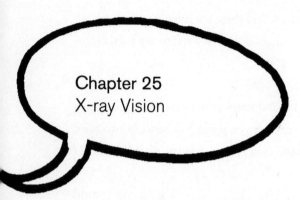

Chapter 25
X-ray Vision

I am the enemy.

Mr. and Mrs. McHale are red eyed and hawklike when I walk into Rusty's room. Mr. McHale's frown deepens, drawing tight lines on his forehead. Mrs. McHale coils, ready to strike. Though they don't move from their seats, they both lean nearer to Rusty, as if they're forming a protective barrier around him. To protect him from me.

I avoid looking at Rusty.

"Mr. and Mrs. McHale," I say softly.

"Why are you here?" Rusty's mother asks. "Why is he here?" she asks Death.

Death wears a friendly smile, even though it's probably killing her to do so. Rusty's parents falter and glance toward the door, almost like they've been waiting for some excuse to get out of this stifling little room.

"The boys need to talk," Death says. "It will be all right."

Mr. McHale shoves his hands in the pockets of his chinos and levels a rimy glare at me. I shiver, and he leaves. Mrs. McHale follows. Neither spares a word for Rusty.

"You have ten minutes," Death says on her way out the door.

Rusty lies in the bed with a single white sheet pulled up to his chest. He's thinner than I remember, his gaunt cheeks stretched tightly over his bones. But even broken, he's still the most beautiful person I've ever seen. And he hates me. He doesn't even look at me. He keeps his hazel eyes focused on a point just over my shoulder.

I catch my reflection in the glass of the television mounted to the wall. "I look like shit," I say, trying to defuse the tension. "My hair hasn't been this long since the summer between my freshman and sophomore years of high school." I'm not sure if Rusty is listening, but I have to try. "My dad spent three months referring to me as 'the hippie formerly known as son.'"

Rusty turns away from me. I'm losing him.

"Lexi died. I'm not sure if you heard that."

Silence.

"I thought you and I could run away together, but I'm no good for you. Everyone I love dies. That's the truth."

Rusty offers me nothing.

"Trevor's gone too. Back to his life out there. We had a funeral for Lexi. Burned that wig of hers I told you about. Fuck, Rusty, I wish you'd met her. She was so brilliant."

I think I see a twitch in his lips, but it's probably just my imagination.

"I had to make a deal with Death to see you. I think she's going

269

to take me away. I don't know what's going to happen to me, Rusty. I'm scared."

No, there's definitely something. Rusty's eyes flicker. It's a little thing, but it's something.

I swallow; my throat is dry. But I keep talking before I lose my nerve. "Meeting you changed everything. I built a family here—Lexi and Trevor, Arnold, and the nurses in the ER—but I never wanted to leave the hospital until I met you. For the first time since my parents died, I wanted something for myself. A life . . . with you. And I thought we could have that, but then Lexi died and I realized that if we left together, you'd die too. I just couldn't bear the thought of being out there. Alone."

I count to ten in my head to give Rusty a chance to respond, but he's still staring over my shoulder when I reach the final number. I turn to leave. This is the last time I'll see this room. The last time I'll see Rusty.

"Fuck you." The words are so low that I almost miss them.

"Rusty," I say, and he screams, "Don't say my name!" in this scratchy yowl that tears at my ears and shatters my heart because I feel the ache of every second he spent waiting for me. Every single one of the seconds that passed that I didn't come, bottled up and stoppered inside him, flung at me like a thermite grenade, and now Rusty's not the only one on fire.

"You promised you'd come." His voice is smaller than I've ever heard it, and I don't know if it's because the infection is making him weak or from the damage I caused by not keeping my promise.

"My parents and sister died, and the little boy in the ER died, and Lexi died. I couldn't bear the thought of you dying too." My heart hurts when I look at him. "I did it for you."

"You're a fucking liar," Rusty says. "You only thought about yourself."

"Everyone I love dies."

"Everyone dies, full stop. Everyone. Even your precious Patient F." There's so much malice in Rusty's voice that every word is a whip, peeling off strips of my skin.

I step toward the bed, but Rusty flinches, so I step back again. "I thought you'd be better off without me," I say. "I thought everyone would."

Rusty closes his eyes and doesn't open them for what feels like a long time. When he reopens them, he says, "I thought that too."

Fragments of thoughts float in my brain, things I want to say right now, but I clamp my mouth shut when I see that desolate look on Rusty's face. It's so like the look I draw on Patient F's face when he travels to his past.

"AJ Crawford was the one who did it," Rusty says. "The one who told me that I didn't matter. He told me in the hallways, in the locker room, in class, on the Internet, with his fists, and when he spit on me. I kept waiting for someone to tell me that he was wrong. But he wasn't wrong."

I start to disagree, but Rusty flashes me a look indicating that he will tolerate no interruptions.

"I lit myself on fire, Drew. I stole a bottle of rubbing alcohol, and I stole a lighter, and I lit myself on fire."

Rusty throws it out there like a slap, but I say, "I know," and there's no way I can look at Rusty right now, but I feel his

271

eyes boring into me. "I think I've always known." Now I have no choice but to look, and he's killing me with those eyes. With all the fire of all the days he spent hating himself. I want to go to him right now, but there's a distance between us so wide, I'm not sure I can bridge it.

"You knew?"

"Yeah."

"Why didn't you say anything?"

"It wasn't my secret to tell." If only I could go to him and take his hand and kiss his lips, maybe this would all be better, but I can't. Or he won't let me. "I hate those boys for making you feel like dying. They should have been the ones to burn."

Tears stain Rusty's voice. "I wasn't just trying to kill myself. I wanted to feel on the outside the way I felt on the inside. I wanted everyone to see what they did to me, to see the damage they'd done."

"Rusty—" I step toward him. To hold him, to kiss him, to tell him that everything is going to be okay, even if that's a lie.

"Fuck you, and fuck your pity." Rusty falters, and I move back again. We're both on our own. Rusty has to go on without my help . . . and he does. "I don't remember jumping into the pool. I don't remember much except screaming."

"I heard you when you came into the ER."

Rusty's eyes narrow, but he ignores me. "I kept begging God to let me die. Every time I opened my eyes, I prayed for the end. All those doctors and nurses trying to keep me alive when all I wanted to do was die. When I opened my eyes and saw you, I thought you were Death, coming to end it all. Only, you didn't. I don't remember exactly when I started wanting to live more than I wanted to die, but hope crept into me the way you crept into my room." Rusty looks away. "Too bad it was all fiction."

Part of me wishes that I'd told him I knew sooner. Maybe then I could have helped him. Maybe then he would have let me. Instead, I say, "That guy was wrong, Rusty. You do matter. And the world needs you in it. More than it needs me."

"I don't believe you anymore." Rusty turns his head away; it's a dismissal. No matter how much I want to, I can't travel into the past and prove to Rusty that he's worth a hundred of those assholes. I can't go to that party and stop him from trying to kill himself.

There's nothing else to say, nothing else to know. "I should have come."

"Maybe I was wrong," Rusty says. "Maybe it *is* you the world would be better off without."

I can't argue. I should have died in the car accident that took my parents and my little sister. There's nothing for me inside the walls, and there's nothing for me out there. There's only one thing left to do.

I cross the distance to the bed and kiss Rusty fast, before he can push me away, because I need to remember what his lips feel like and what they taste like and how his top lip has this ridge that I slide my tongue over. And it's done before he can do anything but kiss me back. Though the kiss is stolen, it's mine all the same.

"Good-bye, Rusty." I stop at the door and look back. "Iloveyou."
Before my words hit him, I run.

Chapter 26
Flight

"Iloveyou," I say as I leave Rusty behind.

Death yells my name as I sprint past her. My real name. I ignore her. Mr. and Mrs. McHale watch as if they knew all along that this would happen. Nina is with them. I am not welshing on my deal with Death. Not really. She'll get what she wants, but it's going to be on my terms.

Doctors and nurses hug the walls as I dash through the brightly lit maze. I don't look back to see if Death is chasing me because, let's face it, Death has been chasing me since the day I arrived. I think I'll welcome her eventual embrace, but I'm going to make her work for it.

I run all the way to the roof of the parking garage. Stopping only when I feel the sun on my face. This—this is as close as I'm ever going to get to heaven. For a few minutes, I just stand with my toes dangling over the edge, basking in the daylight one final time.

"What are you doing?"

I expected Death, but it's Father Mike's voice at my back instead.

"I was supposed to die in the crash." The ledge is barely wide enough to stand on, and I have to concentrate to keep from losing my balance. "I thought I could hang on to my parents by staying here, but all I've done is hurt people. I have to do this." I glance over my shoulder to make sure Father Mike isn't going to try anything funny.

Father Mike takes a tentative step toward me, holding his hands out so I can see that they're empty. He's sweating down his temples. Beads of perspiration pool on his brow. "God saved you."

"God is a fairy tale, Father." I look out over the edge and wonder if it will hurt. It doesn't look that far down, but I know it's got to be far enough. "Any god that would save me over Cady has got his priorities royally fucked up."

"Fair enough," Father Mike says. "And I can't explain why you lived and not her, but this won't solve anything." He takes another step toward me but retreats when I sway forward. I won't let him close enough to pull me down. This is going to happen.

When I'm sure that Father Mike isn't going to come any closer, I look back toward the horizon. "Look at it all. There's so much out there. So much to see and do and experience. But not for me." I run my hand through my hair and try not to remember the night I first came to the ER, but here at the end I can't stop the memories. "After that first night," I say, "I thought I had to stay here because this was the last place my parents were alive. I thought if I lived, they'd go on living too. But that's stupid, isn't it?"

"No, Andy. It's not."

I flash Father Mike a wry smile and nearly lose my balance. "Don't patronize me."

I don't bother turning around, but when Father Mike says, "I'm sorry," he sounds chastened.

"The thing is, I had it all wrong." The memory of my father, his arm dangling limply over the side of the gurney, forgotten as they worked on my mother. Of Cady drowning in her own blood. "I died that night."

"Andy—"

"Death wasn't late to get me. She was there. Only, I was too dumb to see her. Death hasn't been looking for me, I've been looking for Death." I turn around, all the way around. I point my feet toward Father Mike and smile. "I get it now. All my excuses, all my fears, they were just ways I kept myself from seeing the truth."

Father Mike inches closer to me. There is panic on his face, though his voice is exceptionally calm. "This isn't the end of your journey."

"All I have to do is let go."

I hold my arms out and begin to lean back. Death storms the roof, flanked by police. I think I hear sirens in the distance, but I no longer care.

"God's not finished with you yet, Andy."

"My name isn't Andy or Andrew or Drew."

"Please!" he begs.

"Tell God it's my turn to drive." Death and the officers will never reach me in time. Father Mike lunges forward, but it's already too late. All my debts are now paid.

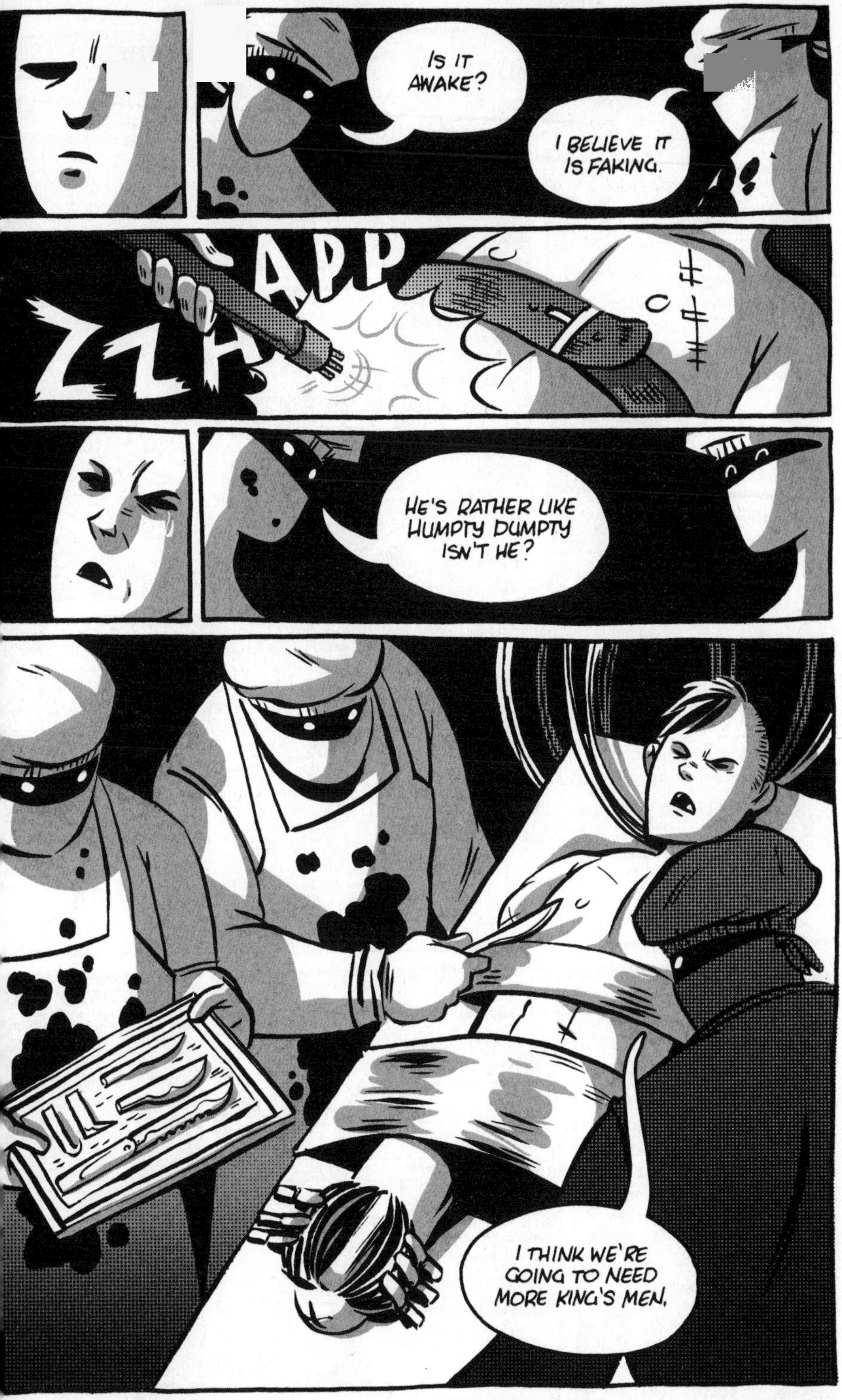
IS IT AWAKE?
I BELIEVE IT IS FAKING.
HE'S RATHER LIKE HUMPTY DUMPTY ISN'T HE?
I THINK WE'RE GOING TO NEED MORE KING'S MEN.

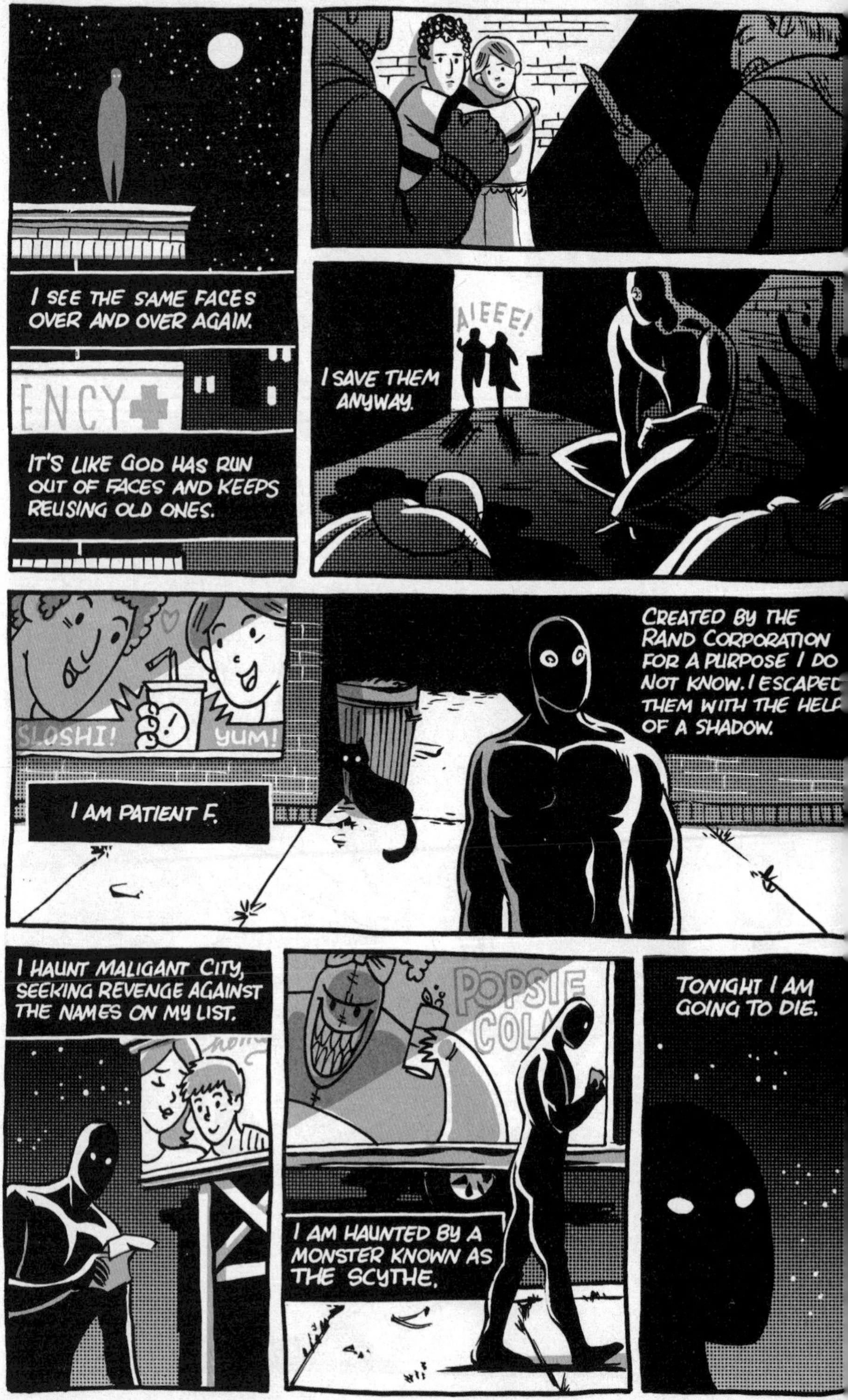
I SEE THE SAME FACES OVER AND OVER AGAIN.
ENCY
IT'S LIKE GOD HAS RUN OUT OF FACES AND KEEPS REUSING OLD ONES.
I SAVE THEM ANYWAY.
AIEEE!
SLOSH!
YUM!
I AM PATIENT F.
CREATED BY THE RAND CORPORATION FOR A PURPOSE I DO NOT KNOW. I ESCAPED THEM WITH THE HELP OF A SHADOW.
I HAUNT MALIGANT CITY, SEEKING REVENGE AGAINST THE NAMES ON MY LIST.
POPSIE COLA
I AM HAUNTED BY A MONSTER KNOWN AS THE SCYTHE.
TONIGHT I AM GOING TO DIE.

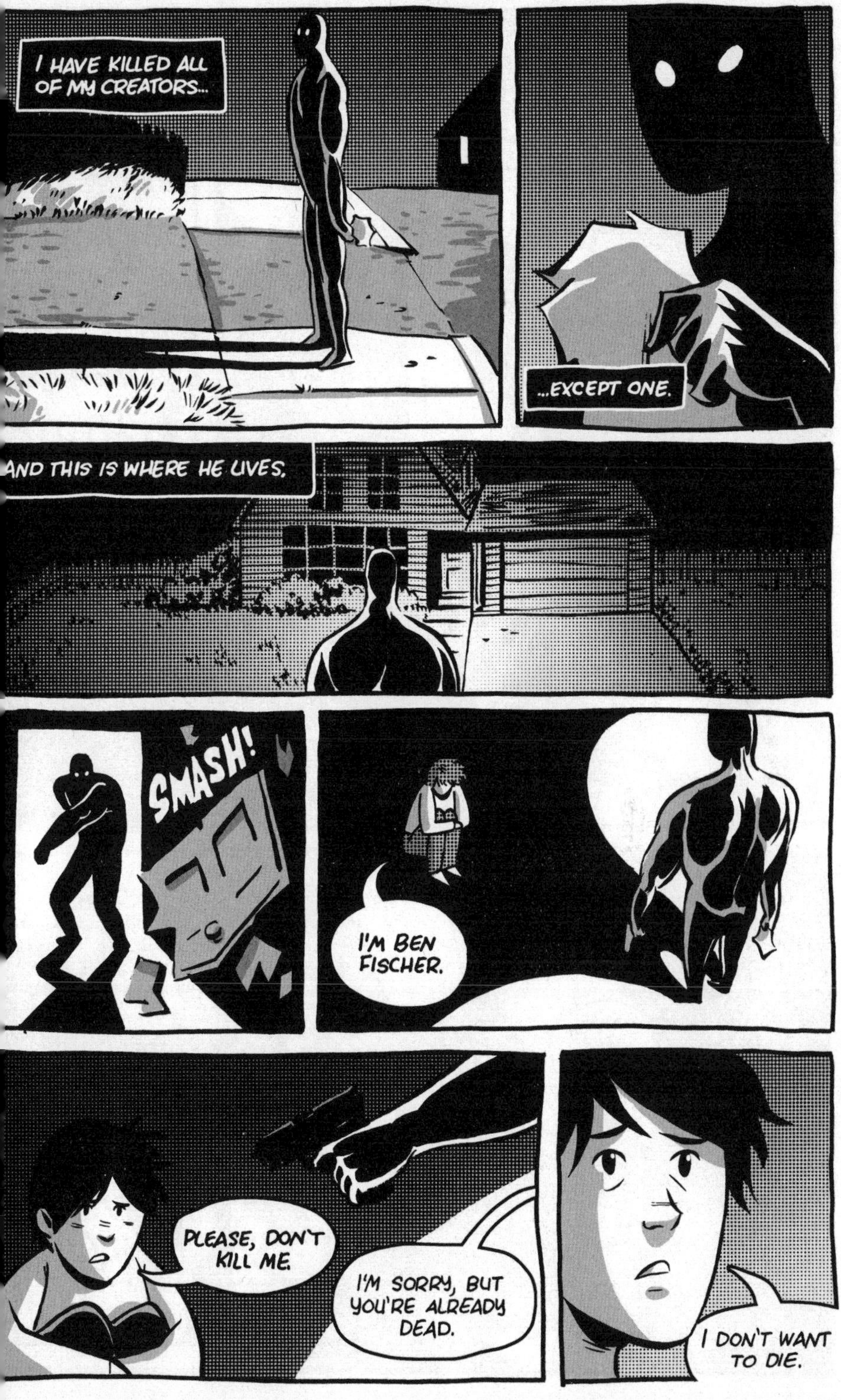
I HAVE KILLED ALL OF MY CREATORS...
...EXCEPT ONE.
AND THIS IS WHERE HE LIVES.
SMASH!
I'M BEN FISCHER.
PLEASE, DON'T KILL ME.
I'M SORRY, BUT YOU'RE ALREADY DEAD.
I DON'T WANT TO DIE.

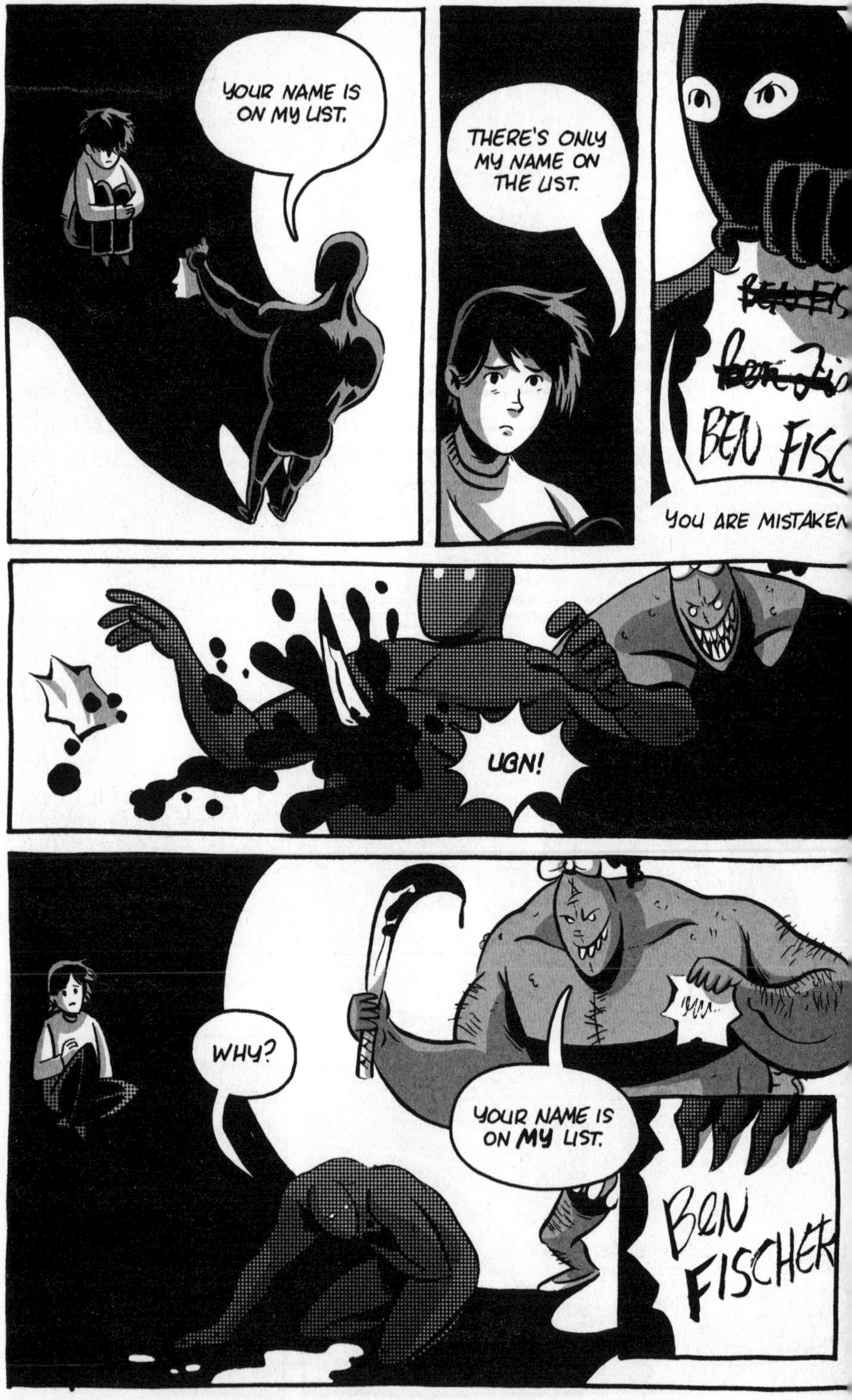
YOUR NAME IS ON MY LIST.
THERE'S ONLY MY NAME ON THE LIST.
BEN FISC
YOU ARE MISTAKEN
UGN!
WHY?
YOUR NAME IS ON MY LIST.
BEN FISCHER

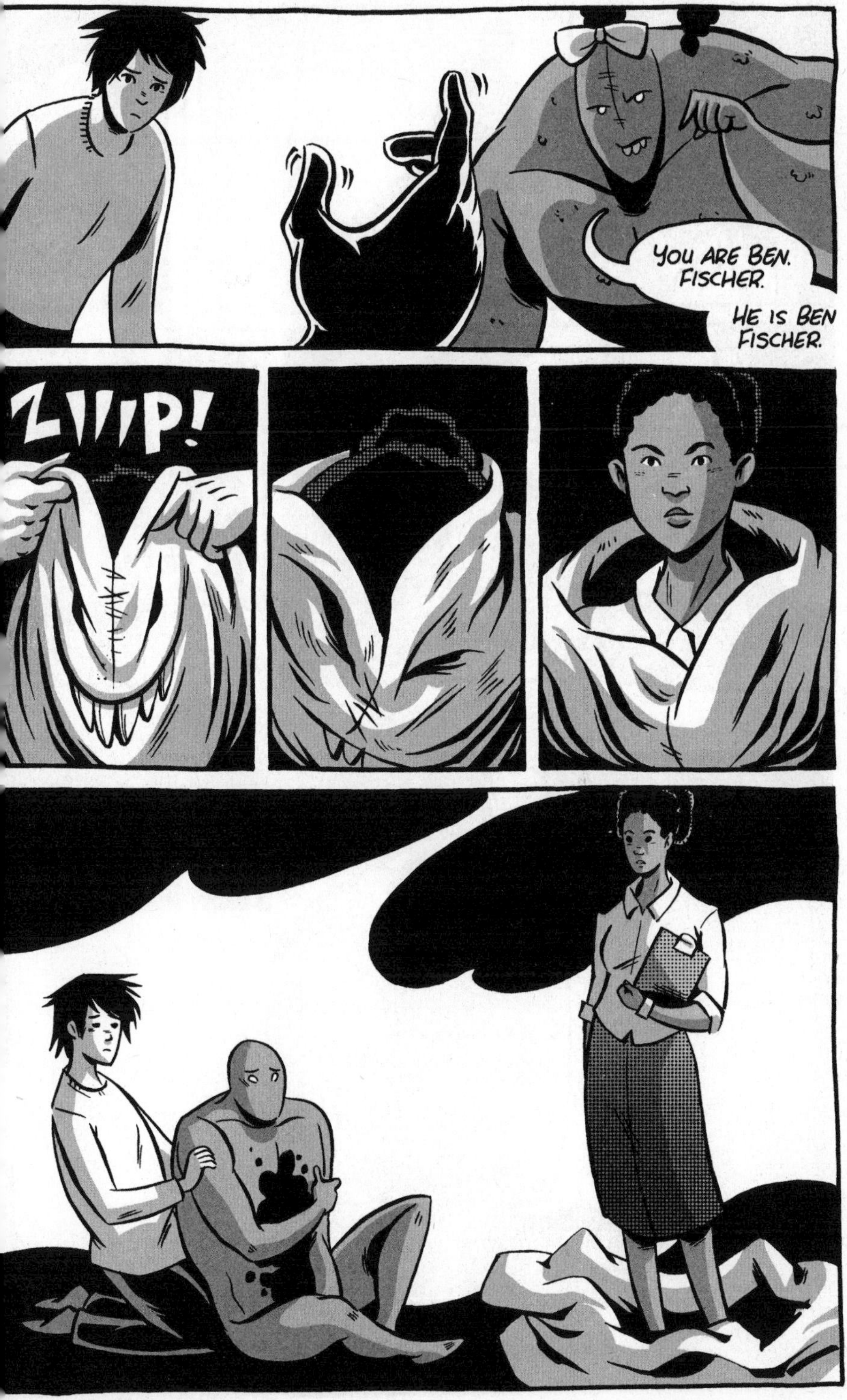
YOU ARE BEN. FISCHER.
HE IS BEN FISCHER.
ZIIIP!

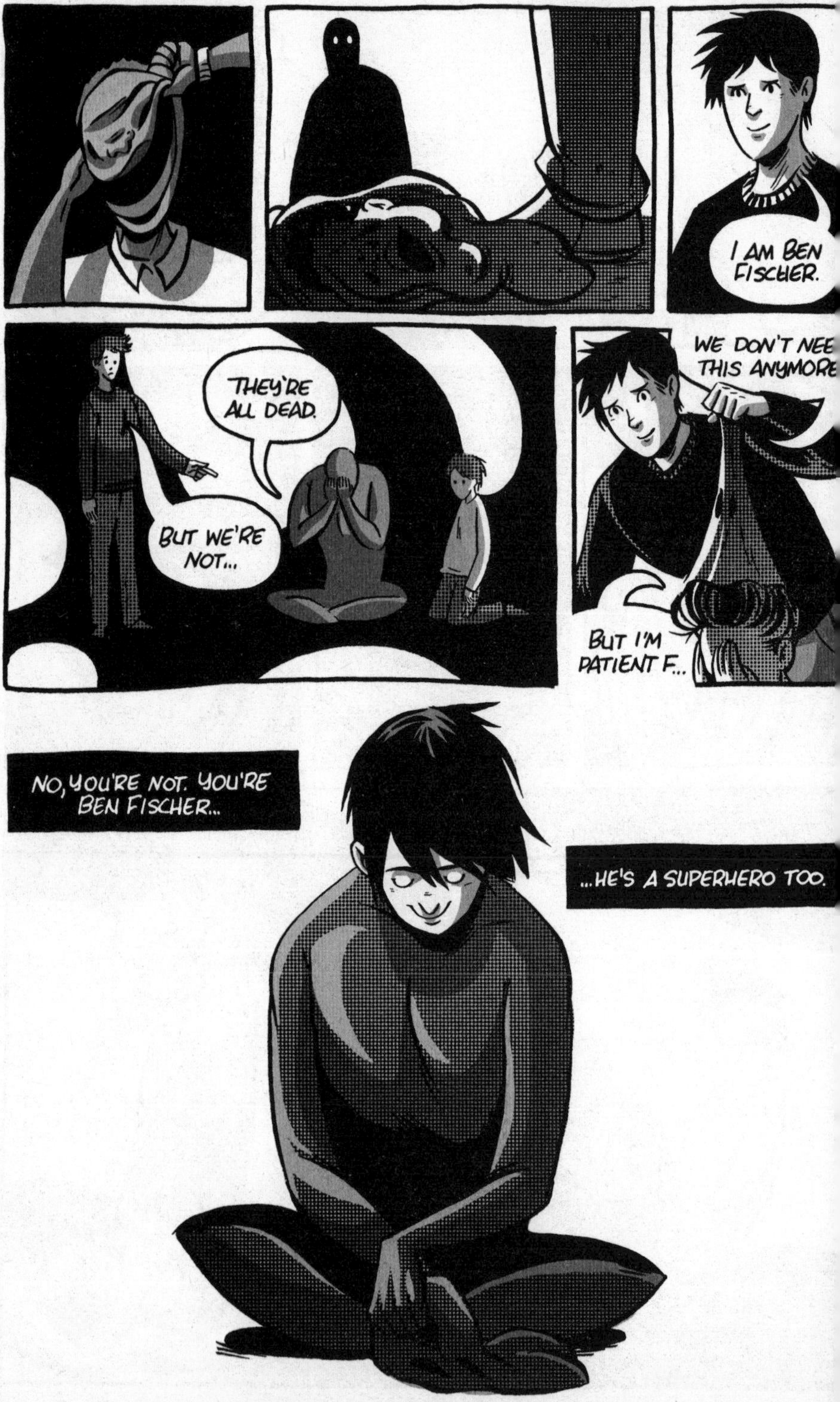
I AM BEN FISCHER.
THEY'RE ALL DEAD.
BUT WE'RE NOT...
WE DON'T NEE
THIS ANYMORE
BUT I'M PATIENT F...
NO, YOU'RE NOT. YOU'RE BEN FISCHER...
...HE'S A SUPERHERO TOO.

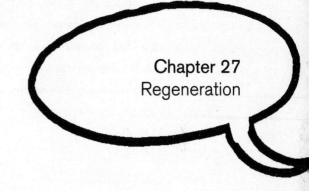

Chapter 27
Regeneration

I am Ben Fischer.

It is the thought that I cling to as the days and nights pass in a blur of tests and needles and doctors whose names I can't remember. The sun rises and sets in the window near my bed. The blinds are open. My left arm is broken and my right leg is mangled; the bones tore through the skin of my thigh. I heard one of the nurses talking about my spleen and some swelling in my brain, but my head aches and I try not to think too much. Every time I do, pain splits my skull and doesn't relent until a nurse pushes more drugs into my IV, sending me back to sleep.

I am Ben Fischer.

When I open my eyes, Miss Michelle is sitting by my bed. She looks like she's sleeping, like she's been sleeping in that chair for days, but when I move she blinks and smiles at me. She doesn't look like Death anymore. She's just a woman, human. Though she looks like she's been through hell.

"I'm Ben," I say. My throat is hoarse and dry, and I start coughing.

Miss Michelle brings me a cup of ice chips, and they are the most brilliant thing I've ever eaten. She doesn't say anything for a while. Just sits there and watches me like she's afraid if she looks away for even one second, I'll disappear.

"You gave us quite a scare," she finally says.

"Yeah."

"You should be dead."

"That's what I used to think."

"Oh?" Miss Michelle asks.

"Not anymore, though."

Miss Michelle seems to weigh my words for truth, trying to make sure that I'm not going to take another header off the top of a parking garage. I know there's nothing I can say to assure her that I'm not. I'll have to earn her trust by living.

"I'm sorry I was late," she says.

I put the ice chips down. Shrug. "I'm not."

Jo comes through the door right then, yelling at me like I didn't almost just die, and Emma and Steven are right behind her carrying a box of doughnuts and a stack of DVDs. They smother me with attention, and I barely notice when Miss Michelle slips out the door.

I drift off to sleep in the middle of Emma's favorite movie, *Better Off Dead*. Jo thought it was inappropriate, but it made me laugh.

Over the next couple of days, I get stronger. Doctors come and go. I have a ton of visitors. Arnold and Aimee. Father Mike. My ER nurses pop in every day. Even Trevor drops by to tell me what a moron I am.

"It's a very special day, asshole," he says. "But if you ever do anything like that again, I'll kill you myself."

He draws a *T. rex* on my cast and tells me he'll visit as often as he can, though I don't expect I'll see him again.

Miss Michelle tells me that my parents left guardianship of me to my aunt and uncle in Colorado. I haven't seen them in years, but they're on their way to get me. I'm not sure what to think of that.

The one person who hasn't visited is Rusty. I'm too afraid to ask about him. Afraid that he's gone, that he never wants to see me again. I wouldn't blame him. Really. But I can't stop hoping.

The day before I'm supposed to leave, Aunt Jess and Uncle Tommy are fussing over me, telling me stories about my parents that I've never heard, talking about them like they're still alive. Uncle Tommy says he's going to teach me to ski, and Aunt Jess signs my cast with, *O Death! where is thy sting?* She's kind of weird, but I like it. They tell me how they came to retrieve the bodies of my parents and Cady and stayed in a crappy hotel for two weeks while the police searched for me. They tell me they never stopped believing I'd find my way home. I'm not sure where home is anymore, but I'd like to find out.

I'd just about given up on seeing Rusty when he walks through the door. Instead of a hospital gown, he's wearing a polo shirt and jeans. He still looks thin and a little pale, but, my God, he's so beautiful. You can forget a lot of things over the course of your life, but not a smile like Rusty's.

"Hey," he says.

Aunt Jess glances at me and I nod. She hustles Uncle Tommy from the room, leaving me alone with Rusty.

"You look like shit," Rusty says.

"You should see the other guy." My voice catches awkwardly. The last time I saw him, he was in the bed and I was standing. "Rusty—"

"I can't do this." He turns to leave.

"Please don't go."

Rusty stops and turns around. He can't look me in the eyes. I think he's going to leave again, but instead he sits on the floor beside my bed, pulling his knees to his chest.

"I thought you'd died."

"I'm pretty sure I did."

"Yeah." Rusty glances up at me. "Drew—" Having a broken arm and leg makes moving pretty difficult, but I do my best to look down at him. I need to see his face.

"Ben," I say. "Ben Fischer." The name still feels wrong in my mouth, but I'm getting used to it again. It's like an old pair of jeans that way.

Rusty takes a deep breath. He's working up to something, that much I can tell, but he's not ready to say whatever it is.

"I'm moving to Colorado," I say. "Some place called Silverthorne. And I finished Patient F."

"Maybe you'll let me read it sometime." Rusty gets up and stands over my bed. He's shaking, trembling. "I hate you." There are tears in the corners of his eyes. There are scars all over his body, and not the ones from the fire. These scars belong to me.

"I know."

Rusty grips the bed rail so tightly that his knuckles turn white. "I mean it."

"I know."

"Stop saying that!" Rusty screams. "I fucking hate you!"

Rusty chokes up and starts to sob. I link my fingers through his and pull him into the bed beside me. He curls next to me and lays his head on my chest. Every movement hurts, but it's so worth it.

When Rusty is done crying, I brush his hair out of his eyes and kiss his forehead. "What are the chances we can get some waffles?"

It takes some smooth talking, but I convince Emma to wheel me outside so that Rusty and I can have a picnic on the lawn. It's the first time I've been out of the hospital since my family died. The world is so big and so fucking scary, but Rusty pushes my wheelchair, and I know that things are going to be okay. I'm not moving on, but I'm moving forward.

Emma couldn't find waffles, but that's okay—I didn't have a checkerboard anyway. Rusty reads to me for a while and, after, we eat and watch the sun set. We're different people now. There are no lies between us. We get to know each other in the negative spaces, where words have no meaning.

"Am I ever going to see you again?" Rusty asks.

"Colorado isn't that far away."

Rusty nods and takes my hand. "I've got rehab and other stuff. I have to see a shrink."

"I'll wait for you."

The silence of the night sets with the sun, and I never want more than this.

Rusty squeezes my hand as if he's afraid to ever let go. "I wish I could see the future."

"It wouldn't help."

"But I want to know that everything is going to be all right."

I smile at Rusty—my best toothy grin—and say, "You just have to have faith."

"Yeah, I guess." Rusty sighs. "I love you too, you know."

Instead of answering him, I pull Rusty to me and kiss him softly on the lips. It's still the best part of everything. So I kiss him again and again and again. . . .

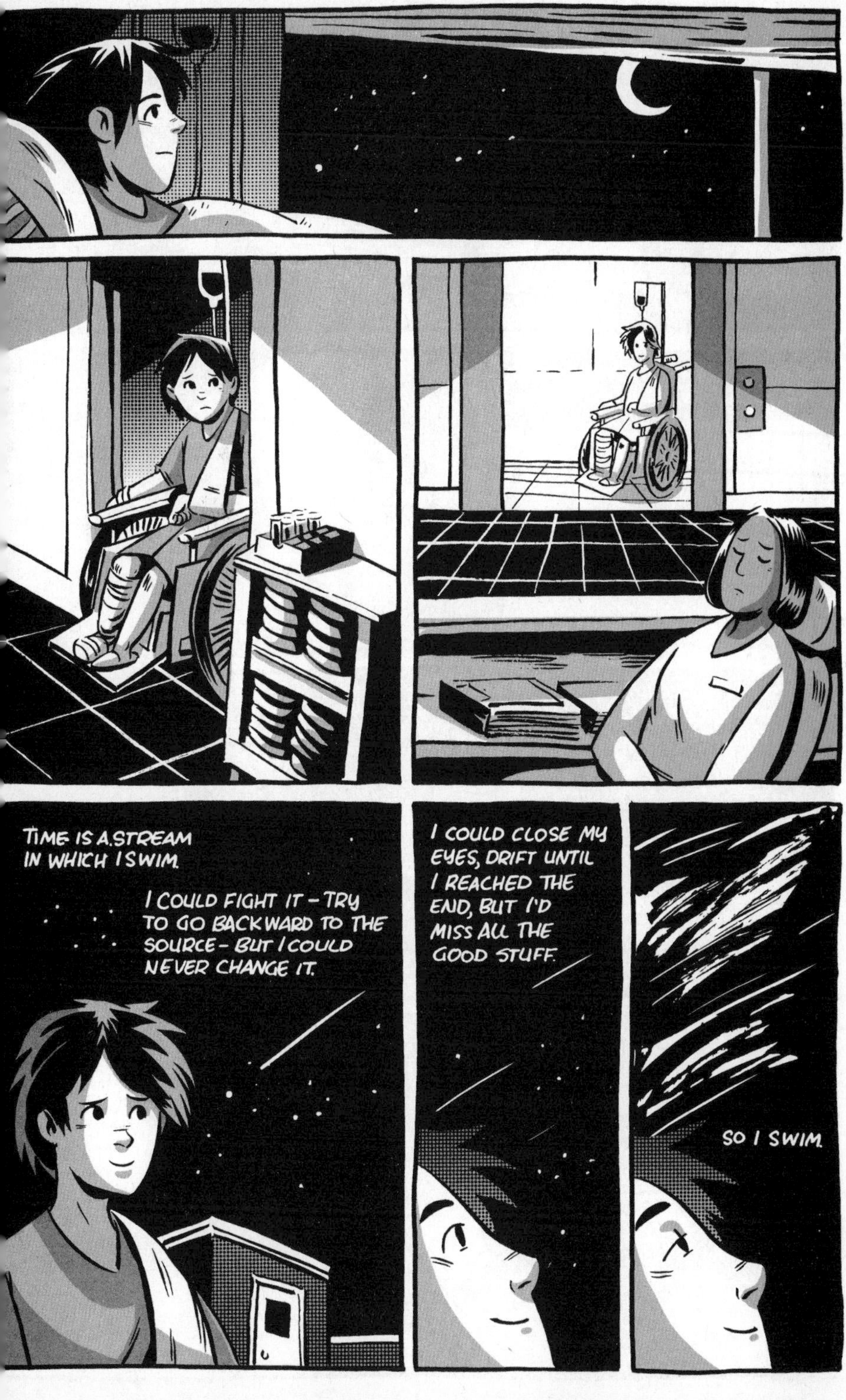
TIME IS A STREAM IN WHICH I SWIM.
I COULD FIGHT IT – TRY TO GO BACKWARD TO THE SOURCE – BUT I COULD NEVER CHANGE IT.
I COULD CLOSE MY EYES, DRIFT UNTIL I REACHED THE END, BUT I'D MISS ALL THE GOOD STUFF.
SO I SWIM.

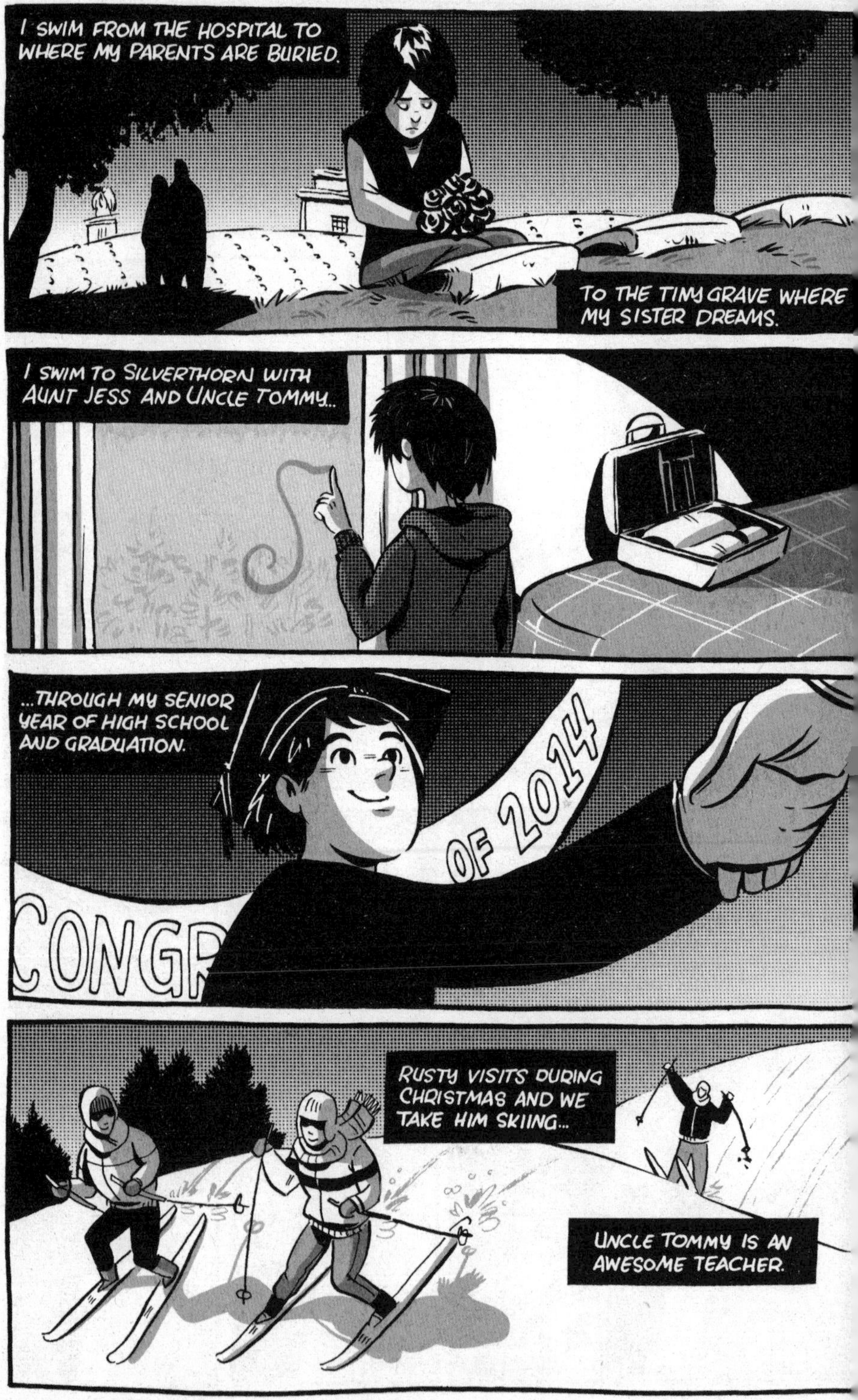
I SWIM FROM THE HOSPITAL TO WHERE MY PARENTS ARE BURIED.
TO THE TINY GRAVE WHERE MY SISTER DREAMS.
I SWIM TO SILVERTHORN WITH AUNT JESS AND UNCLE TOMMY...
...THROUGH MY SENIOR YEAR OF HIGH SCHOOL AND GRADUATION.
CONGR
OF 2014
RUSTY VISITS DURING CHRISTMAS AND WE TAKE HIM SKIING...
UNCLE TOMMY IS AN AWESOME TEACHER.

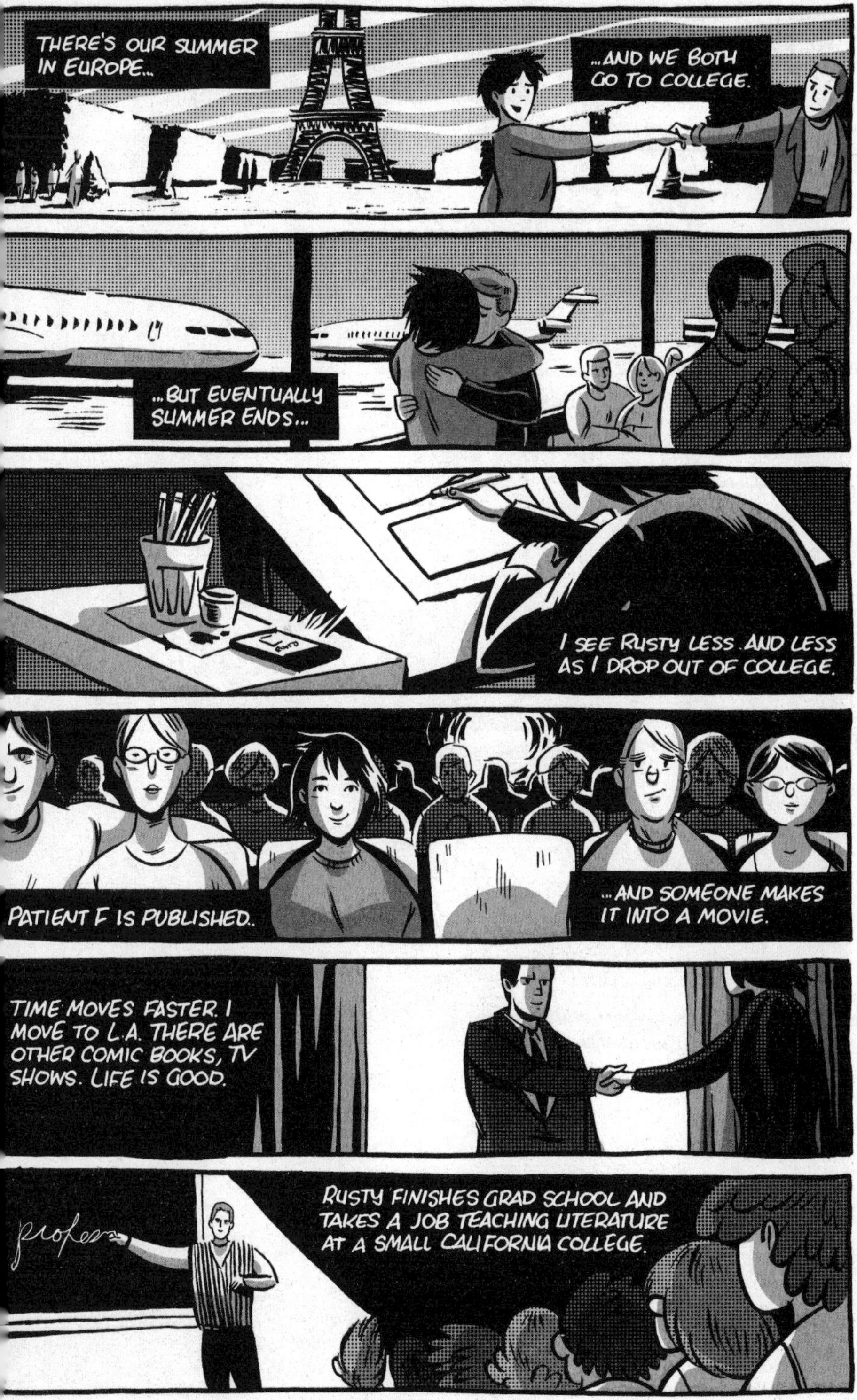
THERE'S OUR SUMMER IN EUROPE...
...AND WE BOTH GO TO COLLEGE.
...BUT EVENTUALLY SUMMER ENDS...
I SEE RUSTY LESS AND LESS AS I DROP OUT OF COLLEGE.
PATIENT F IS PUBLISHED.
...AND SOMEONE MAKES IT INTO A MOVIE.
TIME MOVES FASTER. I MOVE TO L.A. THERE ARE OTHER COMIC BOOKS, TV SHOWS. LIFE IS GOOD.
RUSTY FINISHES GRAD SCHOOL AND TAKES A JOB TEACHING LITERATURE AT A SMALL CALIFORNIA COLLEGE.

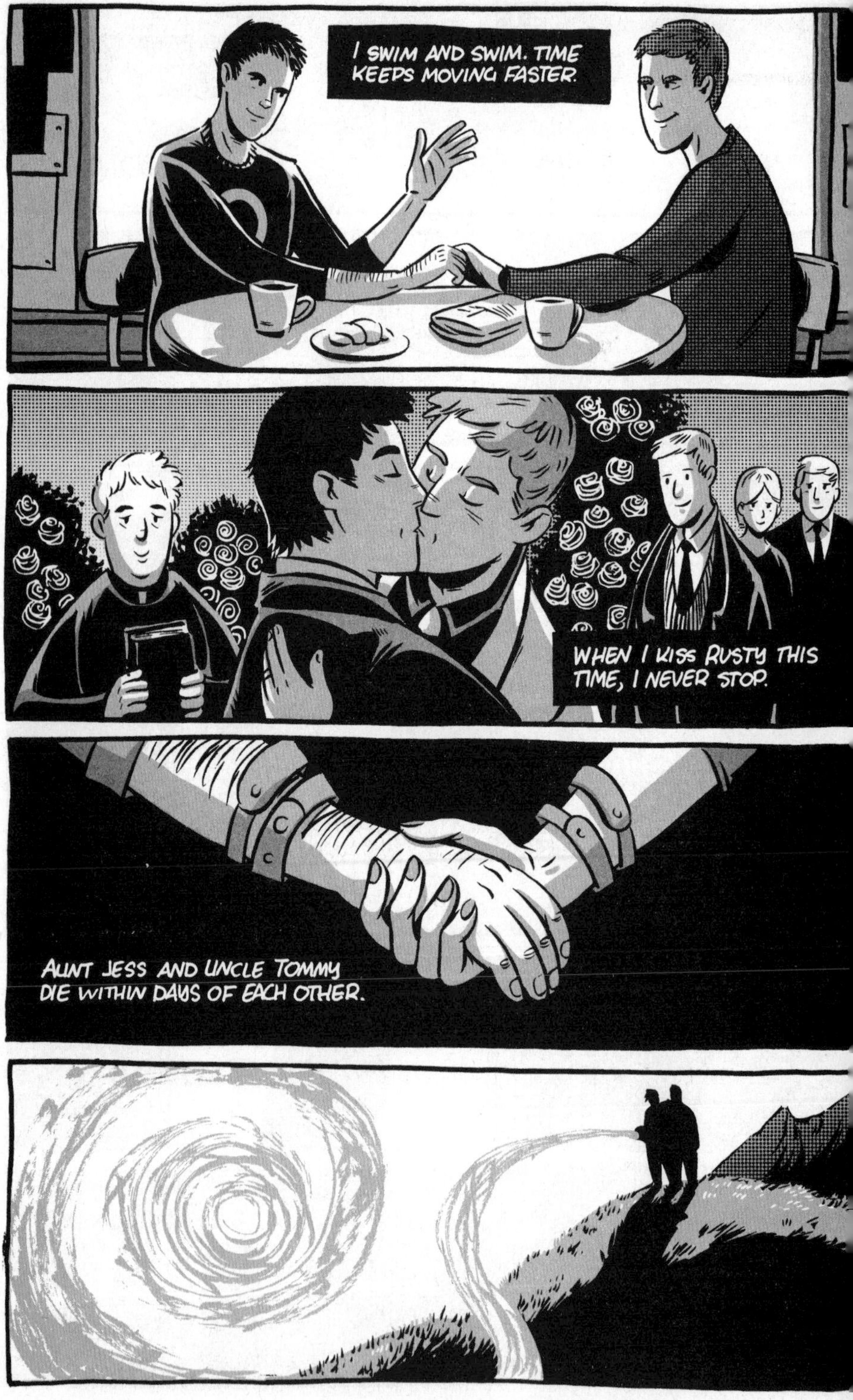
I SWIM AND SWIM. TIME KEEPS MOVING FASTER.
WHEN I KISS RUSTY THIS TIME, I NEVER STOP.
AUNT JESS AND UNCLE TOMMY DIE WITHIN DAYS OF EACH OTHER.

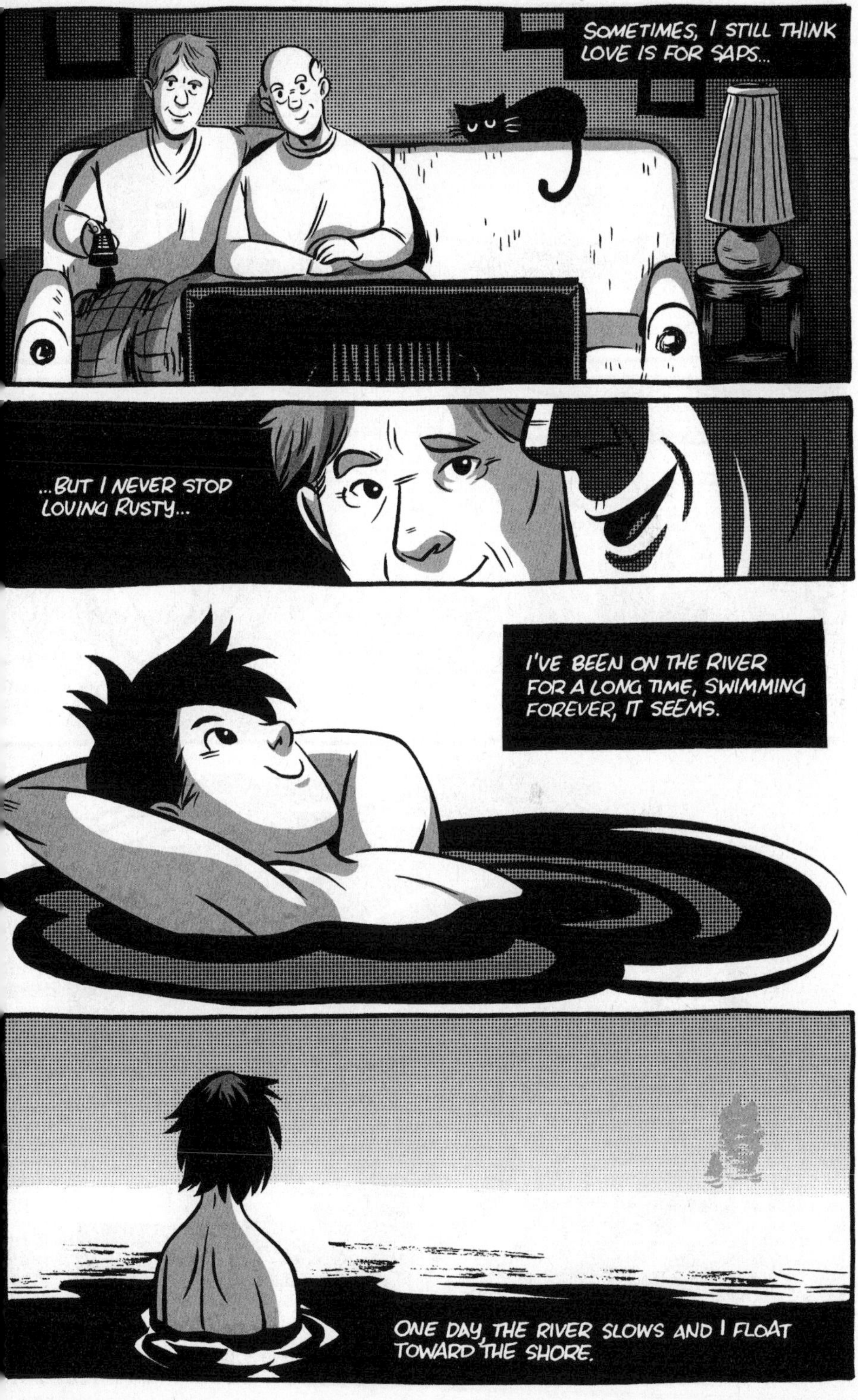
SOMETIMES, I STILL THINK LOVE IS FOR SAPS...
...BUT I NEVER STOP LOVING RUSTY...
I'VE BEEN ON THE RIVER FOR A LONG TIME, SWIMMING FOREVER, IT SEEMS.
ONE DAY, THE RIVER SLOWS AND I FLOAT TOWARD THE SHORE.

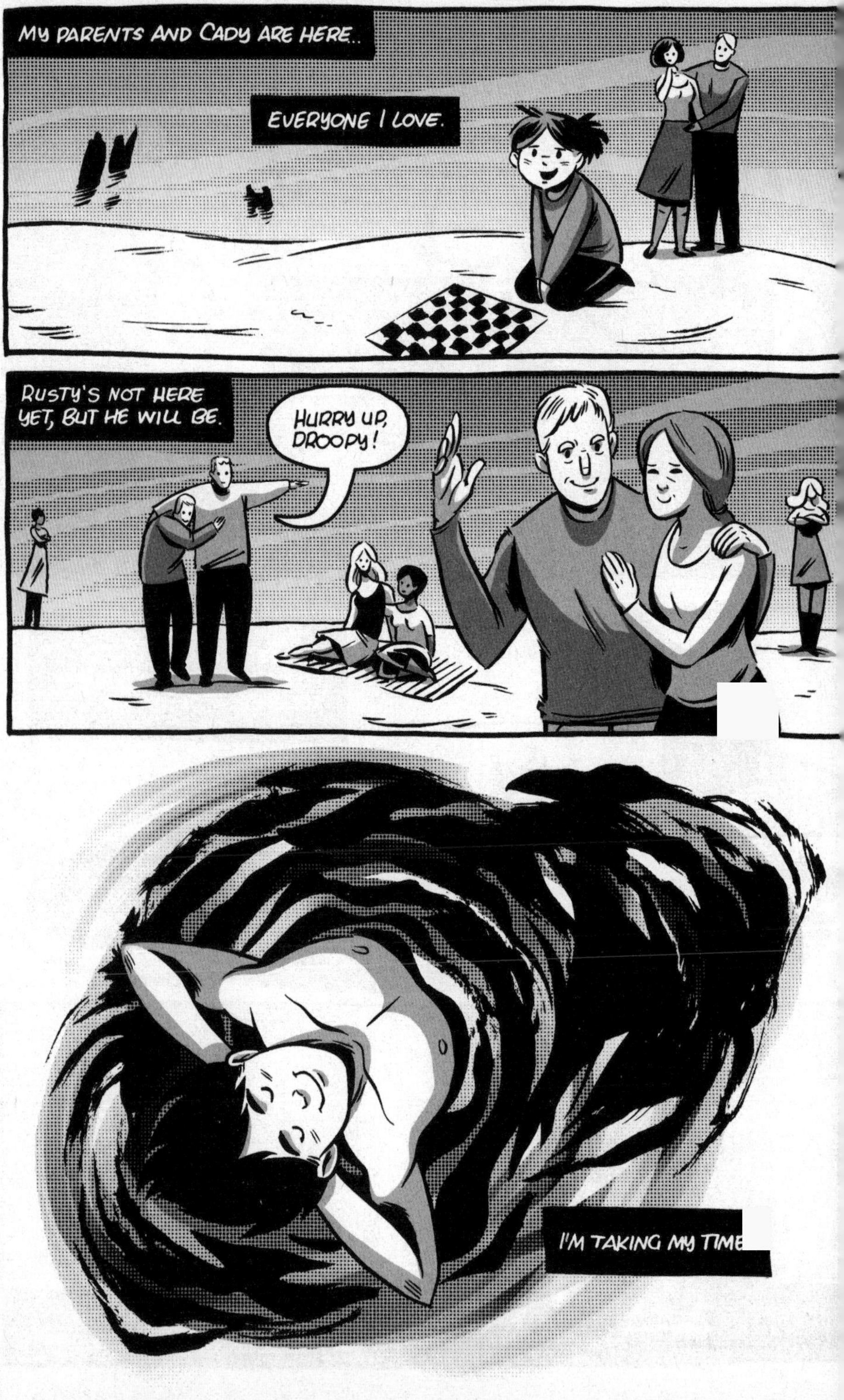
MY PARENTS AND CADY ARE HERE..
EVERYONE I LOVE.
RUSTY'S NOT HERE YET, BUT HE WILL BE.
HURRY UP, DROOPY!
I'M TAKING MY TIME

THE STARS SPIN AROUND ME.

THE SKY BRIGHTENS.

TOMORROW IS TODAY.

THE WALLS NO LONGER HOLD ME. OUT THERE IS WHERE I WANT TO BE.

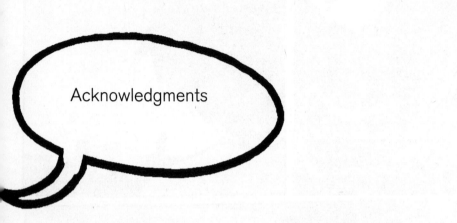

Acknowledgments

The Five Stages of Andrew Brawley has been my baby for about five years, and there were plenty of times I thought I'd never get to see it published. But here we are! I couldn't have done it without the help and support of some amazing people.

I'd like to first thank Amy Boggs, my kick-ass agent, who loved Drew as much as I did, and believed in his story when I thought no one ever would. Michael Strother, my tireless, brilliant, and thoughtful editor, who immediately understood what I was trying to accomplish, and has been a champion, protector, and mentor throughout this process. That Patient F lives and breathes on the page is a testament to the awe-inspiring talent of Christine Larsen. She took my words and made them real.

I'd also like to thank my book designer Regina Flath, my copyeditor Lara Stelmaszyk, the entire Simon Pulse marketing and publicity departments, and everyone at Simon & Schuster for sticking with me through this book. What you all do is magic.

A special thanks goes to the men and women of the Palm Beach County Fire Department, the exceptional nurses at the Jupiter Medical Center and West Palm Hospital, and the instructors at Palm Beach State College's EMT and Firefighter programs. You are all heroes to me.

Throughout this long journey the following people helped me, sometimes without even knowing it. I'd like to thank Suzie Townsend for her invaluable advice about giving Patient F the comic he deserved. Andrew Smith, whose books gave me the courage to follow through with this story when I was ready to give up writing completely. Mike Winchell for repeatedly encouraging me to write my story—here it is! Pamela Deron for throwing an early draft of this book at me and telling me she hated me, and for never letting me quit. Jennifer Diemer, whose editing magic and bottomless kindness made this book a hundred times stronger. Matthew Rush for being a constant source of encouragement, and for his friendship. Margie Gelbwasser for reading every single version of this book, for being my cheerleader through the rough patches, and for always being up for Skyping when I needed an ear. And a special thanks to Rachel Melcher for everything.

As always, I am grateful to my family for supporting me, encouraging me, and forcing strangers to buy my books (welcome to the family, Sy!), and to Matt, who lets me disappear when the muse calls, but never lets me stray too far. You're my happy ending.

Finally, I'd like to thank you for reading. I wrote Drew and Rusty's story, but you give them life.